"A devour-it-like-chocolate page-turner that takes the reader through the vivid landscapes of the times, from grand balls to the bleakest stews of foggy London and across the countryside." — *BookPage*

"Against the backdrop of espionage and intrigue in the court of young Edward VI, Ms. Feather writes a story filled with sensuality, passion and poignancy." — *Romantic Times*

"I recommend *To Kiss a Spy* as a fast-paced, engrossing novel of intrigue, passion and the power of not only romantic love, but love of family, to conquer and heal all."
— *America Online's Romance Fiction Forum*

The Widow's Kiss

"Typical of Feather's novels, the story succeeds as romantic fiction, with fine characterizations." — *Publishers Weekly*

"Rich characters, sophisticated sensuality, and a skillfully crafted story line: a first-class historical romance, wonderfully entertaining." — *Kirkus Reviews*

"Filled with period detail and dynamic characters, Feather's appealing historical romance exemplifies the qualities that make her perennially popular." — *Booklist*

"Feather, whose millions of readers eagerly await each new book, is at the top of her form here." — *Brazosport Facts*

"One of the most intense romances I've read. . . . From the opening scene to the final pages I was glued to this book. I had one of those nights where you keep reading no matter how late it's getting. You keep looking at the clock thinking, 'If I turn off the light right now, I'll get six hours of sleep.' Then it's five hours, then four, and if you're lucky, you'll have finished the book before you get to three." — *All About Romance*

The Least Likely Bride

"Feather's writing is quick, vivid, and upbeat. . . . Her hero is dashing and articulate; her heroine is headstrong and intelligent and ends up saving her lover; and it all adds up to a perfect light historical romance." —*Booklist*

"Ms. Feather's latest is full of intrigue, passion and adventure—a lively read." —*Dallas Morning News*

"A charming, fast read." —*Philadelphia Inquirer*

"I highly recommend *The Least Likely Bride*, and I plan to search out the other books in Feather's Bride Trilogy immediately." —*All About Romance*

"The third in Ms. Feather's Bride trilogy reunites Portia and Rofus, Cato and Phoebe, and brings together Olivia and Anthony in this powerfully crafted story filled with romance and enough adventure to keep the reader turning pages. A keeper." —*Romantic Times*

"Add a bit of 'wrecking' by a dastardly nobleman who wants to marry Olivia for her fortune, along with the skulduggery of a stepbrother she loathes, and you have a typically engaging romance à la Feather." —*Brazosport Facts*

A Valentine Wedding

"A fast-paced book that will keep the reader entertained."
—*Rocky Mountain News*

The Hostage Bride

"The first in Jane Feather's 'Bride' trilogy is a feather in her cap and one of her best stories ever."
—*Atlanta Journal-Constitution*

The Silver Rose

"Well-written and fast moving . . . entertaining."
—Booklist

"Feather's writing style is spirited and her plot is well-paced." *—Publishers Weekly*

Vice

"*Vice* offers everything from sensual romantic scenes to hilarious misadventures to an exposition on the problems facing ladies of the evening in the mid-18th century. . . . Readers will love it." *—Brazosport Facts*

Violet

"Great fun . . . Feather's well-paced plot generates lots of laughs, steamy sex and high adventure, as well as some wryly perceptive commentary on the gender stereotypes her heroine so flagrantly defies." *—Publishers Weekly*

Valentine

"Four out of four stars . . . *Valentine* . . . comes much closer to the Austen spirit than any of the pseudo-sequels that have been proliferating lately." *—Detroit Free Press*

Vixen

"*Vixen* is worth taking to bed. . . . Feather's last book, *Virtue*, was good, but this one is even better." *—USA Today*

Virtue

"Jane Feather is an accomplished storyteller. . . . The result—a rare and wonderful battle-of the-sexes story that will delight both historical and Regency readers."
—Daily News of Los Angeles

Almost
a Lady

Jane
Feather

B A N T A M   B O O K S

ALMOST A LADY

A Bantam Book / January 2006

Published by
Bantam Dell
A Division of Random House, Inc.
New York, New York

ISBN-13: 978-0-553-58756-2
ISBN-10: 0-553-58756-0

Printed in the United States of America
Published simultaneously in Canada

www.bantamdell.com

OPM 10 9 8 7 6 5 4 3 2 1

Almost
a Lady

Chapter 1

The two women walking arm in arm down The Leas along the seafront in Folkestone drew admiring glances from those they passed. There was something striking about their physical differences, one tall and well formed, creamy skinned, dark haired, with large golden-brown eyes, the other small and slight, with the pale freckled complexion that so often went with red hair and lively green eyes.

Meg Barratt paused, slipping her arm out from her companion's, and turned to look across the waters of the Strait of Dover. She rested her folded arms on the wall and lifted her face to the salt spray. The breeze caught her hair, sending red curls flying around her triangular face. She laughed and put a hand to her fashionable straw bonnet.

"I can smell a storm brewing, Bella," she observed.

Her companion, who had stopped beside her, sniffed the wind. "It doesn't look like a storm. The sky's blue, the sea's blue, not a cloud in sight."

"Look over there." Meg pointed towards the horizon. A dark shadow of a bank of cloud was just visible.

The duchess of St. Jules shook her head with amusement. "You always did fancy yourself as a meteorological expert."

"It's my country breeding, lassie," Meg returned in a fair approximation of a broad Kentish accent. "And I can also tell when the tide's coming in."

"Even I can do that," her friend scoffed, peering down at the line of waves creeping up over the sand below the wall. "Besides, you have only to look at the harbor."

Meg glanced towards Folkestone harbor, where a flotilla of boats were at anchor. The air of urgency was clear even from this distance. Sailors and porters rushed hither and thither, leaping from ship to shore as the boats were readied for an on-tide departure. Some were private yachts, some small merchantmen, and out beyond the harbor bar sat two men-of-war, handsome frigates both of them.

Her eye was drawn to a sloop-of-war anchored just inside the harbor. The row of guns on her upper deck gleamed in the afternoon sun. Here too there was the impression of haste and preparation. A dinghy drew up alongside the sloop and a man stepped out of the boat and onto the rope ladder dangling down the ship's side. He went up with an agile speed and grace that Meg could only admire and swung himself over the deck rail in one movement. She watched as he climbed to the quarterdeck, a small figure in the distance but somehow, to Meg's imagination, a significant one.

She shrugged at the fancy and turned away from the wall, preparing to resume the walk. "Where's Jack this afternoon?"

"At dice with the Prince of Wales," her friend returned succinctly. "Prinny will lose his shirt, of course, but in a classic triumph of hope over experience he sits down at the tables with Jack absolutely convinced that this time his luck will change." She chuckled and linked arms with her friend as they continued their promenade. "I think I've had enough of Folkestone, what do you think, Meg?"

"I think it's time for me, at least, to return home for a while. My mother's letters begin to sound plaintive," Meg replied. "Poor soul, she tries so hard not to lament my lack of a husband, but she's really in despair. After all this time I've spent with you and Jack in London, and still not even a hint of a suitor." She shook her head in mock dismay. "I'm a lost cause, clearly."

Arabella shot her a sideways glance. "If you don't mind my saying so, Meg, it's not so much lack of a suitor, it's lack of the right kind," she declared. "You seem to be attracted only to the un-marrying kind."

Meg gave a heavy sigh, although her green eyes sparkled with mischief. "How right you are, my dear. For some reason I'm only drawn to *bad* men. They're the only ones who are any fun."

Arabella grinned. "I can't help but agree with you. Jack's not exactly the epitome of propriety and he wouldn't be so much fun if he were."

"The baby's had an effect on him, though," Meg observed thoughtfully. "Since little Charles was born he's become much more..." She sought for a word. "Not exactly respectable, he's too much of a gamester for that, but *considered* in his manner."

Arabella nodded, a slight smile on her lips at the thought of her husband and child. "Talking of Charles, I must get back. I asked the nursemaid to have him ready by four o'clock so that I could take him for an airing in the carriage."

Meg glanced again towards the horizon. The bank of

cloud was closer and the sea beneath its shadow was dark gray and restless. "I don't think you'll go far with him this afternoon."

Arabella followed her gaze. "Perhaps you're right."

"You go on home. I want to go to the lending library. Mrs. Carson said she would put aside a copy of Mrs. Radcliff's *The Italian* for me, but she won't keep it for more than a day."

"Very well, you take the footman. It's only a step to the house from here, so I'll go home alone."

"No," Meg said firmly. "A duchess needs a proper escort. I, on the other hand, am quite accustomed to racketing around unaccompanied. Besides, the library's only just up the hill." She gestured towards a narrow lane leading up steeply from The Leas towards the High Street.

Arabella didn't argue with her. Her friend needed her solitude at times, and in this tiny seaside town no one would object to a woman past the age of discretion taking a walk unescorted. And even if they did, much Meg would care. "I'll see you later then."

She went off with a farewell wave and Meg turned up the cobbled lane, so narrow that the medieval houses on either side almost formed a roof as they leaned across it and towards each other, casting deep shadow over the damp and slimy cobbles that never felt the sun's warmth.

Out of the sun the mid-April afternoon had a chill to it, exacerbated by the strengthening wind that now and again whistled down the funnel of the alley. Meg drew her cashmere shawl closer around her and wished she had brought a pelisse. Her lavender cambric gown was the height of fashion but too flimsy to offer protection against the elements.

She broke into the sunshine again as the lane debouched

onto the High Street. The wind was still fresh, though, and she was glad to reach the shelter of the lending library at the top of the street.

"Good afternoon, madam," the woman at the counter greeted her warmly. "I have Mrs. Radcliff's book for you." She reached down and placed a volume on the counter. "Two other ladies are waiting for it."

"I'll read it quickly," Meg promised, caressing the book with her fingertips. "If it's anything like *The Mysteries of Udolpho*, I won't be able to put it down."

"I think it's even better," the woman said, dropping her voice a little and glancing conspiratorially around the almost deserted library.

Meg nodded with a smile. "I'll just take a look around, Mrs. Carson, and see if anything else takes my fancy." She wandered off towards the shelves of books lining the rear wall of the library.

She picked out a copy of William Wordsworth's tragedy *The Borderers* and as usual became quickly engrossed. It was with a shock that she realized almost an hour had passed. She had no reason to feel guilty, but absurdly she did as she returned to the front of the library. "I didn't realize the time...I'll borrow this too, Mrs. Carson." She handed over a shilling.

"Best hurry home, Miss Barratt," the woman advised, wrapping the books in brown paper. "Looks quite dark out there now."

Meg glanced towards the bow window. The sun had vanished and it was now as dark as dusk. "There's a storm brewing." She tucked the books wrapped in brown paper under her arm and hurried into the street.

There were few people about now, and those there were

moved quickly, heads down, as they tried to beat the approaching rain. Thunder rumbled. Meg picked up her skirts and walked fast towards the lane that would take her back down to The Leas. Once she reached there the Fortescus' hired house was barely two hundred yards along the seafront. Heavy drops of rain splashed onto the cobbles as she turned into the now dark alley. At least there would be some shelter beneath the overarching roofs of the houses. She looked down the lane and saw a carriage drawn up about halfway along. She frowned. The alley was so narrow there would barely be room for her to squeeze past on either side.

She paused to tuck the books more securely under her shawl just as another crack of thunder rolled across the sky and the rain began in earnest. It was so heavy it penetrated the lane; surprisingly cold and unsurprisingly wet, it soaked her hat in seconds. There were no sheltering doorways, the houses opened directly onto the street, and resigned to a drenching, Meg set off towards the faint glimmer of the sea at the far end. The rain rushed through the kennel in the middle of the cobbled lane heading down the steep slope for the sea below, and the cobbles themselves quickly became even more slimy with mud and floating refuse. Meg's sandaled foot slipped twice and she grabbed onto the doorframe of a house to regain her balance. The carriage below her still hadn't moved and she wondered what business could possibly cause such a large vehicle to enter such a narrow space. She couldn't see the horses, who were at the front facing the sea, but it would need at least four, and they would be impossible to maneuver.

She dismissed the puzzle with a brusque head shake and continued more carefully on her way, rain dripping down the back of her neck. Her skirts were soaked, the hem filthy with mud and slime, her sandals were ruined, her shawl bedraggled, her bonnet resembled a mound of wet straw.

As she approached the carriage the door swung open as if in invitation. Meg frowned and a flicker of apprehension made her heart beat faster. It was ridiculous, of course. There was nothing to be afraid of in this sleepy seaside town, but the open door was barring her from edging past the vehicle. She was still finding it difficult to keep her footing on the steep slippery cobbles and this merely increased her apprehension.

She approached cautiously, and called out, "Could you close the door please, I need to pass." There was no response. Irritation replaced apprehension. Maybe the rain had drowned out her voice but how could the occupants of the carriage not even think that someone might want to pass? And why the devil were they sitting there with the door open in the middle of a rainstorm?

She tried to pass the carriage on the other side, resting her hand on the back as she stepped cautiously around. Suddenly the vehicle lurched forward. Her foot slipped and she fell backwards into the rushing water of the kennel. For a split second she realized her danger . . . the water in its headlong flood was going to carry her beneath the carriage down to the sea. And then she realized nothing more.

She opened her eyes onto a strange and different world. A pitching, tossing world. She was lying flat on a cot that was more like a box than a bed, but when this world gave a particularly violent heave she saw the point of the wooden sides. It was dark and however hard she stared into the gloom she couldn't manage to make out anything that made any sense. Her head was muzzy and aching and her stomach felt somewhat uncertain. It seemed easiest simply to close her eyes again, so she did.

When next she awoke it was to a light-filled world of quiet rocking. A voice cackled, "Wake up ... wake up."

Gingerly Meg turned her head sideways, aware of a tenderness somewhere at the back of her scalp. A large scarlet bird with very long tail feathers was sitting on a perch regarding her with remarkably bright beady eyes. "Wake up," it repeated and gave a cackle of laughter.

Meg wondered if she had died and this was some mad afterlife peopled by scarlet talking birds and an eternally rocking foundation. "Do be quiet," she said to the bird, who was still punctuating its repeated instruction with manic laughter. To her astonishment it fell silent.

Carefully she lifted her head and felt the soreness. There was a lump just behind her right ear. That was reassuring. Bumps belonged to the real world and were inevitable when one fell backwards onto hard cobbles. She'd been drenched and the water from the kennel had been about to carry her in full flood beneath the wheels of the carriage ...

The accident had not damaged her memory at least. Every detail of those moments was as clear as daylight. But what had happened afterwards? She lifted the coverlet and peered along her body, clad, astonishingly enough, in an extremely elegant nightgown.

"G'day ... g'day ..." the bird ventured, tilting its head, the beady eye glinting as it watched her.

"Good day," Meg said, sitting up in the box. An array of windows showed a gently moving sunlit sea. So she was on a boat ... not too difficult a conclusion. But how, not to mention *why*? She looked around at the compact paneled space. It was surprisingly comfortable, a carpet that looked to be Aubusson on the floor, cushioned benches beneath the windows, a table and two chairs in the center, securely bolted to the floor, doors that looked like cupboards set into the paneling. And one door that clearly led somewhere.

A light tap on that door made her heart jump. She swallowed but before she could say anything, the scarlet bird cawed, "Come in ... come in."

The door opened and a man stepped inside, closing the door carefully behind him. The bird rose up on the perch and flapped its wings. Instantly Meg's visitor held out his arm and the bird swooped from its perch to the offered wrist like a falcon returning to his jesses.

Meg stared at him. "Who the devil are you?" she demanded.

Her visitor's slight smile was a gleaming white flash in a deeply tanned face. He leaned his shoulders against the door and regarded her with an amiable curiosity. "Oddly enough, I was about to ask you exactly the same question."

Meg shook her head as if she could somehow clear it of confusion. "I would have thought you'd know the name of a person you've kidnapped," she stated.

"Ah, well, you see, although I can understand you might find this difficult to believe, you were not exactly kidnapped." As he spoke he moved across the cabin, setting the bird onto its perch again.

It went with a slightly protesting caw and a disgruntled flap of its wings, muttering to itself, "Poor Gus ... poor Gus."

Meg gazed at the bird in bewildered stupefaction. This really couldn't be happening. "Gus?" she queried.

"Poor Gus," the bird corrected.

"Gus is a scarlet macaw," the man informed her, scratching the bird's poll. "He's rather talkative."

"I had noticed," she said dryly. *Dear God, why on earth were they having a discussion about a parrot?* She struggled to bring the unruly conversation onto some pointful track. "If I was not kidnapped, how did I come to be here?"

Her host, if that was what he was, hitched himself onto the corner of the table and sat with one leg on the floor, the other carelessly swinging. There was something about the casual grace of his movements that seemed familiar. And then Meg suddenly knew who he was. The man she had watched from The Leas climbing aboard the sloop-of-war.

"This is your ship?" she said, the query purely rhetorical.

"The *Mary Rose*," he returned. "Are you hungry... would you like breakfast?"

Meg realized that she *was* hungry, ravenous in fact. When had she last eaten? "How long have I been here?"

"We picked you up late yesterday afternoon. It's mid-morning now." He reached behind him for a small handbell and rang it. His head moved through a ray of sunshine that caught copper glints in the auburn locks. His hair was a color that Meg, with her own unashamedly red curls, had always envied for its subtlety.

She leaned back against the bulkhead and scrutinized him with narrowed eyes. She didn't feel in the least alarmed, which struck her as a lunatic lack of reaction in the circumstances, but at the moment there was nothing remotely threatening about her companion.

A rotund man opened the door and came into the cabin. He didn't so much as glance at the figure in the box-bed. "Yes, Captain?"

"Bring breakfast, Biggins," the man said. "And coffee ... or would you prefer tea, ma'am?" He smiled politely at Meg. His eyes were the washed-out blue of a distant horizon.

"Coffee, thank you," she said with an enthusiasm that she couldn't restrain.

"G'bye ... G'bye ..." the macaw spoke from his perch as Biggins departed.

"Does he have a large vocabulary?" she asked involuntarily.

"Large enough," the captain of the *Mary Rose* replied. A slight frown drew his copper eyebrows together. "I was told you hurt your head. How is it?"

She touched the bump. "A little sore, but nothing serious. Where are my clothes?"

"You won't wish to wear them again. They were ruined by mud and water." He dismissed the issue of her clothes with a wave and a gesture towards the side of the cabin. "You'll find plenty of replacements in the cupboard in the port bulkhead."

"I see," Meg said, although she didn't. "And what I'm wearing now ...?"

"I don't know," he said. "What *are* you wearing?" He sounded genuinely curious.

Meg closed her eyes on renewed confusion. Maybe some threads of sense would emerge from this tangled conversation. "A nightgown," she stated. "A most fashionable and elegant garment from what I've seen of it."

He nodded without apparent surprise. "You were taken to the sick bay; I daresay the surgeon took care of getting you out of your wet clothes while he was seeing to the wound on your head."

Well, that solved one little mystery at least, and a surgeon's intimate attentions were unimpeachable. The ship

suddenly swung sharply to the left. Meg grabbed the sides
of the box-bed as a cracking sound came from above her
head. Her mysterious host didn't seem to notice the change
in movement.

"What was that?" Meg demanded.

"A tack to port," he informed her, sliding off the table as
the door opened and the rotund sailor reappeared with a
laden tray followed by a lad of about seven, bearing a jug of
coffee.

Meg stayed where she was as the table was laid. The boy
cast her a curious, slightly guilty look before hurrying from
the cabin, but Biggins kept his attention entirely on his
task. When he'd gone, accompanied by a chorus of farewells from Gus, she cast aside the coverlet and edged herself out of the box. The floor swayed beneath her and she
grabbed the back of a chair.

"You'll get used to it," her breakfast companion said
calmly. He ran an eye over her as she stood beside the
table. "Yes, a very elegant garment," he observed. "How
fortunate that it fits you so well . . . I hope you like eggs and
bacon."

Get used to it? Meg stared at him for a second, then decided that food would enable her to take charge of this insane situation. Her bemused weakness was entirely to do
with hunger. She said nothing but sat down and attacked
the full plate before her.

Her host offered no conversation until she had wiped
her plate with a piece of barley bread and taken her last sip
of coffee. Meg set down her cup and thought rather self-
consciously that she must have presented a sight of pure
greed in the face of her companion's rather more decorous
table manners. But then she'd eaten nothing since a light
lunch at noon the previous day. The reminder banished

self-consciousness as the image of that carriage with its open door barring her progress returned in full color.

"So how is it that this kidnapping is not really a kidnapping?" she inquired in tones of deceptive mildness. "I'm knocked unconscious and many hours later find myself somewhere where I have no desire to be . . . imprisoned on a ship, no less. That seems to me a perfect description of kidnapping."

"But as you've already pointed out, I would surely know the name of a person I'd kidnapped," he said, with another flickering smile. The little smile-creases around his eyes were much paler than the rest of his complexion.

"Who brought me here?"

"My men."

"*Res ipsa loquitur*," she declared with an air of triumph.

She hadn't expected a mere sailor to understand the legal term, but he shook his head and said, "Not in this case. My men were under the impression that you were the person they had been sent to collect. A person coming of her own volition. When you slipped trying to get into the coach—"

"*Around* it," she interrupted. "The open door was barring my passage."

"It was open in invitation," he explained with an air of patience. "To make it easy for Ana . . . for the lady my men were supposed to be collecting."

Meg stared at him. "So where is she . . . this Ana?"

His expression darkened and a shadow crossed his eyes. He regarded her with what felt like an uncomfortable closeness before saying rather curtly, "I wish I knew."

She glanced down at the creamy silk folds of her nightgown. "This belongs to her?"

He nodded. "A perfect fit. You see, my dear ma'am, my

men's error was quite understandable. They had never seen their intended passenger in person but had been given a description that in essential details matches your own. They brought you here in good faith."

"Well, why didn't you just take me back?" she exclaimed, rising from the chair with an agitated movement that set the skirts of the nightgown swirling. She stood, one hand on the back of the chair, facing him, her mind now clear, her eyes filled with anger.

He said simply, "I couldn't."

"What do you mean, *you couldn't?*" Biting scorn hid the fear that up to now had been suppressed. For some reason it hadn't occurred to her that this situation could not be rectified.

"Sit down again," he said quietly, but Meg understood it to be an instruction, not a request. She hesitated for a moment, then took her chair.

"The tide was full when you were carried on board wrapped in a cloak. It didn't occur to me to identify a woman I thought I knew, and when I was told that you'd slipped and knocked yourself unconscious, I instructed them to take you to sick bay. After that, with the storm coming up I had no time for anything but sailing us out of the harbor and through the storm." He spoke with the same quiet authority, so that against every instinct she began to feel it all made sense.

"Once matters were under control on the quarterdeck, I inquired after you and the surgeon told me that you would suffer nothing worse than a possible concussion and they had put you to bed in my cabin." He shrugged. "I thought nothing of it... until I came below just before dawn and realized the disaster."

"*Disaster,*" Meg said. "*I'm* a disaster?"

He ran a hand through the wavy auburn hair that was a little longer than current fashion dictated...something that Meg noticed almost in passing. "It's a little difficult to explain," he said vaguely. "The lady you're supposed to be was willingly engaged in an enterprise of vital importance. Her absence and as a consequence your unwitting presence is indeed a disaster."

Meg stared at him as if he was a snake charmer and she the snake. "Who are you?"

"Names would certainly smooth the path," he said with a sideways tilt of his head. "Just whom did my men pick out of the kennel yesterday afternoon?"

"My name's Meg Barratt," she stated and the declaration finally brought the grim reality of an unimaginable situation home to her. She thought of her parents and of Arabella and Jack. They would be frantic. "If I am not returned to Folkestone immediately, I can't imagine what will happen. I *have* to go home." Her desperate gaze fixed upon the cabin's bank of windows...at the ceaseless, inexorable movement of the sea as it slipped beneath the stern, carrying her heaven only knew where.

"I can't do that," he said, and there was an almost regretful note beneath the implacable statement. "Even if the tide was not against us, time is. My mission can only be accomplished at a certain juncture. I cannot lose the opportunity."

And Meg slowly understood that she was indeed trapped. She could not turn this ship around. If its master would not, then where it sailed so did she. "Who are you?" she repeated.

"My name's Cosimo." He gave her a little bow as if in a formal introduction.

"De Medici?" she inquired with unconcealed and disbelieving sarcasm. Such a name was a perfect fit with all this nonsensical talk of missions and vital enterprises.

Disconcertingly he merely laughed. "My mother combined a love of Italian history with a somewhat fanciful temperament."

"So if it's not de Medici, what is it?" Her lip curled a little.

"Just Cosimo," he said, untroubled by her scorn. "You need know me only by that name."

"I have no wish to know you at all." She turned away and went over to the bank of windows. She knelt on the cushioned bench beneath and stared out at the sea, trying to control the tears that filled her eyes.

"When you're ready to dress, you'll find clothes in the cupboard. I'm sure that like the nightgown they'll be a perfect fit." He spoke quietly as ever behind her. "Come to the quarterdeck whenever you feel like it." She heard the door open and close.

"G'bye...g'bye...poor Gus...poor Gus," the macaw muttered.

"Oh, be quiet," Meg said fiercely through the infuriating tears that clogged her throat.

"Poor Gus," the bird murmured and tucked his head beneath his wing.

Chapter 2

Cosimo went up on deck, the serenity of his expression belying the fierce turmoil of his thoughts. The helmsman offered him the wheel as he climbed the steps to the quarterdeck but he shook his head. "I'll take it later, Mike, when we come close to the harbor."

"Aye, Captain. The rocks around the island are as treacherous as any on the Brittany coast," the helmsman said solemnly.

Cosimo laughed slightly and patted the man's shoulder. "I'm not implying that you're not up to the task, Mike. But I like the challenge myself."

A grin twitched the other man's mouth. "And there's none better to do it, sir."

Cosimo looked up at the sails that barely stirred beneath a faint breeze. "It'll take us hours to make landfall with this wind."

"You know what they say about calm following the storm," Mike observed with a sagacious nod. He leaned sideways and spat over the rail. "Sea's a millpond."

Cosimo nodded and walked over to the stern rail, where

he stood leaning his elbows on the topmost bar gazing out at the faint outline of land on the horizon. The Channel Islands, just off the coast of Brittany. With a good wind they'd be maneuvering through the rocks to the harbor on the island of Sark within four hours. At this rate it would be nightfall and they'd have to stand out to sea during the night. Only a fool would attempt the landing in pitch dark. And although his anxiety and the urgency of his mission made him impatient, Cosimo was no fool.

What had happened to Ana? A simple accident that had delayed her arrival at the rendezvous? Or something more sinister?

He forced himself to consider the latter possibility. If Ana had been betrayed to the French, if she was now in the hands of their expert interrogators, it would not be long before they knew everything there was to know, if they didn't already know it. She was a strong woman, a perfectionist, an expert agent who did not tolerate failure, but Cosimo was under no illusions. He would not himself be able to withstand such an interrogation for long, and he could not expect it of Ana.

A simple accident? Most unlikely. Ana left nothing to chance. But maybe, just maybe, she had slipped and knocked herself unconscious and missed the rendezvous. If such a fluke accident could happen to his unwitting passenger, why not to Ana? But he knew that he had to assume the worst. If Ana had been betrayed, then more than the present mission was endangered. Ana knew too many secrets, too many identities. His own life was probably now not worth a farthing.

But maybe there would be a message for him at the naval outpost on Sark. Ana knew he would have had to sail without her. If he missed the tide, he might not reach

Toulon in time to catch Napoleon. If her failure to make the rendezvous had been caused by an accident, she would have used the pigeon courier service to get him a message, knowing that he would stop off there to pick up dispatches. She might already be making her own way to France. There were other crossings, other routes.

He shook his head. There was no point speculating about any of this until he reached Sark.

The sails flapped and he spun from the rail to look up at them, now hanging limply as the last whisper of breeze faded. The midday sun beat down, hot for mid-April, and the blue waters of the Channel danced with light.

"We're making no way, sir?" Mike called.

"No, I can see that. Furl the sails and we'll sit it out. We'll have to hope the wind picks up towards evening." Cosimo pushed himself away from the rail. "Mr. Fisher?" He called to a man keeping a respectful distance across the quarterdeck.

"Sir?" The young man came over briskly.

"Tell the men to stand down. Sleep, cook, do whatever they like for a couple of hours. We're not going anywhere for a while."

"Right y'are, sir." The sailor jumped down the steps to the main deck, hollering through cupped hands.

Cosimo smiled to himself. Such rambunctious informality would not be tolerated on a sloop-of-war belonging to the British navy, but the *Mary Rose* was only loosely affiliated with the official navy and her captain offered his services to the crown according to his own lights. He preferred the freedom of a privateer to the rigid hierarchical structure of the navy, and, because he had proved indispensable on more than one occasion, the British navy bit its stiff upper lip and endured the outrage to its sense of decorum.

The smile faded rather quickly as the thought of Miss Meg Barratt chased away other concerns. He'd invited her to come on deck but there was no sign of her. She hadn't been too happy at finding herself aboard the *Mary Rose*, and he couldn't really blame her for that, but he could put her ashore on Sark and one of the fishing boats would take her back to Folkestone for a consideration.

Could put her ashore or *would* put her ashore?

Cosimo was accustomed to the way his mind worked. It seemed to operate on two levels. While the conscious level blithely did its work, the unconscious was busy as a bee, and the results of its activity just popped up at an opportune time. Miss Meg Barratt was so physically similar to Ana it was almost uncanny. The petite physique, the red hair. Ana's red was a little more subdued than Miss Barratt's, but not so much that someone only vaguely acquainted with Ana would notice. The freckles...they could be concealed. The features...definitely different, but again Napoleon had only met Ana twice and the last time was over a year ago. He wouldn't remember the details but the resemblance would be sufficient to catch his eye.

He turned back to the railing, humming tunelessly as his mind worked. It was, at first sight, an absurd plan. But an assassin was accustomed to adapting and to using what tools came to hand. Maybe he would *not* put Miss Barratt ashore on the island of Sark. But nothing could be done until he'd discovered what he could about Ana's situation.

Meg finally turned her mesmerized gaze from the still and gleaming sea beyond the window, sniffed with a resolute end to tears, and took in her surroundings anew. The breakfast table and its used dishes remained. Gus, still in a huff, sat on his perch with his back to her. A large birdcage, door open, swung from a hook in the ceiling. Her eye fell on two books neatly placed on a shelf below the starboard window. Mrs. Radcliff's *The Italian* and Wordsworth's *The Borderers*. Someone had taken the trouble to rescue her library books from the torrent of water in the kennel. Puzzlingly considerate.

She stared at the door that led to whatever lay outside the cabin. Did she want to venture forth? Even if she did, she couldn't go in a nightgown.

She slid off the cushioned bench and went over to the cupboard in the port bulkhead. There were several gowns, a hooded cloak, shawls, and a neat array of drawers that revealed stockings, chemises, petticoats. Two pairs of serviceable, leather buttoned boots completed the offerings. Serviceable boots on slippery decks seemed an obvious choice, Meg reflected with a sardonic grin that reassured her somewhat. She hadn't completely lost her sense of self and humor in this transformation from reality to sinister fairy tale.

A knock at the door, however, made her heart beat fast and it was with an effort that she was able to steady her voice to call, "Come in." But Gus got there first, and his raucous invitation continued as she turned slowly towards the opening door. The man who entered was not Cosimo, and she was not sure whether she was relieved or alarmed by the stranger.

"David...David..." Gus called, once more a lively host. He hopped off his perch onto the table and picked his way through the dishes, bridling like a harlot on a street corner.

Meg's visitor was a pleasant-faced man with salt-and-pepper hair, wearing a black coat and britches and carrying a leather bag. He gave her an apologetic smile that illuminated light gray eyes as he scratched Gus's poll and returned the greeting. Gus flew up onto his shoulder and sat there with an air of triumph and what Meg would have sworn was a glare in her direction.

"Good day, ma'am," the man called David said.

"Good day," she responded, closing the cupboard door softly behind her.

He set his bag down on the box-bed and said with a smile, "Forgive me, I don't know how to address you, ma'am. But I'm the ship's surgeon. I tended to you last evening."

"Then I'm grateful to you, sir," Meg said with a frank and friendly smile. She came over, hand extended. "My name is Meg Barratt."

"David Porter at your service, Miss Barratt." The surgeon shook Meg's offered hand as he inquired, "How are you feeling? No headache, I trust?"

"No, none. Just a little soreness." Meg touched the spot behind her ear.

"That's to be expected. A little witch hazel will help." He reached up and lifted the muttering Gus down from his shoulder, setting him back on the table. The macaw, apparently restored to good humor, pecked at the crumbs on the breadboard. David opened his bag. "Do you remember what happened?"

"Absolutely," Meg declared. "Down to the last instant before I started to slide beneath the coach."

"Good . . . good. Concussion can do strange things to the brain," he said. "If you'd sit down . . ." He gestured rather tentatively to a chair.

Meg found his courteous hesitancy immensely reassuring. She sat down and tilted her head for a deftly gentle probing of the swelling. He laid a cool pad of witch hazel over the wound and she felt herself relax. "Dr. Porter, do you know where we're sailing to?"

"That's not really my business, ma'am," he said without hesitation. "You should ask Cosimo."

"Oh...I see." She hesitated for a moment, and then said, "Does only he know where we're sailing?"

At that a tiny smile quirked the corners of the doctor's mouth. "We all think we know where we're going, Miss Barratt, but only Cosimo is aware of matters that could change that."

Meg turned her head sharply and the pad of witch hazel fell to the floor. "Everyone on this ship is happily sailing at the whim of one man to a destination that could change at a moment's notice?"

"Basically, Miss Barratt, yes," the surgeon said with the same tranquil smile. "The swelling should go down in a day or two. Until then, don't be too energetic—"

"*Energetic!*" Meg exclaimed. "How could one be energetic confined to this cabin?"

David Porter frowned. "I was not under the impression that you were confined, Miss Barratt. I did not advise it."

Come to the quarterdeck whenever you feel like it. Meg heard Cosimo's quiet invitation and realized that she had no intention of accepting it. "I choose to keep myself to myself, Doctor," she said stiffly. "I'm here against my will...however it came to pass...but until I can return home I don't intend to leave this cabin."

He looked grave. "I see. But I do recommend fresh air and a little gentle exercise...a walk around the decks, for instance. It's not good to stay within doors for an extended period."

"Extended period?" Meg could almost hear a squeak in her voice. "How extended?"

"As I said, you should ask Cosimo." David packed the tools of his trade back into his leather bag. He regarded her thoughtfully for a moment. "You must, of course, do what seems right for you. I understand your situation is rather disturbing. But you have nothing to fear on this ship, Miss Barratt."

Gus flew onto his shoulder as he turned back to the door. "G'bye...G'bye..." the macaw squawked as doctor and bird left Meg to her seclusion.

Nothing to fear? Meg sat down on the bench beneath the window again. Gus's absence was like balm on a wound. The silence was pure heaven. And then she became aware that the motion of the ship had changed. It now rocked gently and when she looked out of the window the sea was not slipping beneath the bow. So they were not moving.

Well, she decided, this was not a situation to be dealt with in a nightgown. She returned to the cupboard in the bulkhead and picked out underclothes and a bronze muslin gown with a paisley shawl. She glanced uneasily at the cabin door. The prospect of changing her clothes became less attractive. As if in confirmation of her lack of privacy there came a brisk knock. "Permission to remove breakfast dishes, Miss Barratt."

She took a minute to swathe herself in the paisley shawl before calling, "Come in."

The rotund Biggins entered, gave her a nod of a bow, and swiftly cleared the dishes onto a tray. "I'll bring hot water, ma'am," he said as he left with another nod. He left the door slightly ajar and was back in minutes with two steaming jugs. "I'll put these in the captain's head, ma'am," he declared, stepping across a narrow lintel into a space Meg hadn't noticed before that was set into the bulkhead.

Curious, she followed him. The tiny area was furnished with a plank with a hole in it, much like a regular privy except that the hole gave access to the sea beneath, and a shallow porcelain indentation with another opening to the sea and a stopper attached on a chain. It was an arrangement that was clearly intended as a makeshift bath. "How neat," Meg observed, surprised into the involuntary comment.

"We do our best, ma'am," Biggins declared setting down the jugs. "Will there be anything else, ma'am?"

"No . . . no, thank you," Meg said swiftly. She'd been uncomfortably aware for the last hour how much she needed the facilities he'd revealed to her. She waited until she heard the cabin door close behind him and then flew to the door in his wake and examined it. There was a keyhole but no key. She didn't fancy stripping naked let alone using the privy behind an unprotected door. The chairs were both bolted to the floor, so they couldn't be used to block the door. She was utterly vulnerable to anyone who chose to walk in. So much for the doctor's assurance that she had nothing to fear on this ship. It wasn't an assurance she could begin to trust.

But her need was now too pressing for such niceties and at least there was a partial wall separating the head from the rest of the cabin. But it was not a situation that could be allowed to continue. She took care of her most urgent business, washed her face and hands, and then returned to contemplate the cabin door.

There seemed only one thing for it. She fetched the

clothes she was going to change into and stood with her back against the door. Swiftly she pulled off the nightgown and scrambled into chemise, petticoat, stockings, before stepping into the bronze muslin. The gown was not quite a perfect fit. The absent Ana had been rather more generously endowed in the bosom than Meg, and a little taller.

Her hands stilled in the process of knotting the sash beneath her breasts, and she stared into the middle distance for a moment or two. Who was she, this Ana? Had she chosen these clothes herself, or had they been put here to await her arrival? If Cosimo's men had never seen her themselves, it was a fair assumption that she had not been on the *Mary Rose* before. So someone else had installed a wardrobe for her. Someone who presumably knew what would both fit and suit her. That indicated an intimacy beyond the usual. And it was clearly intended that she would share the captain's cabin... was Ana Cosimo's mistress?

Meg shook her head vigorously and finished tying the sash. It made no difference to her or her situation whether the absent Ana was anyone's mistress. Her hands dropped to her sides again. But what was this vital enterprise she and Cosimo had been engaged upon? Something so time-sensitive that the ship couldn't return to Folkestone despite the accidental presence of an unwilling passenger.

Another irrelevancy, she decided. It had nothing whatsoever to do with her. The only thing that concerned her was getting off this ship. And until she could do so, she would stay right here in the cabin, minding her own business. She wanted absolutely nothing to do with the ship's captain. In the spirit of this resolution, she ignored the boots and discarded the paisley shawl since the cabin was comfortably warm, then she resumed her seat on the cushioned bench beneath the window and opened a slightly water-damaged copy of Mrs. Radcliff's *The Italian*.

Cosimo's reverie was disturbed by the flapping of wings as Gus landed on his shoulder. Cosimo turned to David Porter. "How is our passenger, David?"

"No ill effects apart from a bump," David said, leaning beside him against the rail. "She's a strong woman... strong nerves, I'd hazard."

"What makes you say that?" Cosimo hid his interest under a casual tone but his friend was not fooled.

David smiled. "In general women of her age and breeding would have succumbed to more than a fit of the vapors at finding themselves in this situation. Miss Barratt appears to find it merely an acute inconvenience."

Cosimo nodded slowly. "I had noticed a degree of resilience... of antagonism, certainly."

"Can you blame her?"

"No," Cosimo agreed. He leaned back against the railing and looked up at a whirling seagull. "You've never met Ana, have you?"

"You know that I haven't." David regarded the captain with a slight frown.

"There's quite a striking resemblance between her and Miss Barratt." His gaze still followed the bird's flight.

David's frown deepened. "I don't know what the object of our present voyage is, Cosimo, but I assume Ana had something to do with it." A faint question mark punctuated the statement.

"Correct," Cosimo responded.

"And there's some point in the resemblance between her and your accidental passenger?"

"We use what clay comes to hand, David."

David was silent for a minute. He had traveled with Cosimo on and off for close to five years and counted him a friend. He knew what he was, although they never spoke of it, and Cosimo never confided details of his missions to anyone who sailed with him. But David, while more than happy to be kept in the dark, was under no illusions. His friend, in the service of his country, was a privateer, and when necessary, an assassin. But even knowing that, this glimpse into Cosimo's cold pragmatism chilled him a little.

He said finally, "You can't use a complete stranger... a woman who accidentally drops into your path, just because it's convenient, Cosimo." It was the closest to remonstration either of them would allow.

Cosimo opened his palms in a what-will-you gesture. "If the tool is willing and can be sharpened, give me one good reason why it shouldn't be employed."

David shook his head. "You're a cold bastard, Cosimo."

"I don't dispute it."

"Do you know what happened to Ana?" David asked the question knowing that Cosimo would answer him or not as he considered proper.

Cosimo's face was shadowed and he turned abruptly back to the sea. "No, I don't. And I don't care to guess." He added so softly David barely heard it, "But I can do nothing to help her now."

David winced at the implications. He could feel his friend's distress as an almost palpable current. "Perhaps you're not such a cold bastard after all," he murmured.

Cosimo turned sideways and gave him a mocking smile. "Don't let that little secret out of the bag, my friend."

"Never," David averred.

Gus flapped his wings and seemed about to take flight over the motionless sea. Both men watched as he flew a few yards and landed on a halyard, where he sat preening himself.

"Is he as intelligent as he seems, truly aware of which side his bread is buttered, or merely accustomed to captivity?" David mused.

"Something of both," Cosimo responded. "It comes to the same thing."

"Yes," David agreed, pushing himself off the railing. "I wonder how the analogy would apply to Miss Barratt." He walked off, exchanging a word with the helmsman before climbing down to the main deck.

Cosimo thought for a minute and then followed the same path. Outside his cabin he paused before knocking. In truth he had no idea how to proceed with his passenger. Getting closer to her, making her more comfortable in his presence, was clearly the first step.

He knocked with what he hoped was a discreet, friendly, but nevertheless assertive rap.

Once again Meg's heart jumped, but she called "Enter" with a creditably steady voice. She didn't move from her seat beneath the window, merely closed her book over her finger and regarded her visitor with a cool, inquiring stare.

Cosimo returned the scrutiny. "Not too bad a fit," he remarked. "And the color definitely suits you." He held the door open for Gus, who hopped delicately over the lintel and flew up to his perch, where, head on one side, he too considered Meg.

Meg decided the comment was far too personal in the circumstances, so she ignored it, merely continuing to regard her visitor in silence.

"It's a beautiful afternoon." Cosimo tried again. He closed

the door but did not advance into the cabin. There was something forbidding in the green eyes fixed upon him. "It seems a waste to spend it immured in here."

"I am as content as it's possible to be in these circumstances, sir," Meg responded coldly.

He leaned his shoulders against the door and gave her a rueful smile. "Come, Miss Barratt, can we not call a truce? I am truly not responsible for your presence on my ship."

"Then who is, pray?"

He seemed to consider this for a minute, before saying, "Well, as I see it, you are. You're the one who slipped beneath the wheels of my carriage, putting your life in considerable danger as I understand. My men actually saved your life."

Meg snapped her book closed and stood up, dropping the volume to the bench. "That is the most disingenuous piece of spurious reasoning I've ever heard, Captain Cosimo."

He threw up his hands in a laughing gesture of defeat. "Pax, Miss Barratt," he said. "This is getting us nowhere. Now tell me what I may do for you to ease matters a little between us."

What a damnably attractive man he was, Meg reflected, angry at the irrelevancy of the reflection but unable to deny it. He had a loose-limbed grace that she'd noticed when he'd climbed aboard the *Mary Rose* in the harbor, and those sea-washed blue eyes were glinting much like the sun-dappled blue water beneath her window. She liked his mouth too. It was wide and full when he smiled, but without the smile it held a calm resolution, an unmistakable authority, that was curiously reassuring. But she wasn't ready to lower her guard simply because her admittedly unwitting captor could probably charm the hind legs off a donkey if he put his mind to it.

"I need just two things from you at this point, Captain Cosimo—"

He held up an arresting hand. "Oh, please, Meg, my name is simply Cosimo. Since we're sharing this cabin we can surely do without the formalities." He frowned suddenly, but she could tell it was an act. "You don't object to my calling you Meg, I trust."

"Would it matter if I did?" Challenge flickered in her eyes and her cleft chin lifted with her arched sandy eyebrows. She didn't like the sound of sharing a cabin.

"Probably not," he agreed amiably. "Now, what are the two things I can do for you?"

Meg folded her arms. "Firstly I would like to know where we're sailing to so I can decide how to get home from there."

"Ah." Cosimo stroked his chin as he frowned in thought. "Well, at this moment we aren't sailing anywhere. You may have noticed that we're becalmed."

"I doubt the wind will remain uncooperative permanently," Meg declared with an icy glint in her eyes and a very dangerous edge to her voice.

"So far in my experience that has never happened," he agreed. "So, when the wind *does* pick up, we will continue our voyage to the island of Sark. Are you perhaps familiar with it?"

"It's one of the Channel Islands," Meg responded, some of the anger leaving her eyes and voice. Sark was not so very far from the English coast, and it was a mere spit across the Channel to the French coast. Of course, France would not exactly welcome an English wayfarer at the moment, but it shouldn't be too difficult to arrange passage back to England from the island.

"Precisely," he said with a nod. "I have some business to do there."

"And presumably you have contacts among the fishermen... the locals... someone who could take me back?"

"It's not impossible," he said.

Meg's anger resurfaced. "Do you have to be so damnably evasive?" she snapped.

"Forgive me... was I being? I merely spoke the truth. It's not impossible." His mouth curved in a half smile. "So much for your first requirement... and the second...?"

"I need a key to this door," she stated flatly, arms still firmly folded.

He shook his head briskly. "I'm afraid that's not possible."

"What do you mean it's not possible?" She took a step towards him. "There's a keyhole, there must be a key."

"Yes, I imagine there is somewhere. I've never had a need of it."

"Well, I, sir, do have." She held his steady gaze with all the considerable resolution she could muster. "I need my privacy."

"Yes, of course, I understand that," he said readily. "And I can safely promise you that you shall have it. No one will enter here in your presence without your express permission... permission I have to add that in my case must not be unreasonably withheld." He made an apologetic gesture that encompassed the cabin. "All my possessions are in here... and, of course, my charts. I can't sail the ship without access to charts."

Involuntarily Meg's gaze followed his to the narrow shelf attached to the bulkhead where she saw the charts and navigation instruments laid out. She said stiffly, "I fail to see what difference it could make to you if I lock the door. I will of course open it at your request."

"No, I regret that this door must remain unlocked at all times," he said quietly.

Meg came forward, her eyes all green fire, one finger jabbing towards his chest. "Now you listen to me—"

He grabbed the finger. "No, *you* listen to me, madam. This is my ship and on my ship *my* word is the last word. Keep that in mind and I see no reason why we should not get along perfectly well."

Meg wrenched her finger free. She didn't like the look of Cosimo at this moment. His expression had undergone a rather alarming change and her stomach was fluttering like a sparrow's wings.

"Do we understand each other?" he asked very softly. "No one will enter without your permission, but the door stays unlocked at all times."

She couldn't drag her eyes from the now cold blue gaze. She tried but was somehow transfixed. Finally she felt herself nod, a bare acknowledgment but an acknowledgment nevertheless.

And his expression changed. He smiled, his eyes once more resembling a summer sky rather than the blue glint of a glacier. "I was sure we could come to some understanding," he said. "It's dangerous to lock doors at sea. If we ran into trouble, a storm perhaps, or even a hostile ship, I'd need access to the cabin and you would need to be able to leave it without delay."

"A hostile ship?" Meg stared at him.

"My dear Meg, we are at war with France. Had that slipped your mind?" He sounded faintly incredulous and Meg cursed her stupidity. She remembered the two ships of war at anchor outside Folkestone harbor, and most particularly she remembered the line of guns shining on the upper deck of this sloop she was sailing in.

"Maybe it had for a minute," she admitted. "There's been rather a lot to think about since I recovered consciousness."

"Yes, of course," he agreed solemnly. "And who's to say what effect that bump on the head could have had on your memory."

It was too absurd. Meg laughed. "You know perfectly well it had no effect at all. I was so busy concentrating on my own present ills I forgot the world's altogether."

"Pax?" he asked again with a lift of his eyebrows and a slight questioning lilt in his voice.

"I suppose so," Meg said. "I can see little to be gained from open hostilities."

"Then come and enjoy the sunshine on deck." He opened the cabin door in invitation. "I know for a fact that we have some excellent bread, cheese, and salami in the stores, and a particularly fine burgundy. There's nothing to do until the wind gets up except eat, drink, and get to know each other."

Meg had no intention of getting to know this man. He was too damnably attractive and she was all too susceptible to attractive men in unconventional situations. Every instinct told her that dropping her guard would be dangerous here.

"I'm quite happy with my reading, thank you," she said, with a gesture towards her book on the bench behind her. "I don't often have the opportunity to read for a long time undisturbed."

Cosimo looked at her, a frown in his eyes. "Are you always this stubborn?"

Meg flushed with annoyance. "I fail to see what's stubborn about preferring my own company to yours, sir."

His well-shaped eyebrows lifted again at this tart rejoinder. "Since you haven't spent any time in my company, I don't know how you could possibly be sure you won't enjoy it."

Meg's flush deepened. He was making her feel like a difficult child, when she was making a perfectly reasonable request to be left to her own devices. "This is a pointless conversation," she said, turning back to the window and her book. "If you have business in this cabin, then please get on with it. If you don't, I would ask you to leave me in peace."

He shrugged. "Please yourself. I'll tell Biggins to bring you some luncheon."

"G'bye . . . g'bye . . ." Gus chanted as the door closed behind the captain. He hopped off his perch and over to the window seat. He flew up onto the cushion beside Meg and began to preen himself, muttering incomprehensibly as he did so.

"Don't think I find your company flattering," Meg said to him. He looked up from his grooming and she could have sworn one bright, beady eye winked at her.

Chapter 3

Cosimo was annoyed and that very fact increased his irritation. He was very rarely put out but Miss Meg Barratt had needled him. He made his way to the galley, where he knew he'd find Biggins. A pot of coffee bubbled fragrantly on the range and the cook was chopping up a large slab of beef for a stew. Biggins was sitting companionably at the table with a mug of coffee, whittling on a piece of ivory. Both men stopped what they were doing when the captain loomed in the narrow doorway.

"Anything I can get you, sir?" Biggins asked, wondering why his usually equable captain had such a frown on his face.

"Yes, take some bread and cheese into my cabin for Miss Barratt, will you, and then bring me some on deck. A carafe of the burgundy too." He turned to leave, saying acidly over his shoulder, "And make sure you knock loudly and get the lady's permission before you open the cabin door. She's rather sensitive on the issue of her privacy."

"Didn't sound too happy, did he?" the cook observed af-

ter a discreet minute as he fetched a wheel of cheddar from
a shelf. "Something's put him out."

"It's that Miss Barratt, I'll lay odds," Biggins stated, filling a carafe of red wine from a barrel. "Summat's not right
there."

"We *was* expecting a lady passenger," the cook pointed
out, slicing cheese deftly before attacking a loaf of barley
bread.

"Aye, but not this one," the other man stated with a significant nod. "I heard captain and the surgeon talking last
night. Right mystery it is, Silas."

"Well, if you ask me, everything's a mystery when you
sail with the captain," Silas stated. "You got any idea where
we're goin' this time?"

Biggins shook his head. "Course not. No one does. It's
just like always."

"Well, he pays well," Silas said with a shrug.

Cosimo returned to the deck, where the wind had done
nothing useful in his absence and the tantalizingly distant
outline of land was barely visible. He leaned on the railing
and stared down at the flat surface of the sea. His present
mood puzzled him. There was no denying that Meg
Barratt had somehow got under his skin. Her stubborn refusal to respond to what he had fondly thought were his
own rather charming attempts at gaining her confidence
had definitely irritated him. Which was unusual. Ordinarily minor miscalculations of that kind ran off him like
water off an oiled hide. He simply returned to the assault
with fresh ammunition and new tactics.

He swung away from the railing with an air of resolution. There was nothing so special about Miss Barratt that

she couldn't be won over by some technique or another. He would try again. He hastened back to the galley, where Biggins was just setting a shiny red apple on a tray with the bread and cheese.

"I'll take that," Cosimo said, lifting the tray from the table. He frowned at it. "Wine," he said. "A glass of burgundy."

"Aye, sir." Biggins, with a raised eyebrow in the direction of the interested cook, hurriedly poured a glass from the decanter he'd already filled and set it on the tray. "Anything else, Captain?"

"There was a salami," Cosimo said. "A particularly tasty one, I recall. Cut a few slices, will you, Silas?"

"Aye, sir." Silas lifted the fat, glistening sausage from its hook above his head. "'Tis a very toothsome one, I grant you, sir. Those Frenchies know what they're doing when it comes to sausage."

"And a good few other things," Cosimo remarked, thinking of their spectacular success at war over the last couple of years. Austria, Rome, Switzerland... all had fallen to Napoleon. What the little Corsican lacked in true blue French blood, he certainly made up for in his ambitions for France, not to mention for himself. Which brought his reflections full circle. Napoleon was the object of his present journey, and if he was to adapt a now ruined plan that had seemed as near to foolproof as such plans could be, then he needed to take this tray of food to Miss Meg Barratt.

He hefted the tray on the palm of his hand in the manner of an experienced waiter and made his way down the corridor to his cabin. He knocked loudly three times. Gus cackled an invitation and he heard Meg say, "Oh, do be quiet, you infuriating bird."

The door was opened by Meg, who gestured wordlessly that he should come in. "I've brought you luncheon as promised," he said cheerfully. "I still think you'd prefer to eat it on deck, but you are your own mistress."

"That's nice to know," she said. "I wish someone would tell this bird that."

"Oh, you can't tell Gus anything," Cosimo declared, setting the tray on the table. "I'm surprised you don't find him a kindred spirit."

Meg gasped at the effrontery of this and then she laughed. This wretched man made her laugh. Very few people could do that. Oh, she had a disgraceful tendency to discover things to laugh *at* on occasion, but very few people could totally engage her sense of humor. It was a trait she and Arabella shared and fostered in each other.

"You have a very engaging laugh, as I'm sure you've been told many times by many men," Cosimo observed, feeling the return of his own good humor.

The amusement froze in her eyes and her laughter died. "Thank you for the tray, Captain," she said in a dry and neutral tone.

Cosimo cursed himself. This lady was not one to respond to lightly given compliments. She would see impudence where another woman would see flirtation. Or would she? He regarded her thoughtfully. "What's your opinion of flirtation, Miss Barratt?"

The question so surprised her that for a moment she was unable to respond. Then she said smartly, "In the right place and at the right time, I have no objection to it. But I don't care for clumsiness on any occasion." On which note, she sat down at the table and began to slice the apple as if her companion was no longer there.

Cosimo recognized that he was bested and swept her an

elaborate bow. "I accept my congé, ma'am." He left the cabin but was unable to prevent himself from closing the door with the hint of a slam.

Meg smiled to herself before she realized that she was contemplating further such engagements with Captain Cosimo and the amusement they would afford. She had already resolved that there would be no temptations in this strange and troublesome situation, however attractive they might be. For a minute there her resolution had faltered.

She sipped her wine and absently passed a slice of apple to Gus, who was sitting expectantly beside her plate.

"Thankee... thankee," he said, tossing the fruit into the air before catching it in his beak.

"You grow oddly endearing," Meg observed, offering him another piece. She caught herself wondering if that could be true of the bird's owner and mentally slapped her wrist. The problem was that she enjoyed the game of flirtation far too much. In the last few months in London she'd had ample opportunity to indulge herself with a variety of totally unsuitable but utterly engaging men, who had no more interest in a serious relationship than she did. And now she found herself trapped on a ship with a man who bid fair to be the most engaging of any of her former playmates, and also the most unsuitable.

What was he? Not an ordinary ship's captain, that was obvious. He was the captain of a sloop-of-war for one thing, and such vessels didn't ply the seas in harmless pursuits. Certainly not in wartime. But he wasn't a naval captain either and this was not a ship of the British navy. No one wore a uniform for a start. It was a private ship. And its captain played the charmer with that delightful smile and the engaging glint in his eye, but she'd seen beneath that surface to a much harder core in their argument over the door key. There had been nothing charming, seductive, or even ordinarily pleasant about his manner and countenance then. No, she had no doubt that this Cosimo was a man to be reckoned with. And whatever he was doing... he and his ship... was rather more complicated than a pleasure trip.

She took a sip of her wine and then rose from the table. Curious she went over to the chart table. She had no experience with naval charts and they revealed nothing to her. She could see the Channel Islands and the coast of France. A few notations had been made on a sheet of paper beside the charts but they made no sense to her. Presumably he'd told her the truth about sailing to Sark. But what kind of business would a sloop-of-war have on such a tiny, insignificant speck of land?

Curiosity now thoroughly aroused, Meg began to explore the cabin. She examined the books on the shelves. Volumes on seamanship and naval history for the most part, but also, surprisingly, a few books on ornithology. The captain of the *Mary Rose* was interested in birds, apparently. He didn't seem much for fiction, which didn't surprise her. There was a Latin dictionary, however, which did surprise her since there weren't any classical volumes to accompany it, a Bible, and a copy of Samuel Johnson's dictionary. She picked the latter out of the shelf and leafed through it. Scattered throughout were odd little marks in the margins beside certain entries.

A loud knock at the door made her jump guiltily. It was Cosimo's knock, she was growing accustomed to its particular rhythm. She shoved the book back on the shelf and went to open the door. Somehow the act of opening it herself gave the illusion of control.

"I trust you enjoyed your luncheon," he said as he stepped past her into the cabin.

"Yes, thank you," she responded with the same formality.

"You'll have to excuse me, I wish to change my shirt." He opened one of the drawers in the bulwark and began sorting through the contents.

Meg resumed her seat on the cushioned bench beneath the window and picked up her book.

Gus, who seemed to have been asleep for the last half hour, took his head out from under his wing and flew onto his perch. "Lovely day," he declared, somewhat irrelevantly Meg thought as she studiously turned her eyes to her book, trying to ignore the man who was calmly stripping to his waist in the middle of the cabin.

She couldn't quite manage it, however. Her gaze slid away from the printed page. He had his back to her as he shrugged out of his shirt. A long, lean, well-muscled back, just a light dusting of reddish hair against the spine. Slim waist.

No, this was not a sensible activity. She forced her eyes back to the page. Arabella had once said quite objectively that Meg's attitude to men was rather masculine. She viewed them in much the same way men viewed women, starting with an unabashed assessment of their physical attributes. There was some truth in the observation, Meg was forced to admit. She, who had enthusiastically given her virginity to a Venetian gondolier who resembled Michelangelo's *David*, tended to abstain from considered reflection on the wisdom of satisfying lust. But that was in situations where she was in control. Here, while she was not afraid of anything, she was not in control of anything.

Except her own reactions. She turned a page with a crisp crackle. ·

"Biggins should have replaced the water in the jugs," Cosimo declared from the head in the tone of voice of one commenting on the lack of sedan chairs on a rainy afternoon. Meg made no response. She didn't want to know what he was doing in there. If he was underlining the fact that they were sharing this intimate space, then he'd certainly succeeded.

Cosimo reappeared, buttoning a crisp white shirt. He shook out the sleeves and fastened the buttons at the cuff. "Ring the bell for Biggins if you need anything."

"When do you think the wind will pick up?"

"By evening . . . it'll be too late to make harbor though. We'll have to stand out to sea until daylight."

Meg remembered the rocky outcrops around the island indicated on the chart. "It's too dangerous to navigate in the dark?"

"Most of these coastlines are," he said. "Brittany is the very devil, and some of the Channel Islands are no different."

"Why are you going to Sark? What about Jersey, or Guernsey, aren't they bigger?"

He had paused by the bookshelf and was adjusting the position of the volume of Dr. Johnson's dictionary that Meg had thrust back. He turned, his hand still on the spine of the book. A smile curved his mouth and a glimmer of knowing amusement sparked in his eye. "Curious, Miss Meg?"

"Is it surprising?" she snapped back.

"No more surprising than your sangfroid," he said. "I'd expect a woman in your situation to exhibit some signs of dismay. Instead you're as challenging as a fox terrier." His eyes narrowed a little. "Who are you, Miss Meg Barratt?"

"Who are you, Captain Cosimo?" she returned. "Answer me and I'll answer you."

"I, my dear ma'am, am the captain of a sloop sailing to the island of Sark," he told her with a hint of laughter in his voice.

Meg shook her head, ignoring the invitation of that laugh. "Not the right answer, Captain."

His bow was pure satire. He left her with her book and her empty tray and empty water jugs in the head. And outside the sun was shining. She could feel its warmth striking the back of her neck as she sat on the window seat. Her legs were twitching. She watched her right foot kick out seemingly of its own volition. Then her left.

Gus hopped to the closed door. "G'bye," he said. It was an order, not a statement.

Meg got up and went to open the door. The macaw hopped over the lintel and towards a flight of steps at the end of a corridor. Sunlight poured down from an opening above and Meg could smell the sea and the sun. Behind her were the stale confines of a space where she'd already spent far too much time. She pulled the door behind her and followed Gus up into the sunlight.

The scene on deck was a mixture of activity and inertia. Men, some shirtless, were sitting around mending sails or splicing rope while a sailor in a loose red smock strummed a guitar. Others washed clothes in big wooden tubs, singing as they did so, while their companions lay stretched asleep in the various patches of sunlight on the decks. The ship rocked lazily on the smooth blue water, while gulls screamed and whirled overhead.

Meg stood taking in the scene, aware of glances that

were openly curious, appraising even, but in no way offensive. She smiled tentatively and one or two touched a fingertip to their foreheads in a half salute. She looked around for Cosimo and saw him up on the quarterdeck, sitting on the deck, leaning back against the railing, face tilted towards the sun, his eyes closed. A picture of relaxation.

She made her way across the mid-deck, the smooth, well-honed boards warm against her bare feet. She passed a pair of sailors fishing over the side, and climbed the short flight of steps to the quarterdeck. No one stood at the lashed helm, but a couple of young men dressed rather more formally, if shirt and britches could be called formal, than the sailors below, sat playing cards on the opposite side of the deck from the captain. They jumped to their feet as Meg appeared.

She waved them down again and ducked beneath the boom with its tightly furled sail, making her way to where Cosimo still sat, comfortably ensconced on a coil of rope and seemingly oblivious to her arrival. However, he opened his eyes as her shadow fell across him.

"Ah, Miss Meg," he said with a lazy smile. "You decided to take the air after all."

"Gus wished to come on deck," she said.

He laughed. "And we all know that Gus is incapable of going anywhere unescorted."

She gave him a rueful smile. "I admit it. I was suffering from acute cabin fever."

"Well, sit beside me." He shifted a little on the coil of rope to make room for her. "In the absence of chairs, we make do. But you'll find this quite comfortable."

"I'm sure I shall," she said, lowering herself to the rope. It was surprisingly comfortable, warmed by the sun and oddly supportive, like an overstuffed cushion. The deck rail made a natural backrest.

"A little wine?" he offered, gesturing to the glass and decanter on the deck beside him.

"There's only one glass."

He shrugged indolently. "If you wish for another, call one of my officers over." He gestured across the quarterdeck to the card players.

Meg hesitated. Ordinarily she wouldn't think twice about sharing a glass with an acquaintance, but in these far from ordinary circumstances it seemed to smack of dangerous intimacy. But she had the impression that Captain Cosimo would be amused if she made something of the issue. Instead she said casually, "I don't like to disturb their game."

He nodded and reached sideways to refill the glass, handing it to her, observing, "Wine and sunshine. Two of the greatest aphrodisiacs in the world."

Meg nearly choked on her first sip. *What was he playing at?* Did he view flirtation as an automatic reaction to the presence of a member of the opposite sex, however inappropriate the setting? Was he some kind of lecher? A Casanova rather than a Cosimo. Non-response once again seemed the most dignified response. She ignored the comment.

Cosimo smiled as he tipped his head back to the sun again. He was enjoying himself. Miss Meg had bested him verbally all too often in their short acquaintance and pressing the attack seemed like a viable tactic. It had certainly caught her off balance and that gave him a little advantage. If she was discomposed by his pointed flirtation, all the better. Even if she did accuse him of clumsiness, he reflected with a slightly caustic edge to his smile.

He realized that his present enjoyment was enhanced by the proximity of her slight frame. Ana's gown was a little big for her, giving her an appearance of frailty that he was confident was merely an illusion. He liked the fact that she'd come shoeless on deck, a lack of interest in the propriety of her appearance that was in keeping with the outspokenness of her personality, as he'd encountered it so far. And a quality that boded well for the use he would like to make of her. She seemed unconcerned by the hopeless tangle of tight red curls that flew every which way around her angular face. The previous day's rain had given her an unruly and distinctly frizzy halo.

As if aware of his reflective assessment of her charms, Meg sat up and adjusted the loose bodice of her gown, retying the sash rather vigorously beneath her small breasts. She glanced sideways at him and didn't know whether to be reassured or not when he didn't even open his eyes.

Gus flew down from the railing, creating a welcome diversion. He hopped onto Cosimo's knee and regarded him with head cocked. "G'morning...g'morning," he declared with what Meg would have sworn was a questioning note.

Cosimo opened one eye. "Surely a man can take a nap on a sunny afternoon, Gus."

"G'morning," the macaw repeated with rather more insistence.

"He is the most extraordinary bird," Meg said. "He makes everyone do exactly what he wants."

"He has us all well trained," Cosimo agreed, opening both eyes and hitching himself farther up against the railing. "Pass me the glass, will you?"

Meg handed him the wineglass. He filled it and drank with a little sigh of pleasure. She remembered something he had said when first they'd met. "This mission of yours," she said rather musingly. "I understood you to say it was a matter of some urgency...so much so that you couldn't possibly take the time to turn around and take me back to Folkestone."

His eyes sharpened a little and he turned to look at her. "Yes, I did," he agreed. "What of it?"

"For a man with a sense of such urgency, you seem remarkably untroubled by being becalmed," she pointed out. "A whole day has been wasted, it seems to me. And if you can't make harbor tonight, then a whole night too."

He smiled again and shrugged lightly. "I'm a sailor, Miss Meg. I know I can do nothing about the wind. It will serve me when it chooses and only then. I await its pleasure with patience."

Once again she had the sense of that deep core of the man existing beneath this carefree, amused façade. A stillness ran there with the hardness that she'd already seen. What else? Power and resolution, she was convinced. Cosimo was no idle dilettante sailor.

"Why do you sail a sloop-of-war?" she asked abruptly. "You don't belong to the navy."

"No," he agreed. "Not in so many words."

"Ah." Meg sat up fully, curling her legs beneath her. "A denial that's not a denial. I've always found those most interesting."

He nodded. "Yes, I can see why."

"But you're not going to say anything else?"

He shook his head this time. "No."

Meg absorbed this, continuing to look at him with interest. Whatever his mission it had something to do with the war. "Did those men-of-war leave Folkestone with you?"

The gleam in his eye intensified. "So you noticed them?"

"They were hard to miss." She turned to look out between the rails and then pulled herself to her feet and scanned the horizon. "They're not in evidence now."

"They too are at the mercy of the same mistress," he said, standing up with her. "The wind plays no favorites." He walked across to the helm and picked up a telescope. "Here, take a good look at your surroundings, Miss Meg."

"I wish you wouldn't call me that," she said tartly as she took the telescope. "It makes me feel like a governess."

At that he laughed. "Oh, no, not you, Meg. No governess ever had such ungovernable red hair and such an asp's tongue."

"I wouldn't know, I never had one," she said, raising the telescope. "At least not beyond the age of five."

"So you attended an establishment...a school for young ladies," Cosimo said.

Meg lowered the telescope. "Drawing, study of the globe, a little pianoforte, a little Italian, a smattering of French?" She shook her head. "No, sir. I didn't have a governess beyond the age of five and I was never educated in some establishment to be one."

Cosimo was puzzled. He knew little about the education of girls, but women of Meg Barratt's position, or at least what he assumed from her manner was her social position, usually had some kind of formal learning. "You had no education beyond the age of five?"

"We had tutors," she said impatiently, scanning the horizon. "Of course we were educated."

"*We?*"

"My friend, Arabella. We grew up as sisters." She lowered the telescope and turned slowly to look at him. "I have family, Cosimo. A father and a mother...as well as Bella and Jack, who will be frantic at my disappearance. Do you not understand how I feel?...How they must be feeling?" She stared at him and for a moment he saw revulsion in the green gaze, and a sheen of tears.

He drew a deep breath. "I can do nothing about it until we make landfall. You must see that." He gestured at the sea, the sky, the empty vista.

"Not at this moment, certainly," she said, the tears gone. "But you could have done when first you realized your mistake, and you can rectify the situation as soon as we reach Sark. There must be someone ... some fishing boat, who will take me back."

He hadn't ignored Meg's situation, Cosimo reflected, but he had put it to the back of his mind. He had been concentrating on plans that didn't involve sending her back to England and so he hadn't allowed such a possibility to interfere with his greater purpose. An error, clearly. He needed her confidence.

"As I said, that's always a possibility, but ..." He held up his hand as she began to protest. "But what is a *certainty* is that once we land I can ensure that a message reaches someone you choose in England within thirty-six hours."

Her eyes widened, lost some of their scornful anger. "How?"

"A pigeon courier." It was a piece of information that gave little away. She had already surmised that he was in some way connected to the navy. It would come as no surprise that he should have access to some of its resources.

Meg absorbed this in silence. It made perfect sense and it would bring relief to her loved ones much more quickly than an uncooperative wind and a fishing boat could. Presumably the pigeon went to its home in England and a human being took the message to its destination. There was something rather cloak-and-dagger about the idea of homing pigeons, however. Questions hovered on her tongue and were quickly swallowed. Cosimo was niggardly with information and she was fairly certain he wouldn't satisfy her curiosity too easily. "Thank you," she said simply. "That relieves my mind."

"Good." He turned to the rail beside her and took the telescope. The distant land was suddenly sharper. He looked up at the pennant flying from the topmast. It stirred faintly.

"Wind, Captain," a voice called, from nowhere as far as Meg was concerned. But the sloop came instantly alive. Men lazing on deck were on their feet, others spilled upwards from the companionways, a broad-shouldered man appeared at the helm, rapidly unlashing it.

"Make sail," Cosimo called between cupped hands and sailors leaped into the rigging. Meg watched with fascination as the sails were unfurled and snapped by a sudden gust before Cosimo, his eyes on the sails, again called an order and the helmsman adjusted the wheel. The *Mary Rose* came on course for Sark, her sails filling slowly as the wind increased.

"In time?" Meg asked.

"No," Cosimo answered. "It'll take us till dark to come within two miles of the harbor. We'll stand to there and go in at first light. Excuse me..." He left her, loping across the quarterdeck, down the steps, and towards the companionway.

Meg stayed where she was until she began to feel superfluous. She didn't think she was in the way but it was hard to be the only spectator in the midst of such activity. She looked around for Gus. He was nowhere to be seen and she guessed that he too preferred the undisturbed peace of the cabin. She picked her way through the hive and climbed down the companionway. The cabin door was closed.

She looked at it for a minute and then, adapting the assumption that sauce for the goose is sauce for the gander, knocked vigorously. Gus invited her in at the same time that Cosimo called, "Enter."

She did so. Cosimo didn't look up from the charts. He was using compasses, making swift pencil notations as he did so. They reminded her of the odd notations in the margins of the dictionaries. He said over his shoulder, "Ring for Biggins. He'll fill the bath for you with the hot water they have to jettison now we're under way. There's nothing for you to do on deck and I'll be out of here in less than five minutes."

Meg realized that a hot bath had become the most unlooked for and therefore most wonderful indulgence imaginable. "Thank you." She let the door close behind her.

"You'll have to endure Gus's company. He doesn't come on deck when we're sailing in a stiff breeze," Cosimo said, still bent over the charts. "You can put him in his cage and cover it, if you like."

Meg glanced at Gus, who was sitting on his perch quietly picking at his wing feathers. "I'll trust him to keep his eyes shut."

Cosimo straightened. "Good." He went to the door.

Meg had the sense that he had almost forgotten who she was and why she was there as he left. She rang the bell for Biggins.

He came within minutes. "Captain says you'd like enough water for a bath, ma'am?"

So he hadn't forgotten. "Yes, thank you, Biggins." She lifted her hair away from her scalp. It would be good to wash it. Perhaps she could dry it in the air on deck. With the wind that she could now feel beneath her feet as the *Mary Rose* lifted to the swell, her hair would dry in no time. She went back to the cupboard with the clothes meant for Ana and looked for something suitable for a woman who wanted to be unobtrusive on a nighttime deck.

Biggins reappeared with the youngster who'd helped with breakfast that morning. "Captain says he'll be dining on deck in two hours when we drops anchor, ma'am," Biggins said, while gesturing with an impatient hand that the boy should take the jugs into the head. "Looks like it'll be a nice evening so he'd like to know if you'll be joining him, or dining in the cabin, ma'am."

Hadn't she already decided that her hair would dry better in the evening air? "Please tell the captain that I'd like to join him on deck."

"Right y'are, ma'am." Biggins clicked his fingers at his companion, who backed out of the tiny space with the empty jugs. "We'll be back in a couple of minutes, ma'am, with more hot water."

Ten minutes later Meg was wallowing in the shallow tub of hot water, while Gus sat companionably in the doorway, keeping up a mindless series of phrases that thankfully appeared to need no response.

Chapter 4

$\mathcal{M}$eg found it difficult to keep her footing as she dried herself after her bath. The *Mary Rose* was skipping over the water under a stiff breeze and the sky beyond the cabin windows was darkening. Wrapped in the towel, her hair in a towel turban, she knelt on the window cushion and looked out. The sea had lost its sparkle and was now the color of pewter, the rolling waves tinged pink by the setting sun. She could see land more clearly now. A small rocky outcrop surmounted by green hills. It looked deserted from this distance.

Cosimo's now familiar knock came at the door. "Just a minute," she called, jumping off the cushion. The towel was no substitute for a dressing gown or even a nightgown.

"Forgive me, I thought you'd be finished with your bath by now," he said through the door and Meg could hear the exasperating lilt of amusement in his voice.

She dropped the damp towel in the middle of the floor and yanked open the clothes cupboard. She grabbed the hooded cloak and wrapped it securely around herself. "All right," she said somewhat grudgingly.

Cosimo came in. His eyebrows lifted in astonishment. "If you don't mind my saying so, that's the most eccentric costume. A turban and a cloak? Is it some new fashion that's passed me by?"

She glared at him. "You didn't give me time to dress properly." She pulled the towel from her head and shook out her hair.

"Why didn't you say?" He bent and picked up the larger discarded towel from the floor.

"I assumed you had urgent business in *your* cabin," she said, waving vaguely in the direction of the charts. "I wouldn't want to keep you from it."

"Nothing that couldn't wait," he said, tossing the towel into the head. "Actually I merely came to fetch a cloak. It's turning chilly up there. You'll need one and something on your feet when you come up." He was opening another cupboard as he spoke. He pulled out a cloak of serviceable dark wool and slung it around his shoulders.

Meg had resumed her seat in the window, hugging her own garment tightly to her. She could find nothing to amuse her in this uncomfortable situation, but Cosimo clearly derived some pleasure out of it. The sooner she got off this ship, the better, she reflected crossly. And then the question reared its head oddly enough for the first time. Where was he going to sleep?

"Where are you going to sleep?" she asked involuntarily.

"When...tonight...?" He seemed genuinely puzzled by the question. "In here, of course."

In silence Meg looked at the narrow box-bed and then back at him.

"It is a little narrow for two," he said. "Unless of course one is particularly fond of cuddling." When she remained silent he said with a chuckle, "You need have no fear for your virtue, Miss Meg. I'll sling a hammock." He pointed to two hooks in the ceiling that she had noticed and wondered about. Then, whistling softly to himself, he left the cabin.

Meg felt she hadn't come too well out of that encounter. In fact, she was beginning to realize that Captain Cosimo was playing with her. He seemed to enjoy teasing her, trying to discomfit her, throw her off balance. Was it simply because she'd annoyed him earlier by refusing to respond to his friendly overtures? If so, she wouldn't really blame him. She'd probably have felt the same herself even though she'd have castigated herself for pettiness. But she didn't think it was that. He didn't strike her as a character who would indulge in pettiness. So what *was* his game?

Well, she wouldn't find out sitting here hugging herself in a cloak. She went to the clothes cupboard again and examined its contents once more. The bronze she had worn earlier would do fine, but she'd just bathed and clean clothes seemed in order. She lifted out a sage green silk gown that seemed more formal than the others. Silver lace edged the three-quarter-length sleeves and a similar band decorated the narrow hem. She'd intended to find something that would allow her to fade into the background but something perverse prodded her to make more of an effort. She laid the gown over a chair and fetched clean linen and a pair of thin woolen stockings.

In fifteen minutes she was dressed. The only mirror was a small round glass set into the wall at the right height for shaving. Even to see her face she had to stand on tiptoe. Her hair was almost dry and she used a comb lying on the shelf below the mirror to bring the curls into some kind of order. The gown, like the one she'd worn earlier, felt a little big, but the addition of the leather buttoned boots gave her a little more height. The color suited her, it was one she often wore, so she would assume that her appearance was more than presentable.

Now, why that should matter was something else altogether. A loud clanging and scraping as of a huge chain being unraveled interrupted her reverie. She spun round from the mirror and ran to the window. The *Mary Rose* appeared to have stopped. The sound of running feet, shouted orders, and the squeak of bolts and halyards came from overhead.

"In port . . . in port . . ." Gus announced, hopping to the door. "G'bye . . . g'bye."

So they'd dropped anchor. That would explain the noise and the bustle. And the macaw was now ready to leave the cabin. Well, Meg was ready too.

She slung the cloak around her shoulders and opened the door and Gus flew up to her shoulder and playfully pecked at her earlobe. "You do me too much honor," she declared, but she was rather pleased nevertheless at this clear indication of the bird's acceptance.

She climbed the companionway and emerged on deck, where the last bustle of furling sails and dropping anchor was almost finished. The light was fading fast now and the evening star shone low in the sky, a three-quarter moon climbing just over the horizon. She stayed at the top of the companionway, unwilling to thread her way to the quarterdeck until it was clear all activity on deck had ceased. Gus showed no such restraint. He took off from her shoulder and swooped towards the lowered boom. He walked along it as delicately as if it were a balance beam and then swooped down onto the quarterdeck.

Meg could see Cosimo at the helm, directing operations in a calm but carrying voice. His cloak hung loosely from his shoulders as he stood braced on the deck, and the evening breeze ruffled the long auburn hair that curled loosely around his ears and flopped over his forehead. There was something almost raffish about him, she thought. An air of careless competence that she knew in her heart of hearts could be her downfall.

His assessing gaze swept his little floating empire and then fell upon Meg in the companionway. He raised a hand in greeting and then gestured imperatively that she should come to him.

Meg obeyed the gesture and climbed up to the quarterdeck.

"Come over here," he called softly. She stepped up beside him at the wheel. He called to the fresh-faced young officer, "Mr. Fisher, summon all hands, if you please."

"Aye, Captain." The young man left his position at the stern rail where he was directing the stowing of the mizzen topsail and came to the front of the quarterdeck. He took a whistle from his pocket and blew a shrill piercing note.

Men poured onto the mid-deck in a jostling yet orderly throng. They fell silent looking up at their captain and the rest of the little group on the quarterdeck. It was a curious rather than an anxious silence, Meg felt. And there was a touch of anticipation in the air as if they were waiting to hear something that would please them.

Cosimo spoke in what seemed like his ordinary voice but the words carried easily. "Gentlemen, as you know we're waiting to make harbor on Sark. We shall be there a day or two. Miss Barratt will be our guest." He put a hand on Meg's shoulder and drew her in front of him. "You will, I know, do her every courtesy. Any questions? Yes, Bosun."

He pointed at a thickset man with a deeply lined face and a thick crop of iron gray hair.

"Beggin' your pardon, Cap'n, but where will we be going after Sark?" A faint stir among the men greeted the question and their air of anticipation grew sharper.

Cosimo laughed, the easy laugh of a man among trusted companions. "My friends, you will know that when I do."

A knowing chuckle greeted this and many of them shook their heads in resignation. The bosun grinned. "Didn't expect nothin' else, sir."

"No, I don't expect you did," Cosimo agreed. "We sail with the dawn tide, until then stand down. We've meat aplenty for a decent dinner, and a hogshead of ale."

A cheer went up, and a couple of caps waved in the air. Cosimo raised a hand in dismissal and turned to Mr. Fisher, who stood ready with another young man who could almost be his twin, Meg thought. The same pink cheeks, still with a hint of puppy fat, the same wide mouth and the same brown eyes. Cosimo said, "Post a crow's nest watch, Mr. Fisher. Let's not forget we're in French waters. And Mr. Graves, check the navigation chart and plot me a course that will take us through those rocks and not onto them."

"Aye, sir." It was said in unison.

Cosimo smiled, "Miss Barratt, allow me to introduce my lieutenants. Mr. Fisher and Mr. Graves."

The two young men bowed. "Pleasure to have you aboard, ma'am," Mr. Fisher said.

"Yes, indeed, ma'am," his companion agreed. "Yours to command, ma'am."

"Why, thank you...thank you both," Meg said with a warm smile of her own. "I will endeavor not to get in your way."

Both young men blushed scarlet and were rendered mute. Cosimo rescued them with a wave of dismissal and they backed away.

When they were out of earshot, Meg asked, half amused, half disapproving, "Shouldn't they still be in school?"

"They are," Cosimo said easily. "The sea is both their school and their tutor. But they're older than they look. Just not very experienced in the ways of the world outside this one."

"They could be brothers."

"In fact they're cousins." He moved away from the wheel as the helmsman came up. "Lash it well, Mike. There's a touch of mischief in the wind."

"Aye, thought so meself, sir," the man said, giving Meg a small nod. It seemed that now she'd been officially introduced, she could be noticed properly. She responded with a friendly nod of her own.

"Let's watch the moonrise," Cosimo invited, steering her towards the stern rail. Meg was aware of a bustle of activity behind her as she rested her forearms on the rail and gazed out over the water. A thin river of silver flowed over the surface as the moon rose.

"How do two nearly identical cousins come to be working on the same ship?" she inquired casually, enjoying the feel of the breeze rustling through her wonderfully clean hair.

"Families often do. You'll find brothers on the same frigates and men-of-war all through the navy. The sea runs in the blood."

Meg turned to look at him. "But this is not a naval ship. I suspect it's a privateer, Captain Cosimo. Why would a family entrust their young men to a ship that has little if any legitimacy on the high seas?"

He chuckled. "Are you talking of the ship or of its captain, ma'am?"

"Its captain, of course."

"Then there, my dear, you have your answer." He said nothing more, merely gazed out towards the invisible horizon.

Meg contemplated this. He was, of course, telling her that he was the reason the families of his lieutenants had entrusted their scions to his ship. "Are they related to you in some way?" she asked.

He turned his head lazily and regarded her with an unsettling gleam in his eye. "You are very inquisitive, Miss Meg."

"Why would it be a secret?" She raised her eyebrows and returned his look with a slightly sardonic air.

"It's not. They're the sons of my sisters. Tell me how else I may satisfy your curiosity."

"Are they older or younger than you? Your sisters, I mean."

"They're twins, and they're four years younger than I am."

Meg nodded. That would explain the cousins' physical resemblance. "So how old are your sisters?"

"I think you mean how old am I," he observed, that gleam intensifying. "It seems I interest you."

"Don't flatter yourself," she said acidly. "I'm merely trying to find out what kind of man has me imprisoned on his privateer. Purely in the interests of self-defense, you understand."

"Tell me honestly, Meg, have you felt threatened even for a second on my ship?"

Honestly obliged her to say no. "But that doesn't alter

the fact that I'm here against my will and you refused to take me back once the mistake was realized," she added.

Cosimo drummed his fingers against the rail in what could only be called impatience. "If it had been possible, I would have taken you straight back. But it wasn't, as I've explained, so can we have done with it, please."

Meg inhaled sharply at the asperity in his tone. She had been singing the same song, she knew, but it didn't alter its truth or its relevance to her situation. She was silent and after a minute Cosimo said in a placatory tone, "My sisters are thirty-three."

Well, that was a droplet of information. "How old are the cousins?"

"Seventeen."

Meg reflected that she had just celebrated her twenty-ninth birthday and Cosimo's sisters, only four years older, had seventeen-year-old sons. She found it an unsettling thought although she hadn't considered herself anxious to be married or even particularly maternal. She was on the shelf and content to be so. *Or was she?*

Well, that was a question that might at some point require some soul-searching, but not at present. Her gaze fixed on Cosimo's hands as they rested lightly on the deck rail. They were very brown and strong looking, the nails unmanicured, the knuckles rather knobbly. His fingers were long and his wrists surprisingly slender and supple. Their strength was taken for granted. Any man who could handle that great helm in the gale-force wind that had blown last night must have extraordinary strength in his hands, arms, and shoulders. Involuntarily her gaze ran up his body. He wore the cloak draped carelessly around his shoulders and the breadth of those shoulders was obvious to the most casual examination. She remembered her earlier covert scrutiny when he'd changed his shirt in the cabin, how she'd been so powerfully aware of the ripple of muscles along his back and in his arms.

Oh, dear. This was not at all helpful, she thought, searching for a neutral topic that would give her some distance from the disturbing proximity of his body. "What part of England are you from?"

He turned his back to the rail and leaned against it, his arms folded across his chest. His eyes were narrowed and Meg had the absolute conviction that he'd been aware of every instant of her examination and her conclusions. "Dorset," he said. "How about you, Miss Meg?"

"Oh, please don't call me that," she begged. "I hate it so."

"Then let's have a pact. If you never call me Captain Cosimo again, I will never call you Miss Meg. How's that for a bargain."

"A good one," she said, responding willy-nilly to his smile. "And I come from Kent."

He nodded, and the smile was still in his eyes as he said, "Now I'm a little stuck for a roundabout way to elicit the personal information you twisted out of me."

"Let me save you the trouble. I am twenty-nine," Meg responded readily. "I don't subscribe to the school of thought that women should never reveal their ages."

"No," he said appreciatively. "I don't imagine you do." He had a slightly questioning look in his eye as he continued to look at her. Meg Barratt was a most unusual woman. Oddly attractive although not by any conventional standards; *jolie-laide*, as the French would say. But while the surface appeal interested him, he was intrigued by whatever lay beneath.

So far he'd seen intelligence and wit. A strong composure as David Porter had noted. She was stubborn and very strong-willed, she'd shown him that much. And she appeared to have adapted to her situation readily if not willingly. What would Ana think of her?

A shadow crossed his face. Ana was a good judge of character, and an expert when it came to assessing the necessary skills for the work she herself did.

"Is something the matter?" Meg asked, chilled by the sudden change in his expression.

He shook his head, saying curtly, "No, nothing at all." He turned back to the rail and gazed out at the silver path of moonlight rippling on the black water. Ana was also expert at looking after herself, he told himself. She had been trained to withstand interrogation, to use information to her own advantage when under duress. He would hold on to that. And in the meantime, concentrate on the woman he had.

When he spoke again his voice was once more light and humorous and the shadows had left his eyes. "So, permit me another personal question, Meg. You talked of your parents, of your friends, but is there no one else who would be concerned by your absence?"

"A man, you mean?" She gave a slightly self-mocking laugh.

"You wear no rings."

She looked at her bare hands. "No. So, no husband. A correct deduction, sir."

"A fiancé?"

She shook her head. "No fiancé."

"A lover?"

"This grows *very* personal, sir."

"My apologies, ma'am, if it's *too* personal."

At that she laughed. "I have no secrets . . . and at present no lover."

"Ah." He absorbed this, most particularly the *at present*. It seemed to imply that Meg Barratt was something of a woman of the world. And that would certainly fit with what he'd observed thus far of her personality.

A cough came from behind them and they both turned. Biggins said, "Supper's ready, Cap'n."

"Thank you." Cosimo offered his arm to Meg. "Allow me to escort you to the table, ma'am."

It was absurd but she entered the game willingly enough. The quarterdeck had been transformed. Oil lamps hung from the yards, throwing a soft golden glow over a table laid with a checkered cloth, silverware, and glass. A wonderful rich aroma rose from a covered stewpot in the middle of the table. Meg realized she was famished. The sea air, she presumed.

The table was set for two and as she took the chair Cosimo formally drew out for her, she said, "What about your nephews and the doctor? Will they not be joining us?"

"The boys have work to do and they'll mess with the men, it's good for morale," he said, taking his own seat opposite. "David has a permanent invitation at my table, but he rarely accepts it. He has a fondness for his books and his own company when at leisure."

"I see." She shook out her napkin and lifted her face to the night sky, now a mass of stars with the three-quarter moon throwing its light across the water. "What a glorious night." There was enough of a breeze for her to be glad of her cloak over her shoulders, but not enough to need to wrap herself up in it. Gus came to land on the deck rail beside the table, cocked his head intelligently, and uttered something that sounded remarkably like agreement.

"Nights at sea usually are beautiful," Cosimo observed, ladling stew into her bowl.

He passed her a loaf of bread and she took it and broke into it hungrily. It was still warm. How did they bake bread on the open sea? She didn't need to know the answer. There was a crock of golden butter that melted into the wheaten bread and the mingled scents were enough to make her light-headed.

Cosimo poured wine and for a while they ate and drank in a silence that gradually, insidiously became charged. When he reached over to refill her glass his hand brushed hers and it happened as she had known all along that it would. A current of arousal crackled between them, jolting her belly and making her toes curl. It was not an unfamiliar sensation but always before she had been in control of the situation, had been able to play it according to her rules. With the exception of the gondolier, she amended. That had been way beyond her control and she hadn't really understood what was happening.

But this was different. She knew perfectly well what was happening, knew that Cosimo knew it too. And she was not in control of any part of this situation. Well, that was not entirely true, she reminded herself. She could control her own body. Not her reactions, her lust, her arousal, but what she did about them. The question quite simply was: *what did she want to do?*

He leaned over and brushed an errant curl from her forehead. "I was afraid of that," he said.

It made it worse that he made no attempt to pretend he didn't notice that charge of lust or to deny it. It was very ungentlemanly of him, Meg decided, but even as she thought that, she couldn't help a soft laugh at her own hypocrisy. She didn't fall into lust with *gentlemen*. Never had, and she suspected never would.

"Why afraid?" she demanded.

He leaned back in his chair again and cupped his wine-glass between his hands. "Wrong choice of word, perhaps."

Meg twirled the stem of her wineglass. "Maybe not," she said. "I suppose it could almost be inevitable when two people are thrown together in these unpredictable circumstances."

He shook his head with a soft laugh. "No, far from inevitable, ma'am, and you know it. Such sparks are few and far between in my experience."

Meg pursed her lips a little. "I'm always attracted to unsuitable men," she confessed.

At that he laughed outright. "And I'm unsuitable of course."

Gus produced a near perfect imitation of the captain's laughter and hopped onto the table.

"I've never met anyone more so, and I've met my share," Meg responded, absently giving the macaw a crust of bread as she continued, "You're a privateer who goes by one name only. You're on some kind of secret mission of such urgency that you couldn't put right a mistake that you called potentially disastrous. Your men don't even know where they're sailing to after Sark. David Porter said no one ever knows where they're going when they're with you, or why they're going there. I'm beginning to wonder if even you know these things." There was distinct challenge in her voice and eyes.

"All that is true," he replied calmly. "Except for the part about my not knowing *why*. Believe me, I know my mission."

Meg looked at him sharply and she glimpsed again that hard cool core beneath the careless, raffish manner. Cosimo knew exactly what he was doing and he had absolute confidence in his ability to succeed. She took a sip of wine.

"I'm not sure I've ever met a woman quite like you," Cosimo observed. "You certainly appear to be a lady of impeccable breeding, but I can't help feeling that appearances in your case are deceptive."

Meg's lips twitched into a grin. He was, of course, absolutely correct. She was no more a lady, as society understood the term, than Cosimo was a gentleman. "My parents wouldn't care to believe that," she said. "My breeding is certainly impeccable."

He inclined his head in acknowledgment and then turned as Biggins's step sounded on the deck behind them. "There's rhubarb pie, sir, if you and the lady wish for it." He set a brown-crusted pie on the table.

"Lovely," Meg said enthusiastically.

"Lovely," declared Gus, examining the pie with a beady eye.

Biggins cleared away the stew bowls and left. Cosimo sliced the pie and placed a large piece on a plate for Meg.

"You're so skinny I can't imagine where you put it all," he commented, handing her the plate.

Meg realized she'd had two laden bowls of stew, most of the loaf of bread, and was now about to eat close to half of a rhubarb pie. "I seem to be particularly hungry this evening," she stated a mite defensively. "I'm not usually greedy."

"I didn't say you were greedy," he protested solemnly. "Merely blessed with a substantial appetite." He took a forkful of pie.

He had barely carried it to his lips before a shout came from somewhere above them. "Sail on the port bow."

Cosimo set down his fork very calmly, murmured, "Excuse me," and pushed back his chair. He took up the telescope and went across to the port rail. In the silvery light of stars and moon, he could just make out the white shape on the horizon and then the dark bulk of a frigate looming against the night's shadows. He had to assume that the *Mary Rose* had been visible to the frigate for no more than a few minutes.

Mr. Fisher came running up. "French or English, sir?" he asked breathlessly.

"I can't tell yet," the captain said, in a tone that held a hint of reproof. "Lower our flag and pennant." If he couldn't yet read the frigate's colors, it was reasonable to hope that they hadn't yet identified the sloop.

"Aye, sir." The young man ran off with an air of what could only be described as excitement. He blew a series of notes on his whistle and two sailors appeared. Meg watched as they lowered the jauntily flying Union Jack and the ship's own pennant.

"Should we fly the French colors, sir?" Cosimo's other nephew, looking both excited and apprehensive, hurried up the steps to the quarterdeck.

"Lad, why would we do that if the approaching vessel is one of our own?" Cosimo inquired. "I'm not about to issue an invitation for friendly fire."

"Sorry, sir." The boy flushed crimson.

"Take the other glass and go up into the crow's nest. As soon as you can identify the colors, shout."

"Aye, sir."

The boy hurled himself at the ratlines, pausing only when his uncle reminded softly, "Telescope, lad."

Meg watched this scene with interest. Cosimo's lieutenants seemed somewhat unversed in their duties and she wondered how reliable they would be in the event of an emergency. But she soon realized that the two youngsters were not of vital importance in the running of the ship.

The grizzled bosun had appeared at the captain's side almost by magic, and Mike, the helmsman, was already at the wheel. Other men, plain sailors as far as she could tell from their clothes, were simply going about their business, standing ready at the sheets, climbing up the masts to be in readiness to make sail, all without any apparent instruction. Cosimo's ship ran on greased wheels.

Gus began to pace along the edge of the table with an agitation that she hadn't seen before. Were his bird instincts telling him something not yet apparent to the humans? It wouldn't surprise her, Meg thought.

She'd lost all interest in rhubarb pie but remained at the table until something decisive happened. The boy who seemed to serve as Biggins's assistant appeared and with a mutter of apology began swiftly to clear away the glasses and dishes. Another youngster swept the cloth away and folded down the table in a few expert moves.

Meg stood up. Presumably the chairs must go too. She was right. The first child returned to carry them away almost immediately. The tension on the ship was now palpable. Everyone stood at their posts, waiting. She looked up at the topmost deck and saw men standing at the row of guns. They hadn't run them out but they were ready to do so at a word. And now she didn't know whether she was frightened or excited. If that was a French ship, would they do battle?

Hesitantly she went over to the port side and joined Cosimo, who was still gazing through his telescope. He said without lowering the glass, "You may stay on deck for the moment, but I'd be grateful if you'd go below the minute I say it's necessary."

"Yes, of course," she said. "If it's French, will you fight?"

"If we can't outrun her, we'll have to."

He didn't sound as if the prospect troubled him in the least. Meg stayed at the railing until the piping voice of young Mr. Graves came from high above. "She's flying the tricolor, sir."

"Very well, gentlemen, make sail." He barely raised his voice, his eye still glued to the glass. He said to Meg, "If you stay right here, you won't be in the way."

"You don't mind?"

He shook his head. "Not if you've the stomach for it." She was not to know that he wanted to see how she would react to a ship under threat. Ana, on another ship at another time, had loved it. She'd stood at the rail with her long red hair streaming in the wind, her green eyes almost wild with excitement, not a nerve in her body even as the guns bellowed and the cannonballs screamed overhead. *Just what was Meg Barratt made of?*

Meg drew her cloak more closely around her and stared out into the darkness until finally she could catch a glimpse of white. Sails. And they seemed to be drawing closer. A little shiver, part apprehension, part excitement, prickled her spine. "Is it bigger than the *Mary Rose*?"

"A frigate," Cosimo answered. "Bigger certainly, but not as swift."

Meg asked no more questions. The man needed no distractions. The *Mary Rose* swung away to starboard under full sail and leaped across the water with the French ship in pursuit.

Chapter 5

Cosimo remained at the rail, his telescope trained on the white sails in the distance. As best he could judge, the *Mary Rose* was holding her lead. He swung the glass across the water, examining the faint shadow of the island of Sark, some two miles distant. In the moonlit night it was visible but only as an outline. He concentrated his gaze on the water around the island, the telltale white foam of waves breaking on rocks. A tiny smile touched his lips.

He lowered his glass. "Mike, hold her steady on this course, I'm going below for a minute. Call me if anything changes."

"Aye, sir," the helmsman said, not taking his eyes from the bellying sails above.

Cosimo, his step more hurried than Meg had ever seen it, swung away from the rail and headed for the steps to the mid-deck. She watched him disappear down the companionway and hesitated about following him. She had seen that little smile. It had not been at all humorous, sinister rather, a smile of satisfaction that one could imagine Mephistopheles wearing when he'd finally bought a soul.

After a moment, she made her way resolutely towards the companionway. The cabin door stood open and Cosimo was bent intently over the chart table seemingly oblivious of Gus, who was pacing the long bar in his open cage with every appearance of agitation, emitting distressed little squawks every few minutes.

Meg entered the cabin quietly, unwilling to disturb the captain's concentration, but he was not as oblivious as he seemed. Without raising his head he said, "Put that red cover over Gus's cage, will you, Meg?"

She looked around and saw a square of crimson silk on the window seat close to the cage. She picked it up and Gus immediately tilted his head towards her and said clearly, "G'night...g'night...poor Gus."

"Poor Gus," she agreed, arranging the cover over the cage. "Should I close the cage door?"

"No," Cosimo responded, still without looking up. "He doesn't like to be locked in, merely tucked away when things get tense."

Meg nodded. It struck her as very sensible of the macaw to opt out of circumstances that upset his equilibrium. She sat on the window seat and watched as Cosimo poured over his charts, making swift notations as he did so. "Do we have a destination in mind?" she ventured.

"Not exactly," he said, straightening and laying down his pen. "Just a plan. Which will lead where it will lead." His eyes were alight with an unholy amusement, that quirk of a smile lingering on his lips. He radiated a certain private exhilaration, as if there was a secret to which only he was a party. But beneath the sparkle of excitement, Meg could sense that cool, hard core she'd been aware of before. It showed in the set of his mouth, the line of his jaw, the subtle tension in his frame. This was a man who was completely in control of his emotions, emotions that were mere adjuncts to the cool steadiness of a ruthless determination.

She found him rather frightening in this guise and, curious though she was, kept a rein on her questions. When he at once left the cabin with his earlier swifter-than-usual step she did not immediately follow him. She glanced towards the macaw's red silk tent, half wishing Gus would resume his usual stream of chatter, but the bird was completely silent. She stood for a minute, her thumbs hooked beneath her chin, her steepled fingers tapping her mouth. She was inhibited from returning to the deck by the sense of her own uselessness. Everyone up there had a task, a clearly defined purpose, while all she could do was try to keep out of the way.

With sudden resolution she left the cabin, closing the door gently behind her, and plunged into the inner recesses of the ship. She had no idea where she was going but exploration seemed a pointful occupation at the moment. It was hard to keep her footing in the dim corridor as the *Mary Rose* danced across the waves under full sail, running before the wind. She passed a kitchen, deserted now, the stoves extinguished, hanging pans secured behind wooden bars, and reached another short flight of steps, at the end of the corridor. These were narrower than the companionway to the deck, more of a ladder than real stairs, but there was a glow of lamplight and she could hear a voice that she recognized as David Porter's drifting up from below.

Without hesitation, Meg swung herself onto the ladder and clambered down. She found herself in a low-ceilinged space, lit by oil lamps hanging from hooks, the smell of oil mingling with pitch and pine and tar. Sacks and roped bundles were stacked against the sloping bulwarks and the sound of water slapping against the wooden sides was very loud. She guessed that they must be below the waterline.

The surgeon, wearing a canvas apron over his shirt and britches, was laying out shiny instruments on a wooden chest; the young boy who usually assisted Biggins was scrubbing a long deal table bolted to the deck in the middle of the space. They both looked up, startled as Meg stepped from the ladder.

"Why, Miss Barratt, is something the matter?" David inquired, frowning in the swaying light of the lamp above him.

"No, not at all," she said swiftly. "Is this the hospital?"

"The sick bay, yes. A temporary use of the space as and when necessary."

Meg nodded, wondering if this was where she'd been brought unconscious the previous night. The table, despite the boy's vigorous scrubbing, bore ominous stains of old blood. Not her own, she knew, but the thought of lying on that table gave her the shivers.

"Are you preparing for wounded?"

"It's wise to be prepared, but with Cosimo's usual luck and judgment there won't be any."

"He doesn't wish to fight then?"

David looked at her a little askance. "Of course not. Why would he?"

She frowned a little and spoke hesitantly, feeling for words. "I don't know, but he has an air of . . . of triumph almost, as if he was contemplating some victory."

David gave a short laugh. "Knowing Cosimo, I'm sure he is doing just that. He'll have a plan of some kind, but it won't include needlessly putting his men or his ship in harm's way."

Once again Meg marveled at the calm, almost blind acceptance Cosimo appeared to inspire in those who sailed with him. David Porter was clearly an intelligent, educated man, and even he placed unquestioning trust in a man who didn't share ahead of time either his actions or his intentions.

"What can I do to help?" she asked, dismissing the puzzle of Cosimo in favor of more urgent matters. The boy was now sprinkling vinegar liberally over the decking and the sharp acrid smell rose above all the others.

"Tear up linen for bandages," David replied promptly, gesturing to a stack of linen on an upturned barrel. "I'll need strips of different widths."

Meg set to the task with willing hands. The deck was bucking beneath her and every now and again plunged forward and then reared up again like an unbroken colt under its first saddle.

"Go up top and get some air," David instructed after a while, seeing her color change. "The motion's actually smoother down here, but the atmosphere is noxious."

"If you don't mind..." Meg said, lurching towards the ladder. She had an overpowering need for great gulps of fresh sea air and was doing her best not to think of the hearty dinner she'd so recently devoured.

She maneuvered her wobbly way back down the dimly lit corridor to the companionway and immediately felt better as the cool air hit her. She drew deep breaths, steadying herself against the rail. The moonlight if anything was brighter than it had been earlier and the sails of the frigate were clearly visible. Cosimo was standing behind Mike at the helm, gazing out towards the French ship through his glass.

"Lower the topgallants," he called suddenly and there

was an instant of complete silence as the command reverberated across the decks. Then men sprang into action, balancing on the yards as they manipulated the ropes that brought down the three great sails.

Meg knew little about the art of sailing but she did know that less sail meant less speed. There was no shortage of wind, so why was Cosimo deliberately slowing his ship? But no one had questioned the order, although there had been that instant of involuntary hesitation.

Cosimo turned his attention away from the sails and swept the telescope towards the rocky outcrops of Sark. They were growing clearer, the white foam of the breakers more pronounced. He said something quietly and Mike stepped away from the wheel. Cosimo took the helm and adjusted their course a fraction.

Meg had forgotten all about her momentary spasm of nausea. She came over to the wheel. "Why?" she asked simply.

He glanced sideways at her and that reckless glitter in his eyes was even more pronounced. "A variation on an old tale," he told her. "Are you familiar with the story of the Piper of Hamlin?"

"Vaguely," she said. "He was supposed to have lured..." She stopped, staring at him.

For answer he merely inclined his head in acknowledgment, then returned the helm to Mike and went to the rail, where he scanned the pursuing ship.

Meg could feel that the *Mary Rose* had slowed and she could almost fancy that she could see the frigate closing the gap between them. Little shivers ran up and down her spine and she drew her cloak closer about her. Cosimo was going to lure the enemy to... to what? She wanted to ask but sensed that he was now so immersed in his own plans that even if he heard her he would choose to ignore her. So she stayed at the rail beside him, gazing out across the moonlit sea, filled with a mingled dread and anticipation.

Cosimo turned abruptly from the rail and called another order. "Fore and mizzen topsails, gentlemen."

This time there was no instant of hesitation. The two sails were down and furled in minutes and the *Mary Rose* pressed on under her mainsail and two foresails.

The frigate grew closer. Meg could now begin to make out details of the ship herself. The array of guns gleamed, all eerie menace, in the moonlight. The air of expectation on the *Mary Rose* was almost tangible, as every man stared fixedly at the pursuing ship.

Then there was a flash of fire, a plume of smoke, and a cannonball burst into the sea to their stern. "I hope, *mon ami*, that you intended that only as a warning shot," Cosimo remarked with a shake of his head. "To do any damage you need to be at least fifty yards closer."

Meg looked at him, astounded. It almost sounded as if he was encouraging the French commander to get close enough to hit them. She could make out figures on the frigate's decks now, hurrying shapes. A loud hail came across the water.

Cosimo listened intently, then he spoke to young Mr. Graves, who was now standing at his side. "Run out the guns, Miles."

"Aye, sir." The young man was pale with excitement that Meg guessed had an edge of fear to it. She guessed too that Cosimo had addressed him informally as a means of reassurance and wondered how many engagements Miles Graves had been a part of. His voice was a little squeaky as he bellowed through cupped hands at the men standing ready beside the gun ports on the upper deck.

The clattering roll of the guns on the casters filled the air as their snubbed muzzles poked through the ports.

"Let's give them a starboard broadside," Cosimo said as casually as if he was ordering a strawberry ice.

Again Miles bellowed, the pitch of his voice still a little squeaky. A sheet of flame accompanied the fusillade, the explosion of gunpowder, and the sea churned, sending up a blinding veil of foam, as the cannonballs crashed into the water.

"If they're too far to hit us, docsn't the same apply to us?" Meg asked.

Cosimo laughed and he sounded truly amused. "We're answering provocation with its like."

As he spoke there was another burst of flame from the French vessel and this time the *Mary Rose* rocked as a cannonball crashed into the stern timbers. A cry went up, "Hit."

Cosimo stepped to the rail, looking down at the mid-deck. "Report."

"Above the waterline, Cap'n." The grizzled boatswain came running to the steps. "Nothing we can't fix."

"Any injuries?"

"Two men, sir. Splinters. They've gone below."

Cosimo nodded and turned back to the starboard railing, raising his telescope once more. "That was a little too close for comfort," he observed more to himself than to any of his small and silent audience. He called, "Raise the topsails, gentlemen," and in a few minutes the two lowered sails were once more filling with wind.

Cosimo strode to the helm and took it from Mike. He called, "Wear ship," and threw the wheel over as men scurried to adjust the sails on the new tack. The great boom swung over and Meg grabbed the rail as the *Mary Rose* listed to port and then came about. To Meg it seemed as if on their adjusted course they were heading straight for the crashing surf that could now be heard on the ugly outcrop of rocks.

Another bellow of cannon came from behind now and she turned to look towards the approaching frigate just as a ball crashed into the side of the ship immediately below where she stood. The sound of splintering wood was appalling and she clutched the deck rail to keep her footing as the ship bucked and rose on the waves.

Cosimo was suddenly beside her. "All right?"

"Yes, I think so," she said, dazed and a little deafened by the racket. She glanced at her arm with some surprise. It didn't hurt, but a jagged splinter of wood stood out from her forearm, blood welling around it, staining the now torn lace-edged sage green silk sleeve. "Oh," she said, frowning in something like disbelief.

"Go below and get David to see to that," Cosimo instructed brusquely.

Meg thought of the cramped and noisome sick bay and the injured men already there. "It's just a scratch," she said. "I'll pull the splinter out and wrap some of this torn lace around it." She was about to yank the piece of wood from the wound when she became aware of an ominous silence. She glanced up at Cosimo.

He was looking at her, his eyes that glacial blue she'd encountered once before. "You have a very short memory, Miss Barratt," he stated softly.

"On the contrary," Meg retorted, refusing to be discomposed, "my memory is remarkably acute." She backed away, still holding her arm, and refusing to drop her own gaze until she had to turn to go down the companionway. On board his ship one had to watch oneself around

Captain Cosimo, she reflected as she made her way along the passage to the sick bay, cradling her arm that was now beginning to throb uncomfortably.

She climbed down into the dark confines of the sick bay. It seemed crowded and she assumed that the second barrage had caused some other injuries. David Porter was putting a splint on a man's foot, while three other men, one bleeding copiously from a gash under his eye, sat on barrels against the curved bulkhead waiting their turn. Meg looked down at her arm, which was still bleeding sluggishly around the shard of wood. She had the uneasy feeling that the wood was somehow preventing a fountain of blood.

David glanced across at her. "Hurt?"

"Just a scratch."

"Give me a minute and I'll be with you."

Meg shook her head. "No, please...there's no hurry. Look after the men first."

He left the man on the table and crossed towards her, head bowed below the low ceiling. "Let me look." He lifted her arm.

"No, really, it's not a problem," she protested. "Please look after the others. I wouldn't have come down except that..."

"That what?" he prompted when her voice trailed away.

"Cosimo gave me his look," she said flatly.

David looked momentarily startled, then gave a guffaw of amusement. "Oh, that look. Questioning an order, were you?"

She shrugged. "It seemed unnecessary to burden you with a scratch when there are others more seriously hurt."

He let go her arm and gestured to a sack spilling what

looked like beans. "Take a seat over there for a few minutes. And whatever you do, don't pull that splinter out."

Meg obeyed. Her choices on this ship were annoyingly
limited. Down here in the bowels of the ship she felt dis-
connected from the action above. The ship's motion was
very different and the immediacy of the danger was somehow distanced, although realistically she knew that they
were not in the least insulated from cannon fire or anything else here below the water level. In fact she was hard
pressed to keep panic at bay at just the image of water
pouring into this space where elongated shadows flitted
against the walls as the lamps swayed violently whenever
the vessel changed course.

She played with the beans, trawling them through her
fingers, fighting to regain her composure. When David
called to her to come to the table she had the panic well
under control. Her arm was now hurting badly and she
had to fight the urge to yank out the foreign body.

She perched on the edge of the stained table while
David looked at her arm. "Cosimo knows what he's talking
about when it comes to wounds," he commented in a casual tone as he took up long tweezers. "They get infected
very quickly if they're not cleaned promptly and properly."
He took hold of the splinter between the tweezers and
pulled steadily. "I can see that his manner might put your
back up if you're unaccustomed to his authority, but as a
general rule his reasoning is faultless."

"One might agree to that if one had voluntarily submitted to his authority," Meg pointed out with a touch of acer-
bity. It helped take her mind off what David was doing.
She watched with an almost detached interest as the long
piece of wood was withdrawn from her flesh. Immediately
the blood flowed quickly, dripping onto the silk skirts of

Ana's gown. David seemed not to notice, or not to care, and began to wash the wound with a vinegar-soaked cloth that made Meg inhale sharply and bite her lip. He probed a little further with the tweezers and pulled out several small splinters.

"I think that's the last of them." He staunched the flow of blood with a pad also reeking of vinegar. "We all find our own ways of adjusting to Cosimo." He reverted to the earlier topic in the same casual tone and as if there'd been no intervening time.

"Sensible if one's *obliged* to do so," Meg returned, pressing her other hand hard on the pad as David indicated that she should.

He gave her a lightly quizzical smile that nevertheless held a hint of concern. "I don't believe Cosimo means you any harm, Miss Barratt."

Meg met his gaze frankly. "Maybe not," she said. "But two days ago I did not expect to find myself trapped on a ship engaging in an act of war with the enemy."

"No," he agreed rather helplessly. "I can see your point, ma'am. But it was an unfortunate accident." He reached over for a strip of the linen that Meg had worked on earlier. He was regretting having started this conversation. Cosimo could defend himself. And if, as he'd hinted to David, he might make use of the unfortunate accident that had dropped an unwitting Meg Barratt onto his ship, David wasn't sure he could defend him anyway.

"Please let's drop the formalities, David," Meg said, sensing the man's sudden unease, although his fingers were deft as they bound up the arm. "My name's Meg."

He smiled at her. "Well, Meg, I don't think that'll scar. It might throb for a while, but I'll re-dress it in the morning."

"If we get through the night," Meg said, grabbing the edge of the table as the ship lurched beneath her.

"Have faith," he responded, bracing himself easily against the motion.

"We're luring the frigate," Meg informed him rather pointedly, sliding off the table. "But I'm not certain what to." She regarded him closely in the wavering light and saw a quick frown cross his eyes. So he was not quite so placidly unquestioning about his captain's plans as he'd implied.

But apart from that fleeting frown he gave nothing away. "Would you like me to fashion a sling for you?"

"No, thank you. I'll be careful." She set off cautiously towards the ladder leading to the decks above.

"Try not to knock it."

Any reply she might have made was lost as a clatter of feet in the corridor above heralded the arrival on the ladder of two men carrying a third between them. "Cannon got loose, sir," one of them said, coming backwards down the ladder supporting the legs of the groaning man. "Crushed Sly against the fo'c'sle. He's hurt pretty bad."

Meg stood aside as the other bearer supporting the man's head and shoulders inched down the ladder. There was little room now in the confined space and she decided she'd only be in the way if she offered to help. Besides, they didn't need it. The man was already on the table, his breathing harsh and ragged, and David was already stripping away his shirt, giving rapid-fire instructions to the boy who acted as his assistant.

She made her way back up to the fresh air. Strangely her fear had vanished and she was now only curious to see what was happening on deck, and how things had changed since she'd gone below.

At first glance everything looked the same. Cosimo was back at the wheel. The French frigate was still in pursuit, but at a slightly greater distance. Meg saw that all the sails were once more set and the *Mary Rose* was speeding over the waves. Ahead the spume from the breaking waves against the rocky outcrop seemed much closer and she felt something clutch in her throat. They seemed on a collision course. But it was clear to her now that Cosimo did not intend for his own ship to founder on those rocks. He was leading the enemy.

But why didn't they notice? she thought, going to the rail to stare out at the pursuing vessel. They had charts. They must know where they were heading. But perhaps they were so eager for the prize that must seem within their grasp they weren't concentrating. Perhaps they assumed that the *Mary Rose* knew where she was going and wouldn't deliberately put herself in danger. Perhaps the French captain didn't know these waters as well as his English counterpart.

But it was useless speculation. Rather tentatively she approached the helm, keeping out of Cosimo's line of sight in order not to distract him. But he was instantly aware of her. His gaze flicked for a second over her pale face, down to the bound arm, then returned to his scrutiny of the sails. "Does it hurt?"

"Throbs," she admitted. "Are we going to run aground on those rocks?"

"O ye of little faith," he scoffed lightly.

Meg swallowed. "Are *they* going to be wrecked?"

He glanced at her again with a slightly mocking glint in his eye. "I assure you they'd have no more sympathy for us were the positions reversed than I have for them."

Meg shook her head in mute denial of such callous pragmatism.

Cosimo said, "If it makes you feel better, there's a sandy shoal just before the rocks. That's where they'll run aground. Now, you're distracting me."

Meg left at once, taking up her station against the deck rail. Things were happening fast now. Cosimo was calling out orders, his feet braced against the deck, his hands on the wheel as he swung it around. She could see the sudden tensing of his shoulders as the wheel fought him, then the ship began to turn, the boom swinging overhead, the sails cracking as they slammed across to the other side. The *Mary Rose* caught the following wind and leaped forward, leaving the frigate still plunging forward towards the rocks.

Meg could hear the cries and shouts from the frigate as they saw what was ahead of them. She had a fair sense now of what the scurrying, clambering sailors were doing as the enemy ship tried to go about, but she was much bigger, much more cumbersome than the dainty sloop and the turn took much longer. There was a great rasping and crashing of timbers filling the stillness of the night air, and the frigate came to a shuddering, straining halt.

The *Mary Rose* danced away towards the open sea and Cosimo after a minute handed the wheel to Mike and came over to Meg, wiping his brow with his shirtsleeve. Despite the cool wind the physical effort of the last fifteen minutes had made him sweat.

"What will happen to them?" she asked.

He smiled. "They'll stay there nice and secure until the navy turns up," he told her, sounding, she thought, rather smug. "There are two English men-of-war somewhere out there in the Channel. They'll come this way sometime after dawn. And they'll find a nice fat prize all wrapped up and beribboned awaiting them."

He looked up at the sky, noticing the first faint graying in the east. Meg followed his eyes. "It seems to have been a very short night," she said, even as she thought that an eternity seemed to have passed since they'd shared that electric supper under the stars.

He nodded. "You're tired. Go below and get some sleep. We'll be making for harbor within the hour."

Meg after a second's reflection decided not to say that she wasn't particularly tired. Or even that she'd prefer to stay on deck. One of those looks in a night was quite sufficient. She made her way to the cabin, where Gus squawked a "G'day" at the sound of the door opening. She took it to mean that he was ready to face the light and removed the silk cover on his cage. He greeted her with a beady eye and hopped along the perch and out of the cage, then he swooped onto the windowsill and regarded the growing light with an air of intelligent interest.

Meg scratched his poll and then stretched out on the cot, careful not to jolt her bandaged arm. She didn't bother to take her boots off; she'd go back on deck shortly.

She didn't hear the door open an hour later, and was unaware as Cosimo removed her boots and spread the coverlet over her. He stood watching her sleep for a few minutes, a considering frown in his eyes.

Meg Barratt had carried herself well that night. She'd shown less wild exhilaration than Ana would have, but she'd managed her apprehension well. She would not cave under danger, he decided. But she showed some awkward scruples. Ana wouldn't have spared a moment's anxiety as to the fate of the enemy vessel and those aboard her. Like him, she had thought only for their goal. The enemy was just that, and all was fair in war.

Could Meg Barratt be persuaded to lend herself to the plan in hand? She had an unconventional streak in her, that much was very clear. She was no ordinary maiden lady. But that aside, she had been sheltered for the most part from the harsh realities of life at war. Could she accept an assassin's task? Understand the need for it?

He pursed his lips. He couldn't act precipitately. He needed to tread carefully, to take his time to learn her, but the devil of it was, he had no time to spare. He was scheduled to remain on Sark for no more than three days, waiting for any dispatches that he could pass on to Admiral Nelson's fleet when eventually he caught up with it. And in those three days he would be hoping against hope that he would get some clue as to Ana's fate. After that, come hell or high water, he had to continue his mission.

Chapter 6

Meg was aware of pain, at first vague and unspecific, as she swam groggily back to consciousness. She lay still for a minute with her eyes shut, feeling the deep throbbing ache in her arm. The events of the night came back vivid in every detail and the acid reflection occurred that the last time she'd awoken in this narrow box-bed she'd also been groggy and in some degree of pain. Sailing on the *Mary Rose* didn't seem particularly conducive to health.

Finally she opened her eyes. Judging by the brightness of the sun, it must be well past mid-morning, she reckoned. Hardly surprising that she'd slept so late considering how she'd spent the greater part of the night. The ship beneath was rocking gently at anchor, and when she dragged herself up in the cot, she could see through the open window green hills in the distance. The air was a delicious mélange of seaweed and salt, and the sound of voices reached her through the window.

Land, Meg thought. The recognition galvanized her and she swung herself out of the box-bed and stood up, holding her arm gingerly against her chest. The bandage was bloodstained but the bleeding seemed to have stopped. The green silk gown was ruined, sleeve torn, the skirts and sleeve stained with blood, which was a pity since she'd rather liked it. Well, there were other garments in the cupboard.

She knelt on the window seat and gazed out across a narrow expanse of water to a quay where fishermen were mending nets. A huddle of cottages crowded behind the quayside and above them rose a green hillside. A slender cart track wound its way up from the hamlet towards the summit of the hill and she could just make out the roofs of several cottages scattered across the hillside.

Hot water and then breakfast seemed the order of the morning. Without much expectation she peered into the head and to her delight saw two water jugs, steam still rising from their contents, and a pile of fresh towels. She glanced once towards the closed cabin door, then shrugged and reached behind her to unfasten the gown. It was impossible to do with one hand and her other arm was stiff and useless except for her fingers.

She struggled in increasing frustration and only succeeded with an unwary stretch in opening the wound on her arm. Absurdly she felt like weeping at her helplessness as she stared at the seeping blood, then with an exclamatory curse tried again with her good hand to undo the top button between her shoulders. Cosimo's familiar knock came as her oaths became more vigorous.

"Oh, come in," she called impatiently.

Cosimo entered with Gus on his shoulder. "What on earth are you doing? It sounded like a bad morning in Billingsgate just then."

"I am trying to unbutton this damn gown with only one

hand," she told him through clenched teeth. "And now the other one's bleeding again."

"Well, for heaven's sake why didn't you come and find me?" he demanded, sounding somewhat impatient himself. "Come here." He moved behind her and swiftly unfastened the buttons before pushing the gown off her shoulders.

His hand brushed the skin of her back and Meg closed her eyes on a jolt of quite unlooked for and at this point unwelcome arousal. He was so close to her she could feel his breath rustling the top of her head. The gown lay in a puddle at her feet.

She stepped away from it and, keeping her face averted, said, "Thank you. I can manage now."

"Are you sure?" he asked with an apparent solicitude that didn't fool Meg one bit. He had enjoyed that moment of contact, whether it had affected him with quite the same jolt she couldn't be certain. But she knew absolutely that her reaction hadn't escaped him.

"The buttons on my chemise are in the front," she pointed out acidly.

"Ah. Pity." His eyebrows lifted. He came up behind her and, reaching over her shoulder, caught her chin on his fingertips, turning her head sideways. For an instant his lips brushed the corner of her mouth. "Are you quite certain I can't help?"

"Positively." Meg didn't bother to pretend outrage at the familiarity; she was growing accustomed to Cosimo's flanking maneuvers, although not entirely sure what he hoped to achieve by them. They seemed more teasing than serious. Anyway she was determined that if and when *she* decided to consummate this attraction, it would be at *her* orchestration. And that wouldn't happen until her situation was clarified and she knew she had a means of getting back to England. Quite apart from the fact that bleeding and grubby as she was now, she couldn't imagine a less enticing moment.

"Very well." Somewhat to her perverse chagrin he sounded perfectly content with her refusal. "I'll leave you then. I'll send David to look at your arm in about ten minutes. I expect you'll need some assistance dressing and he'll be an unobjectionable lady's maid." With that he left the cabin to a chorus of *g'byes* from Gus, who had taken up residence on his perch.

Meg swore under her breath and the macaw cocked his head as if trying to catch what she'd said. "So far I haven't heard you swear," Meg declared. "And I don't think you'd better learn it from me." She managed to undo the buttons and ribbons of her chemise and get rid of garters and stockings. Naked she managed to sponge herself one-handed and then struggled into clean linen. She took out the bronze gown that she'd worn the previous day and shook it out. It would do. But doing it up was beyond her.

Fortunately she didn't have long to wait before David's cheerful voice asked permission to come in.

"Yes do," she said, adding ruefully as he entered, "I need help."

"Yes, Cosimo said you were having trouble." David set down his bag. "Let's take a look at the arm first."

"It opened up again."

"Mmm." He said nothing further as he worked and then when the arm was once more tightly bandaged said, "Now, what else can I do for you?"

"Button me," she said. "I'd ask Gus, but I suspect it's one of the rare tasks that might be beyond him."

David laughed and obliged. "Anything else?"

She shook her head. "No, but thank you."

"My pleasure." He picked up his bag and made for the door.

"David?"

He stopped, his hand on the latch, and looked questioningly at her.

"Cosimo said he would send a pigeon with a message to my friends."

"Yes?" His tone was still inquiring.

"It really can be done?"

"My dear ma'am, if he says it can, it most certainly can. In all the years I've known him, I've never known Cosimo to make a promise he couldn't keep." With another nod, David left her.

Meg wondered why she'd doubted Cosimo, and yet she knew so little about him. In fact she knew nothing about him. Oh, he had twin sisters, he was thirty-seven, he was a skilled and ruthless privateer who relished danger and adventure, but *who* he was remained a mystery. He frightened her a little, and he attracted her a great deal more, but the two were somehow intertwined. This didn't surprise Meg; she knew herself and her own predilection for men society would consider dangerous. But Cosimo was in a different category altogether. There was nothing ordinarily unconventional about him.

Absently she combed her hair, thankful for the fashionably short crop that at least meant she didn't have to wrestle one-handedly with hairpins. She was hungry but more important than food was getting her message to Arabella, who would be a less emotional recipient than her parents, and then finding a fishing boat to take her back across the Channel. Stockings required two hands, so she opted for

sandals and bare feet and went in search of the captain of
the *Mary Rose*.

She found an orderly scene on deck, two sailors scrubbing the planking with holystones, several others polishing
the brass rails. The appetizing smell of frying bacon came
from below. The ship was anchored about a hundred yards
from the quay, a dinghy tethered to her stern.

Meg looked around for someone in authority. One of
the identical cousins, or Mike the helmsman or the grizzled boatswain. Even as she looked around, Miles Graves
materialized from somewhere in the bow and eagerly
skipped over rope coils to reach her. "Morning, ma'am.
The captain said I should look after you. Is there anything
you need?"

"Morning, Miles," she returned cheerfully. "Yes, I need
to go ashore. Could someone row me in that dinghy?"

The eagerness left his face to be replaced with a look of
acute embarrassment. "I beg your pardon, ma'am, but the
captain's not on board. He's gone ashore," he added rather
obviously.

"Really. Well, I wish to do so too," she said, still smiling.

"I'm sorry, ma'am, it can't be done." His pink cheeks
were flushed with discomfort. His uncle had instructed
him to take care of Miss Barratt and see to her needs, but
there'd been no mention of going ashore.

"Why can't it? The boat's there. Surely one of the sailors
could row me the short distance to the quay." Meg was
puzzled and beginning to feel annoyed.

"Not without Captain's permission, ma'am," Miles confessed. "No one leaves the ship without his say-so."

"Ridiculous," Meg scoffed. "I'm not a prisoner."

"No...no, ma'am...of course not," he said hastily.

"But you can't go ashore without the captain's permission."

"Is that what he said?" she demanded, incredulous, her annoyance now edged with real anger.

Miles scratched his head, reflecting that Miss Barratt was becoming rather alarming. "He hasn't authorized shore leave for anyone, ma'am," he said eventually.

"For the men who work for him," Meg said with an attempt at patience. "But I don't. If I choose to go ashore, that's my business. If there's no one available to row me to the quay, then I'll row myself. That way none of the men can be accused of disobeying the captain's orders." Belatedly she realized what an empty threat that was. With her bandaged arm, she certainly couldn't pull an oar, or even manage to tie up the dinghy single-handed. In fact she wasn't entirely sure she could manage to get herself down the precarious-looking rope ladder that hung over the stern just above the bobbing little boat.

Miles merely looked at her helplessly. "Ma'am, I can't let you have the dinghy."

"Well, it's moot anyway," Meg stated in unconcealed frustration. She walked away from him to the deck rail and gazed at the fishermen mending nets on the quay. There was a tantalizing number of fishing boats tied up at the quayside, one or two of them surely big enough to make the voyage to the English coast. It wouldn't be as comfortable a sail as on the *Mary Rose*, but she could handle a little discomfort.

"Ma'am, I'm really sorry." Miles spoke from behind her and she turned again towards him.

Poor lad, she thought. He was really between a rock and a hard place. An angry woman on the one hand and the prospect of one of Cosimo's looks at the very least on the other. "I understand, Miles," she said with a slight shrug and a smile. "I'll settle the matter with your uncle."

Miles looked relieved. "Thank you, ma'am. Is there anything I can get you?"

"Breakfast," she said, settling for the mundane and easily achievable. "I'm famished."

"Right away, ma'am." Beaming, he sprinted across the deck towards the companionway, leaving Meg to resume her watch on the tantalizingly close but unattainable quayside.

Cosimo climbed the hillside behind the village, his long stride easily covering the springy turf. He'd disdained the gravel track that took a more winding and circuitous route to the gray building that crowned the hilltop, and every once in a while paused and turned to scan the blue waters below with his telescope. He wouldn't be able to see the French frigate until he'd attained the brow of the hill and could look out the other side of the island, but he was looking for any sign of the naval men-of-war. If they'd missed the prize awaiting them, they could be alerted by a signal from the hilltop.

He saw nothing but a few fishing smacks, curlews, and seagulls, however, and continued on his way, arriving at the open door of the gray cottage. It was an anonymous-looking building, indistinguishable from the other cottages on the small island, but an armed guard in navy uniform appeared from nowhere as Cosimo approached.

"Oh, it's you, Captain," he said, offering a rather half-hearted salute that he knew wouldn't be returned.

"It is indeed," Cosimo agreed. "Is the lieutenant ashore?"

"Aye, sir." The guard ducked into the cottage. "Sir, the captain of the *Mary Rose*, sir."

The young lieutenant in command of this small outpost of the British navy adjusted his tunic and straightened his shoulders just as Cosimo ducked through the lintel and entered the gloom of the almost windowless cottage.

"Ah, Lieutenant Murray, nice to see you again," he greeted pleasantly, extending his hand.

The young officer stiffened and saluted with rigorous attention to form, then hesitantly shook the proffered hand. Cosimo knew he was an affront to the navy's hierarchy, not least because he refused to observe even the most elementary rules of naval etiquette, but he had the king's writ and a reputation for successful if dubious enterprises that earned him grudging respect.

"A glass of ale, sir?" the lieutenant offered.

"Thank you. It's a hot walk up the hill." Cosimo's smile was amiable and he thrust his hands into the pockets of his britches with the air of one perfectly at home. "Tell me, Murray, have you sighted the *Leopold* and the *Edwina* as yet?"

"Aye, sir." The lieutenant was suddenly animated. "They approached on the other side of the island, and, well, you'll never believe this, sir, but a French frigate was stranded on the shoals just beyond the barrier reef . . . just waiting for them."

Cosimo smiled. "Oh, I'd believe it," he said. "She landed on the shoal just before dawn this morning."

The officer stared at him. "You passed her?"

"Not exactly," Cosimo said. "Oh . . . my thanks." He took the tankard of ale from the guard, who had several roles on this lightly manned station. He raised his tankard in an unspoken toast to the lieutenant, who did the same with his own.

The lieutenant had little difficulty interpreting his visitor's statement. "How did you do it, sir?" Curiosity forced the question from him, although every success of the privateer's stuck in the craw of the regular navy.

Cosimo merely shrugged. "Her captain was overeager for his own prize," he said carelessly. "Let us go outside, it's stuffy in here and we have some matters to discuss."

The two men left the gloom of the cottage and stood blinking in the bright sunlight.

Cosimo knew that if a pigeon courier had brought him a message, Murray would have told him already, but his anxiety was such that he couldn't help asking. "I'm expecting a message . . ." he said, allowing a half question to hang in the warm air.

"From England, sir?"

"I imagine so." But he couldn't be certain. There were pigeon courier outposts manned by covert agents of the British navy dotted around the coastline of Europe, and Ana, as a free agent, would have access to them. Like himself she worked all over Europe, wherever her masters sent her. The dismal reflection occurred not for the first time that if she had been taken by the enemy it could have happened in almost any country. There were French agents aplenty on the prowl across the continent and he hadn't been given any information on her mission before she was due to join up with him in Folkestone.

"Nothing received so far, sir." The lieutenant confirmed what he already knew.

"Send it to me as soon as you receive it," he instructed with a confidence that masked his fear that he might never know what had happened to Ana to keep her from that rendezvous on that rainy afternoon. If she was in the hands of the enemy, there would be no message.

"Aye, sir."

Cosimo drained his tankard. "I'll also have a message to send out to England later today. You have a bird ready?"

"Three, sir."

Cosimo nodded. "Good. I'll bring the message up this afternoon." He handed his empty tankard to the lieutenant, who seemed somewhat disconcerted to receive it and handed it off immediately to the guard.

"I'll wait here for three days in case there are any dispatches for Admiral Nelson," Cosimo said.

"You're joining the admiral, sir?" The lieutenant couldn't hide his envy.

"Eventually," Cosimo said somewhat obliquely. Knowledge of Nelson's planned whereabouts was given on a need-to-know basis. He raised a hand in careless farewell and strode off around the cottage, blithely ignoring Murray's disgruntled salute. On the far side of the building he raised his telescope and scrutinized the churning waters below.

The French frigate was still firmly stranded on the sand, but she'd been boarded by several longboat parties from the two English men-of-war that stood out in the Channel, well clear of the treacherous rocks. They were in the process of winching the frigate off the sand bar and Cosimo watched with a critical eye for a few minutes, before deciding that they seemed to know what they were doing.

He strolled back to the other side of the hill and began to walk down the slope towards the village. He could see his own sloop sitting peacefully at anchor in the harbor. Halfway down the hill he raised his telescope again and trained it on the *Mary Rose*. Meg was standing on the quarterdeck, looking towards the quay and the village. He thought he could detect a certain impatience in her posture. Presumably she was anxious to make arrangements for her return to England. He could delay that event for a couple of days without her even being aware of any deception on his part. It would give him some breathing room.

He folded the glass and set off back down the hill to the quay.

Meg was eating a bacon sandwich with considerable relish as she stood at the deck rail looking at the landscape when she caught sight of the unmistakable figure descending the hillside with long, rangy strides. The lithe athleticism of his step was becoming very familiar. She took a gulp of coffee from the mug that had been provided with the sandwich and watched his progress with a jaundiced eye.

He disappeared from view for a few minutes as he reached the bottom of the hill and vanished into the narrow village lanes but soon reappeared on the quay. He was dressed in britches and shirt, a kerchief tied loosely around his throat, his auburn hair tied back carelessly on his nape. He put two fingers to his lips and an imperative whistle pierced the tranquil scene.

Two sailors materialized as if by a magician's wand on the rope ladder leading to the dinghy. Meg watched as they jumped into the boat, took up the oars, and pulled strongly to the quay. They grabbed the rope dangling from the bollards and pulled the boat close into the bulwark. Cosimo stepped down into the dinghy and sat in the stern as the little craft returned to the *Mary Rose*.

Cosimo swung himself up the rope ladder and onto the

deck with the same agility Meg had noted the first time she'd laid eyes on him. He stood for a minute casting a quick appraising eye over his empire, then, smiling, came towards her.

The smile faded somewhat as he absorbed her expression. "You look as if you lost a guinea and found a penny. Is something the matter?"

"Yes, as it happens," she declared, aware on the periphery of her vision that Miles and his cousin, who'd been hovering close by, were now stepping discreetly backwards. "I've been kicking my heels on this ship for the last hour when I need to send a message to my family and arrange for passage back to England. I could have spoken to a dozen fishermen in the time I've been waiting for you to appear from whatever jaunt you've been on so that you can tell these men of yours that I am not a prisoner and am free to go wherever I choose. Just why would you abandon—"

"Whoa!" he exclaimed as if she were a bolting mare. "When I left, you were in your underclothes and awaiting David's ministrations. I've been gone less than an hour."

Meg took a deep calming breath. "Will you please inform your nephews and anyone else who needs to know that I am not a prisoner on this ship and am entitled to leave it whenever I choose."

He nodded easily. "Certainly. Miles... Frank..." He gestured to the cousins, who were clinging like limpets to the rail on the far side of the quarterdeck. "Miss Barratt is her own mistress. Please accommodate her wishes in as far as it's possible."

"Aye, sir," the two said in unison.

"There." Cosimo turned back to Meg. "Satisfied now? It was a simple misunderstanding."

Meg, with an air of resignation, leaned back against the

rail and tipped up her face towards the sun, closing her eyes against its brilliance. "Very well," she said after a minute. "But now I would like to be rowed to shore so that I can make arrangements for my passage. I realize it might be too late to set out today—one wouldn't wish to spend the night in the middle of the Channel in a small boat— but I'm sure one of those bigger fishing smacks can make sail at dawn tomorrow."

Cosimo shook his head with a considering frown. "Unfortunately storms are in the air for the next twenty-four hours. I don't think you'll find a fisherman willing to risk his boat and his livelihood on such a journey until the forecast is clear."

"How can they know?" Despite her irritation, Meg was curious.

Cosimo waved vaguely towards the sky. "Sailors read the weather in the clouds, they smell it on the air. And they're rarely mistaken. They trust their instincts anyway... right or wrong."

Meg in some agitation rubbed the cleft in her chin with her fingertip. It sounded perfectly reasonable for superstitious folk whose life and livelihood depended on the fickleness of sea and weather. "Well, that makes it all the more imperative that I send a message to my friends at once," she said. "I presume pigeons can fly through a storm?" There was a sardonic edge to the question.

Cosimo ignored it. "They have their own instincts," he said affably. "If they smell danger, they find a safe haven until it's passed."

"In the meantime," Meg persevered, "I will find a room at some local hostelry." She waved towards the village.

"I'm afraid there are no such amenities on the island," Cosimo murmured.

"No tavern?" Meg exclaimed in disbelief. "What is this island? A monastery?"

He laughed. "No, there are certainly several taverns, but none that have accommodation for visitors." He looked at her with a sympathy that Meg did not find in the least convincing. "Sark can only be reached by sea. Those who do come stay on board their own vessels."

Checkmate. Meg's nostrils flared. She needed to feel that she was regaining control of her own destiny, that she was able to make her own choices, and that sense was growing ever more remote. She wanted to stay on Cosimo's ship only if *she* chose to do so. But it seemed choice didn't come into it.

Cosimo read her mind without difficulty. Having won his point, he needed to conciliate. "Let us go below and write your message to your friends," he said. "It has to be written according to a certain formula so that the initial recipients can read it. They will transcribe it and see that it's delivered to the right place. But as you can imagine, the pigeon can't manage to carry an entire scroll."

"Yes," Meg agreed with a sigh. If this was as much as she could achieve at present, it would have to be good enough. "Show me how to do it."

He gestured that she should precede him to the companionway and they went down to the cabin. Gus greeted them with a cheery "G'day," alighting briefly on Cosimo's head before swooping onto his perch.

"Does he ever go ashore?" Meg asked. For some strange reason she found the macaw fascinating. She was used to dogs and horses and farmyard cats, but exotic birds with very strong personalities had never come her way before.

"No, he gets anxious if he ever leaves the ship," Cosimo replied, rifling through a drawer in the chart table. "I tried it once and he dug his claws so deep in my shoulder he drew blood...ah, here we are." He laid a translucent sheet of onionskin parchment on the chart table and took up a quill. "Who's to receive it?"

"The duchess of St. Jules."

Cosimo raised an eloquent eyebrow, observing, "You keep good company. Where is her grace to be found?" He dipped the quill in the ink.

Meg tapped her fingertips against her mouth as she considered. Would Arabella still be in Folkestone? Would she have gone back to London? Or would she have gone to Lacey Court in Kent to be close to Meg's parents?

No, she decided. They wouldn't have left Folkestone as yet. It wouldn't make sense to leave the place where she'd disappeared, not until they'd covered all the possibilities. She gave the address of the St. Jules's residence on The Leas.

Cosimo was making tiny scratch marks on the onion-skin. Meg watched over his shoulder in fascination. They reminded her of the hieroglyphics that adorned the margins of his dictionaries.

"Now give me a word...something that only your friend will understand so that she knows the message is from you."

Exactly the right word popped into Meg's head with such apposite relevance that she spoke it as she thought it.

"Odd," he commented, inscribing the password in another series of scratches.

"What do you wish to say...and keep it very brief."

Meg gave due consideration to this too. After a moment she said, "What do *you* suggest? You know the truth better than I do."

Cosimo, still bent over the paper, glanced sharply up at her. She gave him a sweet smile. His eyes narrowed and without a word he made a few more marks on the paper before holding it up and waving it gently to dry the ink. He took a tiny cylindrical canister from the drawer and began to fold and roll the parchment into the same shape.

"Wait," Meg said as he was about to insert the roll into the canister. "What did you say?"

He didn't answer until he'd completed the task. "That you were safe and sound and they shouldn't worry. I assume that's good enough?"

"You didn't say that I was on my way home?"

"You aren't," he pointed out. "At least, not at the moment." He straightened, dropping the canister into his britches pocket. "Are you?" His eyes were still narrowed, but now they held a gleam that was part challenge, part promise. He didn't touch her... not yet.

Meg moistened her lips. "No," she agreed.

"It would be a pity for you to leave too soon," he said.

She closed her eyes for a second in an attempt to slow things down, but this exchange was up and running at its own speed. "Yes," she agreed with a tiny sigh. "I suppose it would."

"Before we have the opportunity to ... to explore a little." He was watching her closely.

"I'm sure the island has many places of interest," Meg returned. "I would certainly like to see them. It would be a productive use of the wait until I can get passage back home."

"One should never waste time ... or opportunity," Cosimo said. Slowly he smiled, and as slowly reached a finger that lightly brushed the cleft in her chin. He took a step towards her and placed his lips where his finger had been. Then quickly flicked his tongue into the indentation and up into the corner of her mouth.

It was over in an instant but Meg knew as her loins moistened and her belly tightened that she had lost the conductor's baton. This orchestra was following another's direction.

Cosimo took a step back. He nodded as if to himself, then said, patting his pocket, "First things first. Shall we go and find a pigeon?"

"Certainly," Meg responded, adding under her breath, "first things first."

Chapter 7

Arabella gazed out of the long windows of the drawing room that looked directly onto the street. It was a drizzly, overcast day in Folkestone and there were few people passing by, a fact for which she was grateful. Since Meg's disappearance, the gossipmongers seemed to find the slightest pretext for knocking on the door, leaving their cards, or in some cases openly ogling the house through their quizzing glasses.

She turned as the drawing room door opened, asked with a rising note of hope, "Jack, any news?"

The duke of St. Jules cast his beaver hat on the nearest chair. "Nothing," he said. "Mrs. Carson at the lending library insists Meg left minutes before the storm broke. She had two books, Mrs. Radcliff's and some volume of Wordsworth's." He shook his head with an air of frustration as he went to the decanters on the sideboard. "Madeira?"

Arabella shook her head. "No, thank you."

He poured a glass for himself and came to stand beside her at the window, one arm resting gently across her shoulders. "Sweetheart, this is hard to hear when we don't know the truth, but you must understand that we have to stop the gossip." He spoke with uncharacteristic hesitation. "It will add insult to injury for Sir Mark and Lady Barratt to discover their daughter's name and mysterious disappearance on every tongue. Gossip leads to speculation, and while Meg has done nothing overtly to start tongues wagging, in the past she has always sailed close to the edge of propriety."

"I know that," Arabella declared. "And the gossip is entirely of my doing."

The fact that Meg's vanishing act was common knowledge was entirely her own fault. If she'd consulted Jack before setting off the alarm, they could have covered up Miss Barratt's absence without remark. But she'd known that Meg was only going to the lending library. She had said she was coming straight home. When the storm had broken Arabella had assumed that Meg had taken shelter somewhere, but when the skies cleared and then dark fell and she had not returned and there was no message from her saying cheerfully that she'd escaped the storm and was dining with some of the many friends they had in this summer retreat, in thoughtless panic Arabella had sent servants out into the town to knock on doors, ask questions. Which they had done with a thoroughness that spread the story like butter melting in the sun.

"What's done is done," Jack said rather briskly. "What we have to do now is concoct a story."

"But what if she's dead, Jack?" Arabella articulated the question almost without expression. It was such an awful concept she couldn't invest it with emotion.

He exhaled softly. "That's a possibility. It's always a possibility. But I don't believe it, sweetheart. No one makes a victim of Meg."

"Footpads," she said dully.

"It was the middle of the afternoon. She was on the open street in a tiny seaside town."

"So what do we do? I have to notify Sir Mark and Lady Barratt."

Jack ran a hand over the streak of white hair running back from his forehead. He knew Arabella's strengths, her calm competence. She'd pulled him from the mire of guilt and the depths of misery. She'd gone into the dank world of a Parisian prison and brought out his sister. She'd ministered to Charlotte at her death. And he didn't know how to help her when that strength collapsed.

Except by taking charge. "I will do that at once, but we'll imply that Meg is ill . . . a fever . . . nothing too serious but perhaps they should come.

"Then we'll put it about that Meg fell ill while she was walking back from the lending library and was taken in by a shopkeeper. It took her a while to regain consciousness and when she did a message was sent to us and she's safely tucked into bed abovestairs."

"But will anyone believe that?" Arabella asked.

"No, probably not. But they can't disprove it either," Jack stated, draining his glass. "Enough of the megrims, Arabella. I'm convinced Meg is somewhere safe and well and you'll hear from her soon. In the meantime I'm going to London."

"London?" Arabella's eyes widened in dismay. "Why must you leave me now?"

"To enlist the Bow Street Runners," he said tersely. "I'll be there by nightfall and back by noon tomorrow."

"You can't ride there and back in twenty-four hours, Jack," she protested. "You won't have time to sleep."

"Let me worry about that." He turned to the door. "I'll go and write the letter to the Barratts before I leave."

Arabella followed him out of the drawing room. Tidmouth, the steward, was hovering in the hall, looking vaguely disapproving. In his opinion guests did not mysteriously vanish in a gentleman's household, but he'd never really taken to the duchess's best friend. There was something not quite right about Miss Barratt...something a little unstable, he thought.

"Tidmouth, have my horse brought round. I'm leaving for London immediately," the duke instructed over his shoulder as he made for the library.

Arabella followed him into the book-lined room at the rear of the house. It was gloomy, the gray day beyond the windows offering little natural light. She lit the candelabra on the desk so that Jack could see to write. "Do you think perhaps I should write it?" she asked. "They might worry less."

"If you like," he said. "But I think they will be more reassured to think that you're at their daughter's bedside. It's quite natural that I should write in your stead."

She nodded and perched on the edge of the desk while he sharpened his quill and drew a sheet of parchment in front of him. Meg had been gone now for almost forty-eight hours.

"You can't manage the ladder with that arm," Cosimo said when they emerged on deck.

Meg was doubtful but nevertheless determined. "I'm sure I can."

"Mmm." He didn't sound convinced. He glanced around

and beckoned to one of the cousins. "Frank, rig a lady's seat."

"Aye, sir." Mr. Fisher jumped to attention with alacrity and called to a group of sailors who were splicing rope against the mainmast.

"A lady's seat? What's that?" Meg looked down at the dinghy bobbing in the water rather a long way below the deck rail.

"You sit on a plank that we lower on a rope into the dinghy."

"That sounds very undignified," Meg declared. "I can manage."

"No," he declared.

And that, said he, was that, Meg reflected aridly. But on this occasion he was wrong. She watched for a minute as the sailors attached rope to each end of a narrow piece of planking so that it looked rather like a swing. They slung it over the side and made the rope fast with a series of expert and swiftly tied knots, then drew the plank up level with the deck rail.

"Right, I'm going to lift you over the rail and onto the seat," Cosimo informed her in his cool fashion. "Once you're in place, hold the rope with your good hand and the men will lower you very slowly into the dinghy." He paused, seeing her expression. "Unless, of course, you'd prefer to stay on board and let me take care of getting your message away."

"No, I wouldn't prefer it," she declared. "And neither am I going to go down on that thing." She gestured scornfully to the plank contraption, then, before Cosimo had recovered from his surprise at this uncompromising opposition, she hitched herself onto the rail, swung her legs over one at a time, and, ignoring her throbbing arm, grabbed the top of the rope ladder. Her jaw set, she maneuvered herself onto the precariously swaying ladder.

Cosimo, his arms folded, his mouth rather grim, watched her descent in silence. The ladder hung a few feet above the rocking dinghy and Meg reflected that a helping hand here would be useful, but there wasn't one, so she closed her eyes and dropped. The little boat listed violently and she nearly lost her footing. Cosimo found his voice.

"For God's sake, sit down in the stern," he shouted. "*Now.*"

Meg did so promptly and then looked up the sides of the sloop. It seemed a very long way to the railing and she was glad she hadn't seen the climb from this perspective before embarking on it.

Cosimo came down the ladder with enviable speed and dropped lightly into the boat, which barely rocked beneath him. He sat athwart and took up the oars. For a minute he let the blades rest in the water as he regarded Meg with a frown. "You have a singularly annoying streak of independence, Miss Barratt."

"Only because you're so accustomed to getting your own way," she retorted, happily seizing the opportunity to put that oblique declaration of intent in the cabin to one side for the moment. "I'm quite capable of deciding what I can do and what I can't. And I have no intention *ever* of allowing myself to be lowered on that thing like a sack of potatoes."

His expression was unreadable as he dipped the oars and began to pull strongly for the quay. Meg smiled to herself. Such victories had been few and far between in her recent dealings with the privateer, and small though it was, she relished the moment of triumph, the illusion of regaining control.

They reached the quay and Cosimo threw a rope to a waiting lad, who made the dinghy fast. Cosimo stepped up onto the quay and gave the boy a coin before turning to look down at Meg. "Can you get up here alone, or would you like some help?"

It was a giant step up and Meg knew her legs weren't long enough to do it unaided. Just as Cosimo knew it. He had an infuriating grin on his face as he looked down at her in the boat. "I'd like a hand, please," she said with as much grace as she could muster in the face of that grin.

"Certainly." He stepped down into the dinghy again and, catching her by the waist, lifted her bodily up onto the quay.

Meg inhaled sharply. "A hand was all that was necessary," she said, shaking down her skirts.

"Ah, but think of the pleasure I would have missed," he murmured, his grin broadening into a smile that in its complacency rather resembled her own of a few minutes before. He stepped up beside her and touched a fingertip to the cleft in her chin. His eyes gleamed and his mouth curved in a knowing smile. "And you too, perhaps?"

Meg's eyes narrowed and she jerked her chin away from his finger. "What insufferable conceit," she stated.

"Is it? I wonder." He raised a quizzical eyebrow. "Put up your sword, Miss Meg. I thought we'd agreed to acknowledge this..." He opened his hands in a wordless gesture. "This attraction... for want of a better term."

Meg regarded him still with narrowed eyes. She couldn't deny his statement but he was rushing things, taking too much for granted. "Maybe so," she said. "But acknowledging something and deciding to do something about it are very different matters."

He nodded amiably. "Well, just let me know when

you've decided. We go thisaway." He set off towards the village.

Meg followed him rather more slowly. She wasn't sure why they, or rather *she*, was sparring over this. Maybe it *was* because he seemed to be taking her responses for granted and she certainly hadn't given him permission to do that. Or maybe it was because she found the power of this attraction more than a little alarming. She was certain that the privateer was not a safe person to lust after. But then, safety had never appealed to her, so why was it different this time? Coyness didn't suit her, she thought disgustedly. She was known for her frequently disconcerting, straightforward manner.

She caught up with him as they left the narrow cobbled lanes and emerged onto the hillside. He stopped and waited for her, the relaxation in his loose-limbed frame doing nothing to disguise the muscular strength. His copper hair shone in the sunlight, his sea-washed blue eyes, deep-set in the suntanned complexion, were alive with humor and intelligence. Without a doubt he was the most attractive man she'd ever come across, Meg admitted.

"We have to climb the hill," he said, gesturing behind him. "Are you up to it?"

"Of course," she said with a touch of indignation at the implication. "Is that where the pigeons are?"

"Yes, right at the top." He pointed to the gray structure above them and then set off up the hill, Meg climbing steadily behind him.

Her arm was aching again and she cradled it against her chest. It made the going harder since she couldn't swing her arms to help her rhythm and balance, but she pressed on doggedly, pausing once or twice to look back down the hill and out over the blue waters of the Channel. Towards the top of the hill she could make out Guernsey, the Channel Island closest to Sark. It was much bigger and there seemed to be more shipping activity in its vicinity.

"Cosimo..."

"Yes." He stopped at her hail and she hurried up towards him.

"Wouldn't I do better to look for passage home on Guernsey? It's much bigger and seems to have bigger ships around it."

"It has a deeper, more sheltered harbor, that's why," he informed her.

"Well, perhaps I can find a boat here that will ferry me across to Guernsey and then I can get a passage from there." She looked at him closely, brushing a tangle of wind-whipped red curls away from her eyes.

"You could try," he responded with a noncommittal shrug. "Come on, we're nearly at the top."

"*Helpful*," she murmured sardonically to herself as she followed him up the last steep rise to the gray cottage.

Lieutenant Murray appeared in the cottage doorway at the sound of his approaching visitors. "Captain," he said with the inevitable crisp salute.

"This is Lieutenant Murray, of the Royal Navy, Meg. Murray, may I present Miss Barratt." Cosimo gestured between them as he made the introduction. "She's sailing with us, and needs to send an urgent message to her family in England."

Murray couldn't disguise his curiosity as he offered a stiff half bow to the woman accompanying the privateer. She looked disreputable, he thought disparagingly. Bold-eyed and flushed, perspiration beading her forehead. No respectable woman would show herself in public with such a wind-blown tangle of curls and disheveled appearance.

But then, no respectable woman would be sailing on the *Mary Rose*, keeping company with the privateer.

"Ma'am," he murmured faintly.

Meg had little difficulty reading his expression and her eyes flashed, her chin went up. She acknowledged him with a haughty nod. She had no interest in the hidebound opinions of a self-important young sailor preening himself in an immaculate uniform that didn't look as if it had ever seen anything more exciting than a thundershower.

"The pigeon, Murray?" Cosimo prompted. "If you recall, we have a message to send."

The lieutenant cleared his throat. "If you'll come this way." He led the way to a small building that stood just behind the cottage. A soft cooing greeted them as they entered the dim interior. There were half a dozen pigeons sitting on perches and beams that laced the ceiling.

"We have three here at the moment that do the English route," the lieutenant said. "The others have recently flown in from France."

Meg, despite her disdain for the popinjay lieutenant, was fascinated by the concept of a pigeon courier service. "They each know their own route?"

"That's right," Cosimo replied. "Some are able to go direct from France to the English coast, but others stop here. It depends on the message." He put his hand in his pocket and brought out a handful of corn. He held his flat palm up to a bird watching them intently from its perch. The bird hopped forward and delicately pecked at the corn before flying onto Cosimo's shoulder. There was a whirr of wings and two more alighted, one on top of Cosimo's head, the other on his other shoulder. He dug into his pocket for more corn.

Meg remembered the bird books in the cabin. Cosimo

seemed to have an affinity with the species. These pigeons were behaving with him much as Gus did. "They seem to think you're an honorary bird," she observed.

"There are worse things," he responded. "Murray, which one are we using?"

"Number 3 is rested." The lieutenant snapped his fingers at the guard who'd accompanied them. "Get her ready, Hogan."

"Aye, sir." The young man lifted one of the birds off the perch, holding its body securely. He held it for Cosimo, who attached the tiny cylinder to its right leg with a thin leather strap. Cosimo stroked the bird's neck for a minute and then stepped back. The guard placed the bird in a cage and closed the door on it. "I'll send her off now, shall I, sir?"

"Right away," Murray said.

"I'd like to watch." Meg followed the guard carrying the birdcage out into the sunshine. The young man gave her a rather nervous smile. Presumably he didn't have much experience with women, Meg reflected, offering a reassuring smile of her own. "Is she just called Number 3? It seems a bit impersonal."

"That's her navy identification, ma'am. I call her Stella." They had reached the brow of the hill and he set the cage on the ground.

Meg bent to reach in and stroke the bird's shimmering throat. "Fly swift and straight, Stella." She stood up and gazed out towards the invisible English coast. "Where will she make landfall?"

"Dover, ma'am. We've a station just up from the beach."

Her heart jumped. Folkestone was but eight miles from Dover. "How long will it take her?"

"Depends on the wind, ma'am. She should make it by

dawn tomorrow, or soon after, unless she gets blown off course."

Meg thought of the storm that Cosimo said was brewing. That could add a few hours to the bird's flight, but even so, Arabella should know all was well, or at least relatively so, by tomorrow morning.

Hogan extracted the pigeon from the cage and held her high. He checked the cylinder was firmly attached and then threw the bird into the wind. She soared high and they watched for a few minutes as she flew steadily northward.

Meg felt a wave of relief. She'd done all she could for the moment. She felt the privateer's eyes on her and glanced over at him. His gaze held a question. She wondered if it was the same question she was asking herself, and she knew that it was. Now that reassurance was on its way to her friends and family, was there still a truly pressing need for her to arrange passage home without delay? It could wait for a couple of days if she had something better to do. Was a brief sensual interlude with the privateer something better to do?

Her body answered the last question for her. Just the thought of such an interlude made her stomach flip and sent a jolt of arousal through her loins.

Cosimo watched her expression. Meg Barratt was no expert at dissembling. He could read her thoughts as clearly as if she'd spoken them. He was only faintly surprised at her openness about her sensuality; there were women aplenty like her, Ana among them, but he had not before met one straight from the upper echelons of London Society. Unwrapping such a package promised to be as intriguing as he sensed it would be exciting.

He turned to the lieutenant, who was shuffling his feet

impatiently on the turf. "Send to me immediately if there's a message, Murray. It's most urgent."

"Aye, Captain."

"Thank you." He gestured to Meg. "Shall we go back to the ship?"

"It's such a beautiful afternoon, it seems a shame," she said. "Are you needed on board, or could we explore the island a little?"

He nodded. "I see no reason why not. But come and take a look over the other side of the hill."

She followed him around the back of the cottage and looked down at the busy scene in the water below. The two English men-of-war and the French frigate, which now flew the Union Jack and was tied fast to one of the British ships. Longboats scurried around the little flotilla, ferrying men between the ships.

"Will they sail it back to England?" Meg inquired thoughtfully, wishing she didn't feel obliged to ask the question. She knew that naval ships often carried civilian passengers when there was a good reason, and it would be a much more comfortable voyage than in a fishing boat. It would be a pity if the vessel's departure was imminent, she reflected with rueful self-knowledge. Despite her ambivalence she would have to take advantage of it, which would mean she wouldn't be able to explore the possibilities of an interlude with the privateer. But if that was the situation, then she had no choice but to accept it.

Cosimo pretended to give the question some thought. In fact he had nothing to think over. He was not ready for Meg to leave Sark for far more important reasons than the simple satisfaction of his own lust. He needed her here until he knew where matters stood with Ana. If he heard nothing, he'd know there would be no partnership on this mission and then Meg, albeit unwitting, was his trump card. It was highly likely that the French prize would be sent back to England with a prize crew and her own officers and crew as prisoners of war. A small white lie was in order.

"I doubt it," he said finally. "They'll put an English crew aboard and immediately incorporate it into the English fleet."

"But what of the French crew?"

He shrugged. "The officers will be prizes, worth a handsome ransom. I imagine they'll be left here in the charge of the naval outpost until they can be transferred by the next available naval ship. The men will be offered the opportunity to sign on with the British navy or to be held as prisoners of war, also awaiting transport to English shores."

Meg said nothing, but a frown creased her forehead. It sounded perfectly reasonable but she detected something, nothing she could put her finger on, that didn't ring true.

"So none of those ships will be sailing back to England?"

"Not immediately. They'll be chasing Napoleon," he said with an assumption of carelessness.

Meg regarded him with arrested interest. "Where's Napoleon going?"

He hesitated, then decided that sharing such a piece of intelligence with her could do no harm and might help his cause. It would make her feel she was in his confidence. "Egypt, we think."

"Think, or know?" she asked.

He smiled. "An astute question. We know. But strictly speaking, I should not have told you. It's a piece of covert intelligence at present."

She nodded, fitting this with everything else she'd divined about the privateer. Pigeon couriers, spy networks, missing agents, covert intelligence. "I see," she said dryly.

He glanced at her. "Do you?" Then he laughed a little. "Yes, I believe you do. Now, shall we stroll around the island?"

"I think I'd like to ask the captain of one of those men-of-war if there's any chance they might decide to return to Dover," she said with a thoughtful frown, keeping pace with him as he strode off along the lip of the hill. "One never knows."

"Indeed not. It's easy enough to convey a message to the commander of the *Leopold*. If you wish it, you could ask him today."

"So I could," Meg said, casting him a quick appraising glance, but there was nothing in his expression to imply deception, so why did she have this feeling that he was being less than candid? "So I could."

Chapter 8

They strolled along the brim of the hill, Cosimo pausing frequently to look up when a particular bird on the wing caught his eye.

"Have you always been interested in ornithology?" Meg inquired.

"Since I was a small boy," he responded. "Ah, now look at this...careful now." He had stopped and was peering down into the cushiony grass.

"Plover's nest," he whispered when Meg stepped softly up beside him. "Can you see the eggs? They're camouflaged."

"Isn't it dangerous for them to lay their eggs on the ground?"

"Very," he said straightening. "But nature has an odd and sometimes cruel sense of humor. Somehow the species survives. Move away now, the mother's coming back."

Meg walked away hastily, hearing the distressed bird call behind her. "Will we have put her off?"

"No, so long as we didn't touch anything." He dug his

hands into his pockets as he walked, lifting his face to the sun.

He seemed as at home on the land as on the decks of his ship, Meg thought. "How long will you stay here?" she asked. "On Sark."

"We leave on the dawn tide on Wednesday morning."

Today was Sunday; that left the rest of today and two full days. Meg frowned as she walked, still cradling her arm against her chest. It could be seen as just the perfect length of time for a passion-filled idyll with no strings. A couple of days of loving and laughter and no regrets on parting.

"Time is perhaps of the essence." His voice startled her, the comment shocking her with its uncanny tuning into her own thought.

She looked at him sideways and saw that he was smiling, but it was not his usual pleasantly careless smile. There was purpose behind it, a deep lingering sensuality to the curve of his mouth and in the sudden darkening of his sun-bleached eyes. They were walking now in a small copse of wind-bent, gnarled pine trees, the ground beneath them crunchy and fragrant with pine needles. The sun was a mere glint through the overhanging evergreen umbrella.

He moved in front of her, laying his hands on her shoulders, easing her backwards a pace so that she felt the trunk of a tree against her back. A bird whistled somewhere above her and the silence between them was for a moment suspended, filled with a gravity of intent that could not be misunderstood.

Meg tilted her face, meeting the privateer's steady, hungry gaze. His mouth hovered over hers and then his lips met hers. At first it was a cool, firm touch, more of a statement than a caress, she thought, wondering why she always analyzed such initial moves in the lovemaking dance. She liked his smell; it was salty, tinged with fresh air and sunshine, spiced with pine. She touched his lips with a rapid flickering of the tip of her tongue, tasting like a bee testing a flower for its nectar. Salt and sweet. She brought up her good hand and laid it against the side of his face, feeling its shape, the hollow of the cheek, the angularity of the cheekbones, the line of the jaw.

He still had his hands resting gently on her shoulders, but now he moved them to the sides of her breasts, lightly cupping the curve. Fingertips nudged the nipples and Meg felt the frisson as they rose, obedient to encouragement.

She pushed her tongue more insistently against his mouth and his lips parted, drawing in the intruder with a sudden vehemence that for a second took her by surprise. And then all interest in analysis fled as her body took over. She reached her good arm around his neck, pressing herself against him, as their tongues played. His hands moved down her body, holding her hips now, thumbs pressing into the sharp pointy hip bones that she had always wished were not so apparent. But the privateer didn't seem to mind them. In fact, he was playing a tune now that made her catch her breath even as her tongue plunged and fenced and she tasted the salt sweetness of his mouth with a hunger that couldn't be sated. She forgot about the wound on her arm and brought both hands to his buttocks, kneading the hard muscles beneath her fingers with an exhilarating urgency of passion.

Cosimo raised his head, breaking the kiss, looking down at her flushed face, her parted lips, her luminous eyes. "Be careful of your arm," he murmured.

Meg shook her head. She could feel his penis hard and

demanding against her loins and her arm had nothing to do with any of this. "Damn the arm." She laughed with the exhilaration of a moment before, digging her nails into his backside.

He kissed her, tracing the shape of her face with his tongue before returning to her mouth. A swift stroking caress of her lips and then he possessed her mouth and she had no control over this. She received him, gloried in the deep, embracing power of his thrusting tongue and the knowledge of the greater possession it preceded. He lifted her skirts, sliding the material up her thighs with deft movements, his breathing as swift as her own. When his skillful fingers found her center, she braced herself against the tree, her arms once more entwined around his neck, her mouth pressing hard against his so that her soft cry was stifled against his lips as the orgasmic waves engulfed her.

Cosimo kissed her long and deep as he let her skirts fall about her. He stroked her cheek with a flat palm until she had regained her breath, then drew her against him, caressing the back of her head. A tiny smile played over his mouth. It seemed he had been right about Miss Barratt. She was going to prove an exciting and responsive playmate.

She was caressing him now, the fingers of her good hand playing over the hard shape of his penis jutting against his britches, and it was only with a supreme effort of will that he fought the surging arousal and caught her wrist, lifting her hand firmly away from its work.

"I've always believed in give and take," she said, sounding a little indignant as she tried to return her hand to its original position.

"There'll be time enough," he said, a laugh in his voice. "I must get back to the ship."

Meg squinted up at him against a ray of sunshine that fell across her face. "That seems a little unfair," she observed.

He smiled. "Oh, you'll have your turn, ma'am. I promise you."

He had remarkable self-control, Meg reflected. She'd been all too aware of the strength of his arousal. One day, she would really put that self-control to the test. Just the thought made her stomach flip again. "I'll hold you to that," she said, brushing at her skirts. "Do I look dreadfully disheveled?"

"No more so than usual."

"If I weren't in such a state of euphoria, I might take exception to that."

"Oh, please do," he said, taking her good hand and leading her out of the copse. "It sounds as if it might be amusing." .

"You'll have to wait and see," she returned. So the die had been cast. She was going to enjoy a passionate, clearly defined interlude with the privateer. No strings, no harm. Two days, that was all. Nothing could happen in two days beyond a few lustful encounters. And she did enjoy lustful encounters.

They walked down the hill towards the little hamlet in a thoughtful but companionable silence. Meg wondered what Cosimo was thinking, and whether his thoughts ran on much the same lines as her own. She would have been more than disconcerted if she could have read his mind.

Cosimo was thinking of Ana. Involuntarily he caught himself scanning the horizon for a pigeon homing in on the gray cottage. Meg's eager, uninhibited enjoyment of those few minutes in the copse reminded him vividly of Ana. And yet the differences were as striking as the similarities. Ana had a shell, engendered he knew by a life that didn't allow for weakness. She'd grown in a hard school and matured in a harder. He enjoyed that in her, they met and matched each other on an equal playing field, but the Ana that existed deep within her carapace was unknown to him, and sometimes he thought to her too. He dealt always with the part of Ana she was willing or knew how to share. Meg was different. Her core was not so protected. In many ways, he thought, it indicated greater strength than Ana. She was not afraid to reveal her self.

Unconsciously he swung her hand as they stepped through sea pinks and clover on the last stretch to the hamlet. Despite his anxiety over Ana, he felt exhilaration and a purely passionate anticipation. Wherever she was, Ana would not begrudge him that. They had come together when time and events allowed it and parted in the same way. But dear God, he needed to know what had happened. The moment of exhilaration abruptly faded.

Meg felt the change in him through the hand that held her own. A sudden tension, a slight stiffness in his grasp. She glanced at him and saw that the residue of passion had left his gaze. He seemed to be looking inward at something unpleasant. "Is something the matter?" she asked hesitantly.

Instantly his expression reverted to the relaxed humor that she was accustomed to. "What could possibly be the matter?" he said lightly.

"I don't know," she said. "It felt as if some shadow had fallen over you."

She was acutely sensitive, Cosimo reflected. Ana would never have noticed that moment and if she had would have dismissed it as unimportant and no business of hers. Once again he wondered if Meg could be ruthless enough to partner him in his enterprise. Was she perhaps too sensitive? Her emotions running too close to the surface? She was an unusual woman, certainly, but was she unusual enough?

"Oh, just someone walking over my grave, I expect," he said with a careless shrug.

Meg considered this and decided it was a most unsatisfactory explanation, but she was disinclined to press the matter. She didn't know the man well enough to pry. "I'm starved," she said instead. "Aren't you hungry?"

Cosimo, relieved at this change of subject, responded, "I suppose so. It's the middle of the afternoon, after all. A long time since breakfast."

Meg looked at him with curiosity. "You don't normally recognize when you're hungry?"

"Not really," he said, jumping off a low stone wall that separated the hamlet from the bottom of the hill. "Often I don't have time to notice, so I suppose I'm accustomed to ignoring the signs." He reached for Meg's waist and swung her down onto the dirt-packed alleyway. "There's a tavern on the quay. They make a pot of excellent steamed mussels with wine and garlic, accompanied by a tankard of home brew."

"I thought you had to be back on the ship." She caught her foot in a wheel rut and righted herself hastily, grabbing hold of his sleeve.

"Close to it," he said. "The tavern's within earshot of a whistle if I'm needed . . . Are you stable now?"

"As much as I can be with only one arm," she declared. It was a little strange that they could be having this mundane conversation after what had happened in the copse, and yet, at the same time, it increased her anticipation. What had passed between them had been merely the preliminary, and pretending in some way that it hadn't happened heightened her excitement. They would eat mussels and drink ale and return to the *Mary Rose* ... How did one make love in a box-bed? Maybe a hammock ... A chuckle escaped her.

"What's funny?"

"Oh, nothing much. I was wondering how hammocks reacted to activity ... certain kinds of activity."

"It depends on the expertise of those engaged in the activity," he responded solemnly.

Meg let that go and allowed her imagination full rein.

The tavern was low-ceilinged and smelled of ale-soaked sawdust and stale tobacco. A few fishermen sat on the ale bench outside, but within only a surly man in a stained waistcoat leaned against the bar counter, his nose buried in the froth of his tankard.

Cosimo gave him a nod that was barely returned and banged on the counter. A slatternly woman appeared within a few minutes, adjusting a grubby cap on dirty yellow hair. "Aye? Oh, 'tis you, Cap'n." The greeting didn't sound too enthusiastic to Meg's ears. "What'll it be?"

"Mussels, Bertha, if you please, a loaf of bread, and two tankards of your best bitter. We'll be outside." He gestured to the door he'd left open behind them.

The woman merely nodded and disappeared. "Shall we?" Cosimo indicated the door and Meg followed him with alacrity.

"Is it safe to eat from that kitchen?" She was reluctant to show her squeamishness but couldn't help it.

"There's enough garlic in the mussels to ward off a host of vampires." He sat on the low bench and leaned back, resting his elbows against the split wood of the table.

"And if we both eat them, we won't need to ward off

each other," Meg observed, following his lead, lifting her face to the sun.

"Precisely." He laid a hand briefly over hers and the electric crackle was almost audible.

"Should you let your crew know where you are?" Meg asked, trying to put the conversation on an ordinary footing.

"Oh, they know," he said lazily. "Thank you, Bertha." He smiled at the woman who set two foaming tankards on the table.

"Mussels'll be a few minutes," she muttered, hurrying away.

Meg looked towards the *Mary Rose*, bobbing gently a few hundred yards from the quay. Of course at the very least Miles Graves or Frank Fisher would be watching for the captain's appearance on the quay.

The mussels arrived in a steaming fragrant cauldron, with a long thin loaf of crusty bread. Cosimo broke into the bread, passing Meg half of the loaf, and then dipped his fingers into the bowl until he found an empty shell. He used it like a spoon, extracting golden morsels from their shells and supping the juice.

It was a new technique for Meg, who was accustomed to thin pronged forks when it came to eating shellfish, but she adapted swiftly, using her bread to sop up the garlicky vinous liquid, chasing it with deep gulps of the rich brown ale.

Cosimo reached over and scooped an errant trickle of juice from her chin with his finger. He sucked it off slowly and the suggestive little game moistened her loins. Her half smile was alluring as she dipped her bread in the cauldron again and held the succulent morsel to his lips. He took her fingers into his mouth with the bread, and their eyes held, promise dancing between them.

Meg wondered fleetingly what any watcher would make of this little seductive play and then dismissed the thought. It mattered nothing to her. She was unencumbered. No one here knew who she was, and for the moment she was responsible to no one.

It was late afternoon when they got up to return to the ship. Meg felt a certain reluctance to leave the sun-drenched quay and return to the *Mary Rose*. Cosimo was different on land; the watchfulness that was a natural part of him when he was on his ship was relaxed somewhat. On board she had seen how he was constantly on the alert, despite the apparent relaxation of his manner, but the underlying tension in his frame had been absent once they'd left the pigeon cottage... except for that one moment, she amended. She wondered if the inevitable constraints of the ship, the confined space, the presence of others all dependent on Cosimo's authority, would also constrain their time together. Well, she'd discover soon enough.

Cosimo lifted Meg down into the dinghy with a lack of ceremony that earlier would have offended her. He untied the little boat and pulled for the *Mary Rose*, where a waiting seaman grabbed the rope Cosimo threw up and made the dinghy fast. "I'm assuming you'll scorn the lady's seat," Cosimo remarked, indicating the swing still in place against the deck rail.

"You assume right," Meg said, although she regarded the ladder that hung a couple of feet above her head with some dismay, unsure how she could one-handedly grab it and swing herself up.

"I'm also assuming you won't scorn my helping hand,"

he said with clear double entendre and a skimming brush of his lips against her ear.

"No," she agreed.

He lifted her onto the ladder and she climbed up with some difficulty, favoring her injured arm and not refusing Frank Fisher's assistance over the rail and onto the deck. Cosimo swung himself over the side beside her.

"Captain, there's a message from the *Leopold*," Frank said. "It arrived an hour ago."

"Good," Cosimo said, and as she'd expected or feared, it was as if the last couple of hours had never existed. "Is it in my cabin?"

"Aye, sir."

Cosimo nodded and strode off to the companionway. Meg, after a moment, followed him. She still felt uncertain about her position on this vessel, and its captain hadn't done anything to clarify it for her. Indeed, if anything, he'd made it more confusing.

"Cosimo, what do your crew know about me?" she asked, closing the cabin door behind her.

"Nothing," he said, breaking the wafer on a sheet of paper. "Why?"

"No reason." Meg turned her attention to Gus, who was exhibiting considerable pleasure in their return. Or at least Cosimo's, she amended, scratching his poll. "Were they expecting Ana, or just any woman?"

He looked up from the paper, his eyes sharp. "Does it matter?"

She had told herself that this was a short, limited liaison. Why should it matter what anyone on this ship thought or knew? "No," she said decisively. "Of course not."

He smiled slowly. "It shouldn't. I'm invited to dine with

the commander of the *Leopold* this evening. Do you care to join me?"

Meg frowned. It was one thing not to care what the sailors on the *Mary Rose* made of her presence on board in the captain's cabin, quite another for the outside world. There was no knowing who the naval commander was acquainted with. Could she risk the story of her sojourn with the privateer becoming food for the social gossips? No, she had never been foolish in her indiscretions and she wasn't about to start now. Arabella and Jack would scotch all rumors unless they became unscotchable. She was not going to allow that to happen.

"No," she said. "I couldn't do that unless I was asking for their official protection. I'd have to explain how I come to be in need of that protection." She raised her eyebrows in quizzical fashion. The die had been cast in the pine copse. Obviously, asking for the navy's protection and assistance in her return to English shores was not consonant with a liaison, however brief, with the privateer.

"I'll return to England as clandestinely as I left," she continued. "The fewer people who know anything about this misadventure, the better."

Cosimo would have liked her to have thrown her hat over the windmill and propriety be damned, as Ana would have done. But Ana lived outside society and was not subject to its rules. Meg Barratt, for all her unusual conduct, still belonged to an unforgiving world. He couldn't at this point expect her to do anything that would instantly ruin her reputation. She hadn't thrown in her lot with him, merely tacitly agreed to a short, discreet, mutually satisfying liaison.

"I see your point," he said. He contemplated declining the invitation for himself but he was interested in knowing where the frigate's orders were taking them. He might need assistance getting out of Toulon once his mission was accomplished, and it would be useful to know what ships would be in the area.

"I wish I didn't have to go, but I must. I'll be back before midnight." He lifted her chin and lightly kissed the tip of her nose. "Try to stay awake."

"Oh, I will," she declared. "If only to discover the tricks of activity in a hammock."

"Then you'd better take a nap beforehand," he murmured, kissing the corner of her mouth. "It could be an energetic night."

"That had better be a promise," she returned, her flat palm stroking the significant area of his britches. "I too have a promise to keep."

He threw up his hands and stepped hastily away from her. "Enough, now. I have things to do on deck before I leave." He left quickly before temptation got the better of him, but he couldn't prevent a flickering smile as he climbed the companionway.

"Cap'n looks like he's had a saucer of cream," the grizzled boatswain murmured to Biggins, who was sewing buttons on a jacket in a patch of sunlight on the mid-deck.

"Oh, aye?" Biggins glanced up as Cosimo passed him. He grinned a little. "Oh, aye, that he does, Bosun, that he does."

Seaman Hogan stood on the brow of the hill and watched the little gray bird beating its way steadily across the sea towards the island. The last rays of the evening sun lent a pink tinge to its wing tips. As it drew closer to where he stood it began to descend, catching a thermal for a moment and drifting with it, before swooping down, flying straight for the pigeon hut. It landed on a windowsill and folded its wings as fastidiously as a laundry maid folding a tablecloth.

Hogan lifted the bird and examined it carefully. The tiny identifying tag on its left leg was in place and he frowned at it for a minute. "Where have you been, girl?" he murmured. "We thought you were lost." Its heart beat fast against his enclosing hand but it cooed in soft greeting as he stroked its throat.

He unfastened the tiny cylinder from its right leg, then took corn from his pocket, offering it in his cupped palm. The pigeon pecked delicately for a moment or two, then flew up and through the window to a resting place on one of the long perches in the dim interior.

Hogan went into the cottage to where Lieutenant Murray was finishing his supper. "Number 6 is back, sir." He laid the cylinder on the table beside the lieutenant's plate of bread and cheese. "I thought we'd lost her for good."

Murray wiped his mouth with a checkered napkin and took up the cylinder. "It's been what . . . six weeks since we sent her out last?"

"About that, sir."

"Usually they send 'em back within a week," Murray observed and then dismissed the puzzle with a shrug. "I expect they forgot she was there." He opened the container and took out the near-transparent roll of onionskin. He held it up to the lamplight and examined the hieroglyphics. "For the captain of the *Mary Rose*," he concluded. "Must be what he was expecting." He rerolled the paper and inserted it into the cylinder again. "Take it down to the *Mary Rose*, Hogan."

The seaman pocketed the cylinder, saluted, and loped off down the hill in the gathering dusk. A few lamps shone from the windows of the little hamlet but the narrow lanes were deserted. This was a community that lived by the sun. When he emerged from the clustered cottages onto the quay, he saw that the *Mary Rose* was lit by lanterns fore and aft, another two suspended from the yardarm. A couple of men leaned idly against the deck rail and the scent of tobacco wafted across the water.

Hogan caught himself envying them the apparent freedom from restraint. He'd joined the navy cheerfully enough, following in family footsteps, and his present post was far from uncomfortable, although a little isolated, but life on a privateer, or at least this particular privateer, had its appeal.

He put two fingers to his lips and sent a piercing whistle across the intervening water. One of the sailors raised a hand in acknowledgment and in a few minutes the dinghy was bumping up against the quayside.

"Message for your captain," Hogan said, leaning over to give the canister to the oarsman.

"He's on the *Leopold*," the sailor informed him as he took the cylinder. "Is it urgent?"

Hogan shrugged. "No idea. The lieutenant said your captain was expecting it."

"He'll be back afore midnight." The sailor raised a hand in farewell and pulled back to the *Mary Rose*.

Cosimo leaned back in his chair in the *Leopold*'s comfortable wardroom and took an appreciative sip of a rather fine port. "You live well," he observed.

The little group of officers laughed in appreciation of

the truth. "I doubt you live too badly on your ship, Captain," the commander observed.

"Not too badly," Cosimo agreed. He set down his glass on the highly polished table and pushed back his chair. Meg was waiting for him and now that he had the information he'd come for, his impatience was running out of bounds. "I thank you for your hospitality, gentlemen, but I must get back."

"I take it you're sailing for Brest," the commander observed.

It was a reasonable assumption given the course the *Mary Rose* had been following, but Cosimo merely offered a noncommittal smile. "That rather depends."

"Cagey bastard," the commander muttered to his first lieutenant as they followed Cosimo back on board. But he was all polite smiles and renewed expressions of appreciation for their easily won prize as they made their farewells and the captain of the privateer entered the longboat with its bank of oarsmen that would take him back to his own ship on the other side of the island.

Cosimo sat in the stern, to all intents and purposes completely at his ease after a good dinner. He tilted his head back to look at the stars, and none of the oarsmen, or the young ensign directing the crew from the bow, could guess that he was very far from relaxed as he calculated and sorted through alternative courses of action. The frigates had orders to head into the Mediterranean to engage with the French fleet now mustering at Toulon. That was good news for him. Once his mission was completed he might well need all the support he could get.

It would take them close to a month to sail across the Bay of Biscay, around the tip of Portugal and through the Strait of Gibraltar, and it would probably take him almost

as long to reach Toulon by his own route. His present plan
did indeed entail making landfall at Brest and going overland from there to Toulon. He and Ana. But now he didn't
know. If Ana didn't contact him, would it still be safe to follow the original planned route? It was a long haul overland
across the rugged center of France, but not only could they
keep away from major towns and military centers, it was
such an unlikely route for an enemy agent to take, no one
would suspect that they were anything but the casual travelers they appeared.

They. For the mission to have a real chance of success,
he had to have a partner.

The longboat rounded the corner of the island, rowing
close in to the shore. The surf pounding on the dangerous
outcrop of rocks farther out was deafening at times and a
fine mist of spray dampened his coat.

A partner. He had a potential partner. Was she awake
and waiting for him, eagerly contemplating the erotic
prospects of the night ahead? Could he use that night to
bind her to him in such a way that she would be willing to
extend their love affair, to join with him in a very different
enterprise?

He was so lost in the question that he didn't notice immediately when the longboat drew alongside the illuminated *Mary Rose.*

"Good evening, Captain. Welcome back." The fresh
face of Frank Fisher hung over the deck rail as the longboat bumped against the side.

Cosimo shook himself out of his reverie. "Thank you,
Mr. Fisher," he said formally, swinging himself onto the
rope ladder. He climbed onto the deck and raised a hand
in dismissal to the crew of the longboat. "So, all's well in
my absence?"

"Aye, sir," the young man said. "But this came for you." He handed the cylinder to his captain.

Cosimo weighed it in the palm of his hand as his mind raced. Meg would be expecting him to go to her immediately but this couldn't wait. He strode up to the quarterdeck and under the lamplight from the yardarm opened the canister.

Chapter 9

Cosimo unrolled the thin sheet and held it up to the light the better to decipher the faint scratchings. It was from Ana. He'd known that instinctively even before he'd opened it. Or at least, it purported to be from Ana. But she had not composed it even if she had physically written it.

He frowned down at the signature. *Anna*. The signal they had agreed upon as a warning of trouble. The message itself was brief, as it had to be. *Detained. Mission of paramount importance. Continue as planned. Bonne chance. Anna.*

The message had come by pigeon courier. Had one of their own pigeons been captured by the enemy and used to bring a false message? It wouldn't be the first time. French intelligence was as devious and cunning as the British. If they had taken Ana, they would have learned the details of the present mission, and they would be expecting him when he made landfall at Brest. *Continue as planned.*

His lip curled. What arrogant fools. Did they really think he and Ana were such inexperienced simpletons that they would fall for that? They could force Ana to write it, to prime the trap, as indeed he had to assume they had, but how naïve of them to assume they would have no safeguard in place. Whatever they did to Ana, whatever information she was forced to give them, she would always find a way to outwit them. *Whatever they did to her.*

He closed his mind to that thought; it would do neither of them any good. Before he jumped to any conclusions, he needed to talk to Lieutenant Murray, find out if there was anything different about this particular pigeon courier . . . any clues as to where it had come from, and if it was as he suspected, he needed to send an urgent message to his own spy network in England. They had to find Ana. And they would. They were all experienced agents, skilled at infiltrating the enemy networks. They would get to Ana.

He spun on his heel, intending to take the dinghy immediately across to the quay. Lieutenant Murray would probably be fast asleep, but that was just unfortunate. He'd have to wake up. Then he saw Meg standing a few feet away, watching him.

The sight of her startled him. He'd forgotten all about her in the last few minutes. Why hadn't he heard her approach? How long had she been standing there? And now what was he to do? If he abandoned her at this crucial point, he would lose her. Their attraction was still too ephemeral to withstand such a seeming rejection. But he couldn't afford to lose her. There was now much more at stake than a pleasant interlude. His mission now depended on gaining Meg's cooperation. Murray would have to wait. The message to England would have to wait, much as he loathed the idea of wasting a minute in coming to Ana's rescue. But Ana, he knew, would pour scorn on such concerns. For her the mission was always paramount; personal emotions had no place in her working world.

"I heard you come on board," Meg said, not moving from where she stood at the deck rail. "I heard you talk to Frank. I came up to see what was keeping you." His silence confused her. He'd uttered not a word of greeting. Her gaze was intense as she scrutinized his expression. It was unusually grim and his eyes were distracted. Something had happened, something important enough to drive all thoughts of erotic encounters from his mind.

"Just a message," he said with an attempt at an apologetic smile. "I wanted to read it before I came to you." He took the few steps necessary to reach her and pressed his little finger into the cleft of her chin. "I didn't want anything to distract me." His voice was a caress but somehow neither that nor the apologetic smile reassured Meg. He had completely forgotten about her.

"If you have business, you should see to it," she said.

"You are my business," he replied softly, pressing harder into her chin. "Tonight, you and only you, ma'am." His eyes had darkened, his voice was smooth as molasses, and whatever he'd been thinking of before, it was clear that Meg now occupied his whole attention. Only passion was on his mind now.

His ability to switch moods so completely disturbed her. She had seen the shadow on his face, the grim set of his jaw. Where had it gone? It was unnatural to be able to dismiss a troubling thought, wipe it clean away, and replace it with a completely different side to his character. And yet she couldn't find the words to say so. Once again she was confronted with the fact that she did not know this man, and she didn't have the right to pry into areas he chose to keep private. Sexual attraction was no substitute for the kind of intimacy that would permit her questions.

Cosimo sensed the danger, felt her slipping away from him. He needed to do something to rekindle that erotic spark before it was too late. He took her face between his hands and kissed her, his mouth melting into hers in a long, lingering caress. At first, while she didn't refuse the kiss, she was still and unresponsive, as if undecided. But slowly he felt her soften as he stroked her lips with his tongue, grazed her cheek with feather-light taps of his fingertips that made her smile against his mouth. The stiffness left her and she leaned into him, kissing him with increasing fervor.

"Come," he commanded softly, taking her hand. He led her below, running his hand down her back as he eased her into the lamp-lit cabin ahead of him. His hand lingered on the roundness of her bottom and she could feel the heat through the thin material of her gown.

She turned towards him, her eyes now luminous in the golden glow from the lantern suspended from a hook in the ceiling. He held her hips as he gazed down at her, taking in the pearly pink tinge to her usually pale complexion, the scattering of freckles across her small nose, her moistly parted lips. He kissed the corner of her mouth as his hands moved to her back, his fingers deftly unfastening the long line of pearl buttons running from her neck to her waist.

"G'night... g'night."

"Damn!" Cosimo exclaimed. "I forgot about Gus."

"I can't imagine how," Meg said with a choke of laughter. "Can we put him out?"

For answer he picked up the macaw between both

hands and firmly put him in his cage. He threw the crimson cover over it, saying, "Good night, Gus."

"Poor Gus," came the rather mournful murmur from beneath the cover.

"Now, where were we? Ah, yes, I remember. I was unwrapping a present." Cosimo reached for her hands. "New bandage," he observed.

"David re-dressed it," she returned, impatient at this mundane intermission and yet at the same time enjoying the suspense.

"Good," he declared with an approving nod and then laughed a little, aware of both her pleasure and the impatience that exactly mirrored his own. He drew her closely against him, while he continued with the buttons. She could feel the hard lines of his body against her own softness. Her nipples hardened as she felt the back of her dress part and a coolness against her skin. He eased the gown off her hips to fall with a rustle around her ankles.

He kissed the hollow of her shoulder, before beginning on the tiny buttons that closed the bodice of her chemise. He appeared to be in no hurry, instead concentrating on his task as if it were the most delicate operation. She looked down with a curious sense of detachment at his nimble fingers as they worked and the bodice opened, revealing her breasts, their tips hard and tight. He slid his hands under the chemise to her shoulders and pushed the flimsy garment away from her so that she stood naked except for her sandaled feet and the puddle of material around her ankles.

His gaze, now alive with desire, flicked upwards to her face. He smiled slowly before he bent his head and kissed her breasts, cupping the soft swell on the palm of his hand, grazing the nipples in turn with his tongue. He painted a moist path down the deep cleft between her breasts, his hold now spanning her waist as he slid to his knees.

Meg inhaled sharply as his tongue dipped into her navel. She put her hands on his shoulders, heedless now of the slight throb in her arm, and shifted her stance, partly for balance and partly in involuntary invitation as his breath rustled warm across the taut skin of her belly. She was aching for his touch and yet she didn't want it to come too soon.

"My turn," she protested softly, twining her fingers into the wavy auburn hair that was tickling her thighs, trying to pull his head up before he did what she knew he was about to do.

He raised his head, looking up her body. "Ah ... indulge me this once," he murmured. "I need to know you, taste you ... to savor the very essence of you."

And in truth she had no real resistance. He parted her thighs, opened her with his fingers, explored the folds of her sex with his tongue, and she bit her bottom lip until she drew blood to keep from crying out with the pleasure of it.

And as the night in the gently rocking cabin continued, Meg didn't think she had ever encountered a more selfless lover, or a more skillful. His touch was unerring, his awareness of her responses acute, and when at last he yielded himself to her she found nothing but delight in the shape, the scent, the feel of him. She moved above him, beside him, beneath him. His inventiveness matched her own, and when, exhausted, they fell asleep in a sweaty tangle on the box-bed just as dawn broke through the cabin window, she thought she could make love with this man for eternity.

———

Meg awoke alone in the sun-drenched cabin. She was sore, aching, and filled with a deep sense of bodily satisfaction. She hitched herself onto an elbow and looked around. Her own clothes that had been discarded in a heap on the floor last night were gone. Cosimo's clothes were gone too. Gus's cage was empty. How on earth had the privateer got up, dressed, and removed the incessantly babbling macaw without her hearing a sound?

She fell back again on the pillow, a forearm covering her eyes. She felt as if she'd been poleaxed now, so perhaps it wasn't surprising that she'd been dead to the world before. Still, it would have been nice to have been awoken with a kiss. But then, the captain of the *Mary Rose* had more on his mind than dalliance. Presumably he had to deal with whatever she'd interrupted last night.

She sat up abruptly. She *had* interrupted something... something that, if she hadn't reminded him of her presence, would have ensured that there would have been no lovemaking last night. She felt a slight chill at the memory of the way he had suddenly turned on that seductive charm, almost as if he'd had a reason for it. Oh, she was being overly sensitive. What if he had forgotten about their tryst for a minute? This was a man who dealt in covert intelligence, courier pigeons, the luring of enemy ships. A man who went by one name only. And all those were reasons why she found him so exciting.

That and his superlative performance as a lover. She maneuvered herself out of the box and stood up, stretching and yawning. She'd always loved the sense of repletion, of a well-used body, the morning after. It was very indelicate of her, of course, but that reflection as always made her laugh.

She found her nightgown in the cupboard, although

there was no sign of the bronze gown and chemise she'd been wearing. Decently clad once more, she experimented with the little silver handbell on the table. It brought almost immediate results.

Biggins knocked and entered on her invitation. "Yes, ma'am?"

"Would it be possible to fill the bath?" she asked, wondering with slight embarrassment if he was speculating about what had occurred among the tangle of sheets on the box-bed. Was there a lingering aroma . . . some hint she couldn't detect?

But his expression, as always, gave nothing away. "Don't see why not, ma'am," he replied. "The galley fires are lit. I'll heat up water. What about breakfast?"

"Yes, please," she said with enthusiasm. "I'm always ravenous these days."

A glancing smile crossed his stolid countenance. The first she'd ever seen. "Sea air, doubtless, ma'am."

"Doubtless," she agreed, wondering at the significance of that smile. She wanted to ask where Cosimo had gone but in the face of that smile couldn't quite muster the nerve.

"Cap'n says to tell you he'll be back shortly. He had to go to the guard post," Biggins offered as he left the cabin.

Meg went into the head, no longer surprised at her lack of concern for clearly defined privacy. The confined quarters of a sloop-of-war changed one's conception of space.

Biggins returned with a plate of coddled eggs and a pot of coffee. "This do ye, ma'am?"

"Wonderfully," she said, sitting down in front of the plate with an appreciative smile. "It smells delicious. Thank you, Biggins."

"Oh, don't thank me, ma'am. Thank Silas. He's the cook around here."

Meg paused, her fork in the air. "Then I will," she said. "I didn't know, but please convey my thanks."

The man nodded, but for once she detected approval. "I'll be fetchin' that water then," he said.

Meg ate the eggs, drank the coffee, and with each mouthful the night's euphoria faded and reality reared its unmistakable head. Today was Monday. The privateer was leaving at dawn on Wednesday. Now certainly they could enjoy themselves for those two days, but she couldn't let him go while leaving her here without any means to get herself back to England. She had only a few coins in her purse. A trip to the lending library didn't require much in the way of funds. Cosimo would take care of the expenses of her return, she was sure. He hadn't shown any serious inclination to deny his responsibility for her presence here, but he would have to help her find a way to get home before he left.

Except that she wasn't ready to go home.

Meg set down her fork and stared into the middle distance, chin resting in her elbow-propped hand. After such an absence she'd have to return to the parental home in Kent. Whatever story had been concocted to cover her vanishing, it would certainly entail a period of seclusion in the country. She drew in a breath of salt air, the scent of the sea pinks and clover on the hillside. The ship moved gently beneath her and she realized that she no longer noticed the motion.

Was there a way to extend this interlude?

Biggins's knock banished the question for the moment. He entered with his acolyte, both bearing steaming jugs. Meg waited through two more trips before the bath was pronounced deep enough to immerse herself. "Thank you," she said warmly. "I'm sorry to be so much trouble."

"It's no trouble, ma'am," Biggins announced, gesturing to the boy that he should clear away the dirty dishes. "Not much to do when we're in port."

Meg nodded her understanding. She'd seen what life was like on board the *Mary Rose* when they weren't in port. The door closed behind them and she threw off the nightgown and sank with a sigh of pleasure into the bath. Her eyes closed as she revisited the question of whether there was a feasible way to extend this passionate interlude. It could only be a temporary reprieve from the seclusion in the country, but could the possibility be broached with the privateer?

She doubted it. He'd told her he was on a mission and she suspected that extraneous women, however passionate, would interfere with that mission. He'd shown as much last night.

She heard the cabin door open. Cosimo called softly, "May I come in?"

Her heart speeded. She was a naked offering in a bathtub. "You are already, aren't you?"

"Only with your permission, if your remember," he returned. "I always keep my promises."

"Yes, so I've heard." She soaped one foot. "Where's Gus?"

It was an unnecessary question since the macaw at that moment appeared on the lintel to the head. "G'day."

Cosimo loomed behind him, leaning on the frame of the partition. His eyes ran appreciatively over her body, barely immersed in the shallow depression of the bathtub. "Pity there's not enough room for two."

"There isn't," Meg said definitely. She reached for a

towel on the floor and stood up in a shower of drops, wrapping herself in the towel. "What happened to my clothes?"

"Biggins will have dealt with them," he said carelessly. "I expect he decided they needed laundering."

"Why didn't you wake me before you left?" She followed him into the cabin, heedless of her wet footprints on the polished mahogany decking.

"My dear Meg, it would have been the utmost cruelty," he said, taking her towel-wrapped form in his arms. "Believe me, you wouldn't have heard the last trump."

"Maybe not," she conceded, kissing his hovering mouth. "Did you complete your business?"

That shadow crossed his eyes again but it was only for a second, then he said, "Tedious business with Murray. The man drives me insane with his rules and regulations. The navy must have this, navy ships must make such and such a report." He shook his head and moved away from her to the chart table. "Bureaucracy does not win wars."

"No, I'm sure," she agreed. He wasn't telling her the truth, not by a mile and a half. But even after last night's ecstasies she still didn't feel she could pry. She came up behind him as he bent over the chart table, wrapping her arms around his waist. "So will business occupy you all day?" She let the towel fall from her.

He reached behind him, running his hands over the cool naked body at his back. "That rather depends."

"Depends on what?" She nuzzled the back of his neck.

"On what other diversions are on offer."

Arabella had been pacing the drawing room all morning, staring out of the long windows onto The Leas, willing Jack's return from London. Boris and Oscar, her two red setters, lay on the hearth rug watching her uneasily, every now and again going to pace at her side. She touched their heads abstractedly. The atmosphere in the house in the last two days had upset them enough to put them off their food. A highly unusual occurrence.

It was almost noon when, instead of Jack on his raking chestnut gelding, a lumbering old-fashioned carriage drew up at the front door. She recognized it immediately and her heart sank. It was Sir Mark Barratt's. They must have left at dawn to reach Folkestone so quickly. What could she possibly tell them? They were expecting to find an ailing Meg, not no daughter at all.

Why the hell had Jack insisted on going to London? she thought even though she knew it had been the best thing—the only thing—to do. In a curious state of paralysis she stayed at the window watching as Sir Mark descended from the carriage and then handed down his wife. The dogs, recognizing old friends, jumped up at the window barking excitedly, then raced to the door, gazing back impatiently at their mistress.

Arabella knew she ought to run out to the street, greet Meg's parents in person, but she still didn't know what to say. In essence Meg had been in her charge and she had lost her.

Of course, it was ridiculous to imagine that she could be responsible in any real way for a grown woman who had always cleaved to her own path, and Arabella didn't think that Sir Mark or his lady would hold her responsible—they knew their own daughter well enough—but the reflection did nothing to assuage her panicked guilt.

Lady Barratt held on to her bonnet as a gust of wind from the sea threatened to lift it from her head. She grabbed her husband's arm with her free hand and almost dragged his tall stooped figure towards the door, her agitation obvious on her round, pink-complexioned countenance.

Arabella forced herself to move. She crossed the drawing room and the dogs shot between her legs as she opened the door, nearly unbalancing her. She entered the hall just as a footman was opening the door to their guests, Tidmouth standing behind him in readiness to greet them. Boris and Oscar pranced on the black and white marble tiles, their nails skittering.

"Sir Mark...Lady Barratt." Arabella hurried towards them, hoping the rising panic didn't sound in her voice. "How good of you to come so quickly." *Stupid...stupid thing to say*, she castigated herself. There was nothing unusual or praiseworthy about parents rushing to an ailing daughter's bedside. She embraced Lady Barratt.

"Oh, my dear Bella. How is she? Meg is never ill." Her ladyship hugged the duchess tightly, oblivious of the prancing dogs. "Is it a fever? Pray God it's not the typhoid. Or smallpox, I have been in such a worry...couldn't sleep a wink last night."

"No, it's definitely not typhoid," Arabella said, shooting an agonized glance at Tidmouth even as she submitted to Sir Mark's paternal kiss on her forehead. He snapped his fingers at the dogs, who were the progeny of his favorite bitch and well known to him. They sat obediently, open mouths panting, huge black eyes glowing, long feathery tails thumping.

Lady Barratt's voice continued without cease, asking and answering her own questions. "Has the physician been? Oh, but I'm sure he has. You wouldn't neglect such an attention, my dear, of course you wouldn't."

Tidmouth coughed and said, "Perhaps your ladyship

would like to go into the drawing room. You'd like some refreshment after your journey, I'm sure."

"Oh, I must go straight to Meg," Lady Barratt said. "Sir Mark, will you come?"

Sir Mark's sharply shrewd green eyes, eyes that his daughter had inherited, had been on Arabella from the moment she'd appeared, and he had intercepted the glance between the duchess and her steward. He said now, "We'll go up in a minute, my dear. Let's go into the drawing room and compose ourselves first. You wouldn't wish to agitate Meg with your anxieties, I'm sure."

His wife took a deep breath as the calm voice of reason soothed her. "Yes, of course, I'm sure you're right, sir."

Arabella took her arm. "Come, ma'am, you must be cold and tired if you left at dawn. Tidmouth will bring coffee to the drawing room. Sir Mark, would you prefer madeira or sherry?"

"Sherry, m'dear, thank you." He was still regarding her with a question in his eyes, and a deep frown now drew his thick gray eyebrows together over the bridge of his long nose.

Arabella ushered them into the drawing room, the dogs racing ahead of her. "Let me take your bonnet and cape, ma'am. Sir Mark, let me take your stick and your cloak." She beckoned to a hovering footman. "John, please, take Sir Mark and Lady Barratt's cloaks." She was beginning to feel less panicked but she still wished Jack had returned in time for this.

"When did Meg fall ill, Bella? It wasn't clear from the duke's note." Sir Mark stood before the empty grate, his hands laced at his back beneath the long tail of his brown wool coat. Boris and Oscar sat sentinel on either side of him.

Arabella didn't immediately answer as Tidmouth entered with a footman and her guests were provided with refreshment. She was relieved to see that Lady Barratt was less agitated under her husband's calming influence and took her coffee with a hand that trembled only slightly.

She waited until the door had closed on the departing servants, then said, "I don't quite know how to tell you—"

"Oh, my dear, she's dead. My girl is dead," Lady Barratt declared, her complexion as white as marble. The coffee cup clattered in its saucer and her husband moved quickly to take it from her.

"Hush, hush, my dear," he said laying a hand on her shoulder. "Let Arabella speak." He looked at Arabella and there was alarm in his eyes despite his apparent composure and his voice was sharp as he demanded, "Come, Arabella, let's hear it."

"Meg's disappeared," she said, opting for the bald truth. "Three days ago. We were walking on The Leas, I came home, she went to the lending library, and no one has seen her since she left there."

"Disappeared?" Sir Mark sounded incredulous, ignoring the soft moan from his wife. "How could she possibly disappear? She's a grown woman, more than capable of taking care of herself."

"Dead," his wife moaned. "Murdered by footpads."

"Ma'am, don't be ridiculous," her husband said briskly. "They'd have found her body by now."

This didn't appear to comfort his lady, who fell back against the sofa cushions, fanning herself with her hand. "She could be in the sea...thrown into the sea."

"I'll fetch the sal volatile," Arabella said hastily, seeing that Lady Barratt was about to swoon. She hurried to the door. "Tidmouth, will you send Becky for sal volatile, Lady Barratt is not feeling very well."

"I anticipated as much, your grace." Tidmouth produced a small brown vial. "Should I send Becky to attend her ladyship?"

"No, there's no need. Thank you." She closed the door again and went back to the couch, taking the stopper from the bottle. "Sniff this, ma'am, it will help." She waved the bottle beneath her ladyship's nose and the sharp vapor made her own eyes stream.

Sir Mark was tapping his feet impatiently while Arabella attended to his wife. Finally he said, "Where's your husband, Bella?"

"London," she said, rising from her knees beside the sofa. "He left yesterday to enlist the Bow Street Runners."

Sir Mark's ruddy huntsman's complexion lost a little color. The Runners were inevitably associated with scandal of some kind. "I suppose he thought it was for the best."

"Jack said we couldn't waste a minute. If the trail went cold..." She let the sentence fade. "I'm so sorry...I don't know..." Tongue-tied, she wrung her hands and looked helplessly between Meg's parents.

"It's hardly your fault," Sir Mark said. "Meg was not in your charge, Bella. Or your husband's. She'll be thirty next birthday."

Lady Barratt began to weep softly into a lace handkerchief. Arabella knelt beside her again. "She'll come back, ma'am. She *has* to."

The drawing room door swung open and Jack stepped in, dust coating his boots and forming a fine powder on the shoulders of his riding coat. He tossed his curly-brimmed beaver onto a settle as the dogs hurled themselves at his knees with adoring barks. "Down!" he commanded sharply, pushing them off him. "Sir Mark, Lady Barratt, I'm glad you were able to come so quickly." He kissed his wife quickly before bowing to the weeping lady on the sofa and shaking hands with Sir Mark.

"The Runners are looking for her in the countryside," he said. "I've had every square inch of the town combed already, but they'll go over the ground again. In the meantime, we have put it about that Meg is ill and taken to her bed. If you wish it, we could say that you came for her and took her home to recuperate."

"Your staff?" Sir Mark queried.

Jack raised an eyebrow. "My staff, sir, will say only what I tell them to say."

The assurance appeared sufficient for the baronet. He allowed Jack to refill his glass. "I think it would be best for us to remain in Folkestone for a few days. My wife . . ." He gestured to his still-weeping wife.

"Yes, of course," Jack said, pulling the bellrope beside the fireplace. "Much better for you to be here when she comes back." He turned as the steward entered. "Tidmouth, Sir Mark and Lady Barratt will be our guests for a few days."

Tidmouth bowed. "Yes, sir."

"Prepare the Chinese Bedchamber," Arabella said. She smiled at Lady Barratt "It's at the back of the house, away from the noise of the street, ma'am. And Becky will look after you."

"You're very kind, my dear," Lady Barratt said, trying for a watery smile. "I think perhaps I'll lie down for a few minutes. The shock . . ."

"Yes, of course. I'll come with you."

The two women left the drawing room and Sir Mark

said, "Tell me honestly, St. Jules, what do you think has happened?"

Jack pulled at an earlobe. "Quite frankly, sir, I'm at a loss. The distance between the lending library and this house on The Leas is no more than half a mile. It was raining very heavily, and maybe Meg took shelter somewhere, but if so, surely we'd have heard something? Someone would have seen her."

Sir Mark was silent. He sipped his sherry, then said, almost to himself, "Is it possible she left of her own accord?"

"She wouldn't have subjected Arabella to this agony," Jack stated.

Sir Mark nodded. "No, she wouldn't."

"Or her parents either," Jack said.

"Probably not." Sir Mark sighed heavily. "I don't know what to think."

The sound of the great knocker rumbled through the silence and then they heard Arabella's voice. She sounded puzzled, then surprised. She came into the drawing room, looking at a letter in her hand. "This is very odd. Some man just delivered this for me."

"A postman, a courier?"

"He wasn't dressed like either," she said. "He was very elegant in green silk and he was riding a handsome bay. He didn't speak like a postman either." She took up a slim paper knife from the dainty French secretaire and slit the wafer, unfolding the sheet. Her mouth opened. Slowly she looked up.

"It's from Meg."

"What?" Sir Mark bounded forward. "Let me see." He almost snatched the sheet from her. He stared down at it in some degree of incomprehension. "What does this mean? It's not Meg's handwriting."

"May I, sir?" Jack held out his hand. He too stared at the rather masculine script, then looked across at his wife. Her face was radiant with relief, but there was something else in the tawny eyes. A mischievous amusement that he knew well. He looked again at the letter. It read: *An accident befell me but I'm safe and well.* In the top corner was inscribed the single word *Gondolier*.

"Why is it so short?" Sir Mark demanded. "And why did she not write it herself? Can we believe this?"

"Oh, yes, we can believe it," Arabella said flatly. "Meg may not have penned it but she had a hand in its wording, I can promise you."

"I suspect by its brevity and the unknown handwriting that the note came via a rather unorthodox carrier," Jack mused, turning the paper over to examine the back. "It reads as if it was originally written in code ... to be carried by a pigeon for instance."

"Good God, man, what's my daughter doing with a pigeon?" Sir Mark shook his head in disbelief.

"I suspect only Meg can tell us that," Jack said. "Or maybe Arabella can?" He raised an eyebrow at his wife, convinced now that she knew something the rest of them didn't.

"I have no idea," Arabella said, trying to keep a note of slightly hysterical laughter out of her voice. "But at least we know she's all right, and I'm sure that whatever the accident was, it's prevented her from coming home immediately. So we must deal quickly with any possible gossip. But first I'll go and tell Lady Barratt the good news." She whisked herself out of the room before her inconveniently perspicacious husband could ask any more awkward questions.

It was over an hour before she was able to leave a somewhat reassured but still very bewildered Lady Barratt. She closed the door to the Chinese Bedchamber softly behind her and then turned around slowly. Jack was lounging in a window embrasure next to the chamber door, his arms folded, and there was an uncomfortable gleam in his gray eyes.

"So, madam wife, what is the significance of a gondolier?"

"Oh, hush," she said, looking around. "Sir Mark could appear at any moment. It's a miracle he didn't notice himself, I'm sure Meg meant it for my eyes only."

"Maybe so, but you'll share it with me." It was an uncompromising statement.

Arabella covered her mouth to stifle a laugh. "Come away then," she said. "I'll tell you in my boudoir."

He followed her into a pretty sitting room at the rear of the house. The windows were open onto the small town garden below and the faint sounds of waves breaking on the stones of the beach drifted in. Arabella fussed with a bowl of heavy-headed peonies on the round Chippendale table in front of the window while Jack waited with every appearance of patience.

"Do you have the note?" she asked.

"No, I didn't feel I could take it from her father," he said. "But it matters little. You know what it said. I know what it said. Explain *gondolier*."

Arabella brushed a wavy lock of dark hair from her forehead. "It means that Meg is in the middle of some kind of romantic adventure," she said.

Jack stared at her, anger flaring in his eyes, a muscle twitching in his cheek. "So she left on purpose ... put us through this hell for some—"

"No," Arabella interrupted quickly. "Of course not. Meg

would never do that. Something happened." She shrugged. "I have no idea what, but it was nothing she could help. However, she's saying that its consequences are proving not . . . not unpleasant," she finished with another shrug.

The anger died out of his eyes. Jack knew enough of Meg now to believe that his wife was right. She would never have caused such pain to her friends and family deliberately. But the mystery was nowhere near solution.

"What are we supposed to do now?" he asked.

"Stop worrying," Arabella said. Her eyes gleamed with mischief again. "I expect she's been abducted by an Arab sheik and is having a wonderful time in his harem in the desert." She could see from her husband's expression that he didn't appreciate her flight of fancy. "More to the point, why would she send a message by pigeon . . . if you're right, that is?"

Jack frowned. He was beginning to think abduction was not such a far-fetched explanation after all. Pigeons were used when land transport couldn't be. "I have a feeling Meg is no longer on English shores," he said slowly. "She's either on a ship somewhere, or on the French coast. There's no other reason to use a pigeon."

"And you're certain it was brought by a pigeon . . . oh, not the messenger who came here. He was far too elegant to be mistaken for a pigeon, but the original?"

"Sometimes, Arabella, you have a very misplaced sense of levity," he said severely. "Get your pelisse, we're going to walk the dogs down to the harbor."

"Why the harbor?" She fetched the required garment with alacrity.

"Naval stations rely on courier services. Meg's been gone less than three days, so this message has to have arrived somewhere close to Folkestone. I have it in mind to make some inquiries."

"You think Meg's with the navy?" She couldn't hide her incredulity.

"I don't think anything, my dear. I'm merely following a hunch."

"Oh, well, I'm happy to follow it with you." She fastened the top button of her pelisse and arranged a very fetching straw hat on her dusky curls. "Wherever she is, at least I know she's amusing herself."

Chapter 10

"Cosimo?"

"Meg?" He looked up from his charts with a quick smile as she hovered in the cabin door. "What can I do for you?" He infused the question with such languorous sensuality that her knees turned to butter.

"Don't look at me like that for a start," she said. "I want to talk about something serious."

"Oh." He put down his pen.

She came across the cabin and looked down at the charts and the unreadable notations he'd been making. "Are you plotting a course?"

"Mmm." He ran a finger in the groove of her bent neck, up beneath her hair, enjoying the shape of her small skull against his palm.

"For when you leave tomorrow?"

"Mmm." He bent to kiss her nape. "Your skin smells of the sun."

Meg moved her head aside. Every time she'd prepared herself to open this depressing yet increasingly urgent subject, he'd worked some of his magic to banish the issue from her mind, or at least to persuade her temporarily that it was too soon to cast a shadow over the idyll. But the discussion couldn't be put off any longer.

"No, Cosimo, we *have* to talk. Have you given any thought as to how I'm going to get off this island and go home? You can't just put me ashore when you leave and forget all about me."

"Oh, I don't think I could ever manage to forget all about you," he said with a lascivious grin, catching her chin between finger and thumb and turning her face towards him.

"Cosimo, do listen to me," she exclaimed, jerking her chin free and moving rapidly out of range. "I'm serious."

He had done his best to prevent her broaching this subject until it couldn't be avoided. Every minute he had to draw her deeper into their liaison was to his advantage, and he had intended to use their lovemaking that night as a natural introduction to the idea that she stay with him for a while longer. However, it seemed he'd have to deal with it without the benefit of lust's softening.

He perched on the edge of the table, swinging one foot, his arms folded as he regarded her with a quizzical smile. "As a matter of fact I have given it some considerable thought."

"And your conclusion?" she prompted when he didn't continue.

"Well, now..." He tapped his mouth with his fingers. "We *could* decide not to bring this delightful...uh...association...to an abrupt end."

A quiver of anticipation, a little prickle of excitement, lifted the fine hairs along her spine. She said carefully, "How so? You said you *had* to leave."

"Your friends' immediate fears are by now put to rest. Is

there a pressing need for you to return at once to the family fold?"

Her green eyes took on a lustrous sheen. "Go on," she invited.

He'd hooked her, he knew it. That luster in her eyes, the sudden glow of her skin told him all he needed to know. He smiled a slow smile. "We're sailing to Bordeaux with some secret dispatches for our friends there. I shall exchange them for others to be delivered to England. You could come with me for the round trip."

Her blood sang but she forced herself to go slowly. "You're returning to England immediately afterwards?"

He nodded, preferring the deceptive gesture to an outright verbal lie.

"How long will this journey take?"

He shrugged. "That I can't answer, Meg. You've seen for yourself how we're always at the mercy of the weather."

"But weeks ... months ... ?"

"I'd hope weeks, although in the circumstances I'd prefer months." His eyes narrowed and his mouth curved in pure seductive invitation.

It was not an invitation she could refuse. In fact, although she had not allowed herself until now to acknowledge it, it was one she had been hoping for. But the risks ... the risks were enormous.

Reality was a bucket of cold water. Meg suddenly couldn't see how she *could* agree to such a plan. An absence of weeks, maybe even a month or two, would be impossible to conceal.

"I have to think," she said suddenly, feeling his gaze on her, uncomfortably penetrating as if he would read her mind. She couldn't reach a considered decision under that kind of pressure. She hurried out of the cabin, leaving Cosimo still perched on the edge of the table.

A frown chased the seductive softness from his countenance and his mouth hardened. Had he misplayed his hand? Had he misinterpreted Meg's expression, her desire? He would have sworn not, but if he'd jumped the gun, he'd lost the only opportunity he would have. He started to go after her, then stopped. Pressing her wouldn't help. She was far from the most persuadable lover he'd taken.

He turned back to the charts. With or without her, he was leaving for Bordeaux at dawn. His visit to Murray had confirmed the suspicion that the pigeon had been tampered with and he had to assume that the French would be waiting for him at Brest. So he would take the longer route by sea to Bordeaux and from there the shorter overland route to Toulon. It was a more frequented cross-country route and therefore more dangerous, but Ana's capture had left him no other choice. And if he failed in recruiting Meg, he was going to have to complete his mission alone.

He paused, his quill suspended. His chances of successfully completing his mission alone and coming out alive were very slim. He knew he could manage the first part, he had never yet failed at such an enterprise. But living to tell the tale in this instance was much more of a challenge. He needed a partner. And it had to be Meg. The stakes were far too high to consider failure. She was a free spirit, impatient of convention, and with a very healthy appetite for the joys of lust. In the week or so it would take to sail to Bordeaux he would have ample opportunity to feed that appetite, an appetite, if the Bard of Avon was to be believed, that grew whereon it fed.

It certainly did with him, he reflected, with candid self-knowledge. Indeed he could imagine that making love with Meg could become an addiction. He adored the way she moved in sex, the feel of her body, its angles and points, and the surprising softness of curves and indentations. He couldn't get enough of her scent, of the wild fires in her eyes as she approached orgasm, the way she threw her head back, exposing her white throat at the moment of convulsion. And most of all he loved the way he could make her reach a climax over and over again, her cries of ecstasy filling the cabin, her body writhing beneath his hands, his tongue, around the throb of his sex buried deep within her.

He inhaled sharply as his body stirred at the images. Oh, yes, he could imagine sex with Meg could become an addiction; he just had to ensure that it was a mutual one.

Lovemaking didn't figure in Meg's cogitations as she stood in the stern apparently watching lobstermen at work checking their pots in the harbor. In fact, the busy scene made no impression at all. She needed a plan...a plausible story she could concoct to cover an extended absence. One that would satisfy the gossips. Obviously her parents wouldn't be deceived and of course not Jack or Bella, but she had to believe that at some point she would return to her ordinary world and she couldn't do something that would slam the door of social acceptance in her face.

She would write to Bella...enlist her support. That would be easy. She could suggest that her parents fabricate the story that she had gone to distant...very distant... relatives for her health. But where, though? Not Europe, no one in their right minds would visit the war-torn

Continent for their health or their pleasure. But her mother had relatives in the Scottish highlands. Not that she'd ever met any of them, but it was far enough off the beaten track for no one to question an extended absence.

Or she could go home tomorrow.

And miss the adventure of a lifetime? The best lovemaking ever? Absurd. Besides, she liked the idea of contributing her mite to the war against France. Sailing on a sloop-of-war, taking part in the transfer of dispatches, however passive her part, could still be seen as participation in a patriotic act. In fact, she decided, it was her duty to her country to extend her sensual idyll with the privateer.

The hypocritical sophistry made her laugh aloud and the two lieutenants looked at her curiously. Their uncle had just emerged from the companionway and at the sound of that laughter a satisfied smile crept over his countenance. He came over to her.

"What's amusing?"

She looked over at him. "My faultless self-serving reasoning."

"Care to share it?"

She shook her head. "No, I don't think so. If I write a letter of explanation to my friend, is there any way it can be transported?"

He nodded. "The fishing fleet will go out on the morning tide tomorrow. They sell a lot of their lobster catch to fishermen working off the English shore, where they're not plentiful, and they can pass on a letter. It's a relatively efficient postal service."

"Then I'd better start composing."

He put a hand on her back, warm and somehow possessive. "So, is that my answer?"

She smiled at him. "I find I'm in the mood for adventure, sir." Her little attempt at rational consideration of the proposal had been a waste of time, she knew. She'd always intended to accept the invitation and the consequences be hanged. She laughed at herself again. So much for mature reflection.

"Then write your letter quickly," he said. "We'll sail on this evening's tide instead of tomorrow morning."

She looked startled. "Why such a sudden change of plan?"

"Because, my dear, if you're coming with me, there's no need to waste any more time."

"I thought you were waiting for dispatches."

"I got them from Murray this morning."

"Oh, I see." Except that she didn't. Despite the urgency of his time-sensitive mission, an urgency he'd stressed to her more than once, an urgency that had prevented him taking her back to Folkestone as soon as he'd discovered the mistaken identity, he'd been willing to wait unnecessarily just for the sake of one final night of passion. Something was wrong there, but she couldn't put her finger on it.

"I'll write my letter," she said, going below, still thinking about the puzzle. He had left the narrow bed before she'd awoken that morning, as he had done the previous day, so presumably that's when he'd picked up the dispatches. But where had they come from? The only ships she had seen near the island were the naval men-of-war, and it didn't make sense that their commanders had given Cosimo dispatches when they all seemed to be sailing in the same direction and they'd left Folkestone together.

Oh, well, she knew nothing about the mechanics of all this covert activity. At least not yet. There was probably an explanation that hadn't occurred to her. She dismissed the puzzle for the moment with the reflection that she might find this voyage a useful education in more than the joys of the privateer's body.

For the moment blissfully unaware of the questions his glib response had raised in Meg's inquiring mind, Cosimo glanced around his ship from his position in the stern. It was an orderly, leisurely scene. The tide would be full at six o'clock and they would have time to negotiate the reef and be in the open sea before dark. He detested inaction and while he'd accepted the need to stay put while he worked on his as yet unwitting partner, now that that was accomplished his spirit strained to be on the move. He beckoned to the ever watchful Miles, who sprang eagerly across the deck to his side.

Below, Meg heard the abrupt bustle, felt the change in the atmosphere. Voices called, feet ran on the deck above her head, and Gus started to pace his perch, muttering. A knock at the door brought David Porter with his little bag of tricks.

Meg looked up from her composition as she bade him enter. "Good afternoon, David. It seems we're leaving ahead of schedule."

"Nothing unusual about that," he observed, setting his bag on the table. "I'm guessing you're staying with us."

"You guess correctly," she said, aware of a slight heat in her cheeks. It was one thing to behave with blatant indiscretion, quite another to be forced to acknowledge it. But David merely nodded. "It'll be good to have another face around. Sailing can be tedious when you don't make landfall for a long time."

"It can't take that long to reach Bordeaux," she said.

He looked interested. "Oh, is that where we're heading?"

"You didn't know?" She looked stricken, remembering the secrecy that seemed to exist on Cosimo's ship. "Should I have told you?"

"If Cosimo told you, he has no problem with its being general knowledge," David said, lifting her arm to unwrap the bandage.

Meg wasn't sure she liked being lumped together with the entire crew of the *Mary Rose*. It would have been pleasant to cherish the illusion that she was in the privateer's confidence. But it was early days yet, she reminded herself, turning her attention to the rapidly healing wound.

"Does it still need a bandage?"

"I'd prefer it," he said. "Just for another couple of days. If you knock it accidentally, it could open up again. It doesn't take much for that to happen in such close confines." His eyes flickered to the captain's bed and Meg bit her lip hard, unsure whether she should laugh conspiratorially or maintain a haughty indifference to the implication.

She settled for a neutral "Don't worry, I'll be careful."

He looked at her then, a searching, questioning glance, before efficiently rebandaging the arm. "Are you writing letters?" He indicated the parchment and quill.

Meg gave up a pretence that didn't sit well with her anyway. "A difficult letter," she said ruefully. "To my friends in Folkestone. Cosimo said he could send it with the fishing fleet before we leave. I have to give them some explanation." She opened her hands expressively.

"They know you're unharmed? Cosimo sent the pigeon courier?"

"Oh, yes. But I have to concoct some explanation they

can put about for why I'm taking an extended absence from the world . . . well, my world," she amended.

David inclined his head in acknowledgment. "Tricky. I wish you luck." He picked up his bag and went to the door. "But then, I've always believed one should follow one's fancy."

"Really?" It seemed the most extraordinary thing for the reclusive, efficient, unemotional surgeon to believe.

"I'm following Cosimo," he reminded her with a flash of a smile. "Where he leads, there go I, when I could be peacefully and quite lucratively established catering to the whims and megrims of London's society set." He nodded in farewell.

Meg chuckled in amazement as she picked up her quill again. So David Porter liked a little adventure in his life too. *Needed* a little adventure for his own satisfaction, she corrected. Only a pressing personal imperative would persuade a man like David to throw in his lot with a man like Cosimo, on the surface his antithesis.

The reflection spurred her to fresh efforts on her letter. Arabella would sympathize, and Jack would too, once he'd recovered from any residual anger at her for causing his beloved Arabella a moment's anxiety. But it had not been her doing and her conscience was clear on that. This that lay ahead, however, was entirely of her own making, so she'd better do the best she could to ease matters for those she left behind. Most particularly her parents, who would bear the brunt of the inquiries. They would forgive her in the end, at least she hoped they would, but they would do so much more readily if there was no scandal attached to her adventure.

She looked out of the window for a moment, imagining

that she was sitting with her friend in Arabella's conservatory. Bella would be feeding and pruning and spraying her beloved orchids, listening intently to every word. She heard her friend's mischievous chuckle as she regaled her with the more intimate details of her lovemaking with the privateer. A smile touched her mouth and she dipped the quill in the ink anew and attacked the paper with renewed vigor.

When Cosimo came into the cabin fifteen minutes later, she was sanding the closely written, frequently crossed sheet. "Long letter," he commented.

"I couldn't think of a few short lines to describe adequately the complexity of this situation," she retorted, shaking off the sand. "Could you?"

"Probably," he said cheerfully. "I am a man of few words." He was once more at his charts.

Meg folded the letter and affixed a wafer to the fold. "Do you have wax?"

He reached to the shelf above the chart table and took down a stick of red wax. "There's flint and tinder in the drawer under the table."

Meg heated the wax and dropped it onto the wafer. She would have liked to have stamped some identifier into the melted wax but she wore no rings and could think of nothing else, so it would have to go as it was. Then a thought struck her. She took up the quill and scratched a G into the wax. Arabella would make that connection as she'd made the last.

"It's ready," she said.

"Good. Take it to Miles. He's waiting for it. We make sail in an hour." He spoke without taking his attention from his charts.

Meg contemplated the curve of his long back, the tightness of his buttocks as he stood, legs braced apart, while he worked. Arousal flickered in her belly but she knew the privateer was as unaware of her gaze as he was of any desire to arouse her. The passionate lover was clearly taking a secondary role to the working captain and always would. Well, at least she had no illusions about her position in his priorities.

And when she came first, she most certainly came first. Smiling, she went up on deck to deliver her letter to Miles.

They left the harbor on the swell of the tide, the *Mary Rose* tacking across the sheltered body of water towards the open sea, where the crash of the breakers on the reef grew ever louder and more menacing. Cosimo was at the helm, Mike beside him, as the sloop, under full sail, headed for the gap in the rocks.

Meg, wrapped in a cloak against the freshening wind, looked back at the rapidly diminishing hamlet that seemed to represent the last vestige of her normal world. The sea-bound world she inhabited now had rules of its own, and dangers all its own, and she couldn't begin to imagine what her future world would be like after this adventure. Would she be able to fit back into conventional society again?

She'd never been completely at ease in that world, even when she'd known no other. Unlike Arabella, she had not managed to make the ordinary world fit her needs. Bella had molded society to her own tastes, ably assisted, of course, by her unconventional rake of a husband. Meg, without the advantage of such a husband and the social status of a duchess, had had little success in carving her own path. What the duchess of St. Jules could do without scandal, a mere Miss Barratt could not. And she'd opted to appear at least to toe the line. She doubted that she'd be able to settle for that after this adventure with the privateer. So what would the future hold for her?

The question caused a flutter of unease and she spun away from the departing shoreline and looked ahead. Cosimo's tall, powerful frame blocked her view to the bow and the churning waters beyond, and she was content at the moment to have it so. For now, her future lay with the privateer. She had made the decision and she would not allow herself to regret it.

She watched him steer the craft through the rocks, his eyes on the sails, his voice, barely raised as always, calling out a series of orders. Sails were adjusted minute by minute as the sloop entered the gap. Spray from the breakers blinded Meg and dampened her hair, and then the *Mary Rose* sprang free of the narrow gap and the sound of the crashing waves came from safely behind them. Ahead lay a moving sea, white-capped swells racing towards the sloop's lifting bow. The wind was stronger, whipping her hair into a tangle as she stood holding her cloak together at her throat, feeling the deck rising and falling beneath her booted feet, and the salt spray on her cheeks.

The last lingering threads of unease vanished into the wind and Meg yielded to the exhilaration of the moment, to the excitement of knowing that the man holding this ship on course would quite soon be devoting that strength and concentration to a quite different activity. She laughed and the sound was snatched by the wind.

Chapter 11

The weather changed when they rounded the jutting rugged coastline of Brittany, leaving the town of Brest to port as they headed into the rough waters of the Bay of Biscay. Rain clouds scudded across a gray sky and the wind was as cold and bitter as a winter gale.

Meg stood in her usual position against the stern railing, shivering into her thick cloak, her hair frizzed by the damp air. She could just make out the faint line of the French coast and thought longingly for a moment of a warm fireside, a pot of hot soup, a glass of spiced punch. Winter comforts all of them, and things that wouldn't have entered her head yesterday, when the sun had been hot in a brilliant blue cloudless sky and the *Mary Rose* had skipped across sparkling waves. Today she was lumbering through them, climbing up and then pitching forward under only minimal sail.

"Feeling queasy?"

She turned at Cosimo's voice. "No, but it's not very comfortable."

"It isn't," he agreed, coming to stand beside her. "And

I'm afraid it won't be for a while. Biscay's notorious for its heavy seas and bad weather."

"I wish you'd warned me," she said, only half joking.

"Would it have made a difference?" He loosened his boat cloak, then put an arm around her shoulders, drawing her against him, wrapping the voluminous folds around them both.

"No, of course not," she said truthfully, inhaling the mingled scents of his body warmed by the enclosed air inside the cloak. His shirt still smelled of soap and the previous day's sunshine that had dried it, overlaid with a faint earthy tang of sweat from his recent wrestling with a recalcitrant helm.

"We're sailing well away from the coastline," she observed, wondering if closer in it would be less rough.

"For the moment," he agreed. "I don't want to attract unnecessary attention from French patrols. But tomorrow night we'll be going in."

"Why won't it be dangerous tomorrow night?"

"It will be, but I have something to do ashore."

It had been a day and a half since they'd left Sark, and Meg had been content to take each moment as it came, putting aside the war-related purpose of this voyage. Now she experienced that flutter of unease again. "You're actually going ashore?"

"Just for an hour or two."

"To do what?"

He shook his head in mock reproof. "Ask no questions and you'll hear no lies, my dear."

"But I'm not one of your crew," she protested. "They don't seem to mind being kept in the dark. But I do. It matters to me what you do and why."

His expression darkened as she'd known it would, and

the warm humorous light left his eyes to be replaced by that cold blue glitter that she loathed. "You're on my ship," he stated. "You'll know exactly what I want you to know, nothing more, nothing less."

She didn't want to quarrel and yet somehow she couldn't help herself. "That's not good enough, Cosimo. I refuse to be subject to the same rules as your crew. I'm your lover, I'd like to think I was your friend... worthy of some confidence."

"You are both those things but that has nothing to do with it. While you're on my ship you'll receive the same information as everyone else," he said baldly. "Believe me, I have my reasons."

"Oh, I'm sure you do," she said acidly, moving away from the shelter of his cloak. "And tell me, pray, if it was Ana standing here beside you, would you be treating her to the same lack of confidence?"

He had no answer for that, of course. "You must excuse me," he said, leaving her standing there, the formality of his departure conveying his displeasure more effectively than any loss of temper could have done.

If Ana was with him, he wouldn't be making this unscheduled landing at Quiberon. There was a secret courier-pigeon outpost there, manned not by the navy but by members of his own spy network. He'd sent news of Ana's capture from Sark. His agents would have started working on finding her immediately. If there was any progress, news would be sent to Quiberon. If there was none there, the next place would be La Rochelle, farther down the coast. Each landing on the enemy coast was fraught with danger and could only take place at night, but he wouldn't be at peace until he had some news of her.

He wasn't ready to take Meg into his confidence at this

point. She was not committed to his mission as yet. Apart from the fact that it flew in the face of his ingrained habit of keeping his own counsel, he couldn't risk her having information that would betray him if she was forced to give it up. She wasn't a seasoned agent like Ana, and he hadn't had the time or the opportunity to test her strengths and her resourcefulness. That would come later with the training he would have to give her.

And then the thought occurred that perhaps there was no time like the present to initiate such testing and training. It was certainly no time to antagonize her. Meg wasn't Ana, but he needed her to take Ana's place. How could he know what she was capable of if he didn't give her the opportunity to show him?

He glanced back to the stern rail but she was no longer there and he guessed she had gone below to nurse her resentment. Except that he didn't think she was the kind of woman who nursed resentments or held grudges. She would be annoyed, but she would let him know it.

Meg was indeed back in the cabin, and she was indeed annoyed. Gus, who was showing every expression of pleasure at having some company again, hopped onto her shoulder and pecked at her earlobe. "Oh, are you lonely, Gus?"

He muttered sweet nothings in her ear and she felt some of her indignation fade. She lifted him back onto his perch and shrugged off her damp cloak, shivering in the thin silk of the gown beneath. There had been no winter-weight materials in Ana's cupboard, which puzzled her a little. Surely both Cosimo and Ana would have been aware of the way the weather could turn nasty at sea?

Maybe in another cupboard. She hadn't explored the cabin with any thoroughness as yet. She knelt to open the cupboards set beneath the window seats and rifled through their contents. The privateer's undergarments, stockings, cravats for the most part. She sat back on her heels, frowning. Where were the mysterious dispatches he'd picked up from Lieutenant Murray?

Surely they'd be in the cabin somewhere. She forgot about searching for warmer garments and went over to the chart table again and its shelf of books above. Perhaps they were tucked between the volumes. She took out each book, wondering once again why the privateer's library consisted only of dictionaries. Why in particular did he need a Latin dictionary? And a Bible? Did he conduct a Sunday service or something? But she'd passed a Sunday on board, and in port too when the crew had nothing better to do. There'd been no sign of religious ceremony then. Perhaps he was a closet Bible reader. There was an absurdity to that image that restored her usual good humor, but she still wanted to find these dispatches that were the reason for this voyage.

She lifted the charts on the table, opened the little drawer beneath. It held a fresh supply of quills, sheets of onionskin, and a handful of the tiny canisters. She knew, because he'd made no secret of it, that he facilitated courier correspondence, and, because he'd told her, that he was a courier, a carrier of dispatches himself. Important activities, she was sure, in the world of the spy, but somehow they didn't seem important enough for Cosimo. So what else did he do?

She bent to open the cupboard beneath the chart table but it was locked, the only place in the entire cabin that didn't yield up its contents. What secrets did he keep in there? The elusive dispatches, perhaps? But what else?

She was gazing in thought out through the rain-smeared window at the churning gunmetal sea when the door opened. She turned swiftly, unable to help a guilty intake of breath, aware of the open drawer behind her, the volumes that she had not yet returned to their place on the shelf.

"Looking for something?" Cosimo asked, a frown flickering in his eyes.

"Yes," she said. "Something warm to wear."

"In that drawer? Behind the books?" He gave her an incredulous stare as he closed the door behind him.

"No," she agreed, resigned to what this time would be a justifiable use of the glacial look. "I was being nosy."

"Ah." He nodded slowly and remained with his shoulders leaning against the door at his back. "What did you hope to find?"

"I don't know," she said with a helpless shrug. "A clue . . . something . . . anything, really."

"Permit me to tell you, my dear, that you'll never make a spy if you don't learn to cover your tracks." He pushed himself away from the door and crossed to the chart table.

Meg skipped slightly to one side. "I wasn't trying to spy," she protested.

Cosimo returned the volumes to their shelf and closed the drawer of the table. He continued as if he hadn't heard her protest, "And you should always conduct an operation when you're certain you won't be disturbed."

"Without a key to the door, that would be impossible," she retorted, disliking this schoolmasterly tone much more than straightforward annoyance.

He merely shook his head and regarded her thoughtfully. "A clue to what?"

"To you, of course. I can't get a straight answer out of you, so I have no choice but to poke around a little."

"You could always just accept my wishes."

"I could, I suppose," she said, her head tilted slightly as she appeared to consider the appeal of this. But her green gaze held a warning as she met his eyes. "But blind, unthinking obedience to your wishes was never a condition of our agreement. Had it been, I would be back on English shores by now. I'm no puppet, Cosimo, and you, in this instance, are no puppet master. You may pull the strings of your crew, but not mine."

Cosimo wondered with some interest if she had really considered the reality of her situation. She had neither power nor freedom on his ship while they were plowing through the high seas. If she had considered it, her refusal to acknowledge it was certainly indicative of a particularly stubborn, determined nature. Qualities that he had always found appealing in a woman, and that were certainly essential for the work that lay ahead.

"What do you wish to know?" he asked, casting aside the thick, damp folds of his boat cloak.

The question... the capitulation... so astounded Meg that for a second she was dumbstruck. "Tell me about Ana," she said finally, even as she wondered why, of all the questions crowding her mind, that one should have popped out first.

"What exactly do you wish to know about Ana?" He sat down, clasping his hands on the tabletop in front of him.

Meg cursed herself for opening such a fruitless discussion that could so easily imply some kind of pathetic jealousy on her part. She wasn't in the least jealous of the absent Ana. But she *was* interested in other aspects of the missing woman's relationship with the privateer. "Does she work with you?"

"On occasion."

"Is she English?"

"No. Austrian."

"Do you know where she is?"

"Not yet."

"But you expect to soon?"

"I hope to." His countenance had remained expressionless throughout the catechism, his tone neutral, but the wall he'd thrown up was unassailable nevertheless.

Meg accepted defeat at the hands of a master. "It's none of my business," she said. And then she frowned as his last answer sank in.

"Are you going ashore to find out?"

He smiled, the cool neutrality of his expression transformed as the familiar Cosimo returned. "It took you a while, but you got what you wanted in the end."

"You could have simply told me."

"So I could." He stood up. "But that doesn't come easily to me. Other things, however, do. Come here." He crooked a finger. "I have it in mind to demonstrate that even you, my dear Meg, can perform for a puppet master on a certain stage."

And how right he was, Meg thought, as she went into his arms. But she too could play puppet mistress on occasion. Sauce for the goose was most definitely sauce for the gander.

Making love on a pitching sea was a curious business, Meg reflected some considerable time later. It required all the balance of a skilled gymnast. Cosimo had no such difficulty, but then, the sea in all its moods was his natural terrain. He held her against him, cushioning her as the motion threatened to toss her against the hard sides of the box-bed, but not for an instant did he lose his rhythm as he thrust deep inside her, bringing her inexorably closer to her peak despite the distraction of the ever moving space. In the end she relaxed and let her body go wherever the sea took it.

"That was rather like making love on the back of a horse," she observed dreamily, running her hand down his sweat-slick back as he dropped beside her on the cot.

"When have you made love on a horse?" He stroked her belly lazily.

"Well, never, actually, but it's how I imagine it must feel."

"We should try it one day," he said. With a sigh he pulled himself upright and out of the bed. "I've left my ship unattended for too long." He pulled on his britches again and thrust his arms into his shirt. Then he remembered something. "What were you saying about warmer clothes?"

"That I was looking for some," she responded from deep beneath the huddle of blankets. "It's too cold for silk, so if Ana didn't make provision for bad weather, I'm going to have to stay in bed until it gets warm again."

"Well, as it happens there are garments that Ana would have worn in inclement weather," he said, and there was a glint in his eye that put Meg on her guard.

"Where are they?" she asked suspiciously.

"In one of those cupboards, I believe," he said with a vague gesture to the rank of cupboards under the port window seat.

"I looked there, I didn't see anything." She sat up, drawing the covers up under her chin.

That glint intensified. "You might not have recognized them for what they were." He sat down to pull on his boots. "They're a little unusual, but they will keep you warm." He stood up again and reached for his boat cloak. "I own I'm looking forward to seeing you wear them. I believe they will suit you admirably." He came over to the cot and kissed her hard. "Come up on deck when you're dressed." His chuckle carried a note of amused satisfaction that only increased her suspicions.

"Now just what is he talking about?" Meg asked of Gus, who was preening himself on his perch.

"G'day," he said irrelevantly.

"And to you too." Meg climbed out of the box and wrapped herself in the top blanket as the cold air hit her heated nakedness. She went to the port-side cupboards and knelt before them. As she'd found before, they contained only Cosimo's undergarments, cravats, shirts, stockings. She began to pile them up around her and then at the back of the cupboard saw another pile. Heavy cotton shirt, long woolen underdrawers, nankeen britches, thick woolen stockings, a leather jerkin. She took them out and examined them.

A somewhat incredulous smile tilted the corners of her mouth. These garments certainly wouldn't fit the privateer. But they would fit her. "A little unusual" was an understatement, she reflected, experimentally slipping her arms into the sleeves of the jerkin. A little large on the shoulders, a little long in the sleeves, but nothing that would inconvenience her.

She slipped off the jerkin and tossed the clothes on the cot, then knelt again to return the contents of the cupboard to their shelves. As she reached in, her fingers encountered a small hard shape. Curious, she took it out. It was a velvet drawstring pouch. Meg opened it and shook the contents onto the palm of her hand. A small silver key. A key perfectly sized to fit the only locked drawer in the cabin.

She tossed it from palm to palm for a few seconds. Cosimo had hidden it, therefore he didn't want anyone unlocking that drawer. Not a difficult conclusion. She didn't have the right to unlock the drawer, another obvious conclusion. But did she have the right to discover as much as she could about the man who was her lover, on whose mercies at this point she was entirely dependent? Through her own choice, certainly, but that didn't alter the reality. Didn't she owe it to herself to be prepared for anything?

Meg decided that she did. She shuffled on her knees the short distance to the drawer beneath the chart table and tried the key. It fit like a glove and turned with well-oiled ease. The drawer slid open. She stared at its contents, a sudden sick dread clutching at her stomach. A row of knives, highly polished, lay on a baize cloth. There was nothing ordinary about them, nothing that might imply they would be used for a mundane purpose, like whittling wood, or splicing rope, or cutting paper or material. A stiletto blade; a curved blade like a scimitar; a wickedly serrated blade; one shaped like a cleaver; a small silver dagger with the narrow blade of a rapier.

They were knives used to kill. And they were locked away for just that reason.

Meg slammed the drawer shut, locked it with quivering fingers, dropped the key back into its pouch and thrust it into the back of the cupboard, piling the privateer's clothes

on top of it. He'd told her to look for clothes in the cupboard, so if he noticed things were put back out of order,
he wouldn't question it.

Who did Cosimo kill with those knives? She didn't
think they were used for self-defense; there was a deadly
aura about them, about the way they were so neatly laid
out, each one for a specific purpose. Pistols were noisy and
clumsy; knives were silent and lethal.

She thought of his hands, those hands that had been on
her body just a short while ago, brushing her skin, touching with knowing intimacy, so that she moaned beneath
his caresses. Large, powerful, long-fingered hands that
would wield a killer's knife as unerringly as they could
bring her to the heights of ecstasy.

Slowly Meg stood up. Was she being fanciful? Perhaps
there was a perfectly logical explanation for such a collec-
tion. Perhaps he was just that, a collector. But she knew
better. She had seen his dark side, sensed the ruthless core
buried deep beneath the humorous, easygoing exterior.
Whatever this war work was, it was not of the straightforward, fighting-in-the-open kind. Otherwise he'd be in the
navy, commanding a frigate or some such.

Well, she'd certainly learned a lesson about prying,
Meg reflected grimly. One might well uncover something
much better left unknown. She definitely would have preferred not to have discovered the knives. Now she'd be tormented by speculation and she couldn't get at the truth
that might put her mind at rest or at least produce an acceptable explanation because she dare not ask Cosimo
and reveal her invasion of his secrets.

There was nothing to be done about the knowledge except hoard it and watch for further clues. With customary
resolution she put the knives to the back of her mind and

turned her attention to the much less disturbing if somewhat provocative issue of the clothes on the bed. On occasion she'd envied men the freedom of movement their attire gave them, but had never seriously considered how it would feel to dress that way herself.

The idea intrigued her now and she threw off the blanket, hurriedly putting on the shirt. The material was thick but not coarse. She fastened the horn buttons that ran down the front and at the wrists and pulled on the underdrawers, tying the string at the waist. They felt odd. She was not used to having close-fitting garments on her legs. Stockings came next and then the britches. They were of luxuriously soft, warm Saxony cloth. Ana was obviously accustomed only to the best, Meg reflected with a degree of relief. Coarse wool could be hot and scratchy. She flexed her knees, swiveled her hips, did a few experimental high kicks. It was wonderfully liberating. But the waist was too big and she could imagine them sliding inexorably over her almost nonexistent hips. She needed a belt.

Cosimo had a narrow waist, but it was still a man's waist. No belt of his would fit. However, Ana would surely have taken that into account. She was still standing in a quandary, holding up the britches with her hands, when Cosimo entered the cabin on a perfunctory knock.

"Ah, yes," he murmured, looking her over in one long sweeping gaze, an appreciative smile on his lips. "I thought so. You have exactly the figure for them, my love."

"That may be so," Meg declared, "but I can't walk around in them because they'll fall around my ankles within minutes." She let go of the waistband, spreading her hands in dramatic demonstration.

"You need a belt."

"I had come to that conclusion myself. Did...does," she corrected herself hastily, "Ana have one?"

If he noticed the slip, he gave no sign. "No, they fitted her well enough without, but we can adapt one of mine." He rummaged in a cupboard. "Here, let's try this one. It's quite thin." He shook out a thin strip of tooled leather. "Come here and let me measure it."

Meg stood still as he slung the belt around her waist, drew it comfortably tight, and made a tiny scratch with a paper knife. "Are you going to cut it?" The image of the neat array of knives filled her mind's eye.

"Cut it and add a couple of notches," he returned.

"With a knife?" She swallowed.

He looked at her a little oddly. "With what else?"

Meg shrugged. "Oh, I don't know. You could have all sorts of tools...ship things, that sort of thing."

"Oh." He raised his eyebrows. "I'm not aware of any peculiarly specific items that are only found on board ships." He reached into his britches pocket and drew out a small folding knife. He flicked out the blade and deftly sliced through the leather.

That, Meg thought, was an ordinary knife, the kind of knife that ordinary people going about their daily business might carry for just such a mundane purpose. Perhaps in another life he'd been a knife thrower in a traveling fair.

Her absurd sense of humor could come to her rescue on occasion and this was one of them. The idiotic image banished the residue of dread that had come over her when she'd opened the drawer.

Cosimo pressed the tip of the knife into the leather where he'd made the initial mark and turned it to open the hole. "Now, let's try." He fastened the belt, settled it on her waist, and said, *"Et, voilà, mademoiselle."*

"*Et, voilà*, indeed," Meg said, holding her waist, feeling the neat fit of the britches. "Thank you, sir."

He laughed a little, darting a kiss into the corner of her mouth. "My pleasure, ma'am." He folded the knife and dropped it back into his pocket. "Are you warm enough to come on deck now?" He helped her into the leather jerkin.

"Is it still raining?"

He shook his head. "No, but it's cold and damp. The wind's dropped some though, and the sea's less heavy, so I've given order to light the galley fires. Silas will make a hot supper."

"Now, that sounds appealing." She slung her cloak around her shoulders, buttoning the collar high against her throat. "Will we sail all night?"

"Yes, I need to make Quiberon before dark tomorrow."

Meg merely nodded. She guessed that Quiberon was where he was going to go ashore. If he was expecting news there, she guessed too that there would be a courier-pigeon outpost as there was on Sark.

She followed him on deck and the air was like a cold wet blanket on her face, but her body was warm. Miles and Frank, huddled in boat cloaks, were on the quarterdeck. Frank had the helm and Miles was standing behind him, watching the sails and calling out adjustments to the course. Mike, the helmsman, stood laconically to one side, smoking a pipe, the bowl cupped in one hand against the occasional gusts of wind, his eyes on the two young men.

"They have more than one tutor," Meg observed, drawing the cloak tightly around her, suddenly self-conscious at revealing her unusual costume.

"A ship full of them," Cosimo returned. "Miles is a natural sailor; Frank has to work harder, but he'll get there."

"Quiberon," Meg said. "Will you go ashore into the town?"

"No," he answered. "We'll put into a small cove some five miles along the coast."

Meg waited to see if he would say anything more, but after a minute he strode up to the quarterdeck and calmly stood behind Frank, placing his hands over his nephew's. He began instructing him quietly, adjusting the wheel as he did so.

Meg watched them, wondering. She had never heard Cosimo say a harsh word or raise his voice. He had the look, but that was his only weapon, his only obvious manifestation of his authority. And he used it rarely. In fact, she thought ruefully, as far as she was aware, she'd been its only recipient since she'd found herself on the *Mary Rose*. So what was he? He inspired loyalty, but much more than that, devotion. Unquestioning devotion and trust, even from a man like David Porter. An educated, sensitive surgeon, who had no need to cast in his lot with a man who lived on the edge ... a man with a locked drawer of killing knives in his cabin.

Chapter 12

The anchor chain rattled, the sound unnaturally loud in the hush of the night. The *Mary Rose* shuddered to a halt on the swelling waves as the anchor flukes bit into the sandy bottom off the coast of Brittany. The night was dark, the moon showing fitfully between the cloud cover, the stars invisible. But the rain had stopped and the sea was quieter than it had been all day.

Meg, as usual in the stern on the quarterdeck, could just make out the rugged cliffs of the coast about half a mile away. The sound of waves breaking angrily on the notorious Breton rocks was as ominous as the occasional flash of white spume. Somewhere beyond those rocks was the sheltered cove where Cosimo intended to make landfall. Not in the *Mary Rose*, she knew that without asking, but in one of the dinghies lashed to the mid-deck.

She turned her back to the coast and looked along the darkened deck. There were no lights on the *Mary Rose* tonight. Cosimo was talking to Mike and the boatswain, Frank and Miles standing a discreet distance away, but close enough to hear the conversation. Once Cosimo glanced towards Meg in the stern, then returned to his conversation.

Meg had sensed an unusual tension in him as afternoon gave way to evening. She wondered if he was concerned about the news he hoped to receive about Ana. She thought she knew enough to know that something bad had happened to prevent Ana's making the rendezvous in Folkestone. Was Cosimo expecting the worst? That his lover, his partner, his friend, was dead? Killed in the same war he fought. A war that relied on spies and assassins.

She crossed her arms over her breasts in a convulsive hug. She couldn't come to terms with any of the implications of such logical speculations.

"Coffee, ma'am?"

"Oh, yes, please." She took the mug that Biggins was offering, wrapping her gloved hands around it. "An inspiration. Thank you."

"Captain says to put a drop o' this in it," Biggins said, opening a flask of cognac. "Says you'll be needing it."

Meg was too startled to object as the sailor slurped a generous measure into the thick black liquid in her mug. She blew on the cup and took a tentative sip. The cognac instantly warmed her throat and settled comfortingly in her belly. Her next sip was far from tentative. Who was she to argue with a privateer?

They were lowering the dinghy now, and Miles went down the ladder first, followed by the boatswain and a young sailor Meg now knew as Tommy. Cosimo stood at the rail, watching the descent of his men and presumably waiting for his turn. For the first time, it occurred to Meg that he was going to go on this enterprise without a word of farewell. He'd left her with cognac in her coffee and not even a kiss.

Then he looked over at her. "Are you coming? We don't have any time to waste."

Her jaw dropped. *Bastard*. He was laughing, enjoying every minute of his little game. He'd thrown her totally off course and it delighted him. She drained her mug, savoring the last lingering heat of the cognac, set the beaker down on the deck, and strolled over to him. "A little warning would have been appreciated."

"I thought the cognac would have alerted you," he said with an assumption of innocence. He pointed down to the black sea. "You first."

"I'd prefer to follow you."

He shook his head. "I'm behind you, Miles is in front of you. Now, if you're going, go."

Meg swung herself over the rail and onto the ladder. In britches it was a completely different maneuver and she accomplished it with ease, descending the swinging ladder swiftly, trying to ignore the heaving blackness beneath her. Reassuring hands grasped her ankles. "Just step down, ma'am," Miles said, guiding her foot.

She landed in the dinghy with an exhalation of relief and sat down instantly in the stern as the boat rocked. Cosimo stepped in without causing the slightest ripple of the boat on the water and took his place beside her in the stern.

Miles and Tommy took up the oars, the boatswain sat in the bow, and they pulled steadily towards the sound of breaking waves.

"Well, this was an interesting invitation," Meg said with a touch of sarcasm. "Most unexpected."

"I thought you were curious."

"I was . . . am. It would have been nice to have had some

warning though. Time to prepare, use the privy, perhaps...how long are we going to be gone?"

"If the worst comes to the worst, you can use the sea," he said. "My men are very discreet, and we're all accustomed to dealing with such a necessity on the water."

"How very reassuring," she said, but she was smiling to herself even as she wondered whether this invitation was a challenge or a vote of confidence. It didn't seem to matter. She let the hood of her cloak fall back and enjoyed the damp caress of the night breeze on her face. The sound of the breakers grew louder but she was no longer apprehensive.

Then the rocks rose up in front of them, a ragged line of ugly-looking black crags sticking up from the sea that churned white and green at the base. The four men in the little boat showed no consternation. The boatswain called directions softly to Miles and Tommy at the oars. Cosimo sat silently in the stern, but Meg could feel that he was alert, every muscle poised for action, his eyes on the rocks ahead. The tiny gap appeared in a moment of dim moonlight, then was gone again as the clouds scudded over the light, but it was enough for the boatswain and the oarsmen. There were a few minutes of soaking spray and then peace. The water slapped gently against the dinghy; the roaring of the waves was behind them, ahead lay the pale glimmer of a sandy beach, and around them rose craggy gray cliffs.

The oarsmen beached the little boat in the sandy shallows and shipped their oars. Cosimo said briefly, "Hold here for me. If there's trouble, get out at once and return for me the same time tomorrow."

To Meg, he said, "Stay here, right where you are." A smile flickered across his eyes. "That should be sufficient adventure for one night." He blew her a kiss as he stepped over the side of the dinghy.

Sufficient adventure? Meg was not quite so sure. She watched him lope up the beach towards a narrow path that threaded its way up the cliff. Did he have his knives with him? She acted on impulse, stepping into the shallow water that lapped over her boots.

"Ma'am...Miss Barratt...where are you going?" Miles's anguished whisper followed her.

"Come back, ma'am," the boatswain ordered, much more gruffly and with much more authority.

"Soon," Meg whispered over her shoulder. "I'm just going to walk a little way up the path." She guessed rightly that they wouldn't leave the dinghy and follow her. She was their captain's responsibility and theirs was to wait for him to return, preserving their only means of escape back to the ship.

She walked quickly across the sand, not worried about the sound of her footsteps; that would be muffled by the sand. Cosimo was way ahead of her on the pathway when she reached its base. He was climbing fast but using the screening bushes that lined the path as cover as much as possible.

Meg climbed steadily upwards, making no attempt to catch him up, reckoning that the farther away she was, the less likely he was to sense her presence. She ducked behind a scrubby and rather prickly bush when he slowed, and held her breath when he turned to look behind him down the path. His black cloak was pulled tight around him and he was a mere shadow in the black-gray night. From a distance, no one who was not looking for him would make out his figure.

Of course, if someone was...Her heart picked up a

beat and then resumed its normal pace. Cosimo knew what he was doing. If he expected someone to be watching for him, he would be ready for them.

He resumed his climb and Meg climbed steadily after him, choosing to keep as much as possible to the grass beside the path, thinking that there would be even less noise from her footfall than on the sandy pathway.

And then Cosimo disappeared. She gazed upwards and saw only the grayish line of the path leading to the cliff head, the black-gray sky arching above. She looked down and saw only the gray line of the sand and the black water touched with white foam as it broke on the beach. At first she couldn't see the dinghy and had an instant of panic. It was their only way off the shore, and then she thought she could discern a faint shape tucked against the edge of the cliff. She realized that the men had moved off the beach into the shadows so that they were invisible to anyone who might be watching from above.

But now where was her quarry? Had he reached the cliff top? It seemed the only explanation. Meg set off again, her stride lengthening as she grew accustomed to the pitch of the path that at this point was no more than a goat track. She paused once, thinking she heard something, but the night was quiet apart from the chirp of crickets. She still couldn't see Cosimo ahead of her and felt a niggle of unease.

Then it happened. She was grabbed from behind, an iron-hard arm encircling her body so that her arms and hands were imprisoned at her sides. She was pressed backwards and would have lost her footing on the slippery path but for the rock-hard body behind her. Something pricked sharply against her neck just behind her right ear so that she drew breath on a small cry of pain, a cry that was instantly smothered by a hand across her mouth and nose so that she could barely breathe. She could move her arms now and struggled feebly but the sharp point pressing behind her ear dug deeper with her struggles and finally she stopped, gasping for breath. When she was still, the smothering hand lifted slightly so that she could take a gulp of the fresh damp night air. Her heart was banging against her ribs but she knew who held her, although he had said not a word, made not a sound throughout.

His hand was still resting lightly over her mouth, enjoining her own silence, and she concentrated on breathing slowly until her heart stopped pounding and the nausea of fright faded somewhat. Now she could hear low voices somewhere up ahead, and caught the flicker of a lantern among the bushes farther up the path.

Cosimo drew her backwards into the scrub and pushed her down ungently onto the damp grass beneath a bush. He looked down at her, still without making a sound, but she didn't need words to tell her what he was conveying. His mouth was set in a grim line, his eyes frigid. He pointed at her and she nodded her understanding. At the moment, she couldn't imagine finding the strength to move even if he wasn't telling her to stay put.

Cosimo gave her one last hard stare then stepped back onto the path. He was gone from Meg's sight almost immediately and she began to shake in the aftermath of shock and fear. Something trickled down her neck and she touched it tentatively with a fingertip. It was sticky. She looked at the blood on her finger in disbelief. Cosimo had cut her. He hadn't meant to; he couldn't have meant to. But how could she know? The man she'd just seen was capable of anything.

The shaking stopped. Her fear did not diminish, but it

was now infused with rage. How dared he treat her like that? An owl hooted somewhere in the distance and some small animal rustled in the bushes behind her. She resisted the impulse to leap to her feet and instead stood up carefully, trying not to make a sound. She could still hear the low murmur of voices from the cliff above her, and the lantern flickered again.

Meg kept to the bushes parallel to the path as she started upwards again, drawing the cloak tightly around her so that, like Cosimo, she was reduced to a dark shadow. She no longer wanted to follow him but she was driven now by a compulsion. She needed to see what he was going to do . . . to find out exactly who and what this man was.

She dropped to her belly as she neared the top of the cliff and squirmed upwards across the grass until she could just see over the cliff top. A derelict cottage that she guessed had once sheltered a shepherd or goatherd stood a hundred yards or so back from the cliff edge. Two men stood outside talking quietly a few feet from the building, a lantern on the ground between them throwing a golden pool of light. Of Cosimo there was no sign.

And then she saw him. He was coming from behind the building, something bright in his hand. How had he managed to get past the men? But the question seemed irrelevant. She watched in a kind of dread as he sidestepped with his back against the tumbledown wall until he was directly behind the men. Then he moved.

It was over in a second. The two men slipped silently to the ground with barely a cry and Cosimo left them without a backward glance and went into the cottage.

Meg had seen enough. She turned and scrambled back down the path. He'd killed them. In cold blood. They hadn't put up a fight, they hadn't provoked him, he'd just crept up behind them and murdered them. And what on earth was she to do now? She looked frantically for the exact spot where he'd left her and would expect to find her, no longer prepared to risk the privateer's wrath any further. She thought she found the right spot and crouched down again behind the bush.

She heard Cosimo coming down the path, his step no longer stealthy. There was no need for quiet now, she presumed, now that the watchers on the cliff were dead. He stopped on the path and said curtly, "Come along." He held out a hand to pull her to her feet and she hesitated for a split second, suddenly repelled by the prospect of touching him. But he mustn't know what she had seen and she must do nothing to cause suspicion.

She took the proffered hand and scrambled to her feet. "Why is it safe to make a noise now?"

"Because it is," he said shortly, pushing her ahead of him on the path.

Meg paused, asking over her shoulder, "Did you discover what you wanted to find out?"

"No, not what I wanted to find out," he responded. "Hurry up, Meg, we're on enemy soil here, every minute we spend increases the danger."

She said nothing more but increased her speed, trying to formulate the perfectly natural questions that he would have to answer in some form. How would he explain what had happened on the cliff top?

They reached the beach and found the dinghy once more accessible in the shallows. Miles said apprehensively, "I'm sorry, sir. Miss Barratt insisted—"

Cosimo cut him off with a gesture. "Yes, so I understand." He picked Meg up and deposited her unceremoniously in the dinghy, then pushed it off the sandy bottom himself, climbing in over the stern once it floated free. He seemed unaware of his wet boots and britches and sat with his usual apparent calm as they were rowed back through the narrow gap into the open sea towards the dark shape of the *Mary Rose*.

Meg touched her neck where the skin seemed tight and sore. It was still sticky to the touch but the blood was drying. An involuntary shudder went through her. Cosimo shot her a sharp look, his face still grim, his eyes still cold, but he said nothing.

When they bumped gently against the side of the ship, he indicated to Meg that she should go up the ladder first. He followed close behind and as soon as their feet touched the deck he said, "Go below. I'll come down in a few minutes."

Meg didn't argue. She was chilled and depressed, scared and angry all at the same time, and all she wanted to do was crawl under the covers and embrace the amnesia of sleep. A lamp, turned low, offered faint illumination in the cabin, and Gus was already tucked up under his crimson covering. She sat on a chair and wearily pulled off her boots. Her stockings were wet too and she struggled to unroll them without taking off her britches, which seemed too much like hard work in her present state.

Cosimo came in while she was looking at her cold white feet as if she'd never seen them before. He carried a flask and two glasses. He didn't greet her, merely poured a measure of cognac into both glasses and handed her one, before going into the head, reappearing with a cloth soaked in warm water.

"Tilt your head."

Meg took a gulp of the fiery spirit and then did as he

said. He dabbed at the cut with the cloth. "Did you mean to cut me?" she asked.

"No, of course not. I knew someone was following me, but I didn't know it was you. It didn't occur to me that you would do anything so foolish." His mouth was as grim as ever. "Perhaps you'll remember in future that I move fast when I sense danger."

That made some sort of sense, she supposed, and she would have accepted it without question except for what she'd seen afterwards.

"It's only a surface scratch," he said, taking up the cognac bottle and pouring a few drops onto the cloth. He held it against the wound and Meg drew a sharp breath at the sting. "It's as good a disinfectant as vinegar," he stated, tossing the cloth into the head. "Now, I would like an explanation, Miss Barratt."

He perched on the edge of the table in his familiar fashion, one leg swinging casually. "Why did you follow me?"

Meg didn't immediately answer. Her gaze was riveted on the narrow sheath fastened to his belt, and the silver hilt of the knife showing above. The stiletto blade, she recognized it.

"Well?" he prompted.

She shrugged and forced her eyes away. "I was curious. I had no intention of getting in the way."

Cosimo sipped cognac, regarding her thoughtfully over the lip of his glass. Initiative and curiosity were all good qualities, but they had to be tempered with common sense, and her refusal to follow instruction boded ill for a partnership where he had to be able to rely absolutely on her compliance. It was no exaggeration to say that their lives would depend on each doing exactly as had been agreed between them. An unpredictable move on either part would be fatal. But, of course, at this point Meg had no idea of the greater purpose he had in mind for her, so how could she know how vital it was that she adhere strictly to a plan? Well, he'd have to teach her one way or another.

"Did it occur to you that I might have had my reasons for wanting you to stay with the dinghy?"

It did now, she thought bitterly. Of course he wouldn't want a witness to his killings. But had he intended to kill those men? Had their presence surprised him? "Let's drop it," she said. "You needn't worry, I won't do such a thing again." She touched her neck reflexively. "You spring some unpleasant surprises."

"I apologize for that," he said, his voice quiet, although his eyes were still that glacial blue. "I would not have hurt you deliberately for any reason."

Meg took a deep breath. "What did you discover after you left me? Did you find out about Ana?"

"Not exactly," he responded curtly. He stood up. "Go to bed now. You're tired." He picked up the flask of cognac and left the cabin without another word.

Meg stripped off the rest of her clothes, dropped her nightgown over her head, and turned out the lamp before crawling into the box-bed. She lay in the comforting darkness, buried under the covers, listening to the sound of the turning capstan hauling up the anchor. She heard Cosimo's voice calling, "Make sail," and then the snap of the wind in the mainsail. The Mary Rose listed to starboard, then righted herself and began to move steadily ahead.

Meg didn't think she could bear it if he came to her bed that night. Her skin shrank at the thought of his hands on her, the feel of his body close to hers. He was still angry with her, and that would surely keep him away. She would have to find other ways to keep her distance until she could leave the ship at Bordeaux and somehow find her way back to England.

On deck, Cosimo drank cognac from the flask and watched the dark sea slipping past the bow. The Quiberon pigeons had been destroyed. He had found their bodies lying lifeless on the floor of the loft, their handlers, his own men, his friends, killed as they slept. The French had obliterated the outpost, which meant that either Ana had been compelled to give them more detailed information about his operation or someone had betrayed them. Either way, he was now working in the dark. He had no idea what the enemy knew. Had they also destroyed the outfit at La Rochelle?

He would find out only by seeing for himself. They should reach there in two days and there was no point speculating until then. He put the issue away in a separate compartment of his mind, to be brought out and reexamined at the right time. His main concern now was what to do about Meg. Had her actions tonight proved her dangerously unreliable as a partner?

"Penny for them, Cosimo?" David Porter stepped up to the rail beside him.

"They're not worth a sou," Cosimo said, passing him the flask.

David took a hearty swig and passed it back, wiping his mouth with the back of his hand. "Did your mission prosper this evening?"

Cosimo's expression was shuttered as he said, "No, it did not."

David raised his eyebrows at the curt negative. After a minute he said, "If it helps to unburden..."

The privateer put the flask to his lips and drank deep before offering it again to his companion. "The French got there first. Destroyed the pigeons and killed my men. If there had been a message, or some news about Ana, it's now in French hands. So, as you can gather, it's an understatement to say my mission did not prosper."

"I'm sorry." David leaned his elbows on the rail and gazed out across the blackness of the sea. Cosimo rarely expressed dismay at the failure of an endeavor—he tended to change course effortlessly, moving in a different direction towards the same goal—but David guessed that not knowing about Ana's fate, and therefore being unable to help her, was having a much more profound effect on his friend than any ordinary failure. Cosimo might not acknowledge it, but he was not always the callous pragmatist he made himself out to be.

"Why don't you turn back and see what you can discover in England?" he suggested after a minute.

Cosimo glanced at him and gave a short mirthless laugh. "You'll have to believe me when I say that's impossible, David. I have something that has to be done and done within the next six weeks. Otherwise it will be too late."

The surgeon absorbed this. He knew better than to ask what had to be done so urgently. "What about our passenger?" he inquired. "I understand you took her with you this evening."

"And that was a mistake," Cosimo said grimly.

David looked at him with interest, remembering an earlier conversation. "Are you saying this tool is unwilling, or can't be sharpened?"

Cosimo drummed his fingers on the rail. "I haven't

decided as yet. I suspect the steel may need further tem-pering."

"Sometimes you really chill me, Cosimo," the other man declared, revising his earlier gentler assessment of the man. "Are you sleeping with Meg as part of this tempering, as you call it?"

The privateer's fingers drummed faster. A few days ago he wouldn't have denied the accusation; in fact, he would probably have laughed it off. He had always chosen women who enjoyed sensual adventuring without any need for an emotional mutual dependency. He had thought Meg fitted that bill perfectly: she had embraced passion with a lighthearted exuberance that promised the kind of useful and enjoyable partnership he had with Ana. He had certainly intended to use their liaison to draw her into his mission, so to that extent there was a pragmatic purpose behind their mutual desire, but for some reason he found that reflection unusually distasteful.

"I have no reason to believe she doesn't get as much pleasure from it as I do," he said, hearing the stiff, defen-sive note in his voice. "If you'll excuse me, David, I need to set the watch. Keep the cognac, if there's any left."

He walked away, leaving the surgeon staring thought-fully out into the night. Cosimo did not in general set the watch himself; that task fell to Miles or Frank. Neither did the captain of the *Mary Rose* usually sound uncertain of himself. Was Meg Barratt getting under his skin? David tilted the flask and drained the last dregs. A slight smile tilted the corners of his mouth. It might not do the man any harm for once to find his emotional equilibrium a lit-tle off kilter.

Cosimo, fortunately unaware of the surgeon's conclusion, discussed the watch with Frank, the course with Mike, and then took a restless turn around the deck, also unaware of the speculative glances his helmsman cast in his direction. Mike had sailed with the privateer since the *Mary Rose* had first set sail and very rarely had he seen any overt signs of agitation on her captain's part. But something had disturbed the captain tonight, that was for sure.

Cosimo came back to the helm. "I'm going below, Mike. Send to me if you need me."

"Aye, sir, same as always," the man said with a laconic nod. "Everything all right, sir?"

"Of course, why wouldn't it be?"

The helmsman shrugged at his captain's back as Cosimo strode off towards the companionway. *Why indeed?*

Cosimo opened the cabin door quietly. The place was in darkness alleviated only by the grayness that filled the window. He couldn't blame Meg for extinguishing the lamp, but it would have been friendly to have left a tiny glow. He stepped over to the cot and looked down at the formless shape beneath the covers. Her breathing was deep and even and she seemed to be taking up much more of the narrow space than was either usual or warranted by her small frame. Was it deliberate? Or had she been so exhausted she hadn't thought to arrange her limbs in a more hospitable fashion to accommodate her sleeping partner?

He decided he didn't want to speculate on that issue either and opened the cupboard beneath the bed and took out his hammock and a blanket. He slung the hammock from the hooks in the ceiling and sat down to take off his boots, still wet from splashing through the shallows to the beach. He pulled off his damp socks and britches and swung himself with the ease of practice into the hammock, pulling the blanket over him. The canvas bed rocked gently with the motion of the ship but unusually it didn't lull him instantly to sleep. He turned over the events of the evening in his mind, experiencing again the sick desolation he'd felt as he'd looked at his murdered men, the slaughtered birds. Wanton destruction. They could have destroyed the post without killing.

Cosimo was a man who killed to order. He killed from necessity. And he abhorred the wanton infliction of death.

Meg kept her breathing deep and even, sensing that he was still awake. Her relief that he hadn't attempted to share the bed was short-lived. He was still so close to her that he would detect the slightest change in her breathing, the slightest shift of her body that would indicate she was awake. She hadn't the strength to talk to him tonight and for once she couldn't imagine responding to his touch.

Chapter 13

Meg woke dry-mouthed, head and body aching. She'd slept but it had been about as unrestful a sleep as she'd ever had. Images of cut throats, sprawled limbs, the privateer wiping his shining silver blade on his kerchief would not be banished. She knew she'd seen none of that but it didn't seem to help. Nightmares always put pictures to amorphous horrors and she was in the grip of a thoroughly amorphous horror right now.

She hitched herself on an elbow and looked around the cabin. The hammock was gone; Gus's cage was empty and there was no sign of the bird. And extraordinarily, the sun was shining and the *Mary Rose* was once again skipping on her way instead of lumbering through greasy swells. Unfortunately none of this seemed to help Meg's sense of well-being. She lay down again, curling on her side to face the wall, pulling the cover up over her head. If she could stay like this until they reached Bordeaux, surely she could find passage home from there.

Biggins knocked at the door. Meg could now identify every knock on that cabin door. She debated ignoring it, knowing that he would go away, but then reasoned that coffee might help her aching head. She mumbled an "Enter," and the door opened.

"Morning, ma'am," he said without looking towards the bed. "And it's a beautiful one. There's coffee here, and Captain says breakfast will be served on deck. Silas is cooking up a nice dish of kidneys with bacon. I'll be back with hot water." He disappeared without waiting for or seeming to expect any response to this stream of information.

Meg rolled onto her back and gazed up at the ceiling. She couldn't ignore what had happened, just maintain business as usual with the privateer. And short of jumping overboard, she couldn't leave the ship. What had happened was no reason for her to commit suicide. She would just have to find some excuse to keep herself to herself until she could leave the ship and find some way home. In the meantime, the aroma of coffee was irresistible.

Biggins and his little assistant returned with jugs of hot water. "I took the liberty of washing what you wore last night, ma'am, but since it's a nice warm day you'll be comfortable enough, I reckon, in regular clothes," Biggins informed her, still discreetly averting his eyes from the bed.

"Thank you," she managed. She still couldn't quite get used to the idea of this rough-handed sailor laundering her most intimate garments, but she couldn't deny the convenience.

Once alone again, she got up, poured coffee, and took it to the window seat. She drank it gratefully, enjoying the warmth of the sun as it fell through the window onto the back of her neck. The skin still felt tight beneath her ear and she touched it tentatively, feeling the slight ridge of the scab. Cosimo had been correct, it was a superficial scratch. But it had still been made with the point of a stiletto. A quiver went through her at the memory of that moment of panic when she'd felt the blood trickle down her neck.

Her eyes fixed on the locked drawer beneath the chart table. Presumably the stiletto, cleaned of bloodstains, was back with its fellows.

She jumped up, discarded her coffee cup, and went into the head. How to explain her estrangement from Cosimo without letting on that she'd seen what he'd done on the cliff top? She poured water into the basin and dropped the sponge in, lathering it absently. Perhaps she could simply say that after the events of last night she had no stomach for this adventure anymore, that she'd misjudged herself, her own strength and courage. She'd lost interest in their liaison and she wanted to keep herself to herself until they reached Bordeaux, where she would try to find passage home.

It was plausible enough, and no decent man would argue with a woman who wanted to call a halt for whatever reasons to what had been a casual, opportunistic liaison at best. But it stuck in Meg's craw. Apart from the fact that she doubted her ability to be convincing about her abrupt loss of passion, she had plenty of courage, and stomach enough for any adventure that didn't include cold-blooded murder. But if she had to play the feeble little woman to escape gracefully, then so be it. She would play it to the hilt.

She sponged herself with the warm water, and the aches of a restless night dissipated. Once more attired, this time in a jonquil gown of dainty sprigged muslin, she began to feel almost hopeful that she could pull this off without stepping any closer to the brink of the privateer's dangerous edge. She drank more coffee while combing her hair and then set her shoulders. It couldn't be put off forever. She left the cabin.

The tantalizing aroma of kidneys and frying bacon assailed her as she climbed the companionway steps, and when she stepped out into the sunlight she saw Cosimo sitting at the table that had been set up on the quarterdeck. He raised a hand in greeting and crooked his fingers in invitation. Gus, perched on the rail, squawked a "G'mornin'" and unfurled his brilliant scarlet wings.

"Good morning, Gus." She returned the greeting as she crossed the mid-deck. The sun caught the deep red glints in Cosimo's auburn hair, his sea-washed eyes squinted against its brightness, and he looked the picture of relaxation. That now familiar current of desire jolted her loins and prickled her skin. Once again he was the image of the man Meg had known before the events of last night. And for a minute she was tempted to forget what she had seen. But only for a moment.

She stepped onto the quarterdeck and came over to the table, shading her eyes against the sun. "What happened to the weather?" It was a properly neutral greeting and she kept her tone of voice similarly so.

"It turned around," he said pleasantly. "May I pour you coffee?"

"Thank you." She took her seat and shook out her napkin. "I seem to be hungry." Nothing dangerous in this social chitchat. Just keep it up, she told herself.

"After last night it's hardly surprising." He filled her cup and added milk, just the right amount for her taste.

Meg stirred the liquid. He'd brought up the subject and now she needed to pick up the ball. "Yes." She gave an artistic shudder, her fingers quivering a little as she picked up her cup. "I'd rather not talk about it. I angered you by following you and I'm sorry for it." She managed another shudder and lightly brushed the cut on her neck in emphasis.

A frown crossed his eyes, but he said easily, "I don't allow myself to get angry, it's a wasteful emotion, although I admit I was annoyed. But I don't think of it anymore. Let's agree to put it all behind us, Meg." He reached over and ran his fingertips over her hand in a skimming caress. She froze beneath his touch and stared blankly over his shoulder. He moved his hand and sat back, frowning openly now.

Meg picked up her fork and began to eat, avoiding his gaze. She had only to think of those two men crumpling onto the grass to maintain her role. She cast about for some ordinary banal topic of conversation that would skate over the awkwardness but her tongue was tied. She had never discussed banalities with the privateer and didn't know where to begin.

Cosimo regarded her in puzzlement. "What's the matter?"

"Nothing. I'm just tired. I didn't sleep well." She forced a smile.

Cosimo gave a half shrug and continued with his own breakfast, making no further attempt to break the silence that stretched between them until it was almost visible. Finally he pushed aside his plate and stood up. "Excuse me." He walked away towards the bows, his brow deeply creased.

Why had she not responded to his overture? Cosimo wondered. If anyone should still be put out, it was he. Meg had jeopardized his mission, she had been in the wrong, not the other way around. He had hurt her, but not intentionally, and surely she knew that, just as she must have known the danger they were all in on French soil. It was a piece of arrant stupidity to have followed him. Did she think this was some kind of game?

But that deadness in her eyes, the flat tone of her voice, the way her hand had felt like a lifeless bird beneath his fingers... what was behind that? Something much more than an accidental cut for which she had been at least as responsible as he.

On the quarterdeck Gus flew onto the table and picked at breadcrumbs. He regarded Meg with one beady eye. "Mornin'."

"We've already been through that, Gus." she said, offering her forearm as a perch. She scratched his poll, murmuring, "I wish there was somewhere to go on this ship. Something to do." She looked up at the rigging where two sailors were working on the ratlines. It was as hazardous as it looked far up against the mainmast but Meg envied them both the task and the excitement. She had never been bored before on the *Mary Rose*, but then the constant presence of the privateer had been more than enough excitement. Now it was something she needed to avoid, which in such close quarters was not going to be easy.

She got up and went back down to the cabin. One of Ana's gowns had a loose button; it would give her some employment. But she found when she took out the gown that Biggins had been there before her and all the buttons were secure.

A letter to Bella. That would occupy her even if she didn't know when she'd be able to send it. By describing to someone else the events of last night, the whole muddle of her present feelings, her fears about Cosimo and about the immediate future, she might gain some much-needed perspective.

The shelf above the chart table yielded paper, pens, and ink and Meg sat at the table, sharpened a quill, and began her letter. Once begun it was hard to stop and she'd covered three sheets when Cosimo entered the cabin for once without an alerting knock. She was so absorbed that the appearance of the main subject of her detailed correspondence caused her a guilty start. She jumped, dropping the pen, splashing ink over her page, which at least gave her the opportunity to cover her writing with a blotting cloth.

"What did I do to cause that?" he asked with a smile that did nothing to lessen the frown in his eyes. "I don't normally have that effect on people."

"I wasn't expecting you," she said lamely.

"I don't know why not." He came behind her and clasped her nape warmly. She stiffened, her body suddenly motionless, her hand on the cloth covering her letter. He let his hand drop and moved away as if he'd noticed nothing. "Whom are you writing to?"

"Bella, my friend. I assume there'll be a way to send it, but if not I'll just take it with me when I go home." She took a deep breath. "I want to leave the *Mary Rose* at Bordeaux and go home on another ship. How long before we get there?"

"This is rather abrupt." He leaned his shoulders against the bulkhead and watched her, his arms folded, his eyes sharp. "Why are you so anxious to leave me?"

Now was the moment. "I think this has run its course, Cosimo," she said slowly. "It was amusing for a while to pretend that I was an adventuress, but after last night I realize I'm not cut from the right cloth."

"What on earth are you talking about?" He didn't move

from his position but his voice had hardened, and the light behind his eyes was not particularly amiable.

Meg clasped her hands tightly in her lap. "I thought I was stronger... had more courage than I do. It's mortifying to acknowledge it, Cosimo, but I was terrified last night and I had the most dreadful nightmares. This life..." She gestured vaguely around the cabin. "What you do...in this war...this whole uncertainty. I'm frightened and I want to go home." She gazed at him with what she hoped were limpid green pools of feminine frailty.

He continued to look at her, nodding slowly but with a disconcerting lack of conviction. "You do, do you?"

"Please," she pleaded. "How soon can I get back to my world? I wasn't bred for this and I'm too old to learn new tricks."

The look in his eye changed. He stroked his chin, tapping his mouth with his forefinger as if deep in thought. Then he said, "Too old, eh? Well, Madam Methuselah, I see no way to let you off the ship prematurely unless we come across a naval vessel that will take you as a passenger. It seems to me you should have thought of this before we left Sark."

Meg wanted to throw something at him but she kept her hands firmly clasped in her lap. "I couldn't anticipate how I would react to something I'd never experienced," she said, keeping her voice low and unprovocative. "And, be honest, Cosimo, you never told me to expect something like last night."

"My dear, you were the one who insisted on joining us, if you recall." Sarcasm laced his tone. "And, I might add, putting the endeavor in jeopardy."

"I'm sorry for that. I didn't understand the danger, and that more than anything made me realize how unsuited I am to this kind of existence. I'm not made to be a spy or an adventuress. I don't like admitting it, but it's true." She tried for a rueful yet determined smile.

"Well, I don't see that it makes much difference," he declared, dropping his arms and turning to the chart table. "As I just said, barring the felicitous appearance of a ship of his majesty's navy en route to England, you're stuck with me. There's no need for you to embark upon any more extracurricular enterprises."

"But *you* will be?"

"I have one other stop to make." He spoke casually as he applied the sextant to the charts. "But you will stay safely aboard."

Meg swallowed and prepared for the final and most difficult declaration. "If you don't mind, I'd like to . . . to keep to myself from now on."

His put down the sextant and straightened, turning his head towards her. "What am I to understand by that?"

"Isn't it obvious? I made a mistake. I have to correct that mistake *now*. I need to leave this ship at Bordeaux and I want our affair to end *now*, Cosimo. It doesn't feel right anymore."

"I see." His voice was arid as the desert. He returned to his charts, made a few more notations, and then left the cabin, closing the door softly behind him.

Meg let out her breath, realizing only as she did so how shallowly she'd been breathing throughout that confrontation. It was done, over with. He couldn't refuse to honor her wishes. He could despise her for a weak-minded simpleton who hadn't the courage of her convictions, but she could live with that and he would still leave her alone. The next few days promised to be tedious and awkward, but she could get through them. And she didn't believe that

Cosimo was vindictive; he wouldn't simply abandon her at Bordeaux. He would help her find passage home.

On deck, Cosimo did something he now very rarely did. He jumped into the ratlines and climbed steadily upwards to the platform halfway up the mainmast. It was an insecure perch at the best of times but he balanced easily, leaning against the mast at his back, watching his men on the precarious footropes hanging over the deck as they worked the sails. No one paid him any attention, which was as it should be. One instant of inattention could mean death at that height. He enjoyed the cleanliness of the salt air, the swaying of the mast so high above the deck. It gave him detachment and he needed detachment to dig below the surface of Meg's abrupt change of heart. What was behind it? *What exactly was she saying?*

Not for one minute did he believe that flummery about being a weak and feeble woman who'd bitten off more than she could chew in a fit of, *oh, such understandable female confusion and uncontrolled impulse.*

Meg knew exactly what she was doing and had known so all along. So what, that he didn't know about, had happened last night to cause her to put on this farce?

And, as much to the point, how was whatever it was going to affect his plans? The difficulties of counting on her absolute compliance aside, what if she found the whole idea of the mission anathema? Cosimo believed in his own powers of persuasion, particularly when it was a woman he had to persuade. He'd never been given any reason to doubt that power, until now. It was a sobering reflection. At some point the sexual attraction he possessed was going to wear thin, and then what weapons would he have in his arsenal? He laughed with self-mockery. At some point he'd slow down in other areas too. His knife hand would not be so fast, his memory would slip occasionally, his timing would be off kilter, and he would die.

But not yet. He was at the top of his game. This mission was the most important of his professional life and he could not fail. And Meg Barratt was an essential tool.

He climbed down the ratlines to the deck, where his lieutenants pretended they weren't curious about his ascent. "You should keep in practice too," he said. "Both of you."

They took it as the order it was and went up. Cosimo watched them, hands on his hips. "Good lads," Mike observed from the helm behind him.

"Aye, but they've a lot to learn," his captain said. "Frank in particular. He still doesn't understand where his hands are supposed to be."

"He'll get it in the end, sir."

"His mother will kill me if he doesn't," Cosimo remarked a trifle gloomily. "I'll be below. Call me when we're off St. Nazaire; we may encounter French shipping in the area."

"Aye, sir."

Cosimo paused outside his cabin, then, once again dispensing with his customary preliminary knock, opened the door. At first he thought the cabin was empty, and then Gus swooped onto his shoulder with an informative "G'night."

Meg was asleep on the bed, the cover tangled around her knees, her head pillowed on her hand. Cosimo disentangled the cover and drew it up to her shoulders. She didn't move, but he knew it was no feigned sleep. A pile of paper lay on the table and he went over, lifting the top sheet, which was blank. He caught sight of his name and immediately dropped the covering sheet into place. Maybe the clue to this mysterious behavior of Meg's lay in that letter but nothing could make him read it. Which was interesting, since he spent most of his life decoding private correspondence and burrowing for other people's secrets.

Cosimo glanced again at the bed. It would seem he'd developed a conscience, an ordinary human reluctance to pry into someone else's secrets. Or at least, as far as Meg was concerned. And just how had that happened? He picked up the top sheet again, determined to read her letter, and then he let it fall. It couldn't be done. Meg had to tell him herself.

He left her sleeping. If her nightmares at least had been real, then she probably needed a dreamless nap.

The naval sloop appeared on the horizon in late afternoon. She flew his majesty's colors boldly and Cosimo sent Frank to act as signalman with the flags from the port bow.

"They say they're heading for La Rochelle, sir," Frank said excitedly.

"Mmm," returned his uncle, who could read the signals at least as well as his nephew. If the British navy was making for La Rochelle, that meant that one of the fleets of the French navy was preparing to leave the harbor. His own landing point was two miles to the south of the harbor, but if there was going to be a heavy naval engagement, then he would be expected to offer support. But he couldn't afford the time. He had to get to Toulon before Napoleon left.

"Is that a British ship?"

Meg's voice startled him, he'd heard it only in his head

for most of the day. He glanced over at her as she stood at the rail beside him. "I believe so."

"Will they give me passage?"

He shrugged. "Maybe. But I suspect they're on course to join the fleet going to Egypt." He glanced at her. "Would you like to go to Egypt, Miss Meg?"

So they'd retreated to the old sardonic familiarity, and Meg could only be glad of it. It signaled a respite, an acceptance of her earlier statement. She shot him a withering look and ignored the question.

"Did you enjoy your nap...no nightmares?" he inquired pleasantly enough.

"None that haunt me. Will you hail that ship?"

"If you wish it. And how would you like to explain to the commander your presence on the *Mary Rose*?" Once again the question sounded pleasant but Meg wasn't fooled.

It was an awkward question. She'd shied away from meeting the commanders of the frigates at Sark partly because of the possibility of scandal, and now she had to come up with a plausible explanation for her presence on a privateer in the middle of the Bay of Biscay. But she could give a false identity at least. That would be some protection.

"My name is Gertrude Myers and I'd been going for a pleasure sail with friends and we were shipwrecked just off Sark. A fisherman rescued me from the sea and took me ashore, where you found me, and being an upstanding English gentleman, you immediately offered your protection and assistance in returning me home," she said.

Cosimo gave an appreciative whistle. "What a fertile imagination you have," he said. "But I doubt there are too many pleasure sailors in the Channel at the moment."

"It doesn't matter," Meg stated flatly. "It will serve. I'd like you to signal them, please."

"Very well." He beckoned to Frank. "Ask them to heave to."

"Aye, sir." Frank went to work with his flags. "They want to know why, sir," he called back after a minute. "They're in a hurry."

Cosimo glanced at Meg, one eyebrow raised. "Are you certain you're willing to interrupt the urgent mission of a ship of the line in wartime?"

Meg turned away and went below. She knew she couldn't do that simply to get out of a predicament of her own making.

Cosimo waited until she'd disappeared down the steps to the mid-deck and then said to Frank, "Signal that we're under orders to sail for Bordeaux." That should be enough information to ensure that the commander wouldn't expect the *Mary Rose* to join them in their present enterprise.

"They say *bon voyage*, sir," Frank called out, but his captain had already read the signal and had turned away.

In the cabin, Meg sat on the window seat, her knees drawn up to her chest, and watched the great vessel sail with serene implacability into the now setting sun. She realized now that it was foolish to expect salvation from a naval ship. They would all be engaged in the vital pursuit of war. The chances of running up against a vessel that was returning to England were remote, and only such a ship would agree to take on a passenger.

A heavy sigh escaped her. She would have to resign herself to going all the way to Bordeaux, where she would have to find a commercial vessel. There would surely be one. There *had* to be one. Bordeaux was one of the great trading posts, even in wartime.

She wished she didn't feel so low. It was unlike her to get depressed about anything, but nothing seemed right, not even her decision to abandon the privateer and his ship. It was an instinctive decision, a need to run away from a situation she couldn't control. The problem was that deep down she didn't want to leave the *Mary Rose*. She wasn't ready to give up this passionate liaison with a man whose simple presence, let alone his touch, thrilled her to her core. And she wasn't ready to give up the exhilaration she had felt at being part of an adventure.

But her revulsion at that cold-blooded killing on the cliff top cast such a shadow over her soul that she couldn't see how she could possibly forget it sufficiently to continue with the idyll as if nothing had happened. Her own integrity would be compromised by condoning Cosimo's actions. Oh, it sounded pretentious and self-important, but it was true. Every fiber of her moral being was assaulted by the images of those crumpled bodies... images she couldn't imagine forgetting.

So there was nothing for it. She had to leave at the first opportunity.

Chapter 14

Meg stayed below as evening gave way to night. Biggins brought her supper and she ate with desultory appetite, wondering where Cosimo was having his supper. The weather had changed again and a damp drizzle was falling, so she assumed he was not eating on the quarterdeck. Perhaps he and Gus were supping with David in the surgeon's cabin. She would have welcomed Gus's company; keeping herself to herself was a lonely business.

Meg pushed her half-empty plate away and rose from the table. The cabin felt suddenly stuffy and confined and she realized she'd had no exercise all day. She wrapped herself in the thick cloak and left the cabin. Immediately she was struck by an eerie silence and complete darkness. Usually there were voices from on deck or from the galley down the corridor. Always there were the sounds of feet on the decks above as sailors went about the business of sailing the ship. But she could hear nothing except the creak of timbers and the slap of water against the hull. It was as if she were on a ghost ship. And why was it so dark?

Intrigued and a little alarmed, she felt her way to the companionway. And then realized why it was dark. The hatch above was closed so that not even the faintest of star or moonlight penetrated. Her heart jumped into her throat at the sudden fear of being entombed. Why had she been left down here on her own without a word of explanation?

She had of course insisted that she be left alone. Cosimo was taking her at her word, but he was taking it rather too far. She set foot on the stairs and reached up above her head to see if she could push open the hatch. It didn't move. She had seen them latch it closed in a storm, when the wind was really strong and the waves were sloshing across the decks, but there was no storm tonight. It was damp and inclement, certainly, but she'd never seen the hatches battened down for something as mild as a little rain.

Experimentally Meg knocked on the hatch and tried to push it up again. When nothing happened she knocked again, louder this time. And this time had results. The hatch was partially raised and the white face of Frank Fisher showed in the space. He mouthed a *hush* with an air of frantic urgency and Meg froze on the step. Then she tiptoed upwards and Frank lifted the hatch and held it open so that she could crawl out onto the deck.

She found herself in a world of gray wet fog, strands of it coiling around the mast and the deck rail. The silence was almost total, just the slap of waves against the hull. There was almost no wind and she could just make out the single foresail under which the *Mary Rose* sailed. As her eyes grew accustomed to the strange gray light, she made out the figures of men standing immobile against the rail and she could just see Cosimo at the helm, with Mike, as usual beside him. It was a ghost ship, she thought fancifully, manned by these still, silent figures.

Frank had his finger pressed urgently to his lips and she nodded her comprehension. She tiptoed across the mid-deck and up the steps to the quarterdeck. Heads turned towards her and she felt guilty that she was moving at all, but she was sure her feet made no sound as she crept across to the helm.

Cosimo was gazing into the wreathing fog ahead, his hands making minute adjustments to the wheel. He took his hand away from the helm for an instant and pressed his fingertips against Meg's mouth. As if she needed yet another warning, she reflected. It would have been an acid reflection except that it was very clear something very serious was going on.

She moved her head aside and he returned his hand to the wheel. The *Mary Rose* sailed onwards and then Meg heard voices coming out of the fog. She looked at Cosimo, a startled question in her eyes. His shoulders had tensed, but his hands on the wheel showed no strain. A tiny smile tilted the corners of his mouth and it was one Meg recognized. It was that Mephistophelean smile that indicated pure, wicked, gleeful triumph.

She strained to hear the voices and realized with an initial clutch of alarm that they were speaking French. She couldn't at first see where the voices were coming from and then just made out the dark shape of a ship about fifty yards away. And still the *Mary Rose* kept to her course, sliding over the smooth water under the faint breath of wind in her single sail.

And then a voice hailed them, booming out of the fog, and she guessed they were using a megaphone. It was a cheerful hail, the comment slightly ribald, the request for identification a mere formality. Not an eyelid twitched, not a muscle flickered as Cosimo called back in impeccable French. "*Bonsoir, copains. Nous sommes* l'Artemis, *en route à Belle Isle.*"

Meg looked towards the bows and saw that the *Mary Rose* was flying the tricolor. It seemed she'd been missing a fair degree of excitement skulking in the cabin. All her earlier pleasure in the adventure returned in full measure. There was nothing hole-in-the-corner, knives-in-the-darkness about this. They were in the middle of the enemy, practicing a monumental deception. And it thrilled her. Her eyes were shining as she listened to the French response. A casual *Bon voyage.*

Cosimo glanced at her and saw the sparkle in the lively green eyes. So all was not lost, he thought, his quiet smile deepening. He had not been mistaken, and Meg had most definitely been spinning a tale with her feeble-little-woman act. He could sense the energy coursing through her as powerfully as when they made love, and he had always believed that the vibrant pulse of danger was closely linked to the pulse of sexual passion. Once they were out of danger here, he would get to the bottom of whatever had caused her volte-face.

He took her arm and drew her in front of him so that she was facing the helm. In silence he put her hands on the wheel. She gave him one startled glance over her shoulder and then closed her fingers tightly over the smooth wood, feeling the ship beneath her feet. She watched the foresail, and when it fluttered, Cosimo put his hands over hers and adjusted the helm. After that had happened twice, she brushed his hand away the third time and made the adjustment herself. It was a little too far to port and the sail flapped. She swiftly brought it back again and the sail filled. His body was hard at her back, a strong reassuring presence, but Meg felt her own power in the way the *Mary Rose* responded to her hands. It was a heady power and in other circumstances she would have laughed with the sheer exuberance of it, but she was all too aware of the danger that lay around them, sinister dark shapes in the coiling gray fog.

And then the helm spun beneath her hands and she tensed her shoulders, forcing it back, but Cosimo had his hands on it now and she ducked beneath his arm and stood beside him once more. The fog was lifting as the wind got up and the foresail bellied. Cosimo gave no orders but his men needed none. The were scrambling up the ratlines, inching out on the footropes to hoist the mainsail.

The *Mary Rose* sailed out of the fog and into a clear starlit night without a ship in sight.

"What happened?" Meg asked, and then she looked behind her and saw a gray wall and understood. The fog hadn't lifted, they had simply sailed out of it.

"That's a notorious stretch of water for fog," Cosimo informed her. "It was ill luck that we happened to hit it at the same moment as a French convoy."

Meg shook her head in amused denial. "You enjoyed every minute of it, Cosimo."

He laughed softly. "I suppose I did. The idea of slipping through an entire enemy convoy of men-of-war without their being aware has its funny side."

For a moment it was as if their estrangement had never occurred.

"Take the helm, Mike. Hold steady on this course. With luck the trouble for the moment is behind us." Cosimo stepped away from the helm. He took Meg's elbow. "Let's go below."

Meg acquiesced. She had no idea how this situation would resolve itself, but she did know that somehow it had to. There had to be some way to maintain her own moral compass without giving up this adventure entirely. It would be so much simpler to sail back to England on the *Mary Rose*, according to the privateer's original plan. Pragmatic considerations in this case had to take precedence. She couldn't hang around the docks at Bordeaux trying to buy herself passage on a trading ship. It wasn't feasible and she knew it . . . had known it all along.

She didn't know why Cosimo had acted as he had on the cliff top. She'd just seen him steer his ship through an enemy convoy unscathed, and maybe she had to accept that this man was a warrior, fighting a war with unconventional weapons. If she could accept that, then she could manage to stay aboard his ship until they docked in Folkestone. And if making love with the privateer was necessary, then she would see it as payment for her passage.

She'd always wondered what it would feel like to be a whore. The caustic reflection was so far off course that she couldn't help smiling. The fact was quite simple. She was no more ready to give up this passionate adventure than she was to hazard her chances on the docks at Bordeaux. It was a happy concatenation of pragmatics and desire.

Cosimo paused at the cabin door. "I could do with cognac." He went off down the corridor towards the galley.

Meg went into the cabin, shrugged out of her cloak, and sat on the window seat. There was still no sign of Gus, which puzzled her. "Where's Gus?" she asked as Cosimo returned with a flask and glasses.

"Below in the sick bay with David. He hasn't understood the necessity for silence in certain conditions, and he speaks no French."

Meg laughed and took the glass he offered her. "Why didn't you tell me I was going to be battened down?"

"You'd made it fairly clear you wished to be left alone." He perched on the corner of the table and sipped his cognac. "And now I'd like you to explain to me why that was."

Meg swirled the golden liquid in her glass and watched the amber lights dance. What did she have to lose? She had no real choice but to stay on Cosimo's ship until they returned to Folkestone. If he was angry that she'd followed him and seen what she'd seen, so be it. Maybe he'd give her an explanation that would help redirect her moral compass.

Dear God, she was more of a hypocrite than she'd known. Bella would laugh her out of court.

"Why did you kill those men?" She kept her eyes on the contents of her glass.

Cosimo looked astonished. "What men?"

"The Frenchmen on the cliff top by the ruined building. They were just talking together and you came up behind them and killed them."

"I see." He pulled at his chin. "So you followed me again?"

"Yes."

It seemed Miss Barratt was incorrigible. He inhaled and blew out breath in a noisy exhale. "I'd like you to come here."

Meg frowned, hesitating. There didn't appear to be anything threatening in his tone or his posture. She got up and came over to him.

He stood up and said, "Turn around, please."

Meg did so. She felt his hand on her neck, then a slight pressure just in front of her ear. "If I press here, you will lose consciousness," he said in the level informative tone of a man giving a lecture to students. "Can you feel it?" He pressed harder.

Meg swallowed. Something strange was happening to her vision. "Stop it." Instantly the pressure was released.

"It's a very effective method of rendering an enemy *hors de combat*," he continued in the same tone. "Quite silent, and it leaves no marks. When the subject awakes he has no idea what happened to him."

"But you had a knife?" She turned slowly to face him, bewilderment in her eyes.

"Of course." It was a matter-of-fact statement. "I don't risk failure, my dear."

"So you didn't kill them?" she murmured.

"No. But they had killed two men, my friends, as they lay asleep. They slaughtered ten pigeons, took potshots at them while they were caged. You tell me, Meg, whether they deserved my mercy." And now an unpleasant note of derision had entered his voice and she thought that he was challenging her with the realities of this dirty world, this even dirtier war that he fought.

"But you didn't kill them," she repeated quietly.

"I don't kill for pleasure."

It was with an effort that she kept herself from looking at the locked drawer that held the array of knives. He must never know of that prying.

"So that was behind all this nonsense," he mused. "Well, I have to tell you, my dear, it won't wash. I watched you with the wheel, Meg, and you showed not a quiver of anxiety. So could we agree that you don't try to persuade me that you're some weak and feeble member of your sex who couldn't say boo to a goose? If you have concerns, then do me the courtesy of confronting me with them."

There was nothing unreasonable in that. Meg said, "Agreed."

"Good. And could it also be agreed that when I strongly suggest that you do something...stay somewhere...that you will give it your every consideration?" His eyebrows flickered, his query was lightly put, but Meg was in no doubt as to its gravity.

"Have no fear, Cosimo. I'll be staying well clear of any of your extracurricular activities between here and Folkestone," she said with heartfelt conviction. "I'm here only for my passage home, and any extra benefits that passage might afford, of course." She came up to him, putting her hands on his shoulders. "Do you have any requests, sir?"

There was time aplenty for molding. No need to taint a reconciliation with premature disclosure. He kissed her, murmuring, "Well, there was one thing."

Chapter 15

*B*eggin' yer pardon, sir, but I don't think as how it's a good idea, " the boatswain stated bluntly. "Not with the sea as foul as it is...and ye'll have no one to watch your back."

"I appreciate your concern, Bosun, but I'm going in alone," Cosimo returned, his voice pleasant and even, but Meg, from her position behind the half-open door to the cabin, could hear the implacable note.

Obviously the boatswain did too. He said, "Right y'are, sir. I'll have the dinghy made ready." There was a pause, and then he said, "You won't even take one of them young-sters? Rowing the dinghy single-handed in this sea won't be easy."

"No, it's not necessary. We'll take the ship in as close to the beach as possible, and I'll go in from there. You'll hold the ship for twenty-four hours, and if I don't return by then, you'll sail back to Folkestone with Miss Barratt."

"Only twenty-four hours, sir?" The boatswain sounded aghast.

"Precisely twenty-four hours. And then you take Miss Barratt home."

"Aye, sir."

Meg ducked back into the cabin. She'd been about to leave it when she'd heard Cosimo and the boatswain talking at the base of the companionway and something had kept her listening from behind the half-open door. She knew Cosimo was going to make one more shore excursion on the way to Bordeaux, but he hadn't said anything more about it. It seemed that now was the moment. But the boatswain was right, the sea was in a foul temper, and rain was sheeting down from a black moonless sky. Why did it have to be tonight? And surely the crew would resent her if they had to obey their captain's orders and abandon him just to take an unorthodox passenger back to England.

Cosimo came in looking distracted and went immediately to the charts. "So you're going ashore?" Meg said to his back.

"Mmm."

"Tonight?"

"That's right."

"But the weather's foul."

"Can't be helped."

"Bosun doesn't seem to think it's a good idea."

He straightened and turned around. "Now, how do you know that?"

"I was eavesdropping," she confessed. "Just now. I heard you talking. And if the bosun doesn't think it's a good idea, I think you should listen to him."

"Do you, indeed?" He quirked an eyebrow and looked amused.

"It's not funny," Meg said, refusing to be deterred. "Where are you going and why must it be tonight?"

Cosimo scratched his forehead, saying patiently, "I'm going ashore to check for messages. And it has to be tonight because we're just off La Rochelle and that's where I will find such messages." He opened one of the cupboards and took out a black oilskin. "Stay snug and dry while I'm gone."

"And what if you don't come back?" She regarded him steadily.

"Then the boatswain has instructions to sail you home to Folkestone."

"So I heard. And that means abandoning you without knowing what's happened to you. I don't want to be responsible for that."

"My dear, I and only I am responsible for the decisions I make." His tone was crisper now as he dressed in the black oilskin. "My men will follow my instructions without question."

"Yes, I'm sure they will," she said impatiently, "but that doesn't mean I have to. I don't want to sail back home without knowing what's happened to you."

His expression hardened. "Nevertheless, Meg, that's what you will do."

She had no idea why she said what she next said. It went against the firm decision she'd made after the debacle at Quiberon that the privateer's murky business was his own and she wanted no further part of it. But the words spoke themselves. "Why don't I come with you? I'm sure I could be useful. At the very least, I could get a message back to the ship if there was trouble."

She paused, watching him closely for some reaction, and when he didn't immediately answer her, said swiftly, "Ana would have accompanied you, wouldn't she? You would have trusted her."

"Ana was trained," he said. "I could trust her because she knew what she was doing."

"Then train me," Meg said simply. "You tell me what to do and I'll do it." She came up to him, putting a persuasive hand on his arm. "I'm not afraid, Cosimo. And I would much rather be in trouble with you than waiting and worrying, twiddling my thumbs here."

It seemed that Meg was writing her own part in this script, Cosimo thought, without any prodding from him. She was offering herself as a partner of her own accord. And maybe it was a good opportunity to observe her courage and resolve. He didn't expect to run into any trouble on this mission, merely the discomfort and difficulty involved in getting to shore in a gale. If she was willing to put up with that, then why not?

"I'm sure Ana has one of those oilskins hidden around here somewhere," Meg said, seizing on his clear hesitation.

"In that cupboard." He gestured with a jerk of his head to the cupboard from which he'd taken his own foul-weather gear. "It's going to be a very uncomfortable journey, I warn you."

"I'm well aware of that," she returned, shaking out the oilskin. "And I won't melt in a little rain." She struggled into the stiff garment and fumbled with the buttons. "Are we ready?"

Cosimo moved her hands aside and did up the buttons himself, then lifted the hood and secured it tightly beneath her chin with the drawstring. "Now you are."

They emerged on deck into the driving rain. The men were all clad in foul-weather gear; Mike was wrestling with the helm as the *Mary Rose* pitched into the troughs between the heavy swells. "I don't know how close I can put her in this sea, sir," Mike shouted, the wind snatching his words.

Cosimo jumped up to the quarterdeck. "Let me have the helm." He took the wheel and swung the ship onto a port tack, so that she was sailing broadside to the waves. It looked to Meg as if they were now heading straight for the cliff face that loomed out of the darkness. A bell boomed mournfully from somewhere to their right.

Rocks. Meg began to doubt her earlier confident assertion that she was not afraid. Images of shipwrecks crowded her mind, and when she looked down at the churning black sea beating against the sides of the ship, the prospect of being in a small dinghy bobbing on that heaving mass made her feel sick. It wasn't too late to back out. Her pride could stand it.

The *Mary Rose* was within a few hundred yards of the cliff face when Cosimo turned her into the wind and gave order to lower sail and drop anchor. He came over to Meg and said, "Now's the time to change your mind, Meg. It's quite understandable."

"But you're still going?" She was watching them lower the dinghy into the water.

He nodded. "Of course."

"Then so am I."

He scrutinized her expression closely, a frown between his brows, and she met his gaze without flinching. Finally he nodded again. "Very well. I'll go down the ladder first; follow me when I tell you."

She swallowed hard, thinking of that swaying rope ladder that was now lashing in the wind against the sides of the ship. She must be out of her mind, she reflected. Adventures were all very well, but this one seemed to be getting out of hand. It bore no resemblance at all to her illicit adventure with the gondolier in Venice. There weren't any waves on the Grand Canal, for a start. She stared down at the little boat as Cosimo went nimbly down the ladder. He jumped into the boat and steadied the ladder with his hand.

"Come on, Meg."

She sucked in her lower lip, then accepted Miles's help to climb over the rail. He was holding the ladder steady at the top, and Cosimo was doing the same below, so the descent was much less alarming than she'd expected. She sat down promptly, much more experienced now. The little dinghy rocked on the waves and she looked rather longingly up the towering sides of the *Mary Rose* to a deck that from this perspective seemed remarkably stable.

Cosimo had the oars and was pulling strongly towards the cliff face, fighting the wind and the sea, the sheer physical effort clear on his rain-drenched face. Meg wished she could help but knew she couldn't.

"Why wouldn't you let one of your men help you?" she yelled into the wind.

He didn't reply and she realized that he probably didn't have the breath to answer what was, after all, a thoroughly pointless question. The roar of the waves on the rocks at the cliff face drowned out all other sounds and her fingers curled around the edge of the thwart where she sat, her heart thudding with pure terror.

"Meg, grab the painter," he shouted. "When I beach the boat, I need you to jump out with the rope and pull me farther into the shallows."

She nodded and took up the painter, turning to face the bow. Having something to do calmed her somewhat. The sea was a little quieter now, the roaring somewhat abated, and she could just make out a faint white band in the darkness. Presumably the beach. The dinghy scraped bottom and at Cosimo's shouted "Now," she jumped into the water, shocked at how the cold struck even through her boots. She hauled on the boat and dragged it a few yards until it ground to a complete halt on the sand.

Cosimo jumped out, took the painter from her, and secured it around a rock. "The one advantage with a night like this is that no one will be out and about, and certainly not expecting visitors," he observed, sounding remarkably satisfied. "Do you want to wait by the boat?"

"Hell, no," Meg said vigorously. "Where you go, Captain Cosimo, I go. I'm not standing here soaking wet waiting for you."

"It's a tough climb," he said, gesturing to the cliff ahead of them. "The path's a mere goat track and it'll be slippery."

"I'm not waiting here," she reiterated.

"All right. Get climbing." He propelled her ahead of him across the tiny expanse of beach. She could just make out a thin ribbon of a path that wound between jutting rocks.

"I'll be behind you," he said, giving her bottom an encouraging slap. "If you slip, I'll try to catch you."

"Well, thank you, how reassuring," she said sardonically, and set off up the trail.

Cosimo smiled. She was doing well. He had sensed her earlier fear and had guessed what it had cost her to overcome it. If he could rely on her courage, all he had to worry about was overcoming her scruples. And that would be no easy task, judging by her reaction when she thought he'd killed the men at Quiberon. But that was a problem that would come up in its own good time; for the moment, he would concentrate on honing the skills she would need to survive an overland journey across enemy territory.

Meg climbed steadily, recovering her balance easily when her foot slipped. The knowledge of Cosimo behind her made her feel safer, and when she reached a particularly tricky bend in the path she was happy to have his guiding hand on her foot, directing her next step up. Finally they reached the cliff head and she hauled herself over onto wet grass and lay gasping for breath as the rain beat down into her face.

Cosimo came up after her. "Catch your breath," he whispered. "There's no hurry."

"If I'd known I had to turn mountain goat, I might have rethought this," she whispered back, but not seriously. She rolled onto her belly and looked down the path. It was hard to imagine she'd just climbed all that way, and even harder to imagine going back down it.

Cosimo squatted on his haunches beside her until she pulled herself up and stood up. "Where to now?" she asked.

"A cottage, about two miles away," he said. "Keep close behind me and do everything I do. Is that clear?"

"As a bell." She was cold but suppressed a shiver and started off after him across the cliff top. Meg didn't know how long they walked in silence in the teeth of the howling wind. She was fairly certain she had never been so physically miserable before, but took the phlegmatic view that since she'd brought it all upon herself she had no grounds for complaint.

The cottage appeared suddenly in the darkness. A low stone building, a trickle of smoke coming from the chimney, but no lights in the windows. Cosimo stopped in the shelter of the hedge. "Stay here. Don't move a muscle until I come back. Do you understand?"

"What if you don't... come back, I mean?"

"Go back to the beach. There's a whistle in the boat. Use it and someone will come from the *Mary Rose* to fetch you." He spoke in a terse whisper. "From now on I'm not going to think about you. I have my own work to do and I can't afford any distractions. You're on your own. Is that clear?"

"I don't expect any consideration," she snapped, stung by his tone. There was nothing remotely loverlike about this Cosimo. She wondered where his knives were concealed. She had no doubt that he had them somewhere about his person.

He slipped away along the hedge, just another black shadow among many, and within minutes was no longer visible to Meg. She shivered, too cold now for alarm, and despite his instructions started off after him. He wasn't going to think about her, that was fine by her. It freed her to follow her instincts.

The hedge encircled a small garden at the rear of the cottage and Meg heard the soft cooing of pigeons as she crept closer. It reassured her. Cosimo dealt in courier pigeon and dispatches; he was here to pick up messages. Of course there would be pigeons. Also they were alive, unlike the ones at Quiberon, which ought to mean that there would be no nasty surprises.

She wormed her way through the hedge into the garden and then heard the sound of voices. One was Cosimo's. Swiftly she backed her way through the hedge again, and listened. Another voice spoke in guttural French and then they went into the pigeon shed.

Meg slipped back along the hedge towards the front of

the cottage. The wind, it seemed, was dropping, the rain easing. She froze, listening to the sound of galloping hoof-beats along the road that led away from the sea. They were close and coming closer.

She didn't stop to think any further but flew back to the rear garden. Lamplight came from the shed and she burst in, slamming the door at her back. "Someone's coming, Cosimo. Horses...fast..."

Cosimo held a piece of paper in his hand; the man with him was short and stocky and held a pigeon in his palm, caressing its iridescent breast with a fingertip. The two men exchanged one quick glance, then the man extinguished the lamp before opening the pigeon cage to release the birds, shooing them out into the garden with soft encouraging words. Cosimo grabbed Meg's hand and dragged her outside. "The privy," he said, and pushed her unceremoniously into the noxious darkness of the outhouse.

Voices sounded, harsh and demanding. Someone banged and kicked at the cottage door. Meg could make out the flicker of torches through the cracks in the privy door, moving now towards the empty pigeon shed.

Cosimo held Meg against him, his hand over her mouth, as if she needed the reminder to keep silent. Not even Cosimo with his armory of knives could deal with these invaders.

An outraged shout came from the cottage, a stream of angry voices. Meg recognized the voice of the man who had been with Cosimo in the shed. He was yelling furiously, clearly giving as good as he was getting. She could make out protestations of innocence, a simple farmer taking care of his own land and minding his own business, demands to know what they thought they were doing, disturbing respectable folk in the middle of a godforsaken night. She peered up at Cosimo in the dim light and saw a faint smile on his lips, which struck her as somewhat inappropriate in the circumstances. At any moment the privy door could burst open and they'd be confronted by a phalanx of armed men while they cowered in these less-than-salubrious surroundings.

Cosimo glanced up over the bench with its three holes and pointed at the small round aperture that offered some kind of ventilation. "Up," he mouthed, jerking an imperative thumb.

Meg hesitated, wondering how he was going to get through such a small space, but then he gripped her shoulders and gave her a hard shake. He was no longer smiling. She stepped up onto the bench and he seized her around the knees and hoisted her the few inches necessary for her to get her head and shoulders out of the window. She hung there for a second, listening. The noise was still coming from the cottage but from here all she could see was a cabbage patch. She wriggled through with a helping push from behind and dropped to the soft wet earth beneath. But how was Cosimo going to get out?

Knife his way out? No, that was ridiculous. But she reasoned that it would be easier for one person to slip out unnoticed than for two. Particularly if the one person was as skilled at this business as Cosimo...she wouldn't put it past him to make himself invisible.

Before she had time to castigate herself for a misplaced humor that seemed to be catching, Cosimo was suddenly beside her. He didn't speak, merely took her hand and pulled her after him towards the hedge. She could smell the midden and wondered somewhat hysterically if they were going to bury themselves in dung until the danger had passed. Fortunately they skirted the midden and Cosimo jumped into a deep ditch, pulling her with him.

He lay down, dragging her on top of him, then reached up and tore weeds out of the ground to cover them. Then he held her tight and they lay in immobile silence as the chaos raged above them. Meg could feel his heart beating beneath her own. She could smell the sweat and rain on his skin; the stubble of his nighttime beard was rough against her cheek, but she felt his lips caressing her ear in what she knew was a deliberate kiss, and his hand moved down her back to rest on her bottom, cupping the curve against him. To her astonishment she felt his penis harden beneath her, and she buried her face in his shoulder to stifle her laughter. They were lying covered in weeds in a filthy wet ditch in a gale, the enemy rampaging around them, and Cosimo was capable of arousal.

As was she. Her body, cold and soaked though it was, was alive with lust. She moved slightly against him, lifting her head a little, trying to see his expression, but it was too dark to see anything but the gleam in his eyes. Then his hand tightened on her backside without any lustful intention and his body was still as stone. She could feel that his breathing had almost stopped.

Voices came from above. Feet trampled along the edge of the ditch. Torchlight flickered through the rain. And Meg, too, held her breath. Then she heard someone say, "*Allons-y*," and the feet and the torchlight faded away.

Cosimo began to breathe again, slowly and rhythmically, but he continued to lie still, holding her against him, enjoining her silence and immobility for what seemed an incredibly long time. Finally he stirred, reaching up to push aside the cover of weeds. "Get up carefully," he whispered against her ear. "Just in case."

Meg lifted her head above the ditch. The garden was in darkness, the rain still fell, but not as fiercely as before, the cottage was dark, the pigeon shed equally. And she could hear the faint sound of receding hoofbeats. "I think they've gone." She hitched herself out of the ditch and got to her feet, shivering uncontrollably. Whether with simple cold or aftermath, she didn't know and assumed it didn't much matter. Either way, lust forgotten, she was miserable as sin.

Cosimo stood beside her, listening. There was no sound but the wind and the rain. He started off along the hedge and Meg followed. She remembered little about the walk back to the cliff head, keeping her head down, watching her boots squelching through the soggy grass as if they belonged to someone else.

At the top of the path, Cosimo said, "This time I'll go first." If he was aware of her misery, he offered no comforting concern, which, Meg thought, was exactly as he said it would be. She was in this situation because she had chosen to be so, and the consequences were hers to bear.

She began the trek down the goat track, watching her step, clinging to the scrubby plants that lined the path. Below, the roar of the waves, the crash of the surf, grew louder. She stopped to look for the lights of the *Mary Rose*, but there was no sign of them. Of course the ship would be in darkness, anchored so close off the enemy coast. It would have been nice though to have seen just a twinkle from the yardarm.

Eventually they reached the beach and she drew a deep breath, her lungs aching, as she turned to look back up the cliff.

"Not an easy climb," Cosimo said calmly. "You should be proud of yourself."

"I am," Meg returned. "Is the *Mary Rose* still out there?"

He laughed softly. "Of course." He walked across the sand to the dinghy. "Get in and I'll push us off."

Once they were floating free he said, "Under the thwart you'll find a pouch with a whistle. Blow three long and one short, and then repeat."

"I feel like a genuine spy," Meg observed, feeling for the pouch. "Hiding in privies and ditches and signaling ships." She blew on the whistle as instructed and they were rewarded almost immediately by a signaling light in the darkness.

Cosimo pulled strongly towards the light that gradually threw a guiding pathway over the black sea. Miles was clinging one-handed to the bottom of the rope ladder as they came up alongside, and grabbed the painter from Meg, pulling the dinghy close in. He jumped into the dinghy and helped Meg onto the ladder. She climbed rapidly upwards, aware that she was using the last dregs of strength as she toppled over the railing onto the deck.

It was David who helped her to her feet. "Dear God, what madness to go out in a night like this. What were you thinking, Cosimo? The poor woman's a drowned rat."

"There's nothing of the poor woman about her," Cosimo declared as he swung onto the deck beside them. He seemed enviably unaffected by the events of the night. "She's as strong as a horse...Meg, go below," he continued in the same brusque manner. "Biggins, hot water *now*. And tell Silas to make hot grog and bring it to the cabin. Come, Meg, don't just stand there. David, if you want to send some prophylactic against chills to my cabin, feel free to do so."

Meg didn't resist the helping hand that propelled her towards the companionway. The cabin was lit by a lamp, its wick turned down low. There was no sign of Gus, and Meg assumed the gregarious bird had sought company elsewhere.

"Stand still. Let me unfasten the oilskin." Cosimo was now all consideration, undoing the wet, stiff buttons and pulling the garment off her. "God, you're soaked," he muttered. "You'll be lucky not to get a chill on the lungs."

"You're just as wet," Meg retorted through chattering teeth, and he shook his head with a tiny laugh.

"I'm a little more accustomed to it, my dear Meg." He was undressing her as he spoke, and didn't stop when the door opened to admit Biggins with jugs of hot water. "Fill the bath, Biggins."

"Aye, sir."

Meg was too cold to care who saw her at this stage. Her skin was a mass of pimply goose bumps, like a plucked chicken, and her breasts seemed to have shrunk to the size of walnuts. Cosimo passed her the paisley shawl and she wrapped herself up while Biggins continued to fill the tub.

"Get out of your own clothes," she insisted to the privateer when he'd made no attempt even to divest himself of the oilskin.

"Get into the hot water and then I will." He pointed towards the head. "There should be enough to be going on with and I'll pour in more when Biggins brings it."

Meg didn't argue. She slid beneath the water and felt the convulsive shivering ease. Cosimo came in naked with two more jugs and poured them over her. "Move up a little, I have to get in."

She scrunched up to the end as he stepped carefully in opposite her, and then he slid down, shoving his icy feet beneath her backside as he dipped his head beneath the hot water.

"That's better," he muttered, coming up for air. "How about you?"

"Getting better," she said, wriggling against his feet in an effort to warm them up. "Did you get the message you went for?"

He squinted a little through the drops of water that clung to his eyelashes. "Yes."

"So it was worth it?" Meg splashed water on her shoulders as her body chilled.

"It was. And now you need to get out and get dry."

"Was it a message from Ana?" Meg asked, standing up in a shower of drops. "Am I entitled to ask that?"

Cosimo dipped below the water again. He had no desire to tell her anything about the message, anything at all about Ana, not until he'd absorbed all the implications and come to terms with his own emotions. They were too raw at present to be explored, and he certainly didn't want to do it in company. And yet Meg *was* entitled to something, and more to the point, he suspected that if he didn't attempt to satisfy her curiosity, she would go on digging. Better to cut her off at the pass. When he raised his head he said, "Yes, it was."

"Did I do as well as Ana would have?" She wrapped herself in a towel as she asked a question that she didn't know why she was asking. Why did she feel in some kind of competition with this unknown woman?

Trust Meg to go straight to the heart of the matter. She was unfailingly straightforward. "Ana shouldn't concern you," he said dismissively, reaching for a towel as he stood up, hoping that would be the end of it.

"She doesn't," Meg said. "She interests me. They're two

very different things." She walked back into the cabin, toweling her hair and wondering whether they really were.

Cosimo dried himself and followed her into the cabin. Biggins had set a steaming jug of hot spiced rum on the table with two beakers, and the privateer poured the fragrant grog and handed Meg a beaker. "Are you hungry?"

She considered this as she cupped her hands around the comforting heat of the mug. "I don't think so." She took an appreciative sip and then set down the beaker and went to get her nightgown. Once more decently clad, and warmly wrapped in the paisley shawl, she took up the mug again. "So, what did the message say?"

Cosimo, dressed again in shirt and britches, accepted that delaying tactics were getting him nowhere. "You know that I've been trying to discover what happened to Ana in Folkestone." He chose his words carefully; there was much he had no intention of telling her, but he needed to give her just enough to satisfy her. "I was hoping for a message at Quiberon. When that didn't come, La Rochelle was the last opportunity before Bordeaux."

"So Ana is a spy, or whatever it is you are?"

"Among other things," he said evasively. "Anyway, I discovered tonight that she is now safe and well. So there you have it."

"So she told you what had happened in the message?"

The message had not been from Ana, but from one of his agents. They had found Ana and sprung her loose, but she was far from well. The message had been terse, as it had to be, but Cosimo had had no difficulty reading between the lines. The French had not been gentle with her. She had certainly been forced to give up the location of the outpost at Quiberon and he wondered if the raid tonight had been the result of interrogation. It was highly likely. The only saving grace was that Ana had not known the details of their mission. She had known they would make landfall at Brest and would be making an overland journey, and that much she would have been compelled to reveal, but as was customary she would not have known the detailed object of the endeavor until she was safely aboard. So, while she could have given away much that would endanger him and others, she could not have spilled the ultimate secret of his mission. They would be on the lookout for the *Mary Rose*, but he was leaving the ship at Bordeaux, something Ana had not known. The mission was still feasible.

Meg looked at him in puzzlement. He hadn't answered her question and he was clearly thinking deeply about something. Something unpleasant, judging by the hardness of his mouth and the coldness of his eyes. "So now your mind's at rest," she pressed.

"Yes," he said shortly. But his face said the opposite.

She could see that he considered the subject closed, but she couldn't help herself. "So what did happen to her? What delayed her?"

"I don't know exactly," he said in the same curt tone. "Messages by courier pigeon tend not to be detailed, as you can imagine. I only know she's safe."

"Well, that's good," Meg said. He wasn't telling her everything, she could feel the deception in the air. He was a smooth liar, but there was something that didn't sit quite right about this short, glib explanation that was no explanation at all. And she most definitely didn't like the look in his eye, the shadow that mingled with an anger that she had never seen before. She had encountered his frigid look, but that was not an angry look. In fact, Meg thought, she had believed the privateer when he'd said he didn't believe in anger, considered it a wasteful emotion. He'd never appeared more than determined and sometimes annoyed. He was coldly ruthless on occasion, but he never raised his voice, was never discourteous even when giving orders.

She felt a small frisson of fear. Ridiculous because that suppressed rage was not directed at her. But there was a power to it that made her fervently pray that she would never be the cause of it.

And then abruptly he smiled, a slow, lascivious smile that lit his eyes from behind and banished all shadows, any vestige of anger, as if they had never existed. "So, my love, it seems that danger excites you," he murmured, reaching for her, drawing her between his knees as he sat on the window seat. He held her hips lightly, pressing his thumbs into her hip bones. "Cold, wet, filthy, covered in weeds . . . you'd have made love in that ditch regardless of a rampaging army of enemy soldiers just waiting for something to move that they could plunge their bayonets into."

"You started it," she answered, running her hands over his head, twisting an auburn lock around her finger and tugging gently. "You were as hard as a rock."

"Well, I've never denied that for me danger and arousal are closely connected. I just hadn't guessed it would be the same for you." He bunched up the hem of her nightgown and began to ease it upwards inch by sensual inch.

If this was his way of closing a conversation, Meg reflected distractedly, it was certainly effective.

There came a sharp rap at the door and Cosimo swore under his breath. He let the nightgown drop again and called, "Who is it?"

"David."

He got up and went to open the door. Gus flew off

David's shoulder and onto his perch with a cheerful "G'day."

"Bad moment?" David inquired, reading Cosimo's impatient expression. "Forgive the intrusion but Gus was clamoring, and I brought this for Meg. Echinacea." He handed a small vial to Cosimo. "It's proven quite efficacious against chills."

"Thank you, David." Cosimo took the vial. "Good night, now."

"Good night... good night, Meg," David called over Cosimo's shoulder. "Take the echinacea before you go to sleep. Six drops in water."

Cosimo closed the door rather firmly on his departure and with the same firmness put Gus into his cage and dropped the cloth over it. A mournful "G'night" came from beneath the crimson covering and then there was silence.

"Now," Cosimo said, "where were we?"

"In a ditch, I believe," Meg responded, her eyes shining. "With a troop of soldiers with bayonets searching for us."

"Ah, yes." He reached for her hands and pulled her against him, pushing his hands up under her hair. "God, I want you." He kissed her mouth, his teeth nibbling her lip, and the surge of arousal flooded her loins, tightened her thighs.

There was no time now for the niceties. When he spun her to face the bed, she knew what he wanted and toppled forward, bracing herself on her hands. He threw her nightgown up over her head, then held her hips as he drove into her. She pushed back against his belly, reveling in each thrust that seemed to reach further to her core, to fill her with sensation. His nails scribbled down her spine, his fingers kneaded her backside, as she drew closer and closer to the edge, and when her knees finally buckled and she collapsed onto the cot as the joy became almost unbearable, he flipped her over and entered her again, his gaze, dark with passion, fixed upon her as if he would read her very soul.

And when finally he allowed his own climax to engulf him, Meg lay sweat-soaked and exhausted, unable to believe that such heights of passion could be scaled by one mortal woman.

Chapter 16

"What happens when we get to Bordeaux?" Meg asked sleepily, sensing Cosimo's approach across the sun-dappled deck.

"Ah, you're awake at last. I thought you were going to sleep the day away." He stood over her, his shadow blotting out the sunlight.

"The way *you* choose to spend the nights, the days are the only time I have to catch up on sleep," she retorted, squinting up at him. "Could you step out of my sun?"

He moved aside. "I wasn't aware the choice was only mine."

"Well, now, perhaps it isn't," she agreed with an indolent stretch as she lay full length on the deck.

She reminded Cosimo of a thoroughly self-satisfied, contented cat at that moment. He dropped down to the deck beside her, leaning his back against the rail. "So what was your question?"

"What happens when we get to Bordeaux?" she repeated, pillowing her head on his thighs. "I assume there'll be some rendezvous for handing over the dispatches. Is it to another ship, or somewhere on land? Is it in the town itself? Or somewhere outside?"

"Such a lot of questions," he said, his fingers trawling through the sun-fragrant red curls.

"Well, I'm curious. We're half a day's sail from Bordeaux, or so you said this morning. That's the end of your mission, then we go home. I'd like to know how it's going to work."

Cosimo still hadn't decided on the opportune moment to tell her they were not going back to England. "I can't risk the *Mary Rose* by sailing up the estuary to the harbor," he said. "Even if we disguise ourselves as a merchantman, the danger's still too great. So, I'll make a night landfall by dinghy as usual in a little fishing village just this side of the city. That's where I'll deliver the dispatches."

Dispatches that Meg still hadn't seen hide nor hair of, despite her clandestine but nonetheless thorough searches of the cabin. It had become something of an obsession with her. She'd already deduced that the various dictionaries were used for writing and breaking codes. The knives she preferred not to think about. But where were the dispatches? They weren't in the locked drawer and she could find no other safe. They could be somewhere else on the ship, of course. Maybe in David's cabin. She wasn't sufficiently obsessed to poke around there.

"Silas was saying something about supplies," she said. "Where will they get those?"

"Another village," he said casually. "There are those outside the towns who don't mind whom they sell to as long as the price is right."

"And how long do you think it will take us to sail back to Folkestone?"

"Maybe we won't go back to Folkestone," he said.

"Oh? Well, I suppose it doesn't much matter where we

land. I can always take a post chaise home. Only, I'm afraid you'll have to lend me the money." She sat up, and swiveled to face him, brushing the hair away from her eyes. "I didn't have much with me when I fell."

If he'd hoped to lead into a gentle discussion of the possibilities of continuing their journey awhile longer, it was a fond hope, Cosimo reflected. Meg was in no way obtuse, but she was so straightforward herself she didn't suspect a roundabout approach to any subject. He would have to wait for the right moment to spring his surprise without artifice.

"What's the matter?" she asked, leaning forward to rub the little line between his brows with a fingertip.

For answer he took her hand and sucked her finger into his mouth, and felt the quiver run through her, the way her body quickened with lust. Passion *was* an addiction, he thought as he had done once before. They were both enthralled by desire, by the slightest brush of a finger, the merest touch of skin. He could bring her to the brink of arousal by a raised eyebrow, and all Meg had to do was give him her narrow-eyed look, touch her tongue to her lips, and he was lost.

It would serve him well in this greater purpose, but for some reason the knowledge didn't please him as much as it should. He found it faintly distasteful to be considering the openness of Meg's sexual passions as a means to an end. Which was a novel feeling. In his past relations, such a benefit outweighed everything. His own lust was easily subsumed into the greater purpose. His world was dangerous and unstable and there was no room in it for emotion or dependency, mutual or otherwise. And yet he knew he could not bear to hurt this woman who gave herself with such uninhibited delight, and whose passion fired his own beyond anything he had previously experienced. But he was deceiving her, and he intended to go on doing so for as long as necessary. So where did that leave him and his scruples?

"You're thinking too much," Meg said with a soft laugh. "I don't find it flattering to play second fiddle to thoughts that aren't of the pleasantest, judging by your expression."

"Daytime intrusions," he said, turning her palm up and planting a kiss in the middle. "Forgotten now."

"Shall we go below?" Her sandy brows lifted in mischievous invitation. "We could be very quick."

He glanced around. The *Mary Rose* was sailing serenely on quiet waters. There was no sign of other shipping, hostile or otherwise. And Bordeaux and all the disruptive decisions that would have to made there were only a half day's sail. A wise man took the opportunities offered to him.

"Why not?" He stood up, reaching a hand down to pull her to her feet.

"Why won't you let me come with you this time?" Meg demanded, watching as Cosimo pulled his black cloak tightly around him. "It's a perfect night for a row ... unlike the last time."

"The person I'm meeting is expecting me to come alone." He bent to kiss her. "Wait up for me. I'll be back before midnight."

She followed him up onto the deck and stood at the rail in the moonlight as he climbed down into the dinghy, took up the oars, and began to pull towards the sandy cove about half a mile away. She'd been following him around like a dog all day and she still hadn't seen him take the dispatches from wherever they'd been hidden. She couldn't even see where he'd put them for the journey to shore. Dispatches had to be bulky, surely. But there were no bulging pockets in his britches, no lumps beneath his shirt. Nothing she could feel when she kissed him goodbye.

It was yet another puzzle. But when he came back to the ship his work here would be done. They would sail back to England with no more hazardous journeys ashore. There'd be all the perils of French shipping to navigate, but Meg had no fears on that score. She firmly believed the privateer could outsail any admiral of the French fleet. Probably of the Royal Navy, not excluding Admiral Nelson. But that article of faith she kept close to her chest.

She leaned her crossed forearms on the rail and gazed out towards the beach and the small shape of the dinghy. The adventure was all but over. It had to be. She had a world to go back to, not to mention consequences to face. She couldn't begin to imagine how to explain what she'd been doing to her mother, let alone her father. Arabella would help fabricate something, but it was still a daunting prospect. And that would be the end of adventuring. She would be an old maid of thirty, with limited financial prospects, no longer remotely interesting to the social world, even with the patronage of the duchess of St. Jules. If she were a widow, the situation would be brighter. A widow with a decent annuity, even brighter still. But she was just plain Miss Barratt with a sufficient competency to maintain a dignified single life in the country.

Except that she was *not* that person. How could she possibly settle for such a half-existence? She was a privateer's mistress. She knew depths of passion unthinkable to most of the women of her world. Arabella being the exception.

She felt truly alive as never before. And all that lay ahead was being buried alive in Kent.

She turned away from the rail and went below, suddenly too depressed to enjoy the soft night air.

Cosimo took a path from the beach into the tiny village of St. Aubin. He knew it of old. Before the war he had run a healthy smuggling trade in fine wine from the vineyards of Bordeaux to the beaches of Cornwall, and despite changed circumstances he was still welcomed by the occupants of the Lion d'Or as an old friend.

"*Eh, bonsoir, mon capitaine,*" the bartender called, opening the tap on a casket of wine and filling a glass. He set it on the counter. "*Comment ça va?*"

"*Bien, merci, Henri, et vous?*" Cosimo raised the glass in an appreciative toast.

The old man shrugged an affirmative that was not quite convincing. Then spat into the sawdust at his feet. Cosimo nodded his comprehension, and when the door banged open a few minutes later to admit two members of the gendarmerie, he understood even more as he watched his old friend supply them with the best of his cellar with no hope of payment.

He stayed, however, offering monosyllabic responses to the policemen's questions, before offering to buy them cognac, signaling to Henri for the best he had. It worked magic as it always did as they began to talk under the influence of the fine spirit. He learned that patrols had been stepped up in the hills, that Napoleon was going to conquer the world...something he fervently hoped would prove incorrect...and that the port of Bordeaux was now closed to all foreign shipping.

After an hour he threw money on the counter, offered a wave of farewell, and left the tavern, his step just a trifle unsteady. He heard derisive laughter behind him and a contemptuous smile flickered across his mouth.

He reached the *Mary Rose* without incident a little before midnight. Climbed onto the deck, gave orders that they should take the ship out of sight of land, and went below.

Meg was curled up on the window seat, still reading Mrs. Radcliff's *The Italian*. She didn't think she'd ever taken so long to get through a book, and had a moment of regret for the long line of eager ladies waiting for its return to Mrs. Carson's lending library. She jumped up as Cosimo came in and Gus announced, "G'day," swooping from the window seat onto Cosimo's shoulder.

Meg looked him over carefully. He seemed the same as always. "You're back," she said, stating the obvious. "Did everything go well?"

He shook his head as he discarded his cloak. "No," he said.

"Why? What happened?" Concerned, she came over to him. "Are you hurt, Cosimo?" Alarm edged the question.

He shook his head again. "No...no...not a scratch. *I'm* fine."

Meg stepped back a pace. "So who isn't?" She watched his expression.

"The courier didn't appear," he said flatly. "I can only assume something happened to prevent him."

Meg frowned. "Will you try again tomorrow?"

"No, I can't risk it. It's an absolute rule. If a meeting fails, we don't try it again."

"Oh." That made sense in the strange world that Cosimo inhabited. "What will you do?"

"They're vital dispatches," he said.

"Where are they?" Meg asked. "May I see them?"

For answer he unbuttoned his shirt. Tucked snugly beneath his armpit was a tightly folded packet of paper. "Why would you wish to see them?"

And now she felt stupid for her doubts. "No real reason, of course. But what are you going to do with them? Is there someone else who can take them?"

"No." He unfastened the thin leather strap that held the papers in place and took them out, setting them on the chart table. "We work in exclusive circles. It's the only way to keep information safe. This circle is now closed."

"But if they're vital?" Meg wondered why she was pursuing this when she knew perfectly well that he was going to take the dispatches himself. Wherever their final destination was.

He pursed his lips. "You know what I'm going to say."

"Yes. Where do they have to go?"

"Toulon."

Meg's eyes widened. "But that's on the Mediterranean. It's the other side of France. You'll have to sail around Spain, through the Strait of Gibraltar."

"Your geography is impeccable, my dear," he said, regarding her with a smile that was both questioning and rueful. "As it happens, I don't intend to sail."

"Go overland?" She tried to envisage the map in her mind. Such a trek across the center of France in the middle of a war, with sensitive dispatches... "Sweet heaven," she murmured.

"Come with me."

For a moment she was breathless. She looked at him dumbstruck as the prospect of such a journey, such an adventure at the side of the privateer, took shape, the map of

France opening up in her mind's eye. She took a deep, slow breath and asked simply, "How will I get back?"

"The *Mary Rose* will sail into the Mediterranean to meet us. It will take her perhaps two weeks longer than it will take us." He kept his voice calmly matter-of-fact, as if what he was suggesting was a simple and perfectly reasonable, logical adaptation to changed circumstances.

"Will I ever get home?" Meg murmured more to herself than to Cosimo. She wasn't so far lost in the joys of passionate adventuring as to be completely unaware of the very real possibility that such a journey could end in disaster. What would happen if the *Mary Rose* was lost at sea, sunk by a French vessel, leaving them stranded in the center of a French port on the Mediterranean? What would she do if something happened to Cosimo on the overland journey? There were no guarantees, despite the privateer's cool confidence.

But did it really matter? She'd already spent a bleak quarter of an hour contemplating what awaited her when she got home. Was there any reason to hurry that future? She had never been averse to taking risks, quite the opposite. Although this was a risk of such magnitude it required at least a few minutes of thought.

Meg decided she'd devoted sufficient time to thinking. "When do we leave?" she asked.

Cosimo's smile hid his relief. He was only just realizing how worried he'd been about her response. He didn't doubt her courage, but he still didn't know her well enough to be certain she would cast aside her own world as completely as he was asking her to. They would get back to England eventually, but he had no idea when. In agreeing to accompany him to Toulon, she was accepting the fact that her life would never be the same again. He was sure that she had come to terms with that in those long few minutes before she'd agreed, but nevertheless some inconvenient prick of conscience obliged him to be certain.

"Are you quite sure you know what this means?" he asked, taking her hands and drawing her close to him. "We will get back to England eventually, but I can't promise when."

"I understand that," Meg said. "But at the moment I don't have anything to go back for. I would like to write one more letter, though, just to prepare my family for a long time without any communication from me. I don't want them to think I'm dead before I am."

"That can be arranged." He kissed the corner of her mouth. "You are a delightfully unusual woman, Meg Barratt."

"As unusual as Ana?" She raised a quizzical eyebrow to show that the question was not really serious.

"In different ways," he replied. He frowned slightly. "Tell me, Meg, why do you keep bringing Ana up? Does something trouble you about her?"

"As I said before, she interests me," Meg responded. "I'm assuming you were lovers as well as partners?"

He nodded. "Does that bother you?"

She looked astounded and Cosimo realized what a stupid and somewhat arrogant question it was. Meg's nature was far above such petty emotions as jealousy.

"Not in the least," she declared. "How could it?"

"Forgive me, I wasn't thinking straight," he said rather dryly. "But you haven't answered my question."

Meg pressed her finger into the cleft in her chin, trying to find the right words. "It's just rather strange... it feels peculiar, to be living someone else's life," she said slowly. "I look sufficiently like her to be mistaken for her, I wear

her clothes, sleep with her lover, go on her adventures...
her presence is somehow everywhere, and I seem to feel
the need to know all about her...to compare myself, my
actions, my responses."

Cosimo thought about this. It had never occurred to
him that she should have such a complex attitude to a situation that struck him as purely serendipitous. It puzzled
him a little, but then he reflected that women saw certain
issues in a very different light from men. Even Ana had
surprised him sometimes with the complexity of an emotional response. And Meg was much less hardened by life
than Ana had been.

But Ana's life, her secrets, were not his to tell. In fact, he
found talking about her intensely painful, knowing what
she had been through in the last weeks. "I don't compare
you," he stated flatly. "Not in any way, shape, or form."

That was hardly the point, Meg reflected. But perhaps
she couldn't expect him to understand. He was certainly
throwing up that wall again. Ana was off limits to any serious discussion.

A knock at the door broke the moment of rather awkward silence. "Y'are wanted on deck, Captain," Biggins
called.

"Right away." Cosimo released Meg's hands, putting his
own on her shoulders and kissing her again quickly. "I
can't tell you how happy you've made me," he said. "I
don't want to lose you, love."

She smiled. "I'm not ready to leave you either, Cosimo."

When he'd gone she went over to the chart table and
picked up the little packet of paper. Why were these dispatches so vital? Such a tiny parcel, small enough to be secreted under his arm. And they had to be taken all that
hazardous way to Toulon. Reasoning that he'd left them in

full view so she was hardly prying, she unfolded the three sheets. They made no sense, just line after line of unconnected letters and numbers.

Encrypted, of course. Her gaze flicked up to the shelf of dictionaries. It might be an interesting exercise to see if she could crack the code. She smoothed out the papers on the table with the flat of her hand and concentrated on the sequence of letters and numbers, looking for connections, regular repetitions, anything that would make some kind of sense. After a few minutes she reached down Dr. Johnson's dictionary. She turned the pages until she found one with notations in the margin. She read the various entries carefully, glancing at the coded sheets beside the book to see if anything jumped out at her.

She was so absorbed she didn't hear the door open and was totally unaware of Cosimo's presence as he stood in the open doorway watching her. Gus landed on the chart table next to Dr. Johnson and she turned with a start. "I didn't hear you come in."

"So I see." He closed the door and stepped farther into the cabin. "What are you doing?"

"I was trying to crack the code," she responded, trying not to sound guilty or apologetic. "You left these dispatches here, so I assumed you wouldn't mind."

"Mmm," he murmured, reaching over her shoulder to take up the pages. "Quite a big assumption, Meg." He folded them carefully and slipped them into the pocket of his britches, thankful that he'd had the foresight to provide something that could pass as the mythical dispatches. "But it was careless of me to leave them . . . Did you have any luck?" He had to hope that she hadn't, given that the sequences of letters and numbers were utterly meaningless.

"No," she said. "I'm hoping you'll teach me. Since I'm

coming with you to deliver them, what harm can it do if I learn how to read them?"

He shook his head. "A great deal of harm if you think about it." He was looking unusually grave.

Meg frowned. "You trust me to come with you. You trust me to know why you're making the journey. And that's as far as it goes? I don't understand, Cosimo."

"Then let me explain." His expression was still grave. "I'd rather hoped not to have to spell this out, but if I must, I must. If anything happens on this mission . . . if you fall into enemy hands, then what you don't know you can't reveal. Do you understand now?"

Meg did and her scalp crawled. She looked down at her hands, knitting her fingers together. She felt his hand warm on the back of her neck.

"Changed your mind?" he asked softly.

She raised her head, pressing back against the firm, warm clasp, and his fingers tightened with a reassuring strength. "No," she said. "Not for a minute."

He dropped his hand, bent, and kissed her neck. "Now, let's talk practicalities."

"Yes, when do we leave?" Meg was aware of relief. She didn't want to dwell on the dangers; she'd made up her mind and there was no virtue in looking for reasons to change it.

He held up a hand. "First things first. Do you ride?"

She stared at him incredulously. "Cosimo, I was born and bred in the country."

"I'll assume that's an affirmative," he said. "May I also assume that you ride well?"

"I was four years old when I first joined the hunt," she told him with a touch of asperity.

"Sweetheart, it may come as a surprise to you, but not

every horsewoman is comfortable with more than a gentle trot down the tan at Hyde Park."

"Well, you'll be pleased to know that I am."

He offered a smile of appeasement and held up his hands in surrender. "Enough said. Next question, at the expense of getting my head bitten off. How well do you speak French?"

Meg pondered the question. "My accent's not wonderful, at least nowhere near as authentic as yours, but I can hold my own in a conversation."

He nodded. "Then we'll have to find an identity that would explain a slightly foreign accent."

"Swiss, perhaps?"

"Even better, Scots," he said. "The French-Scots connection is still very strong and you could have spent time in France during your childhood with distant French relatives."

"Wasn't Mary, Queen of Scots, a redhead?" Meg inquired with a dry smile.

"I believe so, but her cousin Elizabeth certainly was," he returned.

"Useful discipline, history," Meg mused, a glimmer of laughter in her green eyes. "Particularly in the world of espionage."

"Be serious," he scolded. "We're not playing games, Meg."

She felt a prick of annoyance. "I know that. But we're still safe and sound on the *Mary Rose*. What's happened to your sense of humor?"

"It tends to go absent without leave when I'm planning a mission," Cosimo stated without apology. "It does return, though."

"Well, that's a relief," Meg said, sitting on the window

seat and folding her hands in her lap. "Very well, mine too has taken a holiday. So pray continue with the planning, sir."

There was something about the way she was sitting, the attentive cock of her head, the fixed attention of her gaze, that gave him pause. She was mocking him, still not aware of the seriousness of this. Ana would have been frowning in thought, putting forth objections, ideas, every ounce of her concentrating on the possibly life-saving minutiae of the mission. But Meg was approaching this as a light-hearted venture. Intellectually she knew the dangers, but she'd not yet really experienced them, so how could he expect her to second-guess them? He could lay them out for her in great detail, or he could ease her into them with a little practical experience. She would learn quickly, he was confident of that.

He let himself relax. "It's near dawn but I'm famished," he said. "Why don't you go to bed and I'll rummage in the galley."

Meg jumped up, declaring, "I couldn't possibly sleep. Besides, I'm ravenous too. And we need to discuss this some more. We know I can ride. We have a national identity that will explain my scratchy accent. But I have a host of questions and I need them answered tonight . . . or this morning, rather," she amended, glancing towards the window, where the night's darkness was giving way to a soft gray.

"Then let's go to the galley and see what we can find."

Meg went ahead of him down the corridor. Belowdecks the ship was asleep, but she was sailing under a full crew on deck. It occurred to Meg that she would miss this when they took to the land. The routines of shipboard life seemed to have seeped into her blood, which she thought now seemed to move with the rhythm of the sea. Her gait had certainly changed with the ever-moving decks beneath her feet. And her eyes had grown accustomed to distant horizons.

Cosimo lit the lantern in the galley and looked around the immaculate space. "Sausage," he said, reaching up for the salami on its hook.

"Bread," Meg said, opening the cupboard where Silas kept it. She took out a loaf of barley bread. "Knives ... Oh, yes, they're here."

Cosimo watched her with mingled amusement and amazement. Meg seemed totally at home in Silas's galley. Biggins was the only other person he knew to be welcome there. Silas as a rule guarded his empire with fierce scowls and monosyllabic mutterings.

"Cheese ... could you reach it, Cosimo? I'm not tall enough." She pointed upwards at the wheel of cheddar on a high shelf.

"With pleasure." He lifted it down.

"You'll find wine in that casket over by the washing tub." Meg pointed an authoritative finger. "Glasses in that cupboard ..."

"You seem remarkably familiar with Silas's galley," Cosimo observed, following instruction.

"I've been on this ship for close to two weeks," she informed him. "I don't expect to be waited on, so when I want something, I get it."

He chuckled, opening the tap on the casket and filling two glasses with wine. "Now, that's surprising. I would have expected Miss Barratt to be totally accustomed to being waited upon."

She sliced into the loaf of bread with a decisive cut. "Not by sailors with far more important work to do. Besides, I enjoyed getting to know them. Biggins is almost a friend, so long as I keep a respectful distance, of course." She smiled and sliced salami with the same brisk efficiency. "Will that do, *mon capitaine*?" She turned and curtsied deeply.

"You are an abominable woman," Cosimo declared, seizing her under the arms and hauling her upwards. "You make mock of everything."

"Not quite," Meg said, tilting her head back, offering her mouth. "Not quite everything."

He cupped her head against his linked hands. His eyes held hers. "Are you absolutely certain that this is what you want? Answer me straight, Meg. Think about what it means. *Really* think about it before you answer me, because I will not ask you again."

Her eyes were as serious as his as she said, "I could begin to be insulted, Cosimo, by this reiteration. I have said this is what I want. I *have* considered it carefully. The fact that I can make light of it at this moment takes nothing away from my conviction or my commitment. I will partner you. Now let's eat and discuss what else we have to do. I still don't know who I'm supposed to be as I gallop along beside you and speak Scots-French, tossing my red head to good effect—"

His mouth stopped the rest of her peroration and Meg yielded without a murmur. The carving knife that she'd forgotten she still held fell to the deck with a dull clang.

Cosimo stepped back, picked up the knife, and wiped it carefully on a rag before putting it back in the rack where it belonged. Meg was aware of the delicacy with which he handled it, the way his fingers held the hilt. It was a simple kitchen knife, although certainly sharp. She would have wiped it across the rag and thrust it into the rack without a second's thought. But Cosimo treated it with an almost loving caution.

Chapter 17

"*L*et's go through this again," Cosimo said, pacing the cabin, hands clasped behind his back.

Meg rolled her eyes. "Must we?" she said wearily.

"Yes," he said flatly. "You have to be word perfect in every detail. Now, your name?"

"Anatole Giverny," she said with a sigh. "Or Nathalie Giverny, a widow, depending on what I'm wearing."

"And who are you traveling with?"

"My French cousin, Cosimo Giverny, who is escorting me to my family in Venice. My mother has lived in Venice for five years, ever since the death of my father. She recently married a wealthy Venetian merchant, but fell ill several months ago and they sent for me. It seems that her life hangs by a thread."

"Good," he said with a brisk nod. "Now, how will you conduct yourself on this journey?"

Meg thought if she had to go through this drill one more time, she would scream. For the last two days Cosimo had made her recite the catechism until she heard it in her sleep. She said now, "Cosimo, I can do this in my sleep. The words go round and round in my head all night."

"Good," he said again. "That's what I want to hear. Now, please..."

"I am very shy and retiring," she said, giving up. "As befits a recently widowed woman. I will leave you to do all the talking unless I'm asked a direct question. I will go nowhere on my own and will keep to my chamber with the door locked whenever we are staying in an inn. If anyone asks intrusive questions, I will refer them to you." She threw up her hands suddenly. "Dear God, I'm going to act like a half-wit, stay immured in a tavern bedchamber...I can't imagine a more tedious journey."

His mouth hardened and his eyes took on that arctic glint. "You agreed to abide by my rules, Meg. I intend us both to reach Toulon in one piece, and I know better than you how to make that happen. Do you accept that?"

She sighed again. "Yes, I accept it. But I had hoped we might find some amusement in the journey. Otherwise why am I coming?"

He shook his head. "I understand this is hard, but believe me it's necessary." His expression softened. "And believe me, love, I intend that we shall have plenty of opportunity for amusement." He drew her towards him, tipping her chin with his forefinger. "Trust me."

His eyes were warm again, his mouth curved in the sensuous smile that never failed to arouse her. She could certainly trust him to do that, Meg thought, as his mouth brushed hers in a light butterfly kiss. And she thought she could trust him to keep her safe. What more did she need?

The fact that he gave her nothing of himself but what she saw and felt on the surface was something she'd accepted. Indeed, she preferred not to dig beneath that surface. What she didn't know, she needn't worry about. Cowardly perhaps, but he'd promised her an adventure, a journey filled with excitement and passion, and that was what she'd signed on for. The tedious aspects were all in the preparation, and whatever he was, whatever he did in this war—and Meg was convinced that acting as a courier was an insignificant aspect of his business—Cosimo did well and he could keep the details to himself. She wanted one last passionate, dangerous fling before life closed in upon her again. She could certainly trust him to give her that. It was a partnership where each understood exactly what they were getting out of it.

And she would believe that with every ounce of will.

She parted her lips beneath the insistent pressure of his mouth and allowed her body to melt against him as his hands reached behind her, cupping her buttocks, pressing her against his loins. There were worse reasons than this for embarking upon something as insane as a journey across France in the middle of a war in the company of an English spy.

Two days later Meg stood on the deck of the *Mary Rose* and watched as a trunk was lowered into a sailboat, a craft she had not seen used before. It was quite a bit larger than the rowboat and had a small housing which would provide some shelter.

Cosimo was giving his final orders to his lieutenants, to Mike, and to the boatswain. The ship would continue to the Mediterranean and would anchor in the lee of the Îles d'Hyères just off Toulon. She would wait there until her captain and Meg rejoined her.

Meg wondered vaguely how she and Cosimo were to

get to these *îles* to rendezvous with the *Mary Rose*. But she assumed the privateer had a plan. He would doubtless find a boat to ferry them across.

It was a moonless night, a night Cosimo had been waiting for. He had held the *Mary Rose* just at the mouth of the Gironde, which flowed to Bordeaux and then became the Garonne, which wound its way across France. He and Meg would follow its course as far as possible by this little sailing boat, hoping to get as far as Toulouse by water. From there they would strike out by land across the mountainous region of Tarn towards Vaucluse. There they would drop down through the mountains to Toulon. At least, that was the planned route Cosimo had outlined for her. She assumed it would be subject to change as and when necessary.

"Ready?"

She wheeled round at his voice behind her. "Yes . . . yes, of course." She managed to control the quaver in her voice, but not the fluttering in her belly, as if an entire nest of baby snakes had taken up residence there.

Cosimo wondered, now that the moment had arrived, if she would stay on board the *Mary Rose* if he gave her the option. But he'd told her the last time he'd given her that option it would indeed be the last time. He wasn't going to go back on that now unless she asked him point-blank. And he was fairly certain she would not.

"Everything's on board," he said, sounding cheerfully matter-of-fact as always. "We'll get as close to Bordeaux as we can tonight, and lie up somewhere quiet during the day. We'll need to slip past Bordeaux under cover of darkness tomorrow night. I'm hoping for another moonless night." He stepped back a little. "Let me look at you."

Meg pulled her cap down over her eyebrows and struck a stance, hands on hips, chin lifted, head at a jaunty angle.

Cosimo gave an appreciative grin. "A fine young man you do make, if I say so myself."

Meg grimaced a little. Part of the rigorous training of the last couple of days had involved learning a masculine way to do everything, from sitting in a chair to cutting meat. It had never occurred to her that there were differences between the sexes in such elementary acts. But now she noticed them all the time. Much as she'd disliked the intensity of the education, she couldn't help but recognize and appreciate Cosimo's thoroughness. It gave her much-needed confidence.

She subjected him to a similar scrutiny and couldn't help her own appreciative smile. He was dressed like a fisherman in worsted britches, a loose-fitting shirt, a bandanna tied carelessly at his throat, sabots on his feet, and a cap set at a rakish angle over one eyebrow. Everything was slightly grubby, just as her own britches and shirt were. A little seedy, a little run-down, the clothes of a working man. And nothing about his appearance lessened his magnetic attraction one iota.

She glanced down at the sailboat, where the trunk was being stowed in the stern and covered with a tarpaulin. It contained another wardrobe, her gowns, shawl, petticoats, slippers, and several rather elegant suits of clothes for Cosimo that had appeared from somewhere. She was certain they hadn't been kept in the cabin. It would be interesting to see him dressed formally, she thought. On board ship he was always tidy, but his dress was invariably plain britches, shirt, and jerkin.

"I'm going down now," Cosimo said. "Follow me as soon as I'm in the boat." He gave her one long searching look, waiting for an instant, then when she said nothing he gave an infinitesimal nod and swung over the rail and onto the ladder.

Meg wondered if he'd been silently giving her the opportunity to change her mind. He'd said he wouldn't ask her again, and she hadn't expected him to. But for as long as her feet remained firmly on the deck of the *Mary Rose*, she could still back out. Without further reflection she climbed over the rail and onto the ladder.

"Good luck, Miss Barratt." The cousins hung over the railing and she could see the envy in their eyes as they gazed down at her.

"You too," she said, taking one hand off the ladder to wave. "Look after Gus." Then she climbed down into the sailboat.

Cosimo was hauling up the mainsail, whistling softly between his teeth. It was dark down there on the water, the night air soft. Meg looked up at the deck of the *Mary Rose* and saw men lined up in silence, staring down at the little bobbing craft. Hands were lifted in a farewell that was part salute, part wave, and she smiled, although they probably couldn't see her expression in the dark from such a height.

The sail flapped idly until Cosimo sat down, took the tiller and the mainsail sheet in his hand. He raised his free hand in farewell to his ship and Meg followed suit. The boat scudded towards the mouth of the Gironde.

Meg stepped carefully to the stern and sat on the bench that ran along the side, well away from Cosimo at the tiller. It was a very different matter to be under sail in this little boat than on the *Mary Rose*, but Cosimo was clearly enjoying himself. He had his head thrown back, watching the movement of the sail much as he did on the ship, but here the smallest movement of the tiller seemed all that was necessary to correct a setting.

"I don't know anything about sailing," she said softly, aware of the silence around them.

"You don't need to," he returned, shooting her a quick smile. "All you need to know is how to keep the *Rosa*'s captain happy in his work."

Meg grinned. "I think I can do that. So she's called the *Rosa*?"

"Appropriate enough for a tender to the *Mary Rose*. Why don't you go into the cabin and familiarize yourself with the stores? I'm afraid you are going to be responsible for dealing with food and suchlike. At least while I have the tiller."

Meg did as he asked, taking the two steps down to the low entrance to the housing. She had to crouch as she went in and could barely stand upright once inside. Cosimo would be bent double. She looked around. It was hard to see in the darkness. She poked her head out. "Can I light a lamp?" she whispered.

"There's a lantern on the table. It's ready to be lit. Flint and tinder in a drawer beneath. But keep the light low."

Meg found the table by bruising her hip on a sharp corner. She felt for the drawer, found what she was looking for, and fumbled for the lantern. The soft glow of lamplight showed her a cramped space with a narrow bunk set into the bulkhead. Narrower than the one in the captain's cabin on the *Mary Rose*, so obviously sleeping would be in shifts. But then, sleeping was not the object of this exercise.

Neatly stacked packages filled the bow space. She examined them and found coffee, tea, cheese, half a ham, and a loaf of bread. They could hardly survive on that all the way to Toulouse. So presumably they'd stop to take on supplies. Further exploration revealed a keg of water, a kettle, a pan, and a skillet.

She ducked back into the open air. "How do we heat water?"

"There should be a sack of charcoal and a brazier," Cosimo said. "But we'll do no cooking tonight. You should find cognac and wine in one of the cupboards beneath the bunk. Bring me wine and some bread and cheese."

"Right away, Captain," she said with a smart salute. "May I bring some for myself? Or must the cabin boy eat after his captain?" She raised a provocative eyebrow.

"Don't tempt me, Meg," he said. "I can't leave the tiller if we're to make Bordeaux by morning."

Meg clambered down into the cabin and put together a plate of bread, cheese, and ham. She found the flask of wine and brought the results of her foraging back on deck. "Not very elegant, I'm afraid."

"It'll do fine. You go and get some sleep now."

"I'm not in the least sleepy and I would like to share your picnic," Meg stated. "I can't sleep to order, Cosimo."

"You'll learn," he said carelessly. "You'll learn to take every opportunity you're given. But you'll be your own teacher." He reached for the flask and tipped it to his lips.

Meg frowned into the darkness. He had changed a little, but she couldn't put her finger on quite how. There was something diffcrent about his posture, something contained about his manner, as if he was operating in a private world. Perhaps that was necessary when a spy started work in enemy territory. It interested her and she wasn't foolish enough to take exception.

She accepted the flask as he offered it to her, and broke bread, layered it with ham and cheese, and passed it to him. He accepted it with a nod of thanks and the boat sailed on through the night under a gentle breeze. The water on the river was much quieter than the open sea, although at this point it was wide enough that the banks were hard to distinguish. Meg had studied the charts and knew that that would change as they drew closer to Bordeaux.

There was something hypnotic about the smooth slide across the dark water, the silence broken only by the scream of a gull, the cry of a curlew. Meg realized that a big ship on the sea was a very noisy place even at dead of night. She hadn't noticed before. She ate bread and cheese and absorbed the peace until she felt her eyelids drooping.

"Perhaps I will try to sleep," she murmured.

Cosimo chuckled. He knew what *try* meant. "A wise move."

She laughed a little. "Very well, Captain Cosimo, as always you know best." She stood up, stretching. "Are you sure you don't need me . . . to keep you company at least?"

"I do need you, love, but not at the moment," he returned. "Kiss me and go."

She leaned down and kissed him lightly on the lips, tasting salt and wine. "Call me if you need me. I shan't sleep long."

"No," he agreed. "I'm sure you won't." Meg didn't see his flickering smile.

Cosimo sailed and Meg slept until the dawn light showed and the sky took on an orange tint. They were close to where the Gironde split, with the Dordogne going off to the left and the Garonne to the right straight into

Bordeaux. He'd debated which of the two rivers to take. The Dordogne was less traveled but the Garonne would bring them closer to their destination. In the end he'd decided to take the riskier route. If necessary, they would abandon *Rosa* earlier and take to the roads in another disguise.

He searched for a quiet backwater where they could wait until nightfall. He could get some sleep and then catch a few fish, make a little love, have supper, and start off again as soon as darkness fell and the local river traffic ceased. They would slip past Bordeaux beneath the lookouts on the walls and by dawn would once more be looking for another backwater, but with the fortress city well behind them.

He took a narrow reed-lined stream that the little sailing boat could navigate without difficulty, lowered the sail, and dropped the anchor. He stood and stretched, aware of the stiffness in his shoulders after the hours of maintaining the same position. He relieved himself over the stern and then ducked beneath the housing.

Meg stirred as he came in. She rolled over and opened her eyes on a sleepy smile. "As usual, you were right," she murmured. "That was one of the most blissful sleeps I've ever had."

He hitched his backside onto the corner of the table and shook off his sabots. "I need two hours, and then we can amuse ourselves all day."

Meg struggled into a sitting position and swung her legs to the floor. Her doziness dissipated as she took in the tiredness etched on his face. "What would you like me to do while you sleep?" She stood up, shaking her head to rid herself of the last strands of sleep.

"Only what you wish," he said, falling onto the cot. "It's

quite safe to light the brazier and make coffee. The boat's tied up. If anything changes, wake me at once." He closed his eyes and was instantly asleep.

Meg went up on deck. She could see only reeds, but a faint smell of smoke reached her. There was a cottage or a hamlet somewhere around. Did that still make it safe to light the brazier? The more she thought about coffee, the more the prospect became irresistible. But had Cosimo known of the chimney smoke?

She went below again. Cosimo was dead to the world, so much so that she doubted she could wake him if she tried. But then she revised that opinion. If she gave so much as an alerting cough, he would wake up.

She drank a cup of water from the keg and went back on deck. The smoke still curled above the reeds and she could hear the sound of voices. Then a flat boat, a raft she thought, pushed through the reeds. A pair of children poled the raft close to the sailboat. "*Bonjour, m'sieur?*" They looked up at her curiously.

"*Bonjour, mes enfants,*" she returned.

"*Vous êtes en route à Bordeaux?*" they inquired.

Meg thought quickly. Why would these children think that this little boat was heading for the huge harbor of Bordeaux? Maybe it was the only place they could think of for a boat that appeared out of nowhere, somewhere they'd never been, a city whose existence had a magical quality. But even to children she could divulge nothing.

"*Non, mes enfants,*" she returned with a casual shrug. "*Mon cousin et moi, nous sommes en vacances.*" Now who in the world would be taking a holiday on a river in the middle of a war? She wanted to scream at herself, but the children appeared to find nothing strange about it.

"*Vous êtes pêcheur?*" they asked, miming casting a rod.

"Mais oui, exactement," she said with relief.

"Bonjour, enfants." Cosimo spoke from behind her. *"Un joli matin."*

"Oui, m'sieur. Bon matin." They poled their raft rather quickly back into the reeds.

"You scared them off," Meg said, turning to look at him. "Won't that cause suspicion?"

"I doubt it. A couple of fishermen—"

"I said we were on holiday," she confessed. "Two fishermen on holiday." Cosimo laughed and she added, "But they're not going to believe that. Look at us."

"My sweet, you couldn't have said anything better," he said. "The villages along these tributaries view the fishing rights as their own. They'll assume we're poaching, and, if I'm not much mistaken, will be chasing us off within the hour. So we'd better beat a retreat."

He moved around the boat, hoisting the mainsail, jumping onto the bow to hoist the jib. "Can't I help?" Meg asked in frustration. She could manage anything on land, she was certain, but these boat skills were beyond intuition.

"Sit there." Cosimo gestured to the thwart. "Take that handle, and when I tell you to push it down, do so." He took the tiller and swung it over.

Meg ducked as the boom came across and moved her weight to the other side as he gestured. The sailboat turned in the narrow channel, the wind caught the sail, and the *Rosa* began to move. Meg had her hands on the handle that protruded from the boards at her feet. She had no idea what it did. But as they emerged from the reeds and Cosimo said, "Drop it," she pushed down the handle and felt the little boat surge forward.

"We'll make a sailor of you yet," he said. "Now you can

light the brazier and make some coffee while I find some less crowded spot to anchor."

Meg sat still as stone as they slipped at dead of a moonless night beneath the guns of Bordeaux, only the black jib carrying them, its dark canvas blending into the darkness. Cosimo guided the boat close to the shore so that they wouldn't be visible from above. She could hear voices on the quay, carrying clearly in the still night as they clung to the quayside. Once she heard the unmistakable sounds of a whore and her client, the grunts and groans, the feigned cries of ecstasy. Huge ships of war crowded the harbor and Cosimo threaded his way through them, hiding *Rosa* close against their sides so that the shapes merged and they couldn't be seen from a watcher on deck above. And then finally the harbor was behind them, and the Garonne, while still wide, had become a domestic stretch of waterway once more.

Meg inhaled softly and Cosimo's teeth flashed white. He had enjoyed every second of that, she realized. This man fed on danger. And the pulse of her own exhilaration was telling her that she did too.

"What now?" she whispered.

"We'll see how far we can get before dawn." He crooked a finger at her. "I'm tired, Meg. Would you take over?"

She blinked. He hadn't given her more than an occasional hint as to how this sailing business worked and now he was suggesting she sail while he slept.

Cosimo waited without apparent concern for her response. If she agreed, it would tell him more about her readiness for this mission. If she didn't, then he would learn something vital too. He wasn't going to be asleep while she took the tiller, if she agreed to do so, but Meg wouldn't know that.

"It seems simple enough," she said after a minute. "As long as we're not about to sail into the midst of an enemy convoy."

"Not here. It's plain sailing. The wind is behind you and all you have to do is keep the mainsail filled. You learned a little on the *Mary Rose*; this is much simpler."

"All right," Meg said. "Go and sleep." She took his place and grasped the tiller as he relinquished it.

"I'll be below," he said with a yawn. "Shout if you need me."

"Oh, I will," Meg responded. She settled down, feeling extraordinarily free and competent. She watched the sail, adjusted the tiller, and the little sailboat moved on through the night between quiet riverbanks.

Cosimo, wide awake on the bunk below, listened to the creak of the sail, the slither of the water beneath the bow, and smiled his satisfaction. Soon the time would come when he could tell her exactly what they were going to do.

Meg strained her eyes into the gloom. She *was* seeing what she thought she was seeing. There was another boat coming towards them. A barge, she thought. She had no idea how long she'd been sailing, but the tiller seemed welded to her hand. The hypnotic motion hadn't sent her to sleep, she was far too keyed up for that, but it had induced a kind of trance that had made the initial appearance of the dark shape seem a figment of her imagination. Now it was most definitely no figment and it seemed to be on course to run them down.

"Let me have the tiller." Cosimo appeared as if she'd

conjured him. She eased over and he took her place. "Get below and don't show yourself," he instructed in a voice barely above a whisper. "I don't want them to know there are two of us."

Meg slithered towards the hatchway and vanished into the darkness of the tiny cabin. She crouched on the bunk, her back pressed into the corner, and listened to the shouts above. Cosimo shouted out a greeting in a rough patois that she could barely understand. But she did understand the responding demand that he lower sail and wait to be boarded.

She felt the craft swing as Cosimo turned into the wind, then she heard the creak of the lowering sail. A heavy thump as someone landed on the deck immediately above her head, followed by another. Two of them. Officials of some kind presumably; why else had Cosimo obeyed their orders? She strained to hear what was being said but the exchange was swift and heavily accented.

Silently she dragged the shirt over her head and thrust it beneath the pillow. She was naked now from the waist up. She wriggled under the blanket and held her breath. There was nowhere to hide on this boat, but if they were going to search it, she could hide behind a façade.

When she heard a heavy footstep on the top step leading into the tiny cabin, she gave a little gasp, a small cry of fright. A bearded man stuck his head into the space first, then stepped down. He yelled in that abominable provincial accent, "Come and take a look here, Luc."

A second man appeared, big and heavy, like a boxer running to fat. He leered at Meg, gazing wide-eyed from beneath the blanket. "Thought he said he was alone."

Meg saw Cosimo. Saw him but couldn't hear him. He had cast aside his sabots and his bare feet made not a sound on the steps as he came up behind the two men. She saw the blade of the knife in his hand. She saw his expression, and it was one she had never seen before. Still, utterly concentrated, utterly without emotion, and he held the knife poised in his right hand.

She sat up on the cot, letting the blanket fall to her waist, and screamed. The two men stared at her breasts and then the bearded one cackled with derisive laughter. "*Quelle putain,*" he declared. "Man can't get himself a whore any better than that one?"

His companion laughed uproariously. "Look at those walnuts." He mimed tiny breasts on his own barrel chest. "No wonder he said he was alone."

Meg stared at them in a wide-eyed fright that was not entirely feigned and hastily dragged the blanket up to her throat. Behind them Cosimo was no longer holding the knife. Distractedly she wondered where he'd put it as she pushed herself farther back into the corner of the bunk in a good imitation of a beaten dog. His expression had lost that cold distance and his eyes burned with what she recognized once again as pure, unadulterated fury. And while it sent shivers down her spine, it was infinitely preferable to the emotionless gaze of the killer.

He turned on his heel without a word and went on deck. The men, still laughing as if it was the funniest thing that had happened to them all month, followed him up.

Meg listened to the ribald exchange as Cosimo joined in the barroom vulgarity, making fun of the pathetic whore he had bought from the Bordeaux quayside to provide creature comforts on his journey to the town of Cadillac, where he would pass her on to the highest bidder. She'd chosen the part, she reflected grimly, so she shouldn't object to its consequences. But it still rankled to hear her lack of feminine charm broadcast to the night air. And the bastards would never even know that she'd saved their lives.

They were drinking now, passing around a flagon of beer, presumably from the barge, she thought, huddling beneath the blanket. The memory of Cosimo's expression as he'd stood behind the two unsuspecting men, holding the knife, wouldn't go away. He said he hadn't killed the guards at Quiberon, but what if he'd lied?

She lay down, shivering a little despite the warmth of the night. This man who made such tender, passionate love was a killer. She couldn't fool herself any longer. It didn't matter whether he'd killed at Quiberon, he had intended to kill tonight. Here on this tiny boat. What would he have done with the bodies? Thrown them overboard... dragged them back onto the barge? He would have planned it before he drew the knife, Meg knew. And suddenly the prospect of being immured in a Kent backwater took on a rosy patina.

She heard the two men leave, felt the lightening of the boat as they jumped to the barge, heard the exchange of farewells, and she sat up, pressing her back into the corner again.

Cosimo came into the cabin, ducking his head as he did so. "Well, that was an interesting performance," he observed, sitting on the edge of the cot. The fury had left his eyes but there was a puzzlement in them as if something had happened that he didn't understand.

"I could say the same about yours," Meg returned. "Who were they?"

"Some kind of gendarmerie," he replied with a tiny shrug. "But we've drawn attention, so we'll have to leave the water, I'm afraid."

He leaned forward and twitched the blanket from her hands, revealing her breasts. He put his hands over them, a warm enclosing clasp, and her nipples rose at the touch. "I adore your breasts," he said softly, his gaze holding hers.

The coarse derision of the intruders had cut him to the quick and he didn't know why. Meg had reacted swiftly and inventively to the danger and it should have pleased him; instead a most powerful anger had filled him and it had required all his self-control to keep from slamming his fists into their mocking mouths. He never permitted emotion to interfere with the practical needs of a situation, but he had been within a hair's breadth of doing so. And he had no idea why.

Meg put her hands over his and managed a smile. "I wasn't offended." It was a lie but he was so obviously upset by the insult she felt the need to reassure him.

"They were louts." His mouth hardened for an instant.

"Yes." *And you're a killer.* She laughed with what she hoped was conviction. "My self-esteem is not damaged in the least, Cosimo."

He gave her a searching look and was not entirely convinced. However, it was better to let it go; dwelling on a hurt only made it worse. "It certainly shouldn't be," he said, leaning closer to kiss her, easing her backwards.

She slid down onto the cot and he came over her, moving his mouth to her breasts as his hand slipped into the waist of her britches, reaching farther between her thighs until his fingers found her moistening center.

"You were going to kill them," Meg declared, pushing herself up again so that his exploring fingers lost their destination. "I saw the knife."

Cosimo retracted his hand with some difficulty and sat up, resuming his position on the edge of the cot. Again he looked at her intently. "Meg, do you understand what could have happened? We were boarded by some form of officialdom... there are many such forms along the waterways, some legal, some not, it makes no difference. I had told them I was alone. Once they saw you—"

Meg interrupted him. "They had a great deal of amusement at our expense and then went on their merry way."

"Had they not, both of us would have been suffering in some stinking jail," he said, his voice harsh now. "These peasants have little refinement. I leave it to your imagination."

"You said you don't kill for pleasure," Meg said, watching his eyes, watching for that look that had so chilled her.

"I don't." His expression was unmoving but the cold deliberation she had seen was absent. The Cosimo she knew was now inhabiting his body.

"But you do kill?"

"When necessary, when my own life is in danger... or the lives of those who are important to me." It was an admission he was quite comfortable with. But he was not ready yet to tell her that he also when necessary killed for a purpose... that in essence he was an assassin who needed no personal provocation. She was not ready to hear that yet.

He softened his voice. "This is a dirty business, love. You can't expect to play in the mud and not get your hands dirty."

"No," she agreed. "I don't." She stared into the dimness of the cabin. A man in Cosimo's world had to be prepared for anything. She could imagine what those men would have done to her if they'd had the chance. And she could imagine what they would have done to Cosimo. So, all was fair in war. A man had a right to protect himself and those he loved. Or at least, those he lusted after, she amended wryly. And she had made her own decision and would just have to get over the bits she didn't like. Why should it trouble her so much? This was just an adventure with a wonderfully attractive, deeply sensuous lover. Exploring each other's souls had never been a part of the bargain.

"So what now?" she asked, brightly changing the subject. "Aren't we adrift in the middle of a river?"

"Not exactly," he said, reaching a hand out to her breasts again. "We're at anchor. And if you're prepared for a very quick encounter, we could indulge ourselves."

But she wasn't, Meg realized. She offered a rueful smile. "I'm sorry, but I think that encounter was enough for tonight. I don't seem to feel—"

He stood up at once. "No, of course not. Insensitive of me. That was horrid for you. I'm going to sail until dawn and then find some small town where I can sell the boat and we'll continue overland." He leaned over and kissed her softly. "Sleep, Meg. It will be better in the morning."

She lay down again, wide awake, every muscle tensed and jumping. It wouldn't be better in the morning. She had to stop pretending to herself that this was a game. This passionate adventure was being played out on enemy territory. Her lover was a spy and when necessary he killed without compunction. How had she been foolish enough to imagine that she could subsume that reality into some kind of romantic fiction? How had she been blind enough to imagine that she didn't care what kind of man he was? She cared . . . deeply.

On deck, Cosimo hoisted the sail and took the tiller. The barge had receded into the distance towards Bordeaux. Its crew may have been momentarily satisfied by the vulgar exchange with the sailboat, but somewhere along the line of information, the encounter with the children on the raft a few miles downstream would filter through and coalesce with tonight's badinage and the *Rosa* would be marked. They needed to leave the water at the earliest opportunity.

He wondered if Meg was asleep. Her withdrawal from him shouldn't have troubled him, it was perfectly natural after what she'd just been through, but it did. He would have liked to have comforted her, used the one sure way he knew to heal any damage . . . any hurt inflicted by those peasant brutes. But he had to assume she knew how to heal herself, and maybe she hadn't been lying when she said their coarse insults had not troubled her. Perhaps she was genuinely tired, emotionally exhausted by her quick-witted response to very real danger. It would be quite understandable, particularly when she was not accustomed to responding to dangerous situations. Ana would have been laughing with him now, with that wild exhilaration that always possessed her after danger had been averted. But Meg was not Ana, and he needed to remind himself of that.

Chapter 18

*M*eg stood in the stern of the *Rosa* listening to Cosimo haggle with a burly fisherman from the little town of Cadillac that clung to the banks of the river. They were negotiating a price for *Rosa* and Meg felt rather sad at the thought of leaving the little craft. In the last two days she'd grown accustomed to the gentle motion, the soft sounds of the river, even to sleeping in the narrow bunk.

Cosimo had risked an extra day on the river, reckoning that he would get a better price for his boat in Cadillac, which, although small, was slightly larger than the villages they passed. He also reckoned that he would be able to buy better horses in the town than in the countryside.

At last the two men spat in their hands and shook in the age-old gesture of a bargain completed, and Cosimo came over to Meg. "Well, that's done," he said. "For better or worse. There's a small hostelry in town, not overly salubrious but it'll do for tonight while I make arrangements for tomorrow. A cart is coming to collect the trunk."

Meg nodded. "I shall miss *Rosa*."

He looked at her closely, wondering if her subdued

manner was caused only by the prospect of leaving the water. She had not as yet recovered her usual exuberant self after the encounter with the barge outside Bordeaux, and he'd not pressed her, partly, he was forced to admit, because he didn't want to risk another rejection. He told himself that she was coming to grips with the more dangerous realities of this journey and she was best left to do that in her own fashion.

"Well," he said cheerfully, "you won't miss our makeshift meals, and I can guarantee a good dinner this evening. The accommodations at the Cheval Blanc may be a little basic, but it keeps a good kitchen."

Meg responded with a smile that was slowly becoming less effortful. She had told herself she simply had to adjust her romanticism to reality, not something she would ordinarily find in the least difficult to do. In fact, she would have claimed to have very little romantic sensibility, but she'd certainly let some idealistic version of a passionate adventure rule her head up until the other night. Cosimo was not to blame for her own addle-pated sentimentality and she would manage to shake herself out of it.

"So, we ride from now on?" she said, forcing a note of interest into her voice.

"To start with," he said.

"But what of the trunk?"

"We'll dispense with the trunk, and package its contents into saddlebags. Once we're well clear of this area, then you'll adopt your petticoats again, and some of the time you can travel by carriage."

At that Meg shook her head vigorously. "I cannot abide carriages," she declared. "They make me sick."

He pulled an earlobe. "That's awkward. I don't think

you'll be able to ride all day every day. Are you sure about the carriage? You didn't get seasick."

"I'm quite sure," she said grimly. "I've never been able to stand more than an hour at a time in a carriage without vomiting."

"Well, we'll have to see," he said. He had the urge to hold her, to kiss the little worry lines away from her forehead, but here on an open deck, tied up to the quayside of a bustling little town, was no place for physical demonstrations between a pair of sailors.

"What are you grinning about?" Meg demanded, seeing the wicked gleam in his eye, the curve of his mouth.

He told her and was rewarded with a peal of laughter that warmed his heart. "That's better," he said, then ventured, "Why so glum just recently?"

She shrugged. "I was unnerved, I suppose."

"And now?" His eyes narrowed, his gaze intent on her face.

Meg made up her mind. Moping was a pointless activity. What was past was past. It was time to look forward again, otherwise she was wasting her time completely. "I seem to be getting my nerve back," she responded.

"Perhaps I was expecting you to run before you can walk," he said thoughtfully. "But you think so quickly in a crisis that I tend to forget you're inexperienced at this game."

Meg felt an unexpected rush of pleasure at the compliment. She had noticed on board the *Mary Rose* that the privateer was sparing with compliments to his crew, just as he was with criticisms. His standards were high and it didn't occur to him that a member of his crew would fail to meet them or even exceed them. And as far as she herself was concerned, any appreciative comments had thus far

been confined to the delights of her body and the plea-
sures of lovemaking.

"Well, thank you, kind sir," she said with a mock bow.

He touched the cleft in her chin in a brief caress and
then was all business again. "I want you to go to the inn
and stay there while I clear the boat and arrange for horses.
Now that we've drawn attention to ourselves, the less visible you are here, the better."

Meg offered no objection, although when they arrived
at the inn she did wrinkle her nose at the grimy bedchamber and the flea-ridden mattress. "Is there nowhere else in
this town?" she murmured when the landlord had left
them.

"I'm afraid not. I did ask around when I came in earlier.
But it's just for tonight. We'll be out of here at dawn."

"What the fleas have left of us," she retorted, poking at
the straw mattress with a disdainful finger. "Is there any
spare canvas on the boat? If it's thick enough, they might
not bite through it."

"I'll bring what there is," he promised. "Now stay here
and keep out of sight. I'll be back within the hour." He saw
objection in her eyes, her mouth opening to voice it, and
quickly took her by the shoulders, pulling her hard against
him. He kissed her, intending it to be a light but firm
farewell, except that things changed. He felt her come
alive beneath his mouth, her body suddenly taut against
him. It was the first time in two days that she had responded to him in this way. He ran his hands down her
back, then held her waist as he raised his head for a minute
and looked deep into her eyes, reading the swift upsurge of
passion dancing across the green surface.

"How agile are you feeling?" he murmured, his hands

moving to the fastening of her britches, then pushing them roughly off her hips.

"I'm not going near the bed," she answered obliquely but in a fervent whisper as she kicked her feet free of sandals and then britches. She tugged his shirt out of his britches, pushing her hands up beneath it, her nails scribbling over his back.

"Wait...wait...love," he muttered against her mouth, shrugging out of the shirt, still holding her at the waist. He stepped backwards, drawing her with him, and threw his shirt on the low rough stone of the windowsill.

"Ah, ingenious," Meg said, her eyes widening with mingled amusement and excitement. She jumped as he lifted her so that she was sitting on the stone sill, her bare skin protected by his shirt. "Are we going to provide a spectacle for anyone below?" she asked. "Should we pass the hat afterwards?"

"Our only audience is a couple of cows," he said, glancing over her shoulder into the field below. "Now be quiet. Didn't anyone ever explain to you the detumescent effect of misplaced levity at certain moments?"

"I'm not aware of any such effect," she said, sliding her flat palm down his belly before deftly unfastening his britches. She enclosed in her palm the very clear evidence in support of her claim, then leaned forward and nibbled his bottom lip, reaching behind to push her free hand down inside his opened britches to the cleft between his buttocks.

Cosimo drew a swift breath and pushed his own hands beneath her bottom, lifting her on the shelf of his palms. She reached her arms around his neck and curled her legs around his hips, fitting herself against him, belly to belly. He was inside her in one smooth thrust and held her as he moved. She clung to his neck, his hands, warm and strong against her bottom, holding her in a precarious position that allowed her no initiative. She could only receive. The dismay and the uncertainty of the last couple of days disintegrated as the pleasure filled her. How could she be afraid of a man who could bring her such delight? Only someone she trusted with her soul, someone to whom she could give herself without restraint, could bring her such joy.

Her heels pressed into his buttocks as the sensation rocked her. She buried her mouth in his shoulder, her arms locking around his neck, helpless to slow the tidal wave, and she felt him shudder against her, pulsing deep within her, his seed flooding her. And when it was over he held her gently as her locked thighs relaxed and she slid down his body until her feet touched the floor.

"Sweet Jesus," he murmured, pushing a hand through her tangled curls. "Maybe there's something to be said for a short abstinence once in a while."

Meg smiled weakly. "Except that we forgot to be careful this time."

He *had* forgotten. In that wild, spontaneous moment of ecstasy, he had forgotten his usual precaution. Never before had he spilled his seed inside her.

"I should bleed in two days," she said, seeing his expression.

Cosimo nodded. There was little point worrying about something until there was something to worry about. "I have to go back to the *Rosa*, love. And then to the livery stables, and—"

"And I'm not staying in this cesspit twiddling my thumbs for the rest of the afternoon," Meg interrupted him as she shook out her britches. The physical intensity of those few moments had energized her, restored her initiative, and she had no intention of meekly staying hidden in this filthy chamber.

"I have a good eye for horseflesh—my father breeds hunters—and I will find us what we need. You'll need to give me the funds, though."

Cosimo hesitated for barely an instant. The more involved Meg became in the details of this mission, the easier it would be in the end. "As you wish," he said, tucking his shirt back into his britches and refastening them. "But I think we need to make a few minor adjustments to your appearance in that case."

"Oh?" Intrigued, Meg scrambled back into her clothes, watching as he rummaged through a small valise that he had brought with them.

"Ah, my little box of tricks," he said, taking out a metal tin. "Come here, Ganymede." He opened the tin.

Meg approached somewhat cautiously. He held a thin pencil and a round pot in the palm of his hand. "What's that?"

"A pencil and charcoal," he answered. "I want to enhance your eyebrows a little, and just give the hint of hair on the upper lip. Your figure is convincing, my dear, but your face is all too pure to pass more than a careless glance."

Meg stood very still, controlling her impatience to see the result, as Cosimo deftly touched the pencil to her eyebrows, then to her upper lip. "Are you sure this isn't going to look ridiculous?"

"Be quiet!" he ordered. "How can I do this if you keep moving your mouth?"

"Sorry," she murmured, attempting the utter immobility of a mime, despite the slight tickle that made her want to sneeze.

Cosimo stood back and examined his handiwork critically. "That'll pass, I believe. But a little shadow here, just along the jawline...Yes, that's perfect. Had you thought about your less-than-authentic accent? I don't want to start using the cover story until we're well away from the river. It's no: convincing for a man and a youth on a sailboat." He waited with interest to see whether she had thought through this small impediment.

"Some of the accents around here are so incomprehensible that I don't think my own will be that noticeable," Meg said. "But I'll disguise any English twang with mumbles and monosyllables. It's not that difficult to pick out a couple of horses with staying power, pay for them, and arrange to pick them up at first light without entering into a long conversation."

"Keep the cap low over your eyes, use a lot of gestures, and we'll need a packhorse as well as the riding horses," Cosimo instructed briskly, counting the points on his fingers. "Don't pay more than twenty livres per riding horse, and no more than ten for the packhorse." He counted out coins into her palm. "Be back here in two hours at the latest, Meg. When you leave the inn, turn to your right and you'll find the livery stables in a side alley about a quarter of a mile away."

"That sounds simple enough," she said with a confidence she wasn't sure she felt. She tossed the coins in the palm of her hand. "Until later then." She raised her face for a kiss.

"Until later." Cosimo kissed her, lingered for a second on the sweetness of her lips, then turned and left her, saying over his shoulder, "Two hours, Meg. Not a second longer."

She stood for a minute looking at the door he'd left ajar. She had no mirror to familiarize herself with her adjusted appearance. It was more than a little strange to go out on the street, negotiate for horses, without having a real sense of what she looked like.

But it was all part of the adventure. Meg thrust the coins into the pocket of her britches and ventured forth onto the lanes of Cadillac. She found the livery stable without difficulty and was greeted not by the man she'd expected but by a smiling, apple-cheeked woman who very quickly made it clear that she knew as much about horseflesh and doing business as any man around.

Meg warmed to her even as she realized that her disguise was harder to maintain for a woman's eye. She followed Cosimo's advice and kept the cap low, spoke in barely a mutter, but let her eyes and hands do the work. There was a deep-chested gelding that would do for Cosimo. She ran a knowledgeable hand down his hocks, feeling for warmth or tenderness, stroked his withers, pushed back his lips. His teeth seemed sound and his mouth had no sores from an ill-used curb.

She nodded an affirmative to the woman and moved down the line of horses. She knew exactly what would suit her. A gelding or a mare of medium height with a smooth mouth and good back. A bright-eyed piebald mare was in the last stall, shifting restlessly on her straw. She was a beauty and Meg's eyes sparked with the excitement of the shopper who has found the perfect purchase.

"*Celle-ci*," she said firmly.

The woman named a price. Thirty livres. Meg didn't hesitate. The mare was worth every penny. They would have to forgo the packhorse and travel light. She counted out the money, arranged in the same monosyllabic mumble to collect the animals before dawn in the morning, and returned to the inn, delighted with the success of her errand.

Cosimo was rather less delighted. "You paid thirty livres for a mare?"

"Cosimo, she's worth twice that. She's beautiful."

His lip curled a little. "What has beauty to do with stamina?"

"Everything," Meg stated. "It has little to do with looks, but everything to do with health, and muscle, and temperament."

Now there Cosimo could not disagree. "I'm going to look at her," he said, and left.

Meg paced the small, unpleasant chamber, aware of both hunger and the most appetizing smells coming from below. After a while she addressed herself to the trunk that Cosimo had brought back with him on a cart. There was a sheet of heavy canvas that had been dipped in tar. In ordinary circumstances it would make the most abominable sheet, but she was by now used to the smell, in fact she liked its association with salt and sun, and no fleas would penetrate such a barrier. She occupied her time throwing the canvas over the crackling straw mattress and searching through the trunk for something that would serve as a makeshift cover.

"I can't argue with your judgment on horseflesh," Cosimo announced from the doorway, surprising her as her head was buried in the trunk. "She is indeed beautiful, and the gelding will serve well. I bought a packhorse and they'll all be delivered here at four o'clock tomorrow morning. What are you looking for?"

"Something to cover this canvas. It's so stiff to sleep on. Although I'd sleep on concrete if it would keep the fleas at bay." She sat back on her heels, flushed from her exertions.

"Use my boat cloak." He stood over her with an appraising eye. "My handiwork is smudged. If we're going to eat supper below, then we need to repair the damage."

"I'm famished, and whatever it is it smells amazing," Meg declared, letting him pull her to her feet. "I wish I could see what your artistic efforts are producing."

Cosimo reapplied pencil and charcoal. "I do assure you, it will pass muster," he stated, adding, "in a dim light."

"I'm so hungry I'm not sure I really care." She went ahead of him to the stairs, inhaling the rich fragrant smells from below. "What do they cook here?"

"Fish aplenty, but also duck, goose liver is a specialty, sausage, lentils . . ."

"Enough," Meg said, her saliva running.

They ate at the common board and Meg was relieved to find that the food and wine were the most important elements of the evening. None of their table companions seemed particularly interested in conversation. Bread was passed with flagons of good Bordeaux, and spoons plunged into the communal dishes of a fish stew and a cauldron of potatoes, onions, and bacon. Knives sliced into garlicky sausage and slabs of cheese, and voices rose as the wine flowed. She passed unnoticed, slumping down on the bench, taking care of her appetite, but listening all the time, trying to absorb the accent, identify the vocabulary. She had been taught French by a Parisienne who spoke with a perfect diction that had no affinity with the rough vowels of provincial France. But the more she listened, the more she understood. Whether she could imitate it was another matter.

The conversation grew louder as cognac began to circulate, and Meg thought she could safely slip away unnoticed. She slid off the long bench and beat a retreat to the room upstairs. She found a tallow candle on the windowsill and lit it. The smell of tallow was unpleasant but the light at least softened the contours of the uninviting space. The bed should be safe enough, though. Fleas would have a hard time biting their way through tar-soaked canvas.

Meg didn't trouble to undress. This was no place for the niceties of nightgowns. There was no basin and ewer, so she went in search of the well and the privy. She filled the bucket at the well and dipped the cup to drink, then splashed her face. If she was washing off Cosimo's artistry, so be it. The privy was even worse than she'd expected, but needs must. Keeping as much to the shadows as she could, she returned upstairs.

Cosimo came in a few minutes later. He held two cups of cognac. "As good a prevention against infection as anything else," he said. "Drink it." He gave her one cup. "I'll be back soon."

He left, presumably to take care of his needs as Meg had taken care of hers. Meg drank the cognac and thought about questions that had been nagging at her for days, but that she'd pushed aside as unimportant, irrelevant to her own adventure, merely a part of the mystery that surrounded Cosimo and that added to his attraction. Now, for some reason, she wanted them answered. It seemed she'd had enough of mysteries.

Cosimo returned, his auburn hair glistening with water. Meg tossed him the towel she'd used herself and he caught it with a murmur of thanks, roughly toweling his head.

"Why was Ana traveling with you?" Meg asked without preamble. "Does it take two people to deliver dispatches?"

The question took him by surprise, although he supposed he should have been ready for it at some point. Meg was far too shrewd not to have seen the holes in his concoction. "No, it doesn't," he said, shaking out the towel and spreading it near the open window to dry. "Ana was sailing with me as far as Bordeaux, where she would assume her own mission."

"Oh," she said, nodding, but still frowning. "At the beginning you said your mission could only be accomplished at a certain juncture... that was why you couldn't take me back to Folkestone. I assume you meant delivering the dispatches? It seems strange that they should be so time-sensitive."

"Now why should that seem strange?" He perched on the windowsill and regarded her with a faint smile. "You've seen how difficult it is to make contact along the courier route. I explained to you that we work in closed circles and once an opportunity for contact is missed, it can't be recaptured. I was rather hoping not to miss any of my contacts."

He shrugged. "Had I not done so, I wouldn't be making this journey now, and we'd be on our way back to England." The lie slipped smooth as silk from his tongue and for the first time it made him acutely uncomfortable. Up until now he'd seen the fabrication as a necessary evil, but now it troubled him. He didn't want to lie to her. Deception was so far from Meg's character that she would never understand his reasoning. He wanted to take her into his confidence, he wanted her to partner him fully. He wanted her approval for what he was doing.

That last recognition shocked him. Since when had he sought anyone's approval? Even as a child other people's opinions had mattered little to him. He did what he believed in, without compunction or hesitation. His decisions and choices were ruled by the necessities of his deeply held convictions.

"What's the matter?" Meg asked, seeing his expression. He looked suddenly vulnerable, as if he'd lost a skin. She was so accustomed to believing in his absolute confidence and competence that such a look of insecurity alarmed her. And then to her relief it vanished.

He shook his head as if dismissing whatever it was that had troubled him and said firmly, "Nothing, unless it's the prospect of another visit to that vile privy." He stood up. "Come, let's get some sleep. They're delivering the horses before dawn and we've a hard day's ride ahead."

Meg accepted the change of mood, as much as anything because it was easier to do so. She wasn't sure she wanted to probe into whatever demons had entered his soul for however brief a time. She wrapped herself in her cloak and lay down gingerly on the canvas-covered straw, grateful for Cosimo's boat cloak that offered some softness.

Cosimo wrapped himself in his own traveling cloak and lay down beside her, pushing an arm beneath her to roll her into his side. She rested her head in the crook of his shoulder, flinging her arm over his body, feeling the steady beat of his heart.

"What was Ana's mission?" she inquired sleepily.

"You'd have to ask her," he said. "Now go to sleep."

Ana was off limits as usual, Meg reflected. And she didn't believe for a moment that the mystery woman's mission had nothing to do with Cosimo's. It was her last waking thought before a black cloud of sleep rolled over her.

Chapter 19

*I*t was amazing how one could sense the sea, even when it was two days' journey away, Meg thought, lifting her face to the sun's rays. There was a certain limitless quality to the horizon that was unmistakably connected to the vistas of the sea, even here in the peaceful, verdant green valleys of Vaucluse nestled between two mountain ranges.

On this soft late spring day, they were resting from two days' hard riding, and the inn that they had found was one of the prettiest places Meg had visited. She was sitting now on a wooden seat in the garden on the banks of a narrow river, almost mesmerized by the swooping dragonflies and the dancing light of the sun on the smooth brown water, overwhelmingly thankful that the mountain rides were behind them. Another two days following the path of the Rhône River, and then the coastal route towards Marseilles, then finally to Toulon. At which point this adventure would be over. Or, at least, in essence it would be once they'd made the rendezvous with the *Mary Rose* and were homeward bound.

The last two weeks had had an almost dreamlike quality, a time out of time. Sometimes they had been acutely uncomfortable in filthy inns with unspeakable food. They had ridden through rainstorms and under a burning sun. But then there had been the other side of the coin, breathtaking views and delightful hostelries, and the never-failing delight of lovemaking. There had been no repercussions from that impulsive coupling on the windowsill at Cadillac, and they had never been careless again.

The only difficulty they had encountered thus far on their journey had been her own fatigue. The mountainous roads made hard going for both horse and rider, and at one point towards the end of the first week of the journey, Cosimo had insisted despite her objections that she travel by carriage. Meg had discovered to her astonishment that she was no match for his determination. It wasn't just the glacial look, but resisting the steely insistence that would brook no argument was like pushing Atlas's boulder up the mountain. In the end, although dreading what she knew would happen, she'd accepted the decree, seeing it as the only way to convince him that she was right.

It was a sound decision for all that she suffered for it. Cosimo had been appalled by the middle of the first day after four stops in as many hours for her to crouch retching miserably by the roadside. His remorse had been profound, his apologies reiterated so many times that in the end she'd begged him to stop blaming himself, even though she did get some perverse satisfaction from his guilt-ridden dismay that went some way to compensating her for her wretchedness.

After that Cosimo had accepted the need to rest every third day. Meg knew he fretted at the inaction even though he never said a word, but she also knew she could do nothing about it. She didn't have his stamina, it was as simple as that.

Of course, Ana probably would have matched him mile for mile, she thought with a tinge of resentment, but that reflection remained unspoken.

"*Bonne après-midi, madame.*"

The soft voice startled her out of her reverie and she turned her head sharply. An elegant man, whom she'd seen earlier that day talking to the innkeeper, was crossing the grassy bank towards her. She looked around automatically for Cosimo, but he'd taken the horses to the farrier to have their shoes checked and picked for stones, and he wouldn't be back until close to evening.

She had grown unaccustomed to conversation with strangers, whether she was in the guise of Anatole Giverny or, as today, dressed in Nathalie's petticoats and gown. However, she was more at home in the latter and managed a smile and a "Good afternoon, m'sieur," that was politely restrained.

He came up to her and bowed, his tall shadow blocking the sun. "Daniel Devereux at your service, madame."

Her smile, while unwavering, was cool and she merely inclined her head in faint acknowledgment without offering her own introduction.

"Your cousin is not keeping you company," he observed, glancing around as if expecting to see Cosimo pop out from behind one of the weeping willows that lined the bank.

He must have made inquiries of the innkeeper, Meg thought, and she was aware of a little frisson of alarm even though there was nothing about Monsieur Devereux's appearance or manner to invite such a response. His dark brown coat and britches were impeccably tailored, the expression on his lean face and in the light brown eyes merely friendly. He probably had a perfectly natural curiosity about his fellow guests, with whom he'd be dining that evening.

"My cousin had business in the town," she said in the same cool tone, hoping he would take it as dismissal. Instead he took a seat on the bench beside her.

"Forgive the intrusion, Madame Giverny," he said with a smile that was not in the least apologetic. "Your French is flawless, but I do not think it is your native tongue?"

So he knew her name too. She decided she had no choice but to satisfy his curiosity at this point, as briefly and uninvitingly as she could. "My father had French relatives, m'sieur. I spent some part of my childhood in France. My late husband was Swiss."

"My condolences, madame. You are so young to have such a loss." He nodded gravely. "You are going to Venice, I understand." Then he raised his hands in a gesture of appeal. "Ah, I can see I'm annoying you. My infernal curiosity! I do beg your pardon, madame."

She gave him another chilly smile. "My destination is not a secret, m'sieur."

"*Nathalie?*"

Cosimo's voice, unusually abrupt, came from behind them. Meg looked over her shoulder and saw him in the shadow of the trees a few yards away. "Oh, Cosimo, I didn't expect you back so soon."

"That much, my dear cousin, is clear," he declared coldly. He looked put out, almost angry, his jaw set, no warmth in his eyes.

Meg blinked in surprise. What on earth was the matter with him? "Monsieur Devereux..." she said with a vague gesture to her companion, who stood up and bowed to the newcomer.

Cosimo gave him a curt nod, then said equally curtly, "Cousin, a moment of your time, if you please."

Meg rose, smoothing down the skirts of her cambric gown. In private she would have told him in no uncertain terms that she resented his tone whatever its reason, but in the company of a stranger she would hold her tongue. She took Cosimo's proffered arm and walked away with him towards the tree-shaded path that led back up to the inn.

"What the devil's the matter with you?" she demanded in an undertone, once they were out of earshot.

"*Hush*," he directed in a sharp whisper, placing his other hand over hers where it rested on his arm and pressing hard. His expression didn't soften as they entered the dim hallway of the inn. He took his arm from hers and gestured silently that she should precede him up the narrow flight of stairs.

Meg, puzzled and more than a little discomfited, went up ahead of him, to the small landing where they had a suite of rooms. The innkeeper's wife was just coming out of the little sitting room that connected their bedchambers.

"I've just freshened the flowers for you, madame," she said with a smile and a curtsy. "And Amelie will be pleased to help you dress for dinner. Just ring for her when you need her."

"Thank you, Madame Brunot," Meg responded, powerfully aware of Cosimo looming behind her in scowling silence. The innkeeper's wife looked up at him, then rapidly looked away again, her smile fading. She bobbed another curtsy and ducked past them towards the back stairs.

Meg entered the parlor, then wheeled around upon

Cosimo as he closed the door. "Just what the . . ." Her voice died as she saw his expression. His shoulders shook with his silent laughter, his eyes alight with amusement. "What game are you playing?" she demanded furiously.

"A rather serious one actually," he replied, chuckling. "But you should have seen your face, Meg."

Infuriated, she pummeled his arm with her closed fists. "I will not be made mock of, Cosimo. How dare you do such a thing."

He caught her hands, holding her at arm's length, laughing down into her enraged countenance. "Oh dear, I didn't realize I would make you so angry. I ask your pardon, but I had good reason for it, I promise . . . no . . . no, I'm not going to let you go until you say you forgive me and you'll listen to me." He tightened his grip on her hands as she tried to wrench them free. "Pax, love."

Meg's anger, rarely aroused and never inclined to persist, died down. But she continued to regard him suspiciously. "Very well, so tell me."

"Say you forgive me."

"I don't know whether I do yet. I'll tell you when you've told me what this is all about."

Cosimo released her hands, banishing the amusement from his countenance. "I'm very much afraid that this Daniel Devereux is up to no good," he stated baldly. "I'm guessing he's in the pay of the local municipality, on the lookout for any undesirable travelers. The countryside is crawling with such informers, *canailles* for the most part, only interested in lining their pockets. I don't know about Devereux, but he may be more dangerous than that. So, my sweet, we have to put him off any scent that he might think he's picked up."

"Oh," Meg said, frowning, crossing her arms over her

breasts. She didn't doubt Cosimo's instincts for a minute, but she was still puzzled. "And how does that act you just put on throw him off this scent?"

"It's merely a part of it," he told her. "The rest of it is up to you."

"How so?" She rubbed her crossed arms, still frowning.

Cosimo's smile now was a little rueful, hiding the sharp intensity of his thoughts. He wasn't sure how Meg was going to react, but what he wanted of her was vital, not to deal with the possibility of any threat posed by Devereux, which he thought was unlikely, but to show him whether she was capable of handling the mission that awaited her in Toulon. He'd been watching for the perfect opportunity for this test throughout the journey, and it had just been handed to him on a plate. Everything now depended on Meg.

"You need to convince Monsieur Devereux that you are the genuine article . . . that we are who we say we are," he said carefully.

"And how am I to do that?" She wasn't going to give him an inch. After his amusement at her expense, she wasn't going to make his task of persuasion any easier.

"By charming him," he said, opening his hands in an isn't-it-obvious gesture. His eyes narrowed. "Flirt with him, my dear, flatter him, draw him onto your side. You did once say that you enjoyed flirtation."

"As I recall, I said there was a place and a time for flirtation," she retorted. "It's not the same thing."

A quizzical eyebrow flickered. "But it's a game you enjoy and one I know you're good at."

Meg knew herself to be a mistress at the game of flirtation. And with the right man, one who approached the game in the same spirit, it gave her enormous pleasure.

But this was something different. Cosimo was asking her to initiate the moves with an end that had nothing to do with mutual amusement.

"I don't understand what good it will do," she said eventually, still rubbing her crossed arms as if she was cold. "And why do I want him on my side? My side against whom?"

"Against me, of course. Your predatory cousin-in-law who has his eye on the fortune you inherited on your husband's death, and that will be augmented by the sum that will come to you on your mother's death. He intends to marry you, and he's not going to be in the least diverted at seeing you engaging in a flirtation with another man."

Enlightenment dawned. Her green eyes widened, little golden sparks of reluctant amusement flickering across the surface. So that lay behind the performance. Meg had to admit it was good. But she still wasn't sure she wanted to take on the part he'd laid out for her. She didn't know whether she could flirt convincingly with someone who didn't attract her.

She said as much and saw disappointment cross his eyes. "Well, if you can't, you can't, and there's no more to be said," he replied.

"I didn't say I wouldn't try," she said. "But am I going to do this under your nose?"

"Initially," he responded, hiding his satisfaction. "At dinner. I will fulminate, attempt to interrupt you, behave in short like a boor. This will naturally ensure you the gentleman's sympathy and, since I know how men's minds work, cause him to feel a not unnatural sense of male triumph."

"You mean like two stags fighting over one doe?" she said sardonically.

"Precisely, my dear." He took her hands again, uncrossing her arms, and pulled her towards him, putting her arms around his waist, holding them at his back. "If you play your cards right, love, you can charm the man insensible. Act the cocotte, promise more of the same tomorrow, and we'll be on our way before he wakes in the morning."

"But won't that arouse his suspicions again?"

He shook his head. "No, not when the innkeeper and his wife tell him how I compelled you to leave at daybreak. And how angry you were."

Such a scenario could work, Meg reflected. "Are you certain he's a government informer?"

"No, how can I be certain?" he responded with a touch of exasperation. "But you don't stay alive in this business, Meg, by waiting for hard evidence in such instances."

She felt justly rebuked. "I'll do my best," she said.

He smiled and took her face between his hands, kissing her eyelids, the tip of her nose, the corner of her mouth. Teasing, tantalizing little darts of his tongue. He turned her head and kissed her ear, using his tongue with knowing skill, until she squirmed and wriggled, demanding to be released even as the sensations drove her to a frenzy of tormented delight.

"Bastard," she gasped when at last he raised his head. "You know what that does to me."

"Why else would I do it?" he inquired with a wicked chuckle. He scooped her off her feet and carried her into his bedchamber, tossing her unceremoniously onto the bed.

Meg gave a suppressed shriek of feigned panic and tried to scoot off the side, but he caught her and dragged her back. She laughed up at him as he leaned over her, holding her hands above her head.

"Now what?" he asked.

"What you will, sir," she murmured, moving her slippered foot along the inside of his leg. "I seem to be at your mercy,"

"That'll be the day," he scoffed, then caught his breath as her foot moved higher. "The shoe, my love, is most definitely on the other foot."

An hour later Meg, once more composed, sat before the dresser mirror in her bedchamber watching the maid Amelie thread a black velvet ribbon through her red curls. Her last fashionable haircut had grown out and she thought ruefully of how Monsieur Christophe, the London coiffeur, would throw up his hands in horror at this messy mishmash of different lengths and unruly curls. Not that it bothered the privateer, she thought with a private smile. He seemed to enjoy threading his fingers through handfuls of it, twisting the curls into wild corkscrews.

"There, madame, that is pretty, I think." Amelie smiled at her handiwork. "The black is so perfect with such a vivid red."

And perfect for a widow just out of mourning. "Vivid is one word for it," Meg said, fastening a pin in the neck of the cream lace fichu. "Thank you, Amelie. You've been a great help, and I know you're needed downstairs."

"My pleasure, madame." The girl curtsied and left.

The door to the parlor opened and Cosimo came in. Meg still found it difficult to get used to the sight of him in formal dress. But he'd only worn it once or twice on this journey, when the status of their nightly stops had warranted it, so it was perhaps not surprising.

"How smart you are," she said, admiring the subdued

elegance of his black coat and waistcoat, black britches, ruffled shirt, and starched cravat.

His responding smile was distracted as he looked her over. "You'll achieve a better effect without the fichu," he pronounced. "It's too demure."

"As you wish." She unfastened the pin and flicked away the fichu with a disdainful twitch of her fingers. "Not that there's much of a décolletage to hide."

He came up behind her, sliding his hands down into the neck of her dark green gown, feeling for her breasts. "There's more than enough for those who know." His breath rustled through her hair. "Are you ready?"

"As I'll ever be." She grasped his strong wrists for an instant, then moved his hands aside and stood up. "No shawl?"

"I don't know. What do you think?"

"I think it might prove a useful prop," she said, taking up a filmy strip of black chiffon. "I have no fan, but I can see how this could be used to good effect." She draped it over her elbows. "Shall we raise the curtain?"

"Let me go first, give me five minutes, and then follow. Try for a touch of agitation on your entrance, anger, not tears. You're no subdued young woman with a strict guardian. Rather you need an unimpeachable male escort to make a certain journey in safety and the escort is proving unsatisfactory. Pointedly ignore me and make a bee-line for our friend."

Meg nodded. "Simple enough," she said. "But he might think it a little strange at first. I was very cool this afternoon."

"If you give him half a chance, he'll put it down to the difficulties of your situation." Cosimo was walking to the door. "Five minutes."

Meg went to the open window and drew a deep breath of the scented air. Roses and honeysuckle. It felt as if there'd been some subtle shift in her relationship with Cosimo. It was as if the adventure had taken a different turn; they were no longer simply lovers. But if not that, what? Unconsciously she pressed her fingertip into the cleft of her chin. Partners in a bigger drama? One in which Cosimo was the director, she an actor. But she thought she'd been prepared to expect that on this journey. Cosimo, the privateer, the courier, would encounter situations that required a spy's skills. She just hadn't seen herself as taking any important part in those situations. They were beyond her purview. Very different from joining him on courier expeditions from the *Mary Rose*. That had been play. For her, not for Cosimo, she admitted now.

Five minutes must have passed. Meg checked her image in the mirror and then went downstairs to the parlor that doubled as the inn's dining room. She heard the subdued murmur of voices as she crossed the hallway, and thought that there must be other guests than Monsieur Devereux and themselves. How that would affect tonight's little play remained to be seen.

She pushed open the door. The room was still filled with the late evening sunlight that competed with the candles on the table and the mantelpiece. Apart from Cosimo and Daniel Devereux, there were two other men, whose somewhat elaborately old-fashioned dress of velvet and lace, Meg guessed, was that of wealthy, provincial landowners or merchants. They all looked towards the door as she entered.

Cosimo took a deep draught of the wine in his glass and said, almost as an afterthought, "Gentlemen, my cousin, Madame Giverny."

"Good evening, gentlemen," she said with a nod that passed for a bow. Her lips were set in an angry line and she made no attempt to accompany the nod with a smile.

They bowed and for a moment no one moved, then Daniel Devereux came forward, extending his hand. "Madame, may I pour you a glass of port?"

"Thank you, Monsieur Devereux." She took the hand, this time managing a smile before casting a look of disdain towards her cousin, who had so deliberately failed to offer her refreshment. He turned away from the glance with a flare of his nostrils.

Meg placed her hand on Devereux's arm and moved towards the big bow window that stood open to the garden. "Such a lovely evening. Such entrancing fragrances, don't you find, Monsieur Devereux?"

"Indeed, madame. Late spring is lovely in these parts. More like summer." He was regarding her curiously even as they engaged in this inoffensive small talk, and Meg guessed that the coldness between the cousins had interested him. Well, as the evening progressed he would find much more to intrigue him.

She smiled up at him, allowing the shawl to slip down her arms to reveal what cleavage she possessed. "Are you from Vaucluse, m'sieur?"

"No, alas, madame. I am en route to Marseilles. But I spent many happy months of my childhood in Vaucluse. You've seen the grotto of Petrach?"

"I had hoped to visit it tomorrow," Meg said with a glancing smile that could have been interpreted as shy, but most definitely was not. "I'm not sure whether my cousin will be willing to take me." She allowed her lip to curl just a fraction.

"Then you must allow me to be your escort," he said.

"I know it well. The steps are a little steep, a little treacherous..."

"I'm sure I could manage them with your help, Monsieur Devereux," she said, looking up at him from beneath her eyelashes. "I am most eager to visit the site."

"Then we should agree to do so in the morning, before the heat of the day." His hand lightly brushed hers as he indicated her empty glass. "May I get you another glass of port?"

"Cousin, it's time to dine. Our hostess grows impatient." Cosimo almost snatched her glass from her. "Allow me to seat you." He took her elbow and steered her to the table. Meg made her back rigid, a signal of unwilling acceptance to anyone who would read it as such, and took the chair Cosimo held out for her. He took the chair on her left.

Daniel Devereux glanced at the seat on her right and Meg gave him a tiny smile of invitation, narrowing her eyes just a little, playing coquettishly with the edge of her shawl. He put a hand on the back of the chair in question. "May I, madame?"

"Please, do, Monsieur Devereux," she murmured, fluttering her eyelashes a little as she made a little patting motion towards the seat. She glanced once to her left where Cosimo sat in stony silence, glaring at Devereux, then she turned a brilliant smile back to Devereux.

Devereux took the seat and shook out his napkin. He lowered his voice a little. "Your cousin seems less than pleased with me." The statement was lightly spoken, as if it mattered little to him.

Meg took a sip of wine and dabbed at her lips with her napkin, murmuring under cover of the movement, "My cousin is less than pleased with most men in my company, I fear."

Devereux's eyebrows lifted, but he made no response. Amelie passed out bowls of vichyssoise and for a moment the only sounds around the table were the clink of spoon on china and an occasional rumble of conversation from the two men who seemed to be acquaintances.

"You said you passed some part of your childhood in Vaucluse, Monsieur Devereux," Meg said. "Where do you live now?"

"In Marseilles, madame," he responded. "I own a small export business."

Cosimo gave a snort of derision. "Export business, in the middle of a war. I doubt you'll stay in business for long, m'sieur." He drained his glass and refilled it, not offering the decanter to his table companions.

A smile flicked across Daniel Devereux's rather thin mouth. "I would say, m'sieur, that perhaps you don't know much about such business," he declared. "Madame, may I offer you more wine . . . excuse me . . . ?" He reached across her for the decanter.

"Thank you." She cast another scornful glance at her "cousin." "Indeed, cousin, you know little enough about any kind of business, I believe."

"A *gentleman*, my dear, has no need to sully his hands with trade," Cosimo snarled, draining his glass. He snapped his fingers rudely at Amelie and demanded, "More wine, girl."

Meg was torn between amusement and wonder at this extraordinary transformation of the courteous, even-tempered, exquisitely mannered privateer. How much could he drink without being genuinely affected? she wondered. Not that he would ever lose control; he would know exactly when to stop.

Their two companions across the table were also looking at him in disapproving surprise, and then pointedly ignored him and resumed their own conversation.

Meg returned her attention to Devereux, turning up her eyes in exasperation. "You must forgive my cousin," she said softly, but just loud enough for Cosimo to overhear. "He has had some disappointments just recently."

"Hold your tattling tongue, ma'am," Cosimo hissed. "I'll not have family business broadcast at a public table."

Meg lowered her eyes as if embarrassed at this offensive rebuke, and busied herself adjusting the shawl on her arms.

"Allow me, madame." Devereux helped her with the shawl. "I fear your cousin is deep into his wine. Nothing else would excuse such discourtesy."

She touched a hand to her breast in a fleeting gesture that indicated discomfort and gave him an up-from-under smile. "You are too kind, m'sieur."

"Impossible," he said. "With such a charming lady."

"And now, m'sieur, you flatter me," she said, her smile taking on a coquettish edge, her eyelashes fluttering a little, as she lightly tapped his hand with her own.

"Impossible," he repeated, his free hand brushing hers for an instant.

Cosimo sat in fulminating silence, but beneath the façade he was filled with both admiration and amusement as he listened to the banter. Meg was good. Just the right blend of coquette and innocence, although no one, and certainly not the suave Devereux, would believe in the innocence for one minute. But that was part of the game. She was making it clear that if seduction was in the cards, then she would not be a novice. For every three steps she took forward, there was one delicate step back, drawing him further into the play. Indeed, what man could resist?

For some reason, that reflection had the effect of diminishing both his admiration and his amusement.

He dropped his fork with a clatter onto his plate and then swore under his breath as if the implement had taken on a life of its own. He took up his glass and drank again, then drawled somewhat thickly, "You grow mighty familiar, Cousin Giverny. You'd do well to have a care for your reputation. *I* know your little ways but what passes among family won't do among strangers. Mark my words." He leered at her, managing to look both contemptuous and lustful.

Meg couldn't believe how his face had changed. It had lost all definition, gone soft as if his features were collapsing in on themselves. His mouth was a little slack, his eyes slitted as if he could barely keep them open. She gave him a look of supreme contempt and said, "You are over-drunk, cousin." Then she turned back to Devereux, giving her "cousin" her shoulder.

Cosimo muttered an oath and Devereux flung his napkin on the table, jumping to his feet. "M'sieur, I must protest such language in the presence of a lady."

Meg spoke hastily, her hand reaching for his arm. "N-no, please, m'sieur. I take no notice of my cousin when he's in drink, I beg you to do the same." She pulled at his sleeve with an assumption of urgency and pleaded, "Do please sit down again, m'sieur. I would not have you quarrel with my cousin in this fashion."

Devereux looked down at her, his expression still livid with indignation, then he bowed. "As you wish, madame. Forgive me if I was discourteous."

"No, no, I am grateful for your concern," she said warmly as he resumed his seat. "But my cousin . . ." She let the sentence die with an ill-concealed shudder.

Cosimo judged it time to leave Meg to play the rest of the game alone. He pushed back his chair and stood up, staggering a little. He muttered something about fresh air and weaved his way to the door, pausing to issue a vague threat over his shoulder. "You had best be in your bed by ten o'clock, cousin. I'll not answer for it if you're not." The door banged on his departure.

Meg shook her head in disgust. "Empty words. He has no authority over me and he knows it."

Devereux sipped his wine and refilled their glasses. "Forgive me if this is impertinent, but why do you travel with him?"

"He's the only family escort I have." She grimaced a little over the lip of her glass. "A respectable single woman cannot travel alone, under any circumstances, and most particularly not at this time. There are dangers aplenty for any traveler." She set down her glass. "My cousin has his faults certainly, but he *is* capable of protecting me."

"And when you arrive in Venice?"

She thought she could sense a sharpness beneath the question, as if this interested him more than any previous tidbits of personal information she'd dropped. "I shall give him his congé," she said with a shrug. "Once I am under my mother and stepfather's protection, I will have no need of my cousin's." She made her voice coldly practical.

Devereux absorbed this in silence as he peeled a pear, quartered it, and placed it on her plate. "May I?"

"Why, thank you," she returned, nibbling a piece. "I would like to take a walk along the riverbank when we've finished. It's such a perfect evening."

"Delightful," he agreed. "I trust you'll accept my escort?"

She batted her lashes at him, saying softly, "That was my suggestion, Monsieur Devereux... Daniel."

He looked distinctly complacent as he raised her hand to his lips. "Nathalie... may I?"

"But of course," she said.

"Such a delightful name," he observed. "Are you ready for our stroll, Nathalie?"

Meg pushed back her chair at once and took the hand he held out to assist her in rising. His fingers closed over hers in an intimate squeeze and immediately she gently withdrew her hand. She was happy to lead him on up to a point, but he must not be permitted to take the initiative or push things too fast. That was not how the game was played.

His smile faded for a second, then returned as if nothing had occurred. He offered his arm and she took it with a murmur of thanks, wished their table companions a pleasant evening, and walked with Devereux into the soft air.

"I trust you'll find your cousin easy to dismiss when you reach your mother's home," he said, as they strolled down the path towards the river.

"I'm sure I won't," she stated bluntly. "The situation is a little difficult, Daniel." She gave a tiny but eloquent sigh.

"I beg your pardon. I didn't mean to pry. Please forget I asked." He was all concern, drawing her hand through his arm, then saying cheerfully, "So tomorrow we shall visit Petrach's grotto."

"Yes, that will be lovely," she said. "As long as I can slip away from my cousin. But after a night like this, he'll be inclined to sleep late."

"It seems such a pity that you should have to subject yourself to such an escort," he said, guiding her steps to the seat where he'd found her that afternoon.

She gave another very eloquent sigh. "As long as I don't have to subject myself to a lifetime of it."

"Oh, my dear madame, how should you?" He sounded horrified, stopping just short of the seat.

"He's determined we shall marry. I have a substantial income... my late husband... you understand," she said hesitantly, playing with the end of her shawl, and keeping her eyes on the dark river. "And on my mother's death, there will be more." Another sigh, a little shrug. "I am hoping that my mother and stepfather will support me in my refusal to marry my cousin." She turned her eyes from the river and smiled a little sadly at her companion. "A woman alone is so vulnerable, Daniel." She wanted to laugh aloud at the sudden gleam in his eye.

He took her hand and this time she did not withdraw it. "You must know that you can call upon me, my dear Nathalie. In any way that I can be of service."

"You are too kind," she said softly, lifting her face in an invitation that no man could refuse under the silver light of the moon on the banks of a softly flowing river.

He kissed her cheek, then when she didn't move her head aside, her lips. She allowed herself to lean into him for a bare instant, then straightened. "We must not," she protested. "But you have been so kind."

At that he looked somewhat nonplussed. "Kindness is hardly the issue, Nathalie. I do not ask for gratitude."

"No, no, of course not," she said hastily. "I didn't mean to imply any such thing." Now her mind was working fast. Her task was completed. If he had had any suspicions that she and Cosimo were not what they seemed, she could see that they were now at rest. Now she needed to find a way to bring this to an end without jeopardizing his state of mind. Even if his state of health was somewhat compromised by an abrupt conclusion to this stroll, she reflected with a stab of guilt. True, she enjoyed the pas de deux of flirtation, but her partner in the dance usually had his eyes open. She took no pleasure in leaving a man in all the discomfort of unsatisfied arousal.

She put a hand on his arm. "Please, Daniel, will you escort me back to the inn? The evening has fatigued me ... forgive me ... but when we meet in the morning I shall be refreshed."

Daniel Devereux was a gentleman most of the time, and he could see no way to insist on her staying. He didn't hide his disappointment, though, even as he offered his arm again. "What time will you be ready for our excursion in the morning?"

"Oh, by nine o'clock, easily," she said with enthusiasm. By that time she and Cosimo would be long gone.

"Then I will try to control my impatience until then," he said gallantly, raising her hand to his lips as they reached the door.

She leaned forward to kiss his cheek. "Thank you for being such delightful company, Daniel, and so understanding."

He watched her ascend the stairs, then went to drown his lust in cognac in the taproom.

Meg whisked herself into the parlor, closing the door at her back. She stood leaning against it, her eyes sparkling, her cheeks a little flushed with the triumph of success. Where was Cosimo? She had expected him to be waiting eagerly for her return. "Cosimo?"

He came out of his bedchamber and looked at her for a moment in a way that puzzled her. If she didn't know it was impossible, she would have said he seemed put out, and then he crossed the room swiftly. "Oh, you do have the air of a cat with the cream," he said. "And how well you played it, my sweet." He kissed her full on the mouth with a hard, declarative passion.

"You weren't so bad yourself, at the drunken sot part," she said, laughing against his mouth. "What an unpleasant man you can be." She felt him stiffen slightly and she pulled back her face, but the moment was gone as swiftly as it came and he was grinning down at her with all the usual playfulness, and the only stiffness she could detect was exactly where she wanted it to be.

"I'm glad to see that drink doesn't have an adverse affect," she murmured, moving her hand down his belly. "And I find myself as much in need, love. After such an evening, my appetites are well whetted."

His own had been sharpened too, but by the strange sensations of watching Meg, *his* Meg, take such obvious pleasure in flirting with some other man.

He had been jealous. He astonished himself with such a reaction, but watching Meg, listening to her, had aroused a primitive sense of competition that, never having experienced it before, Cosimo couldn't begin to understand.

Chapter 20

I think we'd be wise to bypass Marseilles in light of our encounter with your friend," Cosimo remarked as they rode along a country lane under a hot afternoon sun. "I would hate to run into him again."

They had left the Rhône behind them several hours earlier and the sense of the sea was now much more pronounced. The salt marshes of the Camargue were not far away to their west and the air had a pronounced salt tang.

"He wasn't *my* friend," Meg objected.

"He certainly believed he was," Cosimo said with a laugh.

"Which was, after all, the object of the exercise." It was a tart rejoinder, but his laugh had irritated her for some reason.

Cosimo glanced over at her as she rode beside him, elegant in a tawny riding habit with a high starched stock and a charming hat with a sweeping peacock feather that he'd bought for her in one of the larger towns they'd passed through. The wide brim of the hat shaded her face but he could see the set of her jaw, the firm line of her mouth.

She had appeared to enjoy her part in the previous evening's theater, but now he wondered.

Well, he would find out soon enough, he thought with grim resolution. The end game must soon be played and tonight he would finally tell her the truth. His spirit quailed at the prospect, and he knew it was because he wasn't sure of her. He had fervently believed that by the time it became necessary to reveal all and recruit her to the mission, she would be ready to join him, if only by virtue of the bond they would by then have forged.

The bond was forged, in many ways stronger than he had ever imagined it could be. But Meg was still as independent and in parts of her being as unknowable as she had been from the first moment he'd looked at her unconscious body in his cabin and realized the potential disaster. He'd acted from that moment on impulse, making steps up as he went along. But now there were no more steps to make up.

He knew what had to be done in Toulon. And he knew how to do it all, from the earliest stage of setting Meg up in her own establishment and guiding her steps towards Napoleon, to the culmination of the mission. Even their escape route was planned to the last detail. And he trusted himself to adapt to any one of the innumerable circumstances that might crop up to force a change in direction. Except for one. If Meg refused to join him.

"I'm sure Monsieur Devereux enjoyed his evening," he said pacifically. "He may have been balked of its continuance, but that's so often the lot of men." He gave a heavy sigh that brought him his reward. A peal of laughter from his companion.

"Women too," she said. "And I'll lay odds, Cosimo, that more women spend more hours of their lives waiting for some man to make an offer, pay a call, or even do so much as leave a visiting card."

"I don't think we'll argue the differing frustrations of the sexes," he said with a chuckle. "I have it in mind to stop for the night in a small village close to Miramas. There's a passable inn there. Tomorrow we'll have to make a detour into the mountains to avoid Marseilles, but it's a much better traveled road than the one through the Laucune, and not at such an altitude."

"Whatever you say," Meg responded. She was fascinated by Cosimo's intimate knowledge of the terrain they had crossed in the last few weeks. He had known almost every inn they'd stayed at, and not once had they taken a wrong turn. She'd asked him early on how many times he'd taken the journey, and he'd given a less-than-concrete answer. It had satisfied her at the time, and then the rigors of the journey had made the issue irrelevant. But now that they were nearing its end, they became relevant again. So she asked him again.

He drew back on his reins as a rabbit darted across the lane almost beneath his horse's hooves. The gelding danced back, shaking its head, the harness jingling. "I have not always taken the same route," Cosimo said, leaning forward to gentle the horse with a hand on its neck.

"But you know where all the inns are?" she persisted.

"Not all," he qualified.

Meg sucked in her lower lip. "I know you're a spy, Cosimo. I know you're a courier. I know you're a privateer. Why won't you give a straight answer to a straight question? You were not expecting to take these dispatches across country from Bordeaux to Toulon. And yet you know exactly what route to take. *How?*"

Cosimo recognized the inevitability of disclosure. He

had been preparing himself to make it tonight, but in the face of that question, it had to be now. Here in the open without any props to assist him, nothing to divert attention. And perhaps it was better that way. Dirty secrets laid out in the fresh air, without artifice.

"I will tell you. But not on horseback." He raised his whip and gestured across a field to where a wisp of smoke hung against the deep blue of the sky. "We'll go over there, find water for the horses, and rest for a while before we continue."

"I wouldn't mind the opportunity to stretch my legs," Meg said, swallowing the surge of unease that rose like bile in her throat. Why was she so certain something bad was about to happen?

They struck out across the field, Meg's mare, never one to toe the line, for once keeping nose to tail with Cosimo's gelding. At the edge of the field that bordered on a tiny hamlet, they came to a narrow stream that was no more than a water-filled ditch. Cosimo dismounted and dipped a finger into the ditch. He touched the fingertip to his tongue. "It's brackish," he said. "Probably has its source somewhere in the Camargue." He remounted. "We'll go into the hamlet. They'll have a horse trough and we can water the animals."

Meg followed him, her sense of unease increasing. Cosimo had never veered voluntarily from their route before.

They broke through the hedgerow into a narrow dusty lane. On either side were small stone cottages, some with kitchen gardens, the soil baked hard in the hot sun of the South. They encountered few people: an old man resting on a hoe, a little girl chasing a scrawny chicken.

Cosimo leaned over the gelding's neck and asked the

man where he would find the horse trough. The man gestured down the lane, and said something that was incomprehensible to Meg, but Cosimo seemed to understand.
He held out a coin with a word of thanks, then nudged the
gelding.

They found the well and the long horse trough in a tiny
courtyard just off the lane. Cosimo dismounted and led his
horse to the trough. This barren spot was not the place
to make his disclosure. It was too public, and there was
nowhere to sit. He saw Meg dismount and lead her mare to
water.

"Hold the horses, Meg. I'll return in a few minutes." He
gave her his horse's reins and those of the packhorse that
he'd been leading, and loped off towards the source of a
certain scent coming from one of the narrow alleys that led
off the courtyard.

When he returned with a rush basket, Meg was drawing
the horses away from the trough. "They've had sufficient,"
she said. "What's that you have?" She indicated the basket.

"Something to refresh *ourselves* with," Cosimo responded. "I followed my nose and it led me to the Holy
Grail." He took the reins of his own horse and those of the
packhorse. "We'll walk the horses just a few yards. There's
a perfect place for a picnic."

Despite her unease, Meg was hungry enough to be intrigued by the contents of the basket. She took the mare
and followed. Cosimo led them to an open space along a
stream into which the ditch opened. Weeping willows
along the stream offered shade, and a grove of pine trees
clustered at the edge of the clearing. She followed suit as
Cosimo tethered his horses in a patch of lush grass.

"Are we dining?" she inquired, trying for a playful note

as she sat on a mossy root and unpinned her hat, setting it on the grass beside her before reaching for the rush basket.

"Not exactly," Cosimo said, sitting down beside her. "I'm hoping that we'll do that when we stop for the night. But we haven't eaten much thus far today, so a little bread and cheese, a ham-and-egg pie, still warm from the oven, and a flagon of wine might be welcome."

Meg propped her back against the willow tree. "They might," she agreed as she drew out the flagon of red wine. She passed it to him and carefully lifted out of the basket a golden-crusted, richly fragrant pie. She sniffed appreciatively, then rummaged some more, coming up with a long loaf of crusty bread and a hefty wedge of ripe, creamy cheese.

Cosimo drew the cork on the flagon with his teeth and took a deep swallow, then passed it to Meg.

She took it, swallowed a draught herself, then looked at him. "Are you going to tell me something I won't wish to hear, Cosimo?"

He returned the look quietly for a moment, then said, "I don't know. I own I would have preferred a different setting for this, but I must use what I have."

Meg set the flagon on the grass and drew up her knees beneath the skirt of her riding habit. The leather britches, which in female riding dress were disguised by the skirt, had become so much second nature in the last weeks that she tended to forget about the skirt altogether.

She clasped her knees and rested her chin on them. "Perhaps you should begin."

"Perhaps I should." But he didn't begin immediately. He drew out the folding knife that was always sheathed at his belt and sliced the pie into four quarters. "Shall we eat first?" He lifted one quarter on the flat blade of the knife and held it out to her.

"Will I need sustaining?" she inquired with a rather unconvincing smile as she took the slice and bit into it.

He shook his head, saying only, "Eat, Meg." He took up the loaf and broke it, then sliced into the cheese, spreading it on a crusty chunk of bread.

Meg was surprised that despite the nagging unease her appetite was as sharp as always. However, they ate in silence, passing the flagon between them, until finally Cosimo brushed off his hands, replaced the empty pie dish and flagon in the rush basket, and stood up.

"I'm going to take this back to its home," he said. "We'll talk when I return." He set off at a fast stride.

Meg stood up and went to the stream. She knelt to wash her hands and splashed water on her face, then sat back on her heels, staring down into the clear bubbling surface of the stream, absently noticing the darting silver flashes of tiny fish caught by the glancing sunlight. Nagging unease had become outright dread, and her picnic now sat like lead in her belly.

She felt rather than heard Cosimo's return and slowly rose to her feet, turning as slowly. He stood beneath a willow tree, hands thrust into his pockets, and met her intent gaze. They were separated by about five feet. She clasped her hands against her skirt and gave an imperceptible nod as if telling him she was ready.

His voice was low and even as he told her. He told her what he was, what he was going to do, how he had deceived her, and what he wanted of her. And throughout she was as still as stone, her eyes never leaving his face, watching so intently it was as if she was seeing the words as they came out of his mouth, until finally there was nothing left to tell, and he was silent.

He was going to assassinate Napoleon Bonaparte.

Meg stared at him, stupefied by the grandeur of such an endeavor...the grandeur and the *enormity* of it. And as she stood there, staring, the implications of everything he'd said finally became concrete.

From the first moment of seeing her he had used her, manipulated her, deceived her. *I don't risk failure, my dear.* His words came back to her with renewed resonance. He'd been grooming her from the first moment of seeing her.

"No," she declared. "I will not help you kill a man."

The rest could wait, her outrage, her disgust, the bitter blow to her sense of self, all that could wait until he understood that every despicable thing he had done to her had been worthless.

It was worse than he'd expected, and Cosimo thought he had been prepared for the worst. But her extreme pallor, the deadness in those always lively green eyes, the death mask set of her features filled him with alarm.

"Meg..." He took a step towards her.

She threw up her hands palms outward. "Don't come near me."

Unwisely he ignored her. He came close, reaching for her hands. "Meg...sweetheart, listen—"

She hit him with all the force she had in her. Her swinging palms cracked against his face, one side and then the other, making a sound in the afternoon quiet that brought an alarmed whinny from the tethered horses.

His nostrils flared, but he didn't move. His hands were still and loose at his sides as the scarlet prints flamed on his cheeks. "You have the right," he said softly.

"I abhor violence," Meg said, spinning away from him.

"And I detest you for making me do such a thing." She walked away into the grove of pine trees.

Cosimo touched his stinging cheeks. For a moment he had been reassured by her attack, action rather than that dreadful deadness, but now he was unsure. An action so out of character would only make Meg feel worse than she did, and would set her even more strongly against him.

He stood irresolute for a few minutes, then shook himself out of his wretched reverie. They couldn't stay here, however ghastly the situation. He followed her path into the trees and called her.

Meg heard his voice but kept on walking, kicking up pine needles with every step. She was numb. She could not in her worst nightmare have imagined something this dreadful. He had played with her. Used the passionate enjoyment she had never attempted to disguise as a means of manipulation. She felt dirty, and as worthless as an abandoned mongrel.

"Meg."

The sharp urgency of his call this time stopped her. Reality told her she couldn't leave this horror behind her, walking away forever through a pine grove. She turned back and walked straight past where he stood a few feet away, back to the horses. She picked up her hat, untethered her mare, and remounted with the aid of a fallen log, then sat, holding the reins loosely, waiting for Cosimo to mount.

He said nothing as he brought the gelding up beside the mare, leading the packhorse. There was nothing to be said at this juncture, he knew that even without looking at her face. He nudged the gelding forward, back towards the dusty road, and Meg dropped back a little but followed throughout the long, hot afternoon.

Miramas stood at the head of an estuary. The hostelry Cosimo had chosen was in a small village on the shores of the estuary. It was an isolated building, at least a mile away from the nearest habitation, and bleakly Meg recognized it as exactly the sort of place off the beaten track that a man of Cosimo's profession would know. They had stayed in many such in the last weeks. Some pleasant, some not.

This one, however, was in the former category. They were greeted warmly, the horses taken from them with promises of good oats and clean hay, and the lady of the house led them into a pleasant garden behind the inn, insisting they sit beneath the grape arbor and try a glass of the local wine. "From my father's vineyard," she said. "A fine Rhône, as good as anything you would get in the valley."

Meg wanted to refuse, but the woman's eager hospitality would not permit the discourtesy. She sat down on the wooden bench at the wooden table and smiled her thanks, leaving the verbal expressions to Cosimo.

The woman brought a dish of olives and a plate of salami with a copper pot of wine. *"Et, Madame Ana, elle va bien, j'espère, m'sieur?"* She beamed at Cosimo as she took two glasses from the capacious pockets of her apron and set them on the table.

"Mais oui, Madame Arlene, merci," Cosimo returned, his voice expressionless.

The woman cast a quick look towards Meg's still figure and set countenance. She looked a little discomfited, bobbed a slight curtsy, and hurried away.

Meg took an olive and spat the pit into the flowerbed beside her. She took a sip of wine. How many times had Cosimo and Ana been here on some clandestine mission? Often enough for the innkeeper to refer familiarly to Cosimo's previous companion and ask after her health.

"I'd like to go to my bedchamber," she said, rising to her feet. "I assume you and Ana always shared a bed. I would prefer my own. I trust that's possible?" Her voice was flat.

Cosimo stood up. "Of course. I'll come with you and talk to Madame Arlène." Meg was already at the brink and he could see no possible virtue in pushing her at this point. He had played his card, and while he was not prepared to accept that he had lost the game, he would accept the loss of a trick. He didn't think he had any aces in his hand, but he had a few lesser cards that he could play to win, if he laid them down skillfully.

He didn't touch her, merely walked beside her into the inn's stone-flagged kitchen. Drying herbs hung from racks above the range and the air was filled with the scents of thyme and tarragon, marjoram and rosemary.

Meg inhaled the scents; they reminded her of quiet kitchens in Kent, of a time when such a betrayal was unimaginable. She listened as Cosimo talked to Madame Arlene. He was saying that he was escorting Madame Giverny to Marseilles. That Madame was tired after the long journey and would like to rest in her bedchamber.

Whether Madame Arlene believed a word of it was unclear. What was clear to Meg was that it didn't matter either way. She followed the smiling innkeeper up the stairs to a small but clean chamber that smelled of lavender.

"*Merci, Madame Arlene*," she said with genuine appreciation. It was a very pretty room. "*C'est très jolie.*"

Madame Arlene murmured appreciation of a deserved compliment, but her eyes ran over her new guest in a quick inquiring examination and Meg guessed that she was being compared to Ana and somehow found wanting. She offered a flick of a smile in dismissal, and the innkeeper backed out, saying she would send up hot water as she closed the door on her departure.

Meg took a deep breath of the fragrant, peaceful quiet. She cast aside her hat and went over to the open casement. And then wished she hadn't. The window looked down on the arbor. Cosimo had returned to the table and was sitting twirling his glass between his fingers, his expression dark. There was nothing easy in his posture. All the composure, the certainty that was the essential Cosimo was missing.

He'd made a mistake. Meg turned away from the window. Cosimo was unaccustomed to making mistakes. He'd miscalculated and he was suffering for it. How often did a plan of his go awry?

Meg dropped onto the bed, linking her hands behind her head. The chintz tester enclosed her in the smell of the sun and sea. Abruptly she sat up to pull off her boots, kicking them across the room. An invincible need to sleep swooped over her.

She opened her eyes onto the same view. The sun was low in the sky but not yet set. She had slept for perhaps thirty minutes. She sat up and struggled to her feet, feeling dry mouthed and headachy. Wine and turmoil under the sun could wreak havoc, she thought with a grimace.

A jug of hot water, still slightly steaming, stood beside the bowl on the dresser. Madame Arlene had fulfilled her promise. Meg undressed with fingers that were all thumbs and sponged herself. The valise that contained her own clothes was on the floor by the wardrobe, but she realized she had no interest in dressing or doing anything except falling into a deep, deep sleep.

Naked, she crawled beneath the lavender-scented covers and curled herself into a ball. She would sleep and afterwards she would be able to face this and find her way through it.

Cosimo stood beside the bed and looked at her. A shaft of moonlight fell across her face, accentuating her pallor, so that the dusting of freckles across her nose stood out dramatically. The hint of bronze that days in the sun had given her countenance was wiped away, as if it had been painted on. He ached as if he'd been racked but the pain etched on her face hurt him more than his own distress. He had come to her now prepared to face the situation, to compel Meg to face it, to accept that there were no alternatives... no alternatives for either of them. She had to partner him because only thus did they have a chance of survival.

But as he looked at her he knew he could not disturb the peace of her sleep. She needed the strength it would give her. He moved away from the bed and leaned out of the window to draw the shutters closed, blocking out the moonlight, then he threw off his clothes and slid under the covers beside her. He didn't touch her, but he needed the sense of her body, the warmth of her flesh to close the distance between them. After a while he fell asleep, soothed by her rhythmic breathing and the familiar scent of her skin.

He awoke with a violent start. Meg was curled on her side, driving her feet into his thighs, trying to push him away.

"Get out," she said furiously. "How *could* you? Get away

from me." She kicked at him, flailing with her hands at his chest. "You disgust me. Get away."

"Wait...wait," he said, seizing her hands. "Meg...sweet, please. Stop for a minute. I'm not touching you...I'm not going to. Be still." He wriggled away from her driving heels, still maintaining a hold on her hands.

Meg wrenched her hands free and sat up. The chamber with the shutters closed was in pitch darkness. Panic caught at her chest and she took several breaths, orienting herself to the world beyond sleep. She had been so deeply asleep, so roughly awoken by the unwelcome knowledge of his body beside her, by the rush of loathsome memory, that it took many minutes to steady herself.

Cosimo had left the bed and now stood beside it, a tall dark shape barely distinguishable from the darkness around him. "I didn't mean to frighten you," he said. "I didn't mean to wake you...I fell asleep beside you...forgive me." He sounded wretched.

Meg's eyes slowly accustomed themselves to the darkness. She pushed the tumbled hair back from her forehead. "Light a candle."

Cosimo felt his way across the chamber to the dresser, where he found flint and tinder beside a fresh candle. He lit the candle and the flame steadied, illuminating the room with a faint golden glow. "I'm so sorry," he said.

"What for?" Meg asked bitterly. "Creeping into my bed and scaring me? Or for the rest? But of course you have no regrets for that, do you? It's who you are...what you do... and it doesn't matter a damn to you who you use to help you on your way."

Cosimo pulled on his britches. Ordinarily his nakedness wouldn't have troubled him in the least but not in this situation. "Actually, it does matter a damn," he said. "You matter to me a great deal more than a damn, Meg."

"Oh, I can believe *that*," she said, as bitterly as before. "I've been a tool from the first moment you saw me. Deny it."

He sighed. "No, I can't."

Meg was silent for a moment. She had expected a fervent denial, something she could attack with the bright sword of righteousness. An admission was impossible to confront.

He spoke swiftly into the silence. "Meg, I ask you to believe that it's been a long time since I thought of you as anything but a lover, a partner, a companion whose wit and strength have been ever a source of delight." He took a step towards the bed, his hands outstretched. "I freely admit that you agreed to join me on this journey because I spun you a tissue of lies. But there hasn't been a day in the last weeks when I haven't regretted that."

"Then why didn't you tell me the truth sooner?" She was sitting bolt upright, the covers tight beneath her chin.

"There you have me," he said ruefully.

She gave a short ironic laugh. "Yes, because you would not jeopardize your mission . . . this assassination . . . by risking my refusal a minute sooner than you had to."

"I don't deny it."

It was impossible to quarrel with a man who admitted every accusation, Meg thought with angry frustration. But it changed nothing.

"I will not help you kill a man," she said steadily. "Leave me here if you wish and I will make shift for myself. But I will go no further with you in this business, Cosimo."

"Napoleon has sworn to conquer England," he said quietly. "And there is every reason to believe that he will succeed. He was given command of the Army of England last October."

"Then why is he going to Egypt?" Meg demanded. "Or was that a lie too?"

"No," Cosimo said. "But his decision to postpone the invasion of England gives us a brief opportunity. The man menaces the entire continent of Europe, Meg. England is protected by the Channel and her navy. Nothing more." He stepped closer to the bed, his hands still open. "Imagine how many lives will be saved by the loss of just this one."

There was something inexorable about that logic. But he was asking her to seduce a man, to lure him to his death. In cold blood. Death in battle was dreadful, but... She thought of the brief and relatively clean engagement the *Mary Rose* had had with the French frigate. She remembered the screams of the sailor who'd been pinned by a loose cannon, his chest crushed. She remembered the blood of wounds caused by something as simple as a splinter. It was not difficult to imagine the casualties of a full naval engagement. And history had taught her all she needed to know about battlefields.

And yet despite logic, everything she was, everything she had ever believed in, shrank from the very idea of taking part in such a way in such a death. "I cannot do it," she said, turning her head away from the light.

Cosimo said nothing for a moment, then he bent to pick up his shirt and the rest of his clothes. "The decision has never been anyone's but yours, Meg." He left the chamber, snuffing the candle on his way out.

Meg threw off the covers and jumped from the bed. She went to the window and flung open the shutters. The moon was setting. She could not do such a thing . . . bring a man to his death. She *could* not.

But Cosimo would do it anyway. With or without her. She knew that without asking him. And she would wait on the sidelines until he had completed his mission, and then join with him to make the rendezvous with the *Mary Rose* and sail merrily back to England.

And how on earth could she do that?

Meg shook her head in amazement at her own stupidity. She was going to sit and twiddle her thumbs while Cosimo trotted off to assassinate Napoleon Bonaparte, then she would happily join him on the way home?

And how would he complete his mission without her?

He would have an alternative plan, she told herself. But what if that alternative had no safeguards? As he'd outlined the plan to her, she would provide the means for his escape, or at least the situation in which he could safely get away. Without her, how would he do it?

Chapter 21

They spoke little the next day as they rode through the mountainous landscape of Chaîne de l'Étoiles, dotted with wind-blasted olive trees above Marseilles. The deep blue of the Gulf of Lions glittered way beneath them and the hot, dry Provençal air was filled with the scent of herbs crushed beneath the hooves of their horses. They rode through small villages of white-washed cottages, their red roofs glowing under the sun's relentless gaze, the massed colors of bougainvillea dazzling the eye. They rode through sandy-soiled vineyards of low-growing knotted vines carefully tended by wizened, deeply tanned farmers, who seemed to have developed a permanent stoop from their work.

They began the descent down to the coast as the afternoon waned. Meg was bone-tired after eight hours of riding, but she thought her exhaustion was more mental than physical. The strain of their silence was intense and her own thoughts were too fragmented, too jumbled for any sort of clarity.

She knew she needed to be thinking of a way out of this

situation, one that didn't involve Cosimo, but she could come up with nothing. She needed him to help her get home. Hard as she tried, she could reach only one conclusion. Stranded as she was in the middle of enemy territory, independent action was not an option. And the knowledge of that made her burn with frustration that only added to her weariness.

Cosimo was aware of her fatigue. He could see it in the set of her shoulders, the angle of her head. Uncharacteristically, he was at a loss to know how best to proceed, to breach the wall she had thrown up. He was still not ready to give up, even after her violent rejection the previous night, but he knew that realistically he would only have one more chance to persuade her to join him. He could not afford to bungle that chance.

It was twilight when they stopped for the night at a tiny hostelry at the edge of the mountain range. In the morning they would drop down to Cassis and continue along the coast to Toulon.

Meg almost fell off her exhausted mare and for a moment wondered if her legs would hold her. They had done other hard riding days but this one seemed to have been the worst of them all.

Cosimo instinctively put out a hand to support her but she brushed him aside and forced her knees to straighten. "I'm all right," she said sharply. "But my horse is done in."

"I'll see to them. Go inside," he returned, his voice even, his tone neutral.

She managed not to totter too obviously as she walked away, resting her hand for a moment on the doorjamb before entering the low building. The light was dim and it took a minute for her eyes to adjust. She was in a square room with a floor of dark red tiles, a single long plank table with benches either side running down its center. The air was heavy with the smell of wine and strong tobacco.

An elderly woman emerged from somewhere in the back and asked a question that Meg could only guess at. The accent in this region was even thicker than she'd encountered before. "*Deux chambres, madame,*" she said tentatively, wondering if indeed this place ran to two bedchambers.

As she'd feared, the woman shook her head vigorously and held up one finger. "*Une chambre,*" she stated flatly. "*Six sous.*"

Well, Cosimo would have to sleep in the barn, Meg decided. She nodded her agreement. Her stomach growled loudly. "*Dîner?*" she asked as tentatively as before. The woman nodded and disappeared into the back regions.

Meg sat down on one of the benches, drew off her leather riding gloves, and unpinned her hat. Dust coated her skirt and the feather in her hat had lost all its jauntiness. Much as had its wearer, she thought aridly. She could even taste dust on her tongue.

A small boy appeared with a copper pot that he set down on the table, regarding her solemnly through huge brown eyes. He didn't offer a glass or cup but scampered away immediately.

Meg lifted the pot to her lips and drank deeply of the pleasantly light red wine that it contained. It washed away the taste of dust and her tongue began to feel a normal size again. Cosimo came in, ducking his head beneath the lintel. He took in his surroundings with one swift glance, then came across to the bench, pulling off his gloves.

"The horses are probably better housed," he observed, taking up the pot and drinking as deeply as Meg had done. "Will they feed us?"

"She says so," Meg answered. "Or at least she nodded when I asked." She stood up abruptly. "I'm going to see if I can wash off some of this dust." She walked towards the back where a door stood ajar. She pushed it wide and stepped into an outdoor kitchen. It had a tin roof, but was open on all sides, and the woman was frying something that smelled wonderful over an open fire.

She looked up as her visitor entered and, when asked about water, pointed towards a courtyard to the rear of the kitchen. There was no well but a filled rain butt, where Meg did what she could to freshen her face and hands before returning to the kitchen to ask where she'd find the bedchamber.

The woman called and the small boy appeared out of nowhere. With a shy smile he gestured to Meg that she should follow him. Instead of returning to the main building, they crossed the courtyard and entered the barn. Well, if she was sleeping in the barn, then Cosimo would have to make do with the table or the courtyard, Meg reflected, following the boy up a rickety ladder into the hayloft.

She was pleasantly surprised when she emerged into the sweet-smelling space at the top of the ladder. It was a lot cleaner and more fragrant than many actual bedchambers they'd been given on the journey. The straw mattress seemed fresh; the linen, though coarse, was clean and smelled of sunshine. A round, unglazed window looked out onto the courtyard. An oil lamp stood on a wooden chest against the wall.

"*Merci.*" She thanked the boy with a smile, and taking it as dismissal, he disappeared down the ladder with the speed of a sprite.

Meg unbuttoned her jacket and dropped it on the bed. The shirt beneath was none too sweet, but her only clean one was in the valise strapped to the packhorse, and Cosimo didn't appear to have brought it into the inn with him. She unbuttoned the wrists and rolled the sleeves up. The cooler evening air was pleasantly refreshing on her bare arms. She lifted her hair from her nape, thinking how wonderful it would be to have it cut again.

"Meg?" Cosimo's voice called from the bottom of the ladder. "I have your things." His head appeared and he reached up and put her valise on the floor before hauling himself up. He looked around. "I've seen worse," he commented laconically. "Madame is putting supper on the table. I don't think she'll appreciate it going cold." With that he went back down the ladder.

Meg thought about changing her shirt and then decided it was a waste of clean linen. She could start the day fresh tomorrow. She followed Cosimo back into the inn and sat down in front of a steaming plate of various cuts of meat, most of which were unidentifiable. She was still hungry but she ate without relish, almost as if it was a duty, although the food was surprisingly good.

Finally she pushed aside her platter and stood up. "How far do we ride tomorrow?"

"No more than half a day," he replied, not looking at her as he ladled red currants onto his plate and added a spoonful of creamy cheese. "The horses need to be cosseted. We won't leave too early and we'll rest every hour."

"Good night then," Meg said. "I won't see you until the morning. I imagine Madame can find you somewhere to sleep." She left him.

Cosimo tapped his fingernails on the edge of the table. This was getting him nowhere. And he was damned if he was going to sleep with the horses, which seemed his only alternative to the hayloft.

He uncorked a flagon that his hostess had provided and inhaled the powerful fumes of a potent fruit liqueur. It tasted of pears, he thought, letting it lie on his tongue. And it went down with a sensation that was both fiery and smooth. Not unlike Meg. The reflection brought an ironic half smile to his lips.

He had three of the tiny glasses before deciding that it was time to do what had to be done. If he lost, so be it. He reached up to turn out the lamp, then made his way by the thin ray of moonlight from a small window to the door. The building was dark and silent, but the courtyard was bathed in silver light.

He looked up at the round window of the barn, but there was no lamplight. He went to fetch his portmanteau from the stables where he'd left it with the horses, half filled the pail with water from the rain butt, stripped and roughly washed off the day's dirt, put on clean linen, took a few things from his portmanteau, and then quietly climbed the ladder to the hayloft.

"Please go away," Meg said from the straw mattress the very instant his head appeared above the ladder.

"You'll have to forgive me, my dear, but there's nowhere else to sleep," he said calmly. "And I have no intention of bedding down with the horses. The packhorse farts pure sulphur."

Meg turned on her side, pulling the cover up to her shoulder. "Please go away," she repeated.

Cosimo ignored the request, instead expertly piling hay into a thick mattress beneath the window. He threw his boat cloak over the makeshift bed, rolled up his discarded clothes into a pillow, and lay down, pulling his riding cloak over him. He fell asleep instantly, his breathing deep and rhythmic, interrupted occasionally by a soft rumbling snore.

Meg had lain beside the privateer for long enough to know when his sleep was genuine, and she knew this was. She had been lying awake, taut as a violin string, waiting for the moment when she would know where he'd decided to sleep.

And now, despite her exhaustion, she could *not* go to sleep. Listening to him slide into the depths of deepest repose, she wanted to jump on him, pull his hair, his ears, anything to get him to wake up and experience her own miserable sleeplessness, a sleeplessness that *he* had caused. Instead she lay there, watching the thin ray of moonlight, throwing herself from side to side, until sleep finally overtook her racing thoughts.

She awoke only a few hours later, just as the first faint graying of the light was visible through the window. She still felt tired, but somehow calm. At some point during the miserable night she had accepted the inevitable, as she had known she would eventually.

Cosimo always awoke at dawn. It didn't matter how late he had gone to bed, and she propped herself on an elbow, watching the pile of hay, waiting for the first stirring.

He awoke gracefully, as he did everything. A small movement of the shoulder, a stretch of his legs, an easy roll onto his back, both arms reaching up in a long stretch that rippled down his body. Then he sat up in one smooth movement and reached his arms languidly sideways and back.

He turned his head towards her. And she knew that he had been aware of her watching him from the first instant of his awakening. But then, he was an assassin. It astonished her that he even allowed himself to sleep. When he was awake, she knew from experience that he did not close his eyes, mental or physical, for an instant.

"You're going to do it anyway, aren't you?" she said. "Without me."

"Yes, of course," he replied.

"Of course," she repeated, the cynicism only barely veiled. "How will you do it?"

Cosimo stood up in one fluid movement. He went to the window and looked out at the gathering light. "I'll establish a pattern of movement, discover everything I can about the man's plans, then pick an appropriate moment and strike."

"Will you use a knife or a pistol?" The questions came so easily now.

"I would prefer a knife, it's quieter and therefore safer," he said in the same level tone. "But if I can't get close enough, then I must use a pistol."

"Will you be able to get close enough?" Meg leaned forward a little as she asked this question, the sheet falling away from her breasts, clearly visible beneath the fine cambric of her chemise.

Cosimo considered this, then he shook his head. "I doubt it."

"But then you won't get away."

"You don't need to worry about that, Meg. Your safety won't be at risk. I'll make all the arrangements so that if I can't take you, then you will be able to make the rendezvous with the *Mary Rose*. They have my orders to take you back to England. They will obey those orders, whether I am there to enforce them or not." He spoke with calm certitude and Meg knew that he was right.

"I'm not concerned about my safety," she said flatly.

"Then what are you concerned about?" He sensed the

line they were both walking. Meg was feeling her way to something and he had to be very careful not to disturb the path.

Meg stared beyond him towards the sliver of pink sky visible in the window. She spoke softly but the vehemence was not blunted. "I loathe what you have done to me. But I love *you*. I would not watch your death."

The declaration winded him. But it was not so much what she said that took his breath away as the unleashing of his own feelings at that one word, a word he had never used...never before felt the need to use. *Love* had no place in his mission. Could not have a place. Such enterprises could not be trammeled by emotion. But Meg had opened a door somewhere inside him that would not now close.

He didn't move, sensing that any physical approach would cross a most delicate line. "Love is not something that should influence such a decision, Meg," he said. "If you would partner me in this, you must lose the ability to feel any emotion."

"As you have done," she stated with an ironic twist of her lips. "Yes, Cosimo, I understand that. If I am to seduce a man to his death, then I cannot feel anything. You had better tell me how this is to be managed." Briskly she cast aside the covers and stood up. "You didn't give me any details of your plans yesterday, but I'm assuming they're honed to the finest detail."

"They are," he agreed. Hating her tone and yet knowing that it was the only one that would carry them through this alive and successful. He'd imposed it, he could only encourage it.

He regarded her in silence for a moment, and she stood

still, waiting, her arms crossed almost defensively over her breasts. "You must understand," he said slowly, thrusting his hands into the pockets of his britches, "that you will not be personally involved at the end. You will see nothing, it will be as if you had no part at all in the business."

Her lip curled again. "Do you think I have to see the consequences in order to accept my part in them?"

He took his hands from his pockets, holding them palms out in surrender. "Some people might find it so. But I should have realized not you. All right, then let's get down to the details."

He tapped the forefinger of one hand into the palm of his other, his countenance almost expressionless, his eyes on Meg but not really seeing her. She guessed he was looking inward, seeing his plan laid out in his mind's eye.

"You will set up your household as a rich widow, with a reputation that is a little on the shady side. We'll maintain the fiction of the widowed Madame Giverny with her French-Scottish heritage, although to make it a little more interesting I think your late husband was a Swiss count with strong French connections. No one will be quite certain where your wealth came from, but there'll be a little gossip, a hint of scandal, around you. Not enough to make you persona non grata, just enough to attract the attention of the men around Napoleon, which will in the end lead you directly to the man himself."

"Where will you be?"

"Directing from the sidelines," he said dryly. "As your majordomo, I shall go into Toulon ahead of you and hire the house, the staff, and of course set the rumors running ahead of your arrival."

"Where am I to wait while you're doing that?"

"There's a small fishing community just outside Toulon.

For a couple of days you'll become Anatole again and stay there, out of the way until it's time for you to make your grand entrance." He saw her face and said swiftly, "It will only be two or three days before I come to fetch you."

"And am I to allow this seduction to come to its logical conclusion?" she asked without expression.

"*Absolutely not,*" he said with a vehemence that shocked him and sent Meg's eyebrows into her scalp. He moderated his tone, explaining, "The game is what will draw him in. The longer you hold out, the deeper he'll sink. In the end he'll agree to any conditions you lay down, at which point you'll propose an assignation, a discreet meeting in an out-of-the-way spot to which he must agree to come alone."

Meg inclined her head in faint acknowledgment. "The honey trap," she remarked. "The oldest trick in the book."

"And also, with the right quarry, almost always successful," Cosimo responded. "Napoleon is very susceptible to women, and he's inordinately vain and arrogant. It would not occur to him that you might not be attracted to him, to his power; it would not occur to him to suspect a trap, just as he will not think twice about going unescorted to an assignation. He considers himself invincible."

Meg nodded. "With good reason."

"Yes," Cosimo agreed aridly.

"But why are you certain he will find *me* attractive enough to seduce?"

Cosimo pulled at his chin. He would much rather not answer her, but the time for deception was past. He said, "Because on one occasion he was greatly attracted to Ana, and you resemble her, as I think I've mentioned before."

"And Ana, of course, was to play the part for which all

along I've been the understudy," she stated, nodding again. "What a fool I've been."

"Meg, I don't know how to make this better," he said helplessly.

"You can't," she retorted with more than a touch of scorn. "Of course you can't. No one could. But I've said I'll do it. I don't want to discuss it anymore." She stood up abruptly. "Are we leaving now?"

"It would make sense to ride before the sun's heat sets in," he said, his voice once more cool and even. "I'll settle up with Madame and see to the horses." He strode back into the inn.

Grimly Meg collected her belongings. Why had she made that declaration? She had flung her heart at him, and he had not responded with so much as the flicker of an eyelid. But then, had she expected him to? Realistically . . . when she'd only realized it herself such a short time ago? No, acknowledged it, she amended. She had known in her heart how she felt for much longer. But it didn't matter anymore, nothing mattered anymore.

She went outside to where Cosimo stood with the horses. "They look refreshed," she observed, sliding her valise into one of the packhorse's panniers.

"They'll manage a couple of hours," Cosimo said. "We'll get down to the coast in easy stages and then rest for the remainder of the day." He cast her a sharply assessing look. "You don't look as if you can manage much more than that yourself today."

"I didn't sleep well," she said pointedly, taking the mare's reins.

"No," he agreed. "But from now on we need to take better care of you."

Meg raised her head smartly. "There's no *we*."

His mouth thinned and when he spoke his voice was hard. "Meg, from this moment until this is over, there is only *we*. We are partners. We work in concert. Your concerns are mine and vice versa. Do you understand that? Because if you don't, then it stops here."

She met his gaze with a hardness of her own. She understood what he was saying. Their lives depended on this partnership. Wasn't that why she'd agreed to join him? She would not abandon him if it meant his death. "Of course I understand."

"Then let me help you mount." He gave her a leg up into the saddle and she could feel now that he had withdrawn from her. His manner was cool, his voice level, and Meg welcomed the distance between them. Once she had agreed to this business arrangement there had never been any doubt but that Cosimo was the controller. He would make the plans, she would execute them. As he had said so insistently, there was no room for emotion in the business at hand.

Cosimo mounted his horse and took the reins of the packhorse. He glanced once at Meg, a look so brief she could not have read it if she'd tried. And at this point she wouldn't have believed what lay behind it anyway. She could not have guessed at the need he felt to hold her, to kiss the worry from her brow, the coldness from her eyes, the strain from her mouth. She could not know how he ached to comfort her and give her strength, how hard it was for him to accept that she would take nothing from him.

However, he had no choice but to respect the barrier she had thrown up between them and keep his distance. All he could do was to make as certain as he possibly could that Meg came through the next two weeks unscathed.

That was all the time they had for her to deliver Napoleon to the fatal rendezvous, and he could not afford to miscalculate a single step in the dance. Meg, unlike Ana, was inexperienced and would need close direction. Some of it she would have to improvise on her own but he wanted to be certain to keep her need for independent action to a minimum.

The following day they reached a tiny fishing village. Cosimo led the way to a cottage set a little back from the beach. He dismounted and rapped on the door. The young woman who opened it was strong-faced, her gaze straightforward, her brown hair braided into a long thick plait down her back. She wore a skirt, kilted up peasant-fashion to her calves, and a shirt with the sleeves rolled up to her elbows, revealing shapely, tanned arms whose muscular ripple indicated a familiarity with hard work.

Her face lit up when she saw Cosimo and she flung her arms around him, an excited stream of greeting issuing from her lips. She was a most attractive woman, Meg noted, remaining astride her mare during this meeting. It seemed that Cosimo certainly found her so, judging by the way he was returning the embrace. At last they broke apart and he turned to Meg.

"Meg, this is Lucille. She will look after you until I return."

"How kind," Meg murmured, dismounting. She bore the young woman no ill will; whatever relationship she might have had, or indeed still did have, with Cosimo was no concern of hers. She followed them both into the cottage.

Cosimo left soon after. He took Meg's hands in a firm,

warm clasp. "I'll be back in three days at the most. Don't leave the cottage, just concentrate on resting, and try to clear your mind of everything but what we have to do. Can you do that?"

"I can only try," she said, letting her hands lie limply in his, so that he quickly released them.

"Meg, I—"

She interrupted him. "There's nothing to be said, Cosimo. Just go. I want to get this over and done."

He turned from her then and swung back onto his horse, taking the leading reins of the mare and the pack-horse. He rode off without a backward glance and Meg turned back to the cottage.

He returned three days later, driving an elegant barouche drawn by a pair of matched bays.

Meg stared at him in disbelief. He was dressed in a coachman's livery, sporting a bicorne hat on a steel-gray close-cropped head that made him look every inch the dignified upper servant. He jumped down and caught her look of stifled laughter. A slow grin spread across his face.

"What d'you think, madame? Do I look the part of majordomo?"

Meg tried to maintain her frigid formality but it was no good. She had told herself in the last couple of days that the hollow feeling she had, the sense of emptiness, was nothing to do with missing the man who'd been her constant companion for more than a month, but seeing him now made nonsense of such self-deception. She had missed him more than she would ever have believed possible in the circumstances, and now that familiar grin and the light in the sea-washed blue eyes were too much to resist. "Yes," she said. "You do."

"Good. Now we have to transform you, Anatole dear, into

a rich, widowed countess." He leaned into the barouche and lifted out a portmanteau. "A coiffeur will take care of your hair this evening, but you must make a most elegant entrance into Toulon."

He carried the portmanteau into the cottage. "Where's Lucille?"

"She went fishing with the men," Meg said, following him. She liked her hostess, who had asked no questions, cheerfully attended to the chores around the cottage, and provided a completely undemanding companionship when they were together. Meg had found her restful and Cosimo's name had never come up between them, not because of any awkwardness but rather as if in this short interlude he was irrelevant to them both.

"Then you'll have to make do with me," Cosimo stated, making his way to the back room where Meg had been sleeping. "Get out of those clothes." It was a businesslike instruction and Meg took it as such.

He put the portmanteau on the bed and opened it up. He took out chemise, a silk petticoat, silk stockings with lace garters, a gown of green-and-rose-striped damask, dainty kid slippers, and a charming cream straw hat with ivory velvet ribbons.

Meg stripped off her Anatole guise. Her nakedness in front of Cosimo felt as natural as always, which still surprised her a little, until she realized that he didn't even seem to notice, so intent was he on the matter at hand. He passed her the garments one at a time, a slight frown of concentration puckering his brow. He buttoned the gown at her back with brisk efficiency and then stood back to look at her.

"I did well," he stated with satisfaction. "They could have been made for you."

Meg thought of Ana's wardrobe that had awaited Cosimo's intended partner on the *Mary Rose*. Presumably the privateer had supplied that with the same accuracy as to fit that he'd managed with these garments for his new partner. The man obviously had a dressmaker's eye, she thought sardonically.

"Do what you can with your hair." He passed her a comb. "The hat will disguise its untidiness until Paul can get his hands on it."

"Who's Paul?" Meg pulled the comb through the unruly, uneven lengths of her hair.

"An excellent coiffeur. You have an appointment at six o'clock this evening. And tomorrow you'll be ready to receive your first, one hopes, inquisitive visitors." He passed her the straw hat.

There was a polished-tin mirror in the little room, offering a rather wavery reflection but Meg was used to it. She adjusted the angle of the brim, arranged a cluster of curls around her ears, and pronounced herself satisfied. It was astonishing how the simple headgear transformed a countenance that had seen a little too much sun for strict fashion in the last weeks. Her freckles, more prolific than usual, were thrown into the shade by the brim.

"Then, milady, we should be on our way," Cosimo said, offering the deep bow of a servant. "If you please..." He opened the door for her and led the way to the barouche.

He put a restraining hand on her arm as she made to step into the carriage. "Just one thing," he said quietly. "From now on, Meg, you take on your role. Once we're on the road into the city, the only communication we can have must be that between mistress and servant."

"I expect to enjoy that immensely," Meg said, stepping

into the barouche and seating herself. "By the way, what are you called, majordomo?"

"Charles," he returned, closing the door. "But if you find it easier to remember the title of the job rather than a different name, address me simply as 'majordomo,' and if you can manage to be haughty enough—"

"Oh, have no fear," she said, taking her seat. "I'll manage that without any difficulty. One question, though. Can I not afford both a coachman *and* a majordomo?"

The sharp-edged tone would have amused him in other circumstances, but it couldn't now. Cosimo turned away and climbed into the driver's seat. "Everyone makes economies at present and it would not be questioned that I would take both positions." He turned his head to look at her, his gaze intent. "It's important that only I drive you. I need to see you safely at your destination, and get you safely home afterwards."

Meg nodded, her ironic levity of a moment ago banished.

"I also speak English, by the way." Cosimo raised his whip to give the horses the signal to start. "You should feel comfortable in either language, it's what people are expecting of Madame Giverny of Scottish descent...who, by the way, is choosing not to use her title in the light of the political situation after the revolution."

"But of course, why would I insist on an outmoded form of address?" Meg asked coolly.

"Of course Madame wouldn't," he agreed with a hidden smile, flicking his whip above the horses' hindquarters. "I should mention, however, that in the company of Bonaparte and his cohorts, you should endeavor to speak only French, for the same political reasons."

"How much easier it would be if I spoke Corsican,"

Meg mused. "To seduce a man in his own language...
wouldn't that make this so much simpler?"

"Enough now," he said as the horses moved forward.
"Remember that the only time you can talk to me in such
fashion is when I say so. Even if you think we're alone, if I
don't give you an indication that it's safe, you must not
drop your role. Is that clear?"

"What do you think?" Meg asked. "I'm not a fool."

"If I thought you were, we wouldn't be doing this now."

It was such an obvious fact Meg didn't trouble to follow
it up. She folded her hands daintily in her lap and settled
back, closely watching the terrain around her, learning
what she could from what she saw. It was clear to her that
any observation, however casual, could prove useful.

As they drove along the coast the road became busier,
with carriages and horse traffic. They passed troops of soldiers and sutler wagons laden with supplies. As the road
followed the curve of a bay the town of Toulon lay ahead.
The harbor was a mass of masts, pennants flying in the
brisk sea breeze.

Meg's stomach clenched, her heart speeded up, sweat
gathered on the nape of her neck and in the hollow of her
throat. They were deep in enemy country and all she had
was the flimsiest of disguises.

*And the partnership of a man who had done all this be-
fore, more times than she wanted to know.*

She took a slow, deep breath, watching Cosimo's back
as he guided the horses through increasingly narrow streets
along the quay. Nothing about his posture indicated tension. And clearly his hands weren't giving any such signals
to the horses, who obeyed the slightest touch of the reins,
walking sedately around obstacles, not so much as flicking
their ears at the raucous shouts coming from the quay.

Cosimo turned the horses away from the quay, into a cobbled lane. He drew up in a quiet square behind a church and in front of a tall, thin, stone row house. A groom appeared as if from nowhere to take the horses as Cosimo stepped down from the carriage and opened the door for Meg.

"Madame," he said with a deep bow.

"Thank you," she said distantly, stepping onto the curb.

Cosimo went up to the front door and it opened before he reached it. "Madame Giverny," he announced, brushing aside the maid who had opened the door. He held it for Meg's ceremonial entrance.

She stepped into a cool, dim hall with a flagstone floor and white plaster walls. A small group of servants were gathered at the foot of a staircase at the rear of the hall.

"Madame, may I introduce your staff." Her majordomo presented her housekeeper, her cook, her personal maid, and with an all-encompassing gesture the various members of the under staff who would keep the household going without her ever needing to address them by name.

Meg acknowledged each one with a vague smile, although she took swift notice of the woman Cosimo had chosen to wait on her personally. Her abigail would be the most difficult servant to deceive.

Estelle was young, rather flustered as she curtsied. Probably not too experienced, Meg guessed, therefore more than willing to ignore any oddities in this household simply for the status of working for a *comtesse*... even if the countess chose to drop the title in the interests of discretion. Cosimo would have reckoned that any shortcomings the inexperienced maid possessed, Meg would be able to deflect. She was accustomed to taking care of herself, after all. And the youngster would not ask awkward questions when she was being given the opportunity to learn a trade at the hands of a kind and understanding mistress.

So, unsurprisingly, Cosimo knew what he was doing.

"I understand Paul, the coiffeur, is expected at six, Estelle," she said, sweeping to the stairs. "Majordomo, have the milliners and dressmakers left their choices for my selection?"

"In your chamber, madame," the majordomo said with a low bow. "And they will wait upon you at your convenience to make any alterations you deem necessary."

Meg gave him a nod of thanks and swept up the stairs, Estelle hurrying behind her.

"This way, madame." Estelle darted sideways at the head of the stairs and flung open a pair of double doors that opened onto a large bedchamber. Another set of doors stood open to a balcony that offered a sliver of a view of the harbor in the distance. "I trust Madame will be comfortable." She stood aside as Meg examined the room.

"Yes, thank you, Estelle," Meg said warmly. "Now, let us look at these offerings of the dressmakers before Paul comes to do my hair."

Chapter 22

"*A*lain, who is that woman who just came in?" The short, thickset young man wore a general's uniform crusted with gold braid and medals that bespoke a triumphant career barely believable in a man not yet out of his twenties. He spoke in a low voice to his equerry, who as always stood in readiness at his shoulder.

"Which one, General?" The equerry peered around the crowded salon. It seemed that the entire French social elite had gathered in Toulon to bid General Bonaparte and the French navy fair winds and victory on the conquering hero's latest campaign. Beautiful women were everywhere to be seen, and hostesses vied with each other to put on the most elegant soirees, balls, and dinners.

"Redhead," Bonaparte said, gesturing with his champagne glass. "She reminds me of someone. She came in with Jean Guillaume." He gave a short laugh. "That one's always the first to latch on to anyone interesting."

The equerry followed the indicating glass and saw a petite red-haired woman in a striking gown of bronze silk with a pronounced décolletage that revealed small but very white breasts, their crowns barely concealed. A collar of emeralds encircled her white throat, and an emerald comb nestled in the fashionably cropped red curls. "*Distinguée*," he pronounced. "Definitely no ingénue." His general, for all his youth, had little or no interest in debutantes.

"No, but who *is* she?" the general demanded impatiently. "I would swear I've met her before."

"I'll find out at once, sir." The equerry melted into the crowd. He paused beside a knot of officers standing in the window embrasure and a murmured exchange took place, accompanied by many extravagant hand gestures and a few knowing chuckles. Now in possession of her name, and even more intrigued by a few other facts he'd gleaned, the equerry continued to circle the room until he reached the side of the red-haired new arrival.

She was in the middle of a group of men, her escort, Major Guillaume, standing beside her with a rather proprietorial air. She turned immediately to include the equerry in the circle, offering him a dazzling smile, her green eyes crinkling at the corners.

Definitely no ingénue, the equerry reiterated. And from what he'd heard, definitely a woman of experience. Very much General Bonaparte's style for the casual liaisons he liked to enjoy before a campaign. Facilitating and monitoring such contacts for his commander had long fallen to the equerry's hand. He bowed. "Madame Giverny, I believe?"

"You believe right, sir," she said in faintly accented French. "But I do not have the pleasure?" She plied her ivory fan with a leisurely movement that somehow contrived to be unmistakably inviting, her eyebrows slightly raised in a question mark, eyes smiling at him over the delicately painted chicken skin.

"Colonel Alain Montaine, at your service, madame." He swept her another deeper bow, taking the hand she proffered and carrying it to his lips. "Guillaume, where have you been keeping the lovely lady?" he demanded of the major.

Meg laughed, a musical trill long perfected in the game of flirtation. "You flatter me, Colonel, but I assure you no one keeps me anywhere."

"Madame Giverny has but recently arrived in town," the major said somewhat stiffly, clearly not enjoying this banter between his companion and the colonel.

"That's true, Colonel," the lady said. "I arrived from Paris two days ago. I *had* to come to Toulon to offer my support to General Bonaparte, his army, and the fleet. Such a bold enterprise." The fan moved slowly, the green eyes sparkling at him over the top.

"Indeed, madame," he agreed, aware of the general's impatient eyes upon him from across the room. "If you'll excuse me, I believe the general wants me." He bowed in farewell and stepped back into the crowd.

"Charming gentleman," Meg observed, turning her smiling attention back to her escort.

The major acceded to this with a faint and unconvincing smile. "May I fetch you a glass of champagne, madame?"

"Thank you, how delightful," she said. "But don't be long now." She batted her eyelashes at him.

"No...no...not a second more than necessary, I assure you, madame." He hastened away, and straight into the ambush prepared for him by the equerry, who had renewed orders from the general.

"What do you know of her, Guillaume? She's very free in her manner."

The major glanced over his shoulder to where Madame Giverny stood chatting easily to the circle of men around her. He fretted at the delay in returning to her side, but the general's equerry could not be put off. "As I understand it, she's a widow...a wealthy widow judging by her household establishment. She has taken a substantial house just behind Ste. Marie."

"Yes, that much I already know. But who are her friends?" The colonel's speculative gaze rested on the woman's animated countenance.

The major shrugged. "I don't know. I came upon her yesterday morning driving along the corniche. Beautiful pair of match bays," he added. "She hailed me, or rather her driver hailed me. He wanted to know how to reach the Place d'Armes. Apparently someone had told Madame Giverny that the troops were reviewed there every morning and she wanted to see the spectacle."

"And no one knows anything concrete about her except her name and that she's a widow," the colonel mused. "A rich widow." He frowned, his intent gaze still on Madame Giverny. "She is *very* free in her manner."

The major looked a little put out. "Just because a woman is alone is no reason to assume some scandal," he declared, well aware now that the equerry had been making other inquiries and knowing full well what he would have heard. "The whispers about her are baseless."

"One would like to think so," the colonel mused. "But she is both alone and *unknown*," he pointed out. "And she has a strange accent. I can't put my finger on it."

"She's only half French," the major stated. "Her mother's family are Scottish. She married a Swiss count, I'm told."

"Giverny." The equerry shook his head. "Not a name I know."

"Why should you?" snapped the major. "Provincial Swiss nobility. There are plenty such in France these days, all too eager to deny their *aristo* roots."

"Quite so." Colonel Montaine nodded. "Well, she's interesting, I grant you that." He strode off towards his pacing general, unconvinced by the major's partisanship. He would lay odds the wealthy widow probably had a checkered past and if the general was interested in her, then it was part of his equerry's remit to examine the lady's past and present credentials very carefully. A discreet exercise usually conducted without Bonaparte's knowledge.

"Well?" Bonaparte demanded as the colonel reached his side.

"There's not much to tell, General. Madame Giverny is newly arrived in town and appears to have no connections here." He told the general what little he had gleaned, omitting the whispers. Bonaparte would consider them irrelevant to a casual and very limited liaison.

"Did you say she reminded you of someone, sir?" he asked when he'd laid out his scanty information.

Bonaparte frowned. "Yes, but I can't remember who or when. I can't put my finger on it." He shook his head, dismissing the puzzle. "Bring her to me."

The colonel bowed. "Immediately, sir." He threaded his way back through the crowd. General Bonaparte was so certain of the power of his position, it wouldn't occur to him that a civilian might resent being summoned with such lack of ceremony. It was up to his equerry to present the command in more palatable terms.

The lady and her escort had moved to another conversational group and he could hear Madame Giverny's trill of laughter above the buzz. She tapped a gentleman on the arm with her fan in mock reproof at whatever he'd said to her. It was striking that there were no women in her circle, but if the whispers had any foundation, it would seem that the lady had little interest in her own sex, he reflected with a dry smile.

"Madame Giverny, I bring an entreaty from General Bonaparte," he said entering the circle without preamble. "He most earnestly requests an introduction." He offered his arm.

So it had begun. Meg was aware of a thrill of fear, and almost immediately a surge of exhilaration. A cool smile played over her lips, which utterly belied the rapid beat of her heart and the slight moistening of her palms. "I'm honored, Colonel," she said, placing her gloved hand on his brocaded arm. "I would never have dared hope for the opportunity to meet General Bonaparte in person." This last was said in a confidential tone that carried a hint of awed reverence.

The colonel said nothing, merely inclined his head in acknowledgment of a sentiment that could only be the truth.

General Bonaparte was pacing restlessly in the window embrasure, his hands clasped behind his back, his gaze watching their progress through the crowd. As they reached him, he bowed and seized Meg's hand, carrying it to his lips. "Madame, this is an honor." His eyes from beneath deeply arched brows were as bright and sharp as an eagle's as they rested on her countenance, and when his large mouth curved in a smile he revealed unusually white, even teeth.

Meg gave him a frank smile that masked her own swiftly assessing scrutiny and said with a sketched curtsy, "The honor is only mine, General Bonaparte. As I was telling the colonel, I had never dared to hope I would meet you in person."

He drew her hand into his arm. "Let us stroll on the terrace, madame, it's a veritable beehive in here. Alain, bring us some champagne, and some of those little lobster patties. I find them delightful."

"Yes, General." The equerry went off to do his errand, glancing over his shoulder at the pair as the general held aside a heavy velvet curtain for the lady to pass through the open French window onto the terrace that looked out over the harbor.

"So, madame, I understand you are Scottish," the general said, patting the hand that rested on his arm. "There are close ties between our two countries."

Be careful now, she told herself. With a cool head she was word perfect in her story, but now with excitement and apprehension warring in her blood she could easily slip up.

"Historically, yes, General," she agreed, pausing at the balustrade and deftly changing the subject. "What a magnificent sight that is." She gestured with her fan towards the mass of ships in the harbor, their lights ablaze. "Will you engage with Admiral Nelson, do you think?"

Bonaparte smiled with a touch of condescension. "If Admiral Nelson is foolish enough to desire such an engagement, then, indeed, madame, we shall embrace the opportunity."

Meg felt the hairs on the back of her neck lift. For two days she had been playing the game, so caught up in her role as the scandalous widow she had almost forgotten how high the stakes were. Now, looking down at the massed fleet in the harbor, the most powerful and dangerous man in Europe standing at her shoulder, she was hit by the full force of the implications of this war with all the impact of a fist in her stomach.

"Perhaps he won't be foolish enough," she suggested with a light laugh from behind her fan. "You are not known for losing engagements, General Bonaparte."

A low rumble of laughter came from deep within his barrel chest. "No, indeed not, madame." He turned his large head to look at her, his gaze lascivious. "I am not known for losing engagements of any kind, dear lady." He became aware of a servant standing discreetly behind them and clicked his fingers at him.

The man stepped forward. The general took a glass of champagne from the tray the man proffered and gave it to Meg, with a half bow, then took one himself. "Try one of these, madame." He took one of the little vol-au-vents from the silver platter and held it to Meg's lips.

Napoleon Bonaparte didn't waste any time, Meg reflected, allowing him to pop the morsel into her mouth. Well, she wasn't interested in wasting too much time herself, but neither could she capitulate too quickly. It was time to beat a strategic retreat.

"You are too kind, General," she murmured as she swallowed what to her tongue was as tasteless and dry as dust. "But if you'll excuse me now, I must rejoin my escort."

"My dear madame, I'm not sure I will excuse you," he said, laying a detaining hand on her arm. "Surely you can spare me a few more minutes of your time. Or is the company of Major Guillaume so enticing?" He waggled an arched eyebrow at her.

Meg's eyes smiled at him over her fan. "Why, of course not, sir. How could anyone compete with General

Bonaparte? I mean only that I would not intrude upon your time. You are the busiest man in France, after all."

"Oh, you flatter me, madame," he said with a careless wave that seemed to encompass the fleet below them as if in denial of his demur.

"I doubt that, sir." Meg adjusted the gauzy scarf draped over her elbows and rested her arms on the balustrade. "When do you intend to make sail? If I may ask such a question..."

"In a little under two weeks, madame. The fleet will be outfitted by then, and the Army of the Orient will set sail for Malta." He spoke with a satisfied confidence that gave Meg another inner shudder. His belief in himself and his prowess was so absolute it was almost impossible not to believe it oneself.

But then, nothing had happened in Bonaparte's meteoric career to dent that confidence, only to boost it. Perhaps it wasn't surprising that his English enemies saw assassination as the cleanest, swiftest way to eliminate the threat he posed.

She could never be truly reconciled to this mission, Meg reflected, it went too far against her nature, but here, facing the reality of Bonaparte's preparations for such a grandiose scheme as conquering the Orient, she could acknowledge its point. Goose bumps appeared on her arms and she shivered, this time openly.

"Ah, but you are cold," he said swiftly. "You must be careful of your health, madame. The salon is overheated and the breeze outside is cool." He was urging her back towards the French doors, a hand on her elbow.

Meg allowed him to escort her back to the buzzing noise of the salon, made stuffy with heated bodies and the blaze of candles. "I have a little headache, General," she said, lightly touching her temples. "But I am so honored to have had the opportunity to talk with you."

"Honored, nonsense," he declared. "But you must go straight home, one should not trifle with the headache. I shall visit you tomorrow. At what hour will you be home?"

"I shall be home at whatever hour in the morning you choose to call, General Bonaparte," she said, giving him an up-from-under smile.

"Then I shall call upon you at ten o'clock," he announced. "Now, my equerry will escort you to your carriage." He beckoned to the ever watchful colonel. "Montaine, Madame Giverny is not feeling quite well. See her safely to her carriage."

The colonel offered the lady his arm. "My pleasure, Madame Giverny."

"Thank you, Colonel." She walked beside him as he expertly threaded a way through the crowd, both of them aware of the interested glances they drew and the rustle of whispers that followed them.

"Madame Giverny, are you leaving so soon? I am heartbroken." Major Guillaume stepped into their path.

"Forgive me, Major, but I have a headache," she said, trying for a wan smile. "The colonel is kind enough to escort me to my carriage."

Guillaume had no choice but to bow his acceptance and step aside.

"Where did you reside in Paris, Madame Giverny?" Montaine inquired casually as he sent a footman for her evening cloak.

"Not strictly in the city, Colonel," she said carefully. "In the Bois de Boulogne." The Bois was large enough to make it difficult to make specific inquiries, even if Colonel Montaine had the time to put them in train. But it would take a week either side to send to Paris for information. And by that time this would all be over, one way or another. Her spine prickled again.

"A charming spot," he said, helping her with her cloak. "And your late husband? Did he have an estate there?"

Meg turned to look at him, a carefully calculated sharpness in her gaze. Her earlier turmoil had ceased almost as soon as she'd left Bonaparte's side and she was aware now of only a cold, detached composure. "Such very pointed questions, Colonel. As it happens I moved to Paris after my husband's death six months ago." She gave a little nod as if to say, *Does that satisfy you?*

"Forgive the intrusion," he said, meeting the challenge of her gaze without flinching. "But when General Bonaparte expresses an interest in someone, it is in *my* interests to ask some questions."

"A few minutes' conversation at a crowded soiree hardly qualifies as interest, Colonel," she said, turning up the collar of her cloak as they stepped into the street.

"You will permit me to say, madame, that you do not know the general as I do."

She inclined her head. "I'm sure that is true, sir. And I'm equally sure I never shall." Her smile was frigid as her carriage drew up and her coachman/majordomo jumped down to hand her in.

"*Bonsoir, madame.*" He bowed as he opened the door of the barouche.

"*Bonsoir, Charles,*" she said, offering her coachman a distant smile as she took her seat. "Good night, Colonel."

"Good night, Madame Giverny." He bowed, then straightened and watched the barouche go off at a brisk trot, a frown in his eye. Was the lady after something more than the satisfaction of a grand conquest? There were many women who would be happy, indeed who had been happy, to add Napoleon Bonaparte to their trophy cupboard. The glory was brief but the triumph resounding. But there was something about Madame Giverny that gave him pause. He just couldn't put his finger on it.

Meg drew her cloak warmly around her as a rather brisk breeze blew off the water. And now she was aware of only one sensation, a pure heady excitement that banished all fatigue, all apprehension. She had played her part to perfection. Worthy of any spy. A bubble of triumphant laughter grew in her chest and she had to fight to suppress it. She'd learned in her time with the privateer what danger did to her, how it filled her with a passionate energy, a wonderful jubilation. And this time was no different. She gazed at Cosimo's back, willing him to say something that would allow her to express some measure of her exhilaration. But she knew he would not, not on the public street, even if there was no one around to hear.

They had had little personal contact since her arrival in Toulon. On that first evening, he had handed her a stack of engraved visiting cards for her to sign, explaining that he was going to deliver them to the prominent households in the town. She could expect to receive visitors the next morning, since, thanks to his undercover preparations while she waited with Lucille, everyone was eager to make the acquaintance of the mysterious countess.

He had known what he was talking about. The door knocker had been banging ever since under a stream of naval and army officers, their wives and daughters, and the wives of the most important members of Toulon society. Meg, to her surprise, had reveled in the game, flirting with the men, pleasantly courteous if a little distant to their womenfolk, and generally bolstering any rumors of a shady reputation that had preceded her arrival.

The invitation from Major Guillaume to accompany him to his brigade major's soiree had been her first real social engagement and her first opportunity to make contact with Bonaparte. The meeting had been a success, but she couldn't decide whether the rather intrusive questioning of the general's equerry was a good sign or not. It was possible it was routine when Bonaparte evinced any interest in a woman, or it could mean that something about her had aroused the colonel's suspicions. But Meg couldn't see how that could be. She hadn't put a foot wrong.

They drew up outside the house behind the Church of Ste. Marie and Cosimo jumped down from the box to open the door with a flourish for his mistress. She murmured her thanks and for an instant looked up at him, her eyes brilliant with excitement and triumph. And for an instant the majordomo's normally gravely sober countenance cracked.

"Later," he mouthed and stood aside so that he could open the door to the house for her.

She swept past him to the staircase, stifling a grin. She still had difficulty reconciling the gray-haired discreet gentleman who kept her household running on oiled wheels with the captain of a sloop-of-war, the privateer, the sometime courier, sometime spy . . . the assassin.

Estelle was waiting for her in her bedchamber, her nightgown laid out, hot water steaming on the dresser. "How was your evening, madame?"

"Pleasant enough, thank you," she said, yawning behind her hand. "But I have a headache. I would like to get to bed quickly." She could think of nothing but that Cosimo would come to her tonight. She sat at the dresser to take off her jewelry, her fingers clumsy in her haste.

"Yes, of course, madame." Estelle hurriedly assisted her mistress to unfasten the emerald collar and remove the comb from her hair. She helped her out of the gown and petticoat and handed her a warm, wet washcloth.

Meg washed off the light dusting of white powder she wore on her face and held the cloth to her neck, feeling herself relax under its soothing warmth. Then she stood up to allow Estelle to drop the nightgown over her head. The maid proffered lavender water for aching temples, tooth powder, and a pot of an aromatic unguent made with glycerin, lemon juice, and rosewater that Meg massaged into her cheeks and bosom. It was supposed to reduce the appearance of freckles and whiten the skin.

"Can I fetch you anything else, madame?" Estelle turned down the bed.

Cosimo would appreciate a nightcap. "Bring me the decanter of cognac, Estelle. A tincture might help me sleep."

She sat back against the pillows, the soft light of the bedside candle throwing a golden pool onto the crisp, white lawn sheet, and waited. Estelle set the decanter and glass on the table beside her, bade her good night, and with a curtsy disappeared to her own bed.

Meg poured a measure of cognac and sipped it, allowing her eyes to close as she replayed the events of the evening, let the jubilation have full sway, remembered how she'd felt that time hiding in the ditch, when the danger raging around them had filled them both with a passionate arousal that they could barely contain. She felt the same now, her loins heavy with desire, her thighs and belly taut with anticipation. She didn't hear the door open until he spoke.

"So, I'm guessing it went well."

Her eyes shot open. He stood in the bedroom doorway, now no longer the perfect servant. Now, despite the clothes and the gray hair, all Cosimo.

"Oh, there you are at last." Meg cast aside the coverlet and sprang from the bed.

Cosimo closed the door softly behind him. He saw and recognized for what it was the glitter in her eyes, the flush on her cheeks. He knew the feeling well. The pure pulsating excitement of the chase in a dangerous hunt.

Swiftly he stepped towards her, hands outstretched. She let him take hers, pulling her into his embrace, and it was as if the estrangement had never been.

"Oh, but you do love adventure, don't you, my love?" he said with a chuckle, running his hands down her back to cup her bottom, pressing her tightly against him.

She laughed giddily and tipped her head back for his kiss, opening her mouth for his tongue, even as she pressed her loins against him. It seemed an eternity since they had had this, a yawning lonely gap of wretchedness that she now realized had made her feel as if she was missing a limb.

Her fingers fumbled with the buttons of his shirt, the waistband of his britches, her hands desperate to feel his skin once again. She ran her flat palms over his ribs, round to his back, pushed them down inside his loosened britches to his buttocks as she kissed his nipples, her teeth nibbling, grazing over his chest.

Cosimo held her tightly against him even as he struggled out of his clothes, shrugging his shirt off one arm at a time, pushing off his britches in the same way, finally falling onto the bed with her as he fought to free himself of his shoes so that he could kick off his britches. Meg seemed oblivious of these gyrations, her mouth, her fingers, all over him. The thin cambric of her nightgown tore as she twisted herself over him, catching the folds beneath her body. She ignored it, her tongue stroking down his belly, following the trail of dark hair farther to take him in her mouth, her hands cupping his balls, rubbing and squeezing gently, reveling in the taste of him, flicking her tongue over the salty tip of his penis, before taking the hot, hard length into her mouth again.

Cosimo moaned softly, pushing his hands up beneath the maltreated nightgown, palming her bottom, kneading the soft rounds as his hips moved beneath the knowing strokes of her tongue. "Stop a minute, for the love of God, Meg," he implored, reaching up to twine fingers into her hair, tugging gently to bring her head up. "I need to feel you...lift up so that I can get this gown off you."

Meg shifted obligingly onto her knees as he yanked the garment up and over her head, then with a tiny sigh of satisfaction returned to her previous position. She obeyed the gentle tap that encouraged her to lift her hips a little for the intimate invasion of his lapping tongue, the delicate exploration of his fingers. Finally he took her waist and manipulated her body so that they lay face-to-face, her length along his. She kissed him, the taste of herself blending with his on her tongue before pushing back, drawing up her knees so that she straddled his hips. Slowly she lowered herself onto him, taking him deep inside her, her lips parted as she felt him slide within her. She sat back on his thighs, circling her hips around his penis, owning him, owning her own pleasure.

He held her hips and watched her face, watching for the obliterating instant of passion before he let his own body follow hers to climax.

He stayed with her until just before dawn when they both awoke, the sweat drying on their now chilled bodies.

Meg sat up, shivering, reaching for the covers that had fallen to the floor. The sheet was still damp beneath her, the candle they'd forgotten to snuff guttered. "Cold," she said, her teeth chattering.

Cosimo got out of bed, rearranging the covers over her, taking a moment to kiss her as he did so. "The sweat of lusty exertion," he observed, brushing her now limp hair off her forehead. "You need a hot bath and a cup of chocolate. But in their absence, I prescribe a small tot of cognac and a warm robe."

Naked, he moved around the chamber, bringing her a thick chamber robe of deep gold velvet, then pouring a small measure of cognac into the glass.

"Aren't you cold?" She inhaled the powerful fumes before taking a sip.

"I'm used to being cold. I'm a sailor," he reminded her with a smile. But he dressed swiftly nevertheless, taking sips from the cognac glass as he did so. He refilled the glass, offered it to her again, and when she shook her head, sat on the end of the bed, drained its contents, then spoke in the tone that meant the lover had been banished for the time being. "Explain to me exactly what happened."

Meg complied, surprised at how clear her head was. Her audience didn't interrupt, although she could see by the occasional flash in his eye that something she had said had caught his particular attention.

"So Colonel Montaine seemed unusually inquisitive?" he mused when she had fallen silent.

"Is that a good sign or not?"

"Probably," he said. "I would imagine that any woman who has caught Bonaparte's attention would be vetted closely. Even if I'm wrong, there's nothing to trace you to anything suspicious."

"So, when the general knocks on my door this morning, I welcome him with open arms," she stated matter-of-factly.

"Certainly, my dear Meg." He stood up, adding, "If he comes."

Meg looked as put out as she felt. "Why would he not? Do you think I failed to attract him sufficiently?"

He laughed softly. "Impossible, love. But Napoleon does not in general go to people, they come to him. He will remember this in the morning. You may expect a summons."

Meg huddled closer into her robe. "And should I obey it?"

"Oh, I think so. But maybe not immediately." He looked at her for a moment and then made up his mind. "Play it by ear. I think you'll sense what's best to do. If you need to consult me, then rearrange the roses on the hall table."

"How very cloak-and-dagger," Meg said, then saw immediately that her lovemaking-induced levity was not appreciated. "It's all right, Cosimo, I understand the seriousness of this. How could I not?"

The light died in her eyes as what they were doing here flooded back with full force. It could never be far from the forefront of her mind, but she had the innate sense that on the occasions when it wasn't paramount, she should indulge them as providing some relief from the relentless tension of the game. "I can't live in the role all the time," she said.

"No, of course not. I understand that," he responded

swiftly. "I'm only concerned that you should not step out of it too often."

"I know that." Meg slipped back against the pillows, her eyelids drooping. "I need to sleep before my next bout with the general."

He bent to kiss her again, brushing the hair off her forehead before pressing his lips to her temples. "I am here," he said. "Always right behind you."

Except in Bonaparte's den, she thought. *There were places Cosimo could not follow her.*

But even as she thought that, she knew that he meant he was in her mind, that she would not take a step without hearing his voice in her head.

That if she needed him, she had only to rearrange the roses on the hall table.

Meg had not sufficiently lost the euphoria of the night's lovemaking to find that idea anything but exquisitely amusing. She smiled sleepily up into Cosimo's face, which hovered over hers with a look of anxious inquiry in his eyes. She reached up a hand and stroked his cheek in benediction. "*Bonne nuit, Charles.*"

He clicked his heels and touched his hand to his forehead in a half salute. "*Bonne nuit, Madame Giverny.*" At the door he glanced over his shoulder and said, "I'm happy to have been of service, madame."

Her muffled laughter followed him into the corridor.

Chapter 23

*M*eg dressed carefully the next morning, choosing a delicate morning gown of apple-green-and-white-striped muslin with little puff sleeves and a high collar. She dressed her hair with a dark green velvet ribbon that matched the wide band that confined the gown beneath her bosom, and powdered her freckles vigorously. Then she dabbed a touch of orange flower water behind her ears, on her wrists, and in the hollow of her throat. Her desire this morning was to present the impeccable image of a society lady about whom there could not be a breath of scandal. The contrast between her performance the previous evening and the interpretation of her role she would offer the general in the light of day should intrigue him even further.

At ten o'clock she was standing partially concealed by the damask curtain at the long window of her salon that overlooked the narrow street. Would he come himself, or would Cosimo be right? She rather thought the latter, since it tended to be the case. And, indeed, it was so. A landau drew up outside and out stepped Colonel Alain

Montaine, resplendent in dress uniform, a cocked hat under his arm. He looked up at the house and Meg drew back fully behind the curtain, then went to the chaise and took up her embroidery frame.

She heard the imperative bang of the door knocker and carefully set another stitch, listening to the voices in the hall. The salon door opened and Cosimo said, "Colonel Alain Montaine, madame."

Meg looked up from her needle and said with a smile, "Why, Colonel, this is an unexpected pleasure."

"Alas, madame, you flatter me," he said with a bow. "I know whom you were expecting and I cannot compete." He came towards her, taking the hand she extended without getting to her feet. He brought the hand to his lips with another low bow. "General Bonaparte is desolated to find he is unable to come to you himself, some work that he must attend to, but he begs that you will do him the honor of joining him for a tisane this morning at his office."

"I would not disturb the general at his work," Meg demurred. "Do pray take a seat, Colonel." She gestured to a chair opposite.

"Forgive me, madame, but I have little time," he said, clasping his hands at his back and rocking a little on his heels. "The general will be most disappointed not to see you this morning."

Meg put her head on one side, seeming to consider this. Then she said, "I own I was looking forward to renewing my conversation with General Bonaparte . . . if you are sure I would not be in any way disturbing him at his work . . . ?"

"Madame, I assure you that the general allows *nothing* to take his mind from his work," the colonel declared with perfect truth. "He awaits you most eagerly. I have a carriage outside."

Meg set aside her embroidery frame and rose gracefully to her feet, the muslin skirts settling delicately around her. "That's most civil of you, Colonel. If you will give me a few minutes, I'll join you directly."

He bowed his acquiescence and she left him with a faint smile, closing the door quietly behind her. "Ah, Charles," she said to the solemn majordomo who appeared to be supervising a maidservant who was polishing the brass door handles in the hall. "I am going with the colonel to pay a call on General Bonaparte." She made her way to the stairs. "Would you bring the carriage to collect me in precisely one hour? I have a luncheon engagement."

Without so much as a flicker of an eyelid, Cosimo bowed. "In one hour, madame."

Meg nodded and went up the stairs to fetch gloves and hat. Cosimo glanced towards the closed door to the salon, then crossed to it and opened it. The colonel spun around from the secretaire at the sound of the latch.

"May I offer you some refreshment, Colonel, while you wait for Madame?" the majordomo asked coolly, even as he mentally reviewed what the colonel might have seen in his exploration of the secretaire.

"No, I have no time," the colonel said harshly, red patches blooming on his cheekbone.

Not a smooth operator, Cosimo reflected with derision. He looked as guilty as sin. Deliberately, the majordomo crossed the salon to the secretaire, straightening cushions as he went. At the desk he carefully tidied the pile of papers as if it was merely part of his general domestic duties, his eyes scanning them. There was nothing there that could arouse suspicions, merely a few visiting cards, several invitations, and a sheaf of suggested menus from the cook. All perfectly in order for the lady of the house.

He offered the colonel a bow as he left the salon. As he went into the hall, Meg was coming down the stairs, drawing on long green kid gloves. She really did clean up nicely, Cosimo reflected with an inner grin, thinking of the britches-clad Anatole and the time she'd dived without a murmur into a muddy ditch to avoid a French patrol. The wide brim of her green silk hat framed her face, giving her a piquant look that was quite enticing. Napoleon would find her irresistible.

"One hour, remember, Charles," she said over her shoulder as she reentered the salon. "I'm ready, Colonel. Forgive me for keeping you waiting."

"Not at all, madame." He offered her his arm. The majordomo opened the front door for them and sprang to open the door of the landau.

"Thank you, Charles." Meg gave him a distant nod as the colonel handed her into the carriage. The majordomo merely bowed in response and waited until the carriage had rounded the corner of the street before returning to the house.

Bonaparte's headquarters was a large mansion on the Place d'Armes set behind high walls and reached through a magnificent pair of wrought-iron gates that opened onto a large square courtyard. Soldiers patrolled the walls in front of the house, a guardhouse was positioned at the gates, and yet more soldiers guarded the massive double doors that led into the mansion itself.

"I trust the general is not anxious for his safety," Meg murmured at this impressive array of military might.

The colonel gave a short laugh. "On the contrary, madame."

Meg made no response, reflecting that this ostentatious display was presumably designed to feed the general's self-consequence and to impress anyone who might have the temerity to doubt the supreme power of the Commander of the Army of the Orient.

She alighted from the carriage at the double doors and the colonel escorted her into a huge, marble-floored entrance hall where there were yet more soldiers, standing at ease around the paneled walls. A magnificent double staircase rose to the upper floors, and the colonel, with a hand under her elbow, urged her forward.

Meg to her surprise realized that she was not nervous, despite being alone and unprotected in the heart of the lion's den. At the head of the stairs, the colonel turned down a wide, door-lined corridor. Two soldiers stood on guard outside the double doors at the end of the corridor. Colonel Montaine opened the door without knocking and ushered Meg into what was clearly a drawing room. A silver tray with a teapot and Sevres cups rested on a loo table beside a damask-covered sofa.

"The general will join you shortly, Madame Giverny," he said, and backed out.

Meg drew off her gloves and went to the bank of windows that gave onto a long balustraded terrace and a splendid view of the harbor. She waited for what seemed a very long time before an inner door opened behind her and General Bonaparte appeared.

"Madame Giverny, forgive me for keeping you waiting."

Meg was reminded of a cocky bantam as he strode towards her, one hand resting on the slight paunch that strained a button of his waistcoat. She considered deliberate unpunctuality the ultimate discourtesy and was rapidly developing a considerable dislike of the man's conceit.

"I'm sure you're very busy, sir," she said with a noncommittal smile. She glanced at the ormolu clock on the mantelpiece. "But I'm afraid I have very little time left. My carriage will come for me in half an hour."

He looked first disconcerted and then annoyed. "Montaine will escort you home, madame."

She shook her head firmly. "I would not put you to any further trouble." She moved towards the table. "May I pour you a tisane, sir?"

"No," he said abruptly. "Never touch the stuff. I'll take a glass of claret." He strode to the sideboard where a row of decanters stood. "But pour for yourself, madame." This last seemed like an afterthought.

Meg calmly poured a thin verbena-fragrant stream into one of the delicate cups and turned back to the general, who stood in front of the window, a full wineglass in his hand and a glower on his face.

"Perhaps something troubles you, General," she suggested with a coaxing smile, crossing the Aubusson carpet towards him, holding her cup and saucer. "The cares of campaigning, I dare say."

"Nonsense," he said with a snort. "I never worry, Madame Giverny, about the conduct of my campaigns. I make decisions and I abide by them." He drank wine and stood with his short legs apart, regarding her now with less of a glower, a gleam of interested appreciation in his bright eyes as he took in her appearance properly.

Meg perched delicately on the scrolled arm of a chaise longue and sipped her tea, giving him a coquettish look over the rim of her cup. "You don't appear careworn, I'll admit, General."

He laughed. "Never, madame. I am as confident of my success as I am that the sun will come up at dawn." He came over to her, taking the cup from her and placing it on the sideboard, before grasping her hands and drawing her to her feet. "Come, now, Nathalie, let us be a little less formal. Such a pretty name, Nathalie."

She smiled. "And how am I to address you, sir?"

"You may call me Napoleon," he stated, pulling her closer to him. "Ah, what a delicate scent." He bent his head and darted a kiss behind her ear.

Meg drew back with a startled protest. "Sir... Napoleon, please."

"Oh, come now," he said, laughing. "Don't play the ingénue with me, Nathalie. You did not come here just to drink that insipid liquid. You came to spend time with Napoleon." He pulled her closer again, his mouth hovering over hers.

Meg allowed him to kiss her, but without responding herself, then she firmly stepped back, shaking her hands free of his clasp. "You presume too far, General," she declared, but with a half laugh that took any sting out of the accusation. "Now, indeed I must go, or I shall be late." She picked up her gloves. "I can find my own way downstairs, I believe."

He was glowering again, a man who clearly didn't like to be gainsaid... a man who was not in the least accustomed to being denied his will. "You will dine here with me tomorrow evening," he pronounced after a moment.

Meg hesitated, in no doubt that he meant a *dîner à deux*. This man was not one for a long, drawn-out seduction. Would she be able to hold him off in such an intimate setting while drawing him in close enough to suggest her own assignation? There was something frighteningly predatory about Napoleon Bonaparte, but would he attempt to force an unwilling woman? Well, she had no choice but to risk it. It was a fine line to tread but she had the sense that he would lose interest quickly if she put him off too much.

"Perhaps," she said, drawing on her gloves finger by finger, making a sensual game of each movement as she stroked the fine kid over each finger. His fascinated gaze was riveted on her hands.

"Tomorrow night," he insisted, moistening his lips. "I will send my carriage for you at eight o'clock."

"No," Meg said, making a minute adjustment to the brim of her hat. "I will come in my own carriage, Napoleon, and it will wait for me." She stepped closer to him and lightly brushed his cheek with a gloved finger. "I am an independent woman, General. I like to make my own arrangements."

His face darkened and for a moment she thought he was going to explode, then suddenly he threw back his head and guffawed. "Do you, indeed, Nathalie Giverny?" He grasped her hand at the wrist. "Well, I appreciate independence, madame. Come to me at eight o'clock tomorrow evening." He turned her hand and pressed his lips to the inside of her wrist. "I will await you most eagerly."

"Until tomorrow then," she said, gently extricating her hand and walking to the door. Only when she was safely on the other side of it did she realize how fast her heart was beating.

"A short visit, madame," said the colonel, stepping out of a shadowy embrasure where clearly he had been waiting for her reappearance.

"I have a luncheon engagement," she informed him with a haughty toss of her head. "My coachman will be in the courtyard."

"Allow me to escort you." He offered his arm and ushered her downstairs and outside into the brilliant sunshine. Her carriage and coachman were waiting at the gates to the courtyard, and Charles jumped quickly down the minute he saw them.

"Good morning, Colonel," Meg said, giving him her hand with a cool smile of dismissal. "Thank you for your escort."

"My pleasure, madame." He regarded her with a puzzled frown in his eyes. She was unlike any of Bonaparte's other fancies. For the most part the women he took a fancy to were all too eager to fawn over him, to hang on his every word, to eke out the last minute of any visit. The colonel knew that the general would have kept the lady waiting for close to half an hour. It was his habit to do so, to impress upon visitors the honor he was conferring upon them, carving out a precious slice of his day for an interview.

Montaine had never taken a woman to the general who left in such a collected manner so very soon after the meeting would have started. It would not have pleased the general, that much he knew. He waited politely for the carriage to start, then, curious to see what effect Madame Giverny had had on General Bonaparte, hurried back into the mansion.

He found Bonaparte in his study, pacing restlessly between the desk and the windows.

"An independent woman, that Madame Giverny, Montaine," the general declared. "Says she'll come to dinner tomorrow night but in her own carriage." He gave a short laugh. "Most refreshing, I find."

"Indeed, sir," the equerry said. "I would like to make further inquiries about the lady. Perhaps it's a little premature to invite her to a private dinner."

The general turned a scowling gaze on the colonel. "What are you implying, man?"

Montaine cleared his throat. "Nothing … as yet, sir. But the lady is newly arrived, no one seems to know anything about her. She's not…" He paused. "She's unusual, General."

"Yes, exactly," Bonaparte said impatiently. "That's what I like about her. She's refreshing."

Montaine tried again. "I would like to be certain she has no ulterior motive in her pursuit of you, General Bonaparte."

The general's eyebrows rose. "What possible ulterior motive could she have, man? I am Napoleon." Then a disarming smile changed his countenance completely. "Besides, you have it wrong, Alain. *I* am the one in pursuit."

"Yes, sir, so I understand," the colonel said. "But nevertheless, I would like to make further inquiries. The lady's reputation—"

"Oh, fiddle that," the general interrupted with a wave of his hand. "I have no interest in her reputation, only in a brief liaison. And I trust that will be forthcoming. If you don't like it, then you may take tomorrow evening off, and Gilles will do the honors."

"Sir, I—"

"No, I won't hear another word." He turned petulantly towards his desk. "I have work to do and so have you. Bring me the supply orders for the *Arabesque*."

"Yes, sir." Montaine saluted and left the study, his expression grim. He was powerless to stop his general pleasing himself in such matters. And he had no evidence for his unease. *At least not yet.*

———

"I trust you passed a pleasant time, madame?" Cosimo said over his shoulder as he drove away from the mansion gates.

"Pleasant enough, Charles. Although the general is a busy man. Our meeting was rather short." She smoothed out imaginary wrinkles in her close-fitting gloves, her hands moving restlessly among the folds of her skirt. "He has invited me for dinner tomorrow evening."

"I'm sure Madame will enjoy herself," Charles said gravely. "Where will this dinner take place?"

"In the general's private apartments, I believe."

"A privilege," he said, turning the horses expertly into the narrow lane alongside the church.

"Yes," she agreed, her voice rather flat. She saw his shoulders tense a little at her tone and wished she'd managed to keep the flood of uncertainty that had provoked it at bay. She knew they would have to wait until night, once the house was asleep, before he would be able to bolster her flagging courage.

It was the early hours of the morning before he came to her bedchamber. He wouldn't let her talk until they'd made love, a much gentler form of the exercise than the previous night, with Cosimo wielding the conductor's baton and Meg, for once, willing to yield the initiative. Afterwards he lay on her bed, hands linked behind his head, listening quietly to her as she paced around the chamber giving him the details of her morning's encounter.

"He didn't like the fact that he couldn't dominate me," she said as she finished the account. "But I think it intrigued him."

"It would certainly put him on his mettle," Cosimo

stated. "As we had planned, if you remember. It was the one surefire strategy to hook him quickly."

She nodded. "I know. But he does frighten me a little, Cosimo. What if he gets angry when I refuse him tomorrow night and...and well..." She extended her hands in an eloquent gesture.

He sat up, swinging his legs over the side of the bed, and reached for her hands, drawing her down onto his knee. "First you need to remember that I will be at the gate the whole time. If you feel the need for me, then find a way to move the curtains aside just for a second. That will bring me."

"You know which windows are his?" She was surprised.

"Of course," he said simply, and Meg was no longer surprised.

"But if I summon help, won't that ruin everything?" she objected.

"Not necessarily. No one need know you summoned me, and you may safely leave the management of such an intervention with me. It'll be sufficient to dampen the general's ardor temporarily and we'll trust not permanently." There was a grim edge to his customarily even tones.

"And if I can't reach the window?" She swiveled on his knee to look into his face. His expression was as grim as his voice.

"As a last resort, you will faint," he said. "Bonaparte detests weakness of any kind, and embarrassment even more. A swooning woman in his bedchamber would be enough to send him scuttling."

"But that would put him off permanently," she said.

"It would certainly be a setback," Cosimo agreed. "But I have faith in you, love. You will bring this off with aplomb, I promise."

And there was something about the utter confidence of the statement that gave Meg all the courage she needed.

She would bring this off and bring Napoleon Bonaparte to his assignation with death.

"You need to sleep," Cosimo said swiftly, seeing her sudden pallor, the darkening of her eyes. "One last thing, though." He turned her face towards him. "You need to watch Montaine. It's his job to vet candidates for the general's bed. Be very careful around him, he was snooping around the secretaire this morning."

"He was asking some very pointed questions," Meg said. "But I can't think what he could discover about Meg Barratt from Kent."

"No, neither can I," Cosimo said, but he had a little niggle of doubt that he kept from Meg. She had enough to concern her. He lifted her off him and tucked her into bed, kissing her eyelids shut. "I will be watching that window every second you are in there." He snuffed the candles and left soundlessly.

Meg curled up on herself under the coverlet. How would she feel when her part in this deadly mission was completed? It was so close to fruition now that for the first time she could see a time after it was over. How could she ever resume an ordinary life again?

Cosimo had said they would rejoin the *Mary Rose* and return to England. But how could she ever continue with a love affair tainted by the blood that would stain both their hands? Oh, she understood the reasoning behind this mission, but her intellect had very little to do with her gut. She had no stomach for it.

But she had even less stomach for seeing Cosimo's death.

The next day passed minute by minute. Meg paced the salon, resenting every interruption and yet welcoming it. The usual parade of officers came and went and she smiled, bantered easily. She accepted an offer from Major Guillaume to ride with him along the corniche in the afternoon and regretted it immediately. But then she reflected that riding would clear her head, and she hadn't been on the mare's back for two days.

"You seem to have attracted illustrious attention, madame," the major observed as they turned their horses onto the broad green swathe of grass that bordered the harbor.

"Indeed, Major?" Meg raised a questioning eyebrow, but there was a warning in her eyes.

A warning the major foolishly failed to heed. "General Bonaparte, madame. It's said that he is smitten with you."

"Is it, indeed?" she said, her nostrils flaring a little. "I'll thank you not to bandy my name about, Major Guillaume, and most certainly to keep the gossip of scuttlebutts to yourself." She nudged the mare with her heels and the horse, responsive as always, picked up her gait.

Guillaume urged his horse forward, his face rather red. "Forgive me, madame. I was out of order."

"Certainly you were," she said coldly and rode on in a flinty silence. The major kept pace, made a few hopeful conversational gambits, and then lapsed into a defeated silence. At which point Meg took pity on him.

"It's very hard for a woman alone to avoid malicious tongues, Major. I had thought you above such gossip mongering." She sounded hurt and sorrowful.

"Oh, my dear madame, I pay no heed to the rumors, I swear it," he said earnestly. "Forgive me, I wished only to alert you."

"Then I thank you for a warning that is, however, quite unnecessary," she said with a wan smile. "I am not unaware of the honor General Bonaparte's notice does me, but I own Colonel Montaine's disapproval is hard to bear and I'm afraid I took that out on you. He doesn't say anything openly, but there's something about the way he looks at me that makes it clear what he thinks of me." She gave a heavy sigh.

"Oh, my dear Madame Giverny," the major said, leaning over to pat her hand. "You need have no fear. Everyone knows that Montaine is a suspicious gossip. Rest assured no one takes any notice of him."

With the possible exception of Bonaparte, Meg reflected, as she thanked her champion with a sweet and slightly sad smile. When he left her at her door, she went up to her chamber, satisfied that Guillaume would defend her in the officers' mess with sufficient vigor to give his fellow officers second thoughts before deriding the widow's reputation. It might even give Montaine pause, at least in the short term, which, after all, was all that they needed.

Chapter 24

Meg was once again surprised at how calm she felt as she swept down the stairs that evening, the train of her dark red silk evening gown caught over one arm to facilitate her step. The gown was strikingly sophisticated, its slender cut skimming her body, the waist high enough under her bosom and the neckline low enough to make the most of her breasts. A black scarf provided a dramatic counterpoint to the deep red silk and she wore black opals at her throat and in her hair.

When she'd asked Cosimo how he'd managed to provide the jewelry that augmented her wardrobe, he'd merely smiled and shaken his head, leaving her to wonder whether someone else had been involved in their acquisition, someone whose identity she mustn't know. Either that or he'd been carrying them with him across France, in which case she had no idea where he could have hidden them. But that was hardly surprising. The privateer's secrets were too numerous to imagine. The jewels themselves would have been chosen with Ana in mind, of course, which explained why they so perfectly suited her own coloring.

As she stepped down into the hall she unfurled her Chinese fan of black painted silk and raised her eyebrows infinitesimally at her majordomo, who stood at the front door waiting to escort her to her carriage.

He gave a tiny nod, then opened the door with a ceremonial flourish. "Madame, your carriage awaits."

"Thank you, Charles." She bestowed a distant smile on him as she walked past him, and gave him her hand as she stepped up into the carriage. He squeezed her fingers in quick reassurance before leaning in to tuck a rug over her lap.

"You are magnificent," he whispered.

"I know," she murmured back and was rewarded by the flash of appreciative amusement in his eyes as he straightened.

She knew that if her appearance was vital to the part she had to play, then it was faultless. It was that, perhaps, that gave her this unexpected confidence.

Cosimo drove the carriage through the gates and into the courtyard of the general's mansion. They were obviously expected. The guards at the gate jumped to attention with a salute, and when they drew to a halt in front of the doors at precisely eight o'clock, an equerry hurried to the carriage.

"Good evening, Madame Giverny." He opened the door for her. "General Bonaparte is expecting you." He gave her his hand to help her down.

Meg, who had prepared herself for the dour Montaine, was relieved at the fresh face and gave him a warm smile as she stepped down. "My coachman will wait with the horses at the gate," she said, sending a haughty nod in the direction of said coachman, who sat ramrod still on the box, not presuming to glance at his mistress.

"If you will come this way, madame." The equerry gestured towards the doors that stood open, sending a river of yellow light into the courtyard.

Meg's heart seemed to pause for a second and her earlier calm vanished, but then she swallowed once, let her shoulders relax, and was in control once more. "Thank you." She put her hand on his proffered arm and was escorted into the house, the doors closing behind her with a decisive click.

This time the general was waiting for her in the drawing room, standing before the empty hearth, hands clasped at his back. He beamed at her when she entered, and hurried over, taking both her hands and bringing them to his lips. "My dear Nathalie, how charming you look, how delightful. Do let me give you a glass of champagne... Gilles, a glass of champagne for Madame Giverny." Still holding her hands, he took a step back and gazed at her in clear appreciation. "Charming," he said again. "Absolutely charming."

"You are too kind, General," she responded, gently removing her hands from his clasp and turning to take the glass from the equerry. "Where is Colonel Montaine this evening?"

A frown crossed Bonaparte's bright eyes. "Montaine is off duty," he stated. "You should not concern yourself with him."

"Oh, I wasn't. I'm simply accustomed to seeing him at your side." Meg offered a careless smile as she sipped her champagne, wondering if the frown and the absence were significant. Had the colonel unwisely warned his general off the widow? She didn't think Napoleon would take kindly to personal advice from his equerry. If Montaine had queered his own pitch, so much the better for her.

"That will be all, Gilles." Bonaparte dismissed the man with a wave. "You may tell them to serve dinner in fifteen minutes."

The equerry bowed and left the salon.

"Now, Nathalie, we must become properly acquainted." Napoleon reached to take her hand but she gave him a little smile and said quietly, "Excuse me one minute." She went to the door the equerry had closed behind him and opened it a fraction. "It is a little soon for a tête-à-tête, Napoleon."

His frown was more of a glower, then he gave a short laugh. "I didn't think you so nice in your notions, madame."

"In my position, I cannot be too careful, sir," she responded, smiling with a touch of invitation that took any offense out of her words as she came back to him, extending her hands. "It is a little different for women, Napoleon."

The glower faded as he took her hands. "I suppose it is. But come and tell me about yourself." He drew her towards a sofa and sat down, urging her to sit beside him.

Meg gave him the version of her history that was now so familiar to her she almost believed it herself. "My husband, Comte Giverny, was quite elderly," she explained as the story came to an end. "His death was not unexpected. Although he was more like a father to me than a husband, I feel his loss every day. He was always a tower of strength." She touched her eyes with a fingertip as if to brush away a tear.

"Ah, my dear, how sad for you," Napoleon said, seeming genuinely moved by her story. "To be alone in the world so young."

"I am not so young, Napoleon," she said, with a faint, self-deprecating smile. "I believe we are exactly the same age. And you have accomplished almost as much in ten years as Alexander the Great."

He smiled, taking her hand between both of his. "Believe me, my dear Nathalie, I have barely begun. My victories will cast Alexander's into the shade before I'm finished. The world has seen nothing yet."

He spoke with such calm conviction, his eyes glowing with absolute faith, that it took her breath away. She knew he was adored—worshiped even—by the men who served under him, and experiencing the wash of that utter confidence in himself, she could begin to understand it.

"I was wondering how it felt for you to be in Toulon again," she said. "After you recaptured it from the British five years ago. I had always understood that that military success was the turning point for the new Republic."

His white teeth flashed in a broad smile. "Ah, Nathalie, every minute I spend in this city reminds me of that most satisfying victory."

"You were but twenty-four," she prompted, thinking that if she could keep the conversation centered on his exploits, his military victories, his Jacobin philosophy, she might be able to steer a safe course through the evening. "Will you tell me about it? Now that I know Toulon a little, the details of the campaign will make more sense."

"At dinner," he promised as an inner door opened to admit a bowing manservant.

"Dinner is served, sir."

"Ah, good. I'm famished." He rose to his feet, patting his round belly in emphasis. "Nathalie . . ." He offered his arm and escorted her into a small, private dining room, where the round table was set for two, and discreetly placed candles shed a soft intimate light over the white linen, heavy silver, exquisite cut glass.

He drew out a chair for her and then took his place opposite, saying heartily as he shook out his napkin and spread it over his lap, "What do you have for us tonight, Alphonse?"

A man in a white apron was supervising a server placing dishes on the sideboard. He turned and bowed, reciting reverently, "For the first cover, General, a dish of ortolans braised with white grapes, a roasted bass with a sauce of *écrevisses*, a ragout of rabbit, and the pièce de résistance, a saddle of lamb with a sauce bordelaise and a delicate mousse of sweet garlic and baby peas." He permitted a small smile of satisfaction to touch his rather thin lips.

"Excellent...excellent," pronounced the general. "I trust it will satisfy you, madame."

"Amply, sir," Meg said somewhat faintly. She had a good appetite but so many dishes for the first cover would daunt an appetite much heartier than hers. Not so Napoleon, it seemed, who began to eat with relish.

Alphonse removed himself from the dining room after a few minutes of anxious observation as his master tried each dish and pronounced it good, but the servant remained to serve them, keeping the wine goblets fully charged.

Meg drank sparingly, knowing that she would need her wits about her even more when the servant finally left them. She nibbled the flesh off the tiny leg of an ortolan and dabbled her fingers in the finger bowl at her elbow. "From what I've read of the engagement at Toulon, General, it was your decision to attack the fort at Point l'Eguilette that drove Admiral Hood and the British into retreat. I rode there with Major Guillaume and he tried to describe the action to me, but of course he was not there in person. I would dearly love to hear you tell it."

Napoleon wiped his mouth vigorously and took a deep draught of wine. "I will show you, my dear, exactly how the engagement was conducted." He began to move cutlery, cruets, glasses around on the cloth to indicate the various positions, and Meg, despite her tension, was quickly absorbed by the general's enthusiastic re-creation of the battle for Toulon. Whatever she might think of Napoleon Bonaparte personally, he was inspired to the point of genius when it came to warfare.

She drew him out about Toulon, his subsequent victories, and about his imprisonment at Antibes as a suspected traitor four years earlier. The strategy worked. He was delighted to talk about his career and to describe his triumphs to such an admiring, attentive, and clearly knowledgeable audience. Conversation didn't affect his enthusiasm for his dinner either and Meg observed with something like awe the quantities of fowl, fish, and flesh that disappeared into the rotund body.

At last, however, he set down his fork and sat back. "Most satisfactory." He gestured to the hovering manservant. "Ask Alphonse to introduce us to the second cover."

Alphonse returned to supervise the arrangement of dishes that this time were laid directly upon the table. A basket of peaches, bowls of jellies and syllabubs, mushrooms and melted Roquefort on rounds of brioche, and an astonishing gâteau elaborately decorated with a naval frigate in full sail, flying the tricolor.

"Magnificent," Napoleon declared, rubbing his hands. "Alphonse, you have outdone yourself."

"Thank you, sir." The chef bowed himself out.

"You may leave us now, Claude," the general said to the manservant. "We can serve ourselves."

Meg helped herself to one of the savory brioches and waited until the servant had left, closing the door behind him, before she said, "You must forgive me, Napoleon, but if we are to be alone, I would like to keep a door open."

"Good God, madame, what are you afraid of?" he demanded. "I am not in the habit of ravishing my dinner companions."

"No, of course not," she said with a laugh. "And I didn't mean to imply any such thing. But I would prefer it to be generally understood without possibility of a mistake, that you and I are simply dining together."

He pushed back his chair and went to the door that led into the drawing room, opening it wide. "Will that suit you, madame? Or should I send for Gilles to stand guard?"

Meg looked dismayed at the sarcastic tone. "It seems a little unjust that you should be angry at such an understandable request. Perhaps I should leave now." She made a move to stand up.

Instantly he crossed back to the table. "No...no... please, Nathalie. I didn't mean to sound unreasonable, but I really don't see why you should concern yourself. You are among friends. The only people around are my staff, all loyal to me to the last drop of their blood."

"I'm sure they are," she said, resuming her seat. "But I would like them to be able to tell the truth about our meeting with a good conscience." She gave a deep sigh, watching him out of the corner of her eye. "Malicious tongues will wag at the slightest opportunity. You may already have heard some of the innuendo whispered about me—"

He reached over to take her hand. "My dear, I never

listen to rumor," he stated. "And I don't permit my staff to do so either."

"I very much fear that Colonel Montaine..." She gave a slightly sorrowful smile as she dabbed at her lips with her napkin.

"The colonel knows better than to bring tales to me," Napoleon declared.

"It's very hard for a woman alone to preserve the purity of her reputation," she said, hammering the point home with another deep sigh.

"Quite so," he said. "Now, may I tempt you to a slice of this gâteau?"

Obviously he was no longer comfortable with that line of conversation, Meg reflected, but she'd sowed the seeds for the moment. "Just a sliver, thank you. The news from Paris is very confusing these days. I heard talk of another coup d'état before I left."

The change in topic distracted him as she'd hoped, and he launched into a detailed commentary on the uncertainty of the Directory that at present controlled the government. "Without the support of the army, the Directory would have been overturned long since," he stated. "If it hadn't been for my 'whiff of grapeshot' three years ago, the political face of France would be very different."

"Will you continue to support the Directors?" she asked, picking at a meringue-covered hazelnut.

He shot her a sharp glance over the bowl of syllabub. "That remains to be seen, madame."

She smiled. "First, of course, you must conquer the Orient."

"I shall," he declared through a mouthful of whipped cream.

The manservant knocked and entered. "Would you prefer to take coffee in the drawing room, General?"

Napoleon regarded his guest thoughtfully. "Madame?"

"As you wish, Napoleon."

"Very well, then, we shall adjourn. Bring port and cognac, Claude." He wiped his mouth and pushed back his chair. "Madame."

Meg accepted his arm and they returned to the drawing room. The long curtains were drawn across the windows and the door to the corridor that she had opened earlier was now closed. She glanced at it and the general himself opened it a fraction of an inch.

"There, madame, is your modesty satisfied?"

"My modesty does not concern me, General," she said softly, suggestively. "But my reputation does. I will not compromise that lightly."

His bright eyes were suddenly piercing as he absorbed both words and tone. "Of course not, Nathalie. I understand perfectly." He sat down on the sofa beside her, watching her hands as she poured coffee. One arm slid surreptitiously around her, his hand flattening against the small of her back.

The warmth of his palm seemed to sear her skin through the delicate silk of her gown, and it took a supreme effort of will for Meg not to jump to her feet. Soon this would be over, she told herself. She just had to keep this up for another half an hour, no more. Arrange the assignation and then it would be over... *her* part would be over. She need never see Napoleon Bonaparte again.

She declined the glass of port he offered and sipped her coffee, trying to ignore the hand still firmly in place on her back. The fingers started to creep up towards her neck and he leaned sideways, saying softly into her ear, "You know I find you utterly alluring, my dear."

She shifted very slightly on the sofa, turning herself a little to face him. "As I said, Napoleon, I don't compromise my reputation lightly." A slight seductive smile lifted the corners of her mouth, leaving him no doubt that she returned his sentiments.

He was silent for quite a few moments, his fingers absently playing a tune along her spine. Meg held herself still, allowing the tune to come to an end, waiting for whatever response would emerge from the deliberative silence.

Finally he let his hand drop and stood up, going over to the sideboard to refill his goblet with cognac. Then he turned, cradling the glass between his hands, considering her with a slight frown. "So, Nathalie, how then should we arrange this?"

Meg decided to meet the straightforward question with a straightforward answer. Her role was not that of simpering ingénue, fluttering in pretended innocence. She wouldn't know how to play such a part even if it were. The sardonic thought flitted across her mind to be swiftly dismissed. The moment was too crucial for distraction.

She opened and closed her fan as if in deep thought, then closed it with a decisive snap and looked across at him. "Should we decide upon an assignation, Napoleon, it must be in complete privacy," she said, her voice low but clear. "We must meet somewhere outside town, just the two of us. I would ask that you come quite alone, as I will."

She opened her fan again, half concealing her expression as she watched his face. "No one must know of it. In less than a week you will be gone from here, our liaison barely a memory, and I will still be here. I cannot, *will* not be left the butt of every scandalmonger and gossip along the Mediterranean coast."

"I understand, my dear," he said. "I believe I can meet your conditions with little difficulty."

"You give me your word you will tell no one." She rose with a degree of agitation. "Oh dear, I'm such a fool in these matters. I have no control sometimes, when I meet…" She opened her palms in a gesture of helplessness. "When I meet someone who attracts me so deeply."

He smiled and unconsciously grasped the lapels of his braided scarlet dress coat. "Attractions are meant to be acted upon, my dear."

"Maybe so," she said with a rueful smile. "But it's the woman who takes the greatest risk." Even as the glib words dropped from her lips her scalp crawled and a wash of nausea rose into her throat.

"Trust me, Nathalie, I will take no risks with your reputation," he said, coming towards her, taking her hands and bringing them to his lips, before pulling her sharply towards him and kissing her hard on the mouth.

She struggled against him, turning her head away. "Please, please, Napoleon. Not here, I beg of you."

Abruptly he released her. His eyes were rather wild and he was breathing heavily. "Forgive me, but you drive me to distraction. I cannot wait to…" He didn't complete the sentence but there was no need to do so.

Meg stepped away from him, moving closer to the window. She didn't think he would press further at this point, but the knowledge of Cosimo watching the curtains from the gate was more than reassuring. "In the right place at the right time," she said, thankful that her voice remained steady.

He exhaled noisily and mopped his brow with his handkerchief. "You drive a hard bargain, my dear Nathalie. But it will be as you say. I will arrange matters. Wait to hear from me."

"Most eagerly," she said, coming over to him. She leaned into him and lightly kissed the corner of his mouth. "A promise," she whispered into his ear. "And now I must leave you . . . for the present."

Napoleon pulled the bellrope with sufficient vigor to yank it out of the wall and the equerry answered before the last peal had faded. "General."

"Escort Madame Giverny to her carriage," Bonaparte instructed curtly. He gave his guest a curt bow. "I bid you good night, madame," he said before spinning on his heel and stalking into his adjoining office without waiting for her responding goodnight.

"General," she murmured to his back and swept past the interested-looking Gilles, who held the door for her. Bonaparte had played that rather well. The rumor now would be that the widow had displeased him in some way. She managed a look of confused discomfort as she was escorted from the mansion and across the courtyard to her waiting carriage, and returned the equerry's goodnight with a bare whisper.

He saluted and returned to the mansion to report to Colonel Montaine on the interesting conclusion to the general's evening.

Cosimo had never spent a more uncomfortable evening. He hadn't taken his eyes off the curtains at Bonaparte's window, and every muscle in his shoulders and neck ached. All his customary cool detachment had fled as he'd sat there waiting, trying not to imagine how Meg was managing, and failing miserably. His imagination ran riot. He cursed himself for hurling her into such a dangerous situation. Meg was not Ana, as he'd told himself over and over in the last weeks. She had none of the other woman's experience, and none of the motivation that drove Ana to play her part in this war.

Ana had survived the Terror but she had lost her family. Her Austrian mother had been one of Marie Antoinette's closest companions from the moment the princess as a young girl had left her own mother in Vienna to be thrown unprotected, uneducated, and unadvised into the vicious turmoil of the French court. Ana had survived on her wits, escaping to England with a visceral loathing of the revolution and all that it stood for. It hadn't taken her long to find a home with the antirevolutionary networks spreading across Europe. She and Cosimo had first partnered each other on a mission four years earlier.

Meg Barratt had grown up in the quiet English countryside, well educated certainly, but not in the world of dirty experience. What did she know of the blood and viscera that informed Cosimo's own world? She was doing what she was doing not out of conviction but out of loyalty to him. Out of *love*, she had said.

His hands tensed on the reins. His world did not admit such an emotion. And this evening, waiting with churning guts for that great door to open and Meg to walk out unharmed, was most definitely not the time to wonder why. The horses reacted to the tension on the reins and raised their heads, pulling against the curbs. It was enough to bring him back to the world that he controlled, the world that existed outside the tumult of anxiety. He quieted them and sat back on the box, forcing himself into the trance that would give him calm and strength.

He was aware instantly of the moment when the door across the courtyard opened. He jumped down from the box and let down the footstep. He watched her as she walked across the paved courtyard. Her step was firm, her color no paler than usual, the slight smile she gave the equerry as he handed her into the carriage perfectly steady.

Cosimo draped the lap rug over her and noticed that her hands were quite still in her lap. He didn't look at her, spoke only the brief courtesy greeting of a good servant, climbed back upon his box, and drove away.

Meg didn't begin to shake until they turned the corner behind the church and the house was in sight. Her teeth began to chatter, her heart pounding in her chest like a bolting racehorse.

She couldn't make herself move when Cosimo came around to open the door for her. Her body was somehow petrified on the seat. She looked at him, murmured, "I feel so *filthy*. What have I *done*?" Then she fell silent because if she said any more, the words would pour out in an undammable flood and they could not be retracted.

Cosimo without a flicker removed the lap rug, said calmly, "Here we are, madame. A beautiful night as usual. May I help you?" He took her hand as he spoke, his grip closing tightly over her fingers. His other hand moved to her elbow and he half lifted, half pulled her from the vehicle. When she set foot on the pavement he steadied her with an arm around her waist.

There was no one on the street, but there could be watchers in the house, and Meg found that just the simple pressure of his arm, the firmness of his hand on hers, gave her the strength she needed to get herself through the front door.

"Send immediately for Estelle," the majordomo instructed a hovering servant. "Madame is feeling a little faint...Madame, if you will permit, I will help you upstairs."

"My thanks, Charles," she managed, putting a hand to her forehead. She was beginning to regain control but the scene once instigated must come to a natural close. "The heat, I think. It's such a warm evening."

Estelle came bounding down the stairs with all the exuberance of youth, flourishing sal volatile that she waved vigorously under her mistress's nose. "Oh, madame, are you ill?" She took Meg's other arm.

"No, much better now, thank you, Estelle." Meg pushed away the sal volatile, her eyes beginning to stream from the potent vapor. "Just a touch of the heat. Charles will help me to my room."

The majordomo escorted her as far as the door and then when instructed stood back and left her to the ministrations of her abigail. His expression was dark. Meg must have succeeded in preparing the trap. She would not otherwise have said what she'd said. But he felt nothing...not one iota of the satisfaction that he would have expected. None of the quick thrill of the chase that would usually accompany this moment. The trap was set, the rest was up to him. Such moments of anticipation had always been the spur to completion. Once he began the operation, his mind was in control, his body automatically performing the moves carefully rehearsed over hours of meticulous preparation. And when the operation was completed, he was simply satisfied. No sense of triumph, merely the knowledge of a mission completed.

But something here was awry. And whatever was awry was within himself.

He waited until the household was asleep before he went to her, and it took every ounce of the control born of experience to wait. There was no line of candlelight beneath her door, but he knew she was awake. He opened the door softly, stepped in, and closed it as softly behind him. He saw immediately that the bed was empty.

"Meg?"

"Yes." She stepped out from the shadow of the window curtains where she'd been standing looking out onto the dark street and the bulk of the church. "I haven't gone anywhere."

"No, I didn't imagine you had. May I light a candle?" He lit the taper without waiting for her permission and set it on the table. "You had a hard evening." It was a statement.

"I didn't realize how hard until it was over," Meg confessed. She drew the sides of her peignoir around her with a shudder. "I don't think I was ever intended for this work, Cosimo."

"No," he agreed. "Neither do I." He took her in his arms, carrying her to the bed and lying down with her, nestling her into the crook of his arm. "But your task is finished, love."

She reared up onto an elbow. "And will you feel nothing... nothing at all when you do this?"

He answered her honestly. "I will think of the countless lives that will be saved if this war is over."

"And I cannot argue with that logic," Meg said, sliding down again into the curl of his arm. "Napoleon will make the arrangements and he'll inform me of them. Is that right?"

"Yes," he said. "He will feel safer if he dictates the rendezvous. You said it must be close to the city?"

"Close enough for me to go alone." Her voice was dull.

Cosimo lay on his back, holding her, feeling the dullness resonate in her body. "Your part is over," he repeated.

"Is that supposed to make me feel better?" Meg sat up again, suddenly the wretched fury of the evening catching up with her. "I've lured a man to his death, Cosimo. And knowing you, nothing will prevent that death. You once told me you don't risk failure. I believe it. If you did, I wouldn't be here. I've done what you wanted; now I want you to leave me alone." She got off the bed, tugging the peignoir around her again, and went back to the window.

Cosimo stood up too. He looked at her averted back, the rigidity of her pose, and admitted defeat. Nothing he could say tonight would help either of them. He went up to her and softly kissed her nape.

A shudder ran through her and he stepped back as if he'd been burned. His mouth grim, he left her.

Chapter 25

"The door was open the whole time?" Colonel Montaine regarded Gilles skeptically.

"Yes, Colonel, and Claude was on duty in the dining room for the whole of the first cover."

"What did they talk about over dinner?"

"The general's military career for the most part, according to Claude. That and some discussion about the political situation in Paris."

Montaine drummed his fingers on the tabletop, where he sat over a late supper. "The general showed no *special* interest in the widow?" He gestured in invitation to the wine decanter.

"Thank you, sir." Gilles filled a goblet and sat down opposite the colonel. "Not that anyone could detect, sir. And when she left he seemed displeased."

"Hm." The colonel frowned. "Because she was leaving, perhaps? Or had she offended him in some other fashion?"

"I don't know, Colonel. But he was curt to the point of rudeness."

Montaine rubbed his chin. Something didn't sit quite

right. Women never turned down Bonaparte's advances, but could the widow Giverny be the exception, could she be impervious to the general's power and seductive charm? Unlikely. If so, why would she have accepted the initial invitation?

"Does Madame Giverny remind you of anyone, Gilles?" he asked abruptly.

The equerry shook his head. "No, I don't believe so, Colonel. Should she?"

The colonel's frown deepened. "Bonaparte said she reminded him of someone, it was what caught his attention in the first place. I see no resemblance to any woman I've met before, but you've been with him longer than I have."

Gilles shook his head again. "No, she rings no bells. But the general keeps a meticulous log. Perhaps there's some reference there."

"Perhaps." Montaine picked up his wineglass. "I don't relish the general discovering me snooping through his journals, however. I wouldn't even know which year to start." He drained his glass and reached again for the decanter.

"Do you suspect Madame Giverny of something?" Gilles regarded him curiously.

The colonel shrugged. "It's just a feeling, Gilles. Nothing I can put my finger on. If Bonaparte goes to bed before dawn, I'll try to take a look at his journals." He didn't sound too hopeful. The general survived on remarkably little sleep. Usually it was dawn by the time he lay down for the catnap that sufficed for a night's rest, and by then headquarters would be a hive of activity again, making discreet spying a much more difficult operation.

"You could always ask him," Gilles suggested.

Montaine gave a short laugh. "The last time I mentioned the lady to the general, I got my head snapped off. I
don't think I'll risk it again. Good night, Gilles."

The other man accepted this abrupt dismissal without
surprise. The colonel was not known for the niceties of
his manner. He drained his glass and stood up. "Good
night, sir."

Montaine twirled the stem of his wineglass between his
fingers, gazing sightlessly into the middle distance. Finally
he pushed back his chair and got to his feet.

He strolled casually down the hallway towards the
general's apartments. The drawing room door stood open
and the general's manservant was tidying the room. The
colonel paused in the doorway. "Has General Bonaparte
retired, Claude?"

"No, sir. He went out riding about half an hour ago."

"Riding? But it's past midnight."

"Yes, sir. He said he needed some exercise."

"Who accompanied him?"

"I believe one of the officers on duty, Colonel."

"I see." Montaine looked thoughtful. "I want to check
the general's diary for tomorrow." He crossed the drawing
room and entered the office. It was brightly lit as always;
the general had unpredictable working hours and candles
were kept burning throughout the night.

Montaine left the door slightly ajar and went to the
shelves behind the desk where the general's leather-bound
logbooks were kept easily to hand. Each book bore the year
on its spine and his hand hovered uncertainly. He had
joined the general's personal staff early the previous year.
He had not come across a woman who closely resembled
Madame Giverny, so the year before, perhaps? He drew
out the relevant volume. Gilles had no recollection of

such a woman either, and he had joined the general's personal staff six months before the colonel.

He opened the book at January, 1796, the year the general had married Josephine Beauharnais. Montaine smiled a little grimly. Bonaparte adored his wife, but was so busy campaigning he barely saw her. Hence the need for these impulsive liaisons. He thumbed through the entries for the early months after the general had been put in command of the Army of Italy. They were meticulous accounts of the various engagements of the Italian campaign, interspersed with the general's judgments of his own decisions, and occasional descriptions of social events. Interesting enough, but not what he was looking for. Although he was somewhat uncertain as to what that was. And then his eye fell on an item at the bottom of a page.

During the armistice of Cherasco, when Bonaparte was dictating the terms to the King of Savoy in Milan, the general noted a meeting with an Austrian woman, Ana Loeben.

April 30th: Introduced tonight by Giovanni Morelli to Countess Ana Loeben, delightful redhead, petite and charming, well educated, a fascinating conversationalist. Complaisant husband apparently. Worth pursuing?

Montaine tapped the question mark with a fingertip. *Was this it?* Had the general pursued Countess Loeben? More to the point, had he *caught* the countess? The colonel turned pages, but there was no other reference to the lady, which seemed to imply that she had not been caught. It could, of course, be pure coincidence that a woman so like the one that Bonaparte had noticed in Milan should appear from nowhere. But it was also a possibility, however faint, that someone had intended the Countess Giverny to catch the general's susceptible eye.

And as far as Montaine was concerned, a possibility of danger threatening his general must be considered a probability and acted upon.

He slotted the volume back onto the shelf and then froze at the sound of voices in the outer chamber. The door flew wide and Bonaparte stood there, tapping his riding crop against his boots.

"You're here, Alain," he observed without apparent surprise.

"I came to check your diary for tomorrow, General," the colonel said calmly, knowing perfectly well that it would never occur to Bonaparte to question such an explanation. "The brigade majors requested a staff meeting to discuss leave policy."

"Good God, man, that doesn't require my attention," the general said. "You can handle it, surely?"

"Yes, of course, sir," Montaine said as calmly as before. "But before I arranged the meeting I wished to be sure that you didn't require me yourself at that time."

"Oh, I see." The general nodded, apparently satisfied. "By the way, tomorrow evening I shall be going out, Alain. You may have the evening off, I won't be requiring the services of any of my staff."

"May I ask where you're going, sir?"

"No, you may not," Bonaparte stated, sitting at his desk. "Now, leave me. I have work to do." He waved towards the door.

Montaine wished his general good night and left, his mind working overtime. He went downstairs and demanded to speak to the duty officer who had accompanied the general on his ride.

The junior lieutenant responded to the summons at a

run. "Colonel." He saluted, almost skidding to a halt in front of his superior.

"Where did you go with General Bonaparte this evening?"

"We rode out of town and the general stopped at a cottage. He told me to wait and he went inside. Then he came out and we rode back here."

"He went inside? Did someone open the door for him?"

"I believe so, but I couldn't really see. He told me to wait on the pathway. I waited for perhaps ten minutes, then General Bonaparte came out again and we rode back."

"You had better take me there now."

An hour later, Colonel Montaine gazed at the unremarkable lime-washed cottage set back from the path behind a low stone wall. He recognized it. A week earlier he and Bonaparte with a small group of officers had passed by here, and an elderly woman weeding in her garden had rushed out to greet them with voluble delight. She had pressed pieces of freshly baked cherry pie upon them, and Napoleon, whose sure touch with ordinary folk never failed him, had dismounted and strolled with her into the garden, where he'd eaten pie and talked with her and her husband for a few minutes before rejoining his men.

So what had brought him out here again so late at night? Why had he roused the old couple from their beds? What had he wanted from them?

Whatever it was, Montaine didn't like it. Any more than he liked the idea of his general going off alone tomorrow night. Was Bonaparte intending to come here? Had he been arranging something with the old couple?

An assignation with Madame Giverny...

It seemed the obvious explanation. But usually the general's fancies were smuggled into his quarters and smuggled out again at dawn. Why was this different? Why was *she* different?

Montaine rode back in abstracted silence. He knew Bonaparte wouldn't listen to him if he expressed his unease with this assignation and his reservations about the widow, so he would have to take precautions without the general's being aware. If he was wrong, then the consequences would be hard to bear, but if he was right and did nothing, the consequences for Bonaparte... for France herself... were unimaginable.

Meg awoke the next morning from a sleep so deep and dark it took her a few minutes to identify the source of the weight that seemed to be pressing on her chest. She sat up against the pillows and bleakly took stock. They were in the end game and to all intents and purposes her part was played. But it would never really be over. She would never be able to forget her part in a man's death.

The door opened and Estelle entered with Meg's morning chocolate. "Good morning, madame. A beautiful one it is again," she said breezily. "I trust you're feeling better this morning." She set the tray down on the bedside table and went to open the curtains, letting in a flood of buttery sunlight that made Meg blink. It certainly didn't suit her mood.

"Yes, thank you, Estelle," she said, closing her eyes against the cheery light.

"A letter came for you, madame," the abigail said, handing Meg a wafer-sealed paper before she poured a fragrant stream of chocolate into a shallow cup. "Bright and early the messenger was. I don't even think M'sieur Charles was around."

Meg murmured something in response and turned the folded, sealed paper over in her hands. There was nothing to identify the sender. No imprint on the wafer, no initials, no crest. Just her name written in bold black script.

She took the cup Estelle handed her and said, "I'll ring when I'm ready for you, Estelle."

The maid looked a little surprised. "Shouldn't I put out your dress for the morning, madame?"

"Not right now," Meg said with a touch of impatience. "I'm not ready to get up just yet. I'll ring when I am."

Estelle bobbed a curtsy and left. As soon as the door had closed, Meg slit the wafer with a fingernail and unfolded the sheet. It bore a time — 10:30 p.m. — and a meticulously drawn map. The artist was a skilled cartographer. There was nothing else. No signature, no salutation, nothing but the time and the map.

Napoleon had clearly taken her insistence on secrecy to heart, she reflected. No one but herself could identify the author of this missive. No one but herself would understand what it meant.

She let the parchment drift to the coverlet and sipped her chocolate. It was for tonight, since there was no date. Could Cosimo be ready at such short notice? But it was really a rhetorical question. He would have been ready long since, just waiting for the time and the place to spring the trap.

Slowly a cold detachment descended upon her. If she was to get through this day and evening, she had to insulate herself from her imagination. She finished her chocolate, set the cup aside, and reached for the handbell.

Cosimo was in the hall when she came downstairs half an hour later, the message from Bonaparte tucked into her sleeve.

"Good morning, madame." He bowed with a polite smile but his sharp blue gaze scrutinized her appearance.

"Charles," she said in response, moving towards the salon. "I have some errands I would like you to run for me this morning. Wait upon me in the salon...oh, and bring me coffee, please."

"Certainly, madame." He made his way to the kitchen, reflecting with a half smile that Meg had very little difficulty with the haughtiness aspect of her role.

He took a tray of coffee into the salon and set it on the table. Meg was sitting with her back to him at the secretaire and for a few minutes didn't appear to acknowledge his presence. He coughed and said, "Shall I pour for you, madame?"

"Oh, yes, thank you, Charles," she said rather absently.

Cosimo glanced around the deserted salon. The windows were closed, the door was closed, there were no pricked ears in the vicinity. There was no real need for Meg to maintain the act quite so punctiliously. He poured coffee before saying, "I understand you have some orders for me, madame."

She turned then and he looked in vain for the glimmer of mischief he'd expected, but her pale face was sculpted in porcelain, not a hint of emotion of any kind. Silently she held out the parchment to him.

He looked at it, then nodded. "You have a luncheon engagement with Madame Beaufort?"

"Yes."

"Then you must keep it. Do everything that you intended to do, don't change your plans."

"But this evening I'm engaged to attend a concert with a party of Major Guillaume's."

"Obviously you'll cry off from that. I think it would be best if you were to mention casually at luncheon that you're feeling a little under the weather... nothing serious, just a touch of the sun perhaps. I'll deliver your message of excuse to Guillaume after I've brought you home from the Beauforts'." He spoke swiftly, decisively, refolding Bonaparte's map and tucking it into the inside pocket of his waistcoat.

"And then what?" Meg asked in the same distant tone.

He looked at her, noting anew her pallor, the deadness in those usually lively green eyes. "Sweetheart, I know this is hard—"

"Yes, it is," she interrupted brusquely. "And the sooner it's over, the better. You haven't told me yet how we're to get away from here, back to the *Mary Rose*."

"You don't need to know that at present," he said, his tone once more decisive, all the tenderness banished. "You already know what you do need to know. We've been over it several times. Go to bed early and tell the household to do the same, dress in your britches, and at precisely eleven o'clock let yourself out of the house and make your way to the stables, where I'll be waiting. Is that clear?"

Meg nodded. "Yes, it's clear."

"Good. I shall go off now and run these errands you have for me..." He tried a conspiratorial smile but received no response. With a shrug he turned to the door. "I'm going to follow the map but I'll be back in time to drive you to the Beauforts' at one o'clock."

Meg heard the front door close almost immediately after he'd left her, and hurried to the window. Cosimo was striding down the street with the air of a man on a mission. He couldn't possibly be checking out the rendezvous on foot, she thought. And then she shook her head dispiritedly. What did she know about his plans? He'd gone to considerable lengths to keep her from knowing anything except what was essential for her to play her own part.

Cosimo walked to a livery stable on the edge of the city and rented a nag that had seen better days. He didn't argue the price, however, or comment on the animal's woeful condition. He had no desire to draw attention to himself. He followed the beautifully drawn map and within a short space of time arrived at an isolated cottage set back from the pathway.

An old man was sitting on a wooden bench dozing in the sun while a woman picked beans in a kitchen garden. The only other buildings Cosimo could see were a lean-to outside of which a goat was tethered, and a hut that he guessed was the privy way off to the side of the cottage.

Humble quarters for General Bonaparte, he reflected. Were the old couple to be allowed to remain in situ for the assignation? Not that it would matter. They could offer no obstacle to the assassin. He dismounted and went to the gate. "M'sieur?"

The old man jerked awake. "Eh...eh?" He stared at the visitor as if he had dropped from the sky. The woman, on the other hand, set down her basket of beans and came over, wiping her hands on her apron.

"M'sieur?"

He smiled warmly and apologized for disturbing them. "*Pardon, madame.* I am looking for the road to La Valette."

"Ah, m'sieur." The woman threw up her hands in horror. "You are going in quite the wrong direction. Thataway, m'sieur." She pointed back the way he had come.

He exclaimed suitably at his own stupidity, and wiped his brow pointedly with his handkerchief.

"Ah, come in...come in..." the old woman urged. "A drink of milk fresh from the goat will set you right. This way now. And my good man will water your horse."

Cosimo with profuse thanks and apologies followed her into the low-ceilinged cottage. It was clean, freshly swept, and there was a ladder leading upwards into what he assumed was a loft. Well, Bonaparte would not think twice about such sleeping accommodations, he had enjoyed much worse on campaign, but it was still an interesting choice of venue for a night of passion with a gently bred lady. In other circumstances the thought would have made him chuckle.

He accepted a cup of warm goat's milk, controlling a grimace of distaste even as his eyes darted around the small space looking for the right place to position himself for the ambush. The old couple would have to receive an urgent message that would take them out of the cottage, but from whom?

Gently he drew the woman out about her family and her circumstances. She was more than happy to chat and when her husband came in he proved even more garrulous. Cosimo learned of the daughter in the neighboring hamlet who was expecting a baby any day, and the son who had joined the army of the Republic under the flag of the great Bonaparte. He listened, prodded a little, and finally took his leave, discreetly putting two livres on the table in ostensible payment for the milk.

He rode the pathetic nag back to the livery stable, his plan now shaped in his mind. He walked back to the house, fetched the carriage from the mews, and brought it round to the front door.

Meg was waiting for him, dressed in filmy jonquil muslin, a high-crowned silk hat perched atop her red curls. She was still paler than normal, and with a knowing eye he could see that she had powdered her freckles rather more than usual, but he could also detect a resolution, a hardness in her that showed in the tight smile she gave him, the set of her shoulders, the swing of her hips as she walked to the carriage.

They said nothing. He left her at the Beauforts' and went to his own apartments to check and double-check the weapons on which his life would depend. He chose his knives, sharpened them, practiced sliding them smoothly and swiftly out of the sheath. He cleaned his pistol. Now he was not thinking of anything but what his hands were doing. And when he was satisfied, he sat down and wrote to Meg.

It was a letter he hoped she would never have to read. But if he did not come back for her, then she needed to know how to get out of Toulon to rendezvous with the *Mary Rose*.

By the time his preparations were complete, it was time to return to the Beauforts' for his mistress.

Meg emerged from the house looking wan, leaning on the butler's arm. "Madame is not feeling very well, Charles," the butler informed Madame Giverny's coachman as he helped the ailing lady into the carriage.

"Oh, it's nothing," Meg said weakly. "I find the heat so oppressive."

"I'll have Madame home in no time," her coachman said, sending a curt nod in the butler's direction. He snapped the reins and the horses started off at a brisk trot.

"How are you?" Cosimo asked quietly, for once risking a personal conversation in the public street.

"I don't know," Meg said candidly. "This day is interminable."

"Yes," he agreed. "But it's always like that."

Always. Meg felt as if her breath had stopped. How could he say that so casually? *Always.* How many assassinations had he accomplished, for God's sake? How many days had he spent like this? She let her head fall back against the seat and closed her eyes. This was not her world. She had yearned for adventure, for passion . . . and she had found both. But sweet heaven, at what a price.

When they reached the house, Cosimo helped her down from the carriage and then said in a bare whisper, his lips hardly moving, "I will not see you again until this is over, Meg." He put a paper into her nerveless hand. "If I am not in the stables when you get there, then follow these instructions to the letter. Do you understand?"

"I understand." She scrunched the paper in her hand and began to walk away from him up to the front door. Halfway she stopped, looked back to where he stood beside the carriage. The sun glinted off the silver streaks in his gray hair and seemed reflected in the sea-washed blue of his eyes. She wondered if she would ever see him again. She lifted her hand in a tiny gesture of farewell, then went into the house.

The remainder of the afternoon Meg spent in the relative cool of her bedchamber. She could find no peace.

Whether she paced the carpet, or tried to read, or lay down and closed her eyes, images, red and twisted and violent, rose relentless in her mind's eye. She thought of taking a dose of laudanum that would at least grant her a few hours of sleep, but knew she didn't dare risk muddling her mind.

Where was he now? What was he doing?

Cosimo reached the cottage at eight that evening, more than two hours before Bonaparte would arrive for the rendezvous. It would give him ample time to make his preparations.

"Shall I go now, m'sieur?" the lad demanded eagerly as they stood a hundred yards down the pathway in the deep shadow of a plane tree.

"In a minute," the assassin said, laying a hand on the boy's shoulder. He'd found the lad on the beach, searching for driftwood, and it hadn't taken more than the promise of five sous to persuade him to deliver an urgent message.

The boy danced impatiently, anxious for his payment, anxious for his supper. At last Cosimo said, "Now, you remember what you're to say?"

"Yes, baby's coming. They have to hurry," the child said, holding out his hands. "I can do it, m'sieur. Honest I can."

"I know you can," Cosimo responded, reaching into his pocket and carefully counting the coins into the grubby palm. "Now go." He gave him an encouraging pat on the shoulder and watched as he scampered away to the cottage.

The lad was back in minutes and gave his paymaster a cheeky grin as he ran back along the path towards his own home. Cosimo swung himself into the branches of the plane tree and settled down to wait. He didn't have long. The old man and his wife hurried out of the cottage, each carrying a bundle, and without a backward glance set off up the path.

Cosimo waited in the tree until they had disappeared from sight. They had a five-mile walk ahead of them for which he was sorry, but at least they were out of harm's way. And once they realized there was no emergency they would not walk back tonight.

He moved stealthily to the cottage, circling it once. The goat was tucked up in its shed, the chickens put to bed away from the fox. Conveniently there was no dog. And neither was the door locked. He lifted the latch and entered the cottage. They had extinguished the cooking fire but a lantern stood upon the table with its wick freshly trimmed and its oil chamber filled, flint and tinder beside it. The old couple had not forgotten their august visitor.

The assassin went up the ladder to the loft. It smelled of lavender and apples. The linen on the straw mattress that formed the couple's bed was clean and fresh. A flagon of cider and two cups stood on a wooden crate beside the bed, and, most touching, two apples had been placed on the bolster, a gift for the lovers.

Cosimo exhaled on a long slow breath. Then he retreated down the ladder and slipped into the inglenook, where he waited, his body so calm and still now that he barely needed to breathe. His hand rested on the rapier knife in the sheath strapped to his thigh, and every sense was stretched into the silence, listening for the first hoofbeat on the sandy path.

———

Meg heard the front door knocker soon after eight o'clock. The loud, insistent sound made her heart jump. She went out onto the upstairs landing. Cosimo was not there to open the door, he'd told the staff that Madame Giverny had given him the night off, and the head footman did the honors.

Meg listened, stunned, as Alain Montaine's voice rose from the hall below. "Tell Madame Giverny that General Bonaparte's equerry wishes to speak with her." There was something about the tone, an insolent edge, that set her teeth on edge, but that also screamed danger.

Her first thought was that he had been sent by Napoleon with a message to cancel the assignation. But that arrogant, importunate tone was not that of a messenger. Had they discovered something? Was Cosimo even now in their hands?

She slipped back into her chamber and sat down at the dresser, examining her reflection in the mirror. A touch of rouge, a dusting of powder, and in the soft light of candles her pallor would be less noticeable. She glanced over her shoulder as Estelle burst in.

"Who's that at the door, Estelle?" Meg was astounded at her calm detachment. She felt not a flicker of panic. Her mind was working fast but with absolute clarity. She would greet Montaine with a haughty indignation at such an unceremonious intrusion on an evening she had intended to spend in peaceful solitude. If she *had* been keeping her rendezvous with Napoleon, it would be more difficult to carry off, but as it was she would merely be telling the truth about her evening's plans. Or at least, the first part of the evening.

"General Bonaparte's equerry, madame." The abigail

twisted her hands in her apron in her agitation. "He said he wants to see you."

"Indeed?" Meg sounded incredulous. She turned around, her eyebrows raised. "Come now, girl, I cannot believe he would have made such a demand."

"Oh, but he did, madame. He said to tell you that he wants to see you."

"Well, he must wait in that case," Meg said, turning back to the mirror. "I'm not yet dressed for dinner. Run down and tell Denis to put our visitor into the salon. He may tell him that I will be down shortly."

Estelle, breathless, bobbed a curtsy and went to do her mistress's bidding.

Meg drew several deep breaths, and held out her hands. Not a quiver. She touched her forehead. Dry and cool. She would not think about Cosimo. If she allowed the slightest chink in the fortress she'd built around her imagination, the whole structure would tumble into ruin. She would simply play the part she had to play and trust Cosimo to take care of himself.

She touched the hare's foot to her cheeks and opened the jewel casket, taking out a string of matched pearls. She was fastening them around her neck when Estelle reappeared, closing the door at her back with a dramatic click.

"Colonel Montaine, madame. He said he'd wait, madame."

"So I should hope," Meg said, rising from the stool. "Bring me the ivory negligee, Estelle. If the colonel insists on disturbing the peace of my evening, then he must take me as he finds me."

Dishabille was perfectly acceptable dress for an informal evening at home, and the colonel would find he had rudely interrupted a lady enjoying such an evening. A dainty lace cap and a pair of satin slippers completed her outfit, and thus attired, Meg made a stately descent of the stairs.

She caught her breath at the phalanx of soldiers ranged in the hall, then lifted her chin and sailed past them into the salon.

"Colonel, delighted though I am to see you, I must protest at such a martial display in my hall."

The colonel bowed and gestured towards the sofa. "Madame Giverny, you will be pleased to seat yourself."

She frowned. "Unless I am much mistaken, sir, this is *my* house. If I choose to sit, I will. If I choose to invite you to do so, I will. However, I find I do not so choose."

"You may not leave here tonight, madame," he stated.

Meg indicated her negligee with an airborne hand. "I had no intention of doing so, Colonel. As it happens I have not been feeling too well. I was intending to take a light supper in my boudoir and retire early." She turned back to the door. "I trust you have no objections to my doing that."

"Madame, I insist you remain in this room," Montaine said, trying not to show his discomfort at the lady's composure. He had expected to catch her preparing herself for her assignation, not lounging around in a negligee complaining of ill health.

Meg very slowly turned around. She gave him a look that would have stopped a charging elephant in its tracks. "Colonel Montaine, do you have any reason for treating me with this discourtesy? Have I committed some crime? Has General Bonaparte authorized such an outrage?"

"You were expecting to meet with General Bonaparte this evening," Montaine said, at last given an opening.

Meg shook her head. "Not to my knowledge, Colonel." She went to the fireplace and pulled the bellrope. "You must be mistaken, but I have to tell you, sir, that it is an even greater mistake to treat *me* with such rudeness."

Montaine was now truly uncomfortable but he was sticking to his guns. He'd started this, and whatever the consequences, he had to complete it. He moderated his tone. "Madame Giverny, forgive the discourtesy, believe me I meant none. But I must ask you to remain within doors this evening."

She gave a light laugh. "Colonel, that is no hardship. As I've been trying to explain, that was my intention all along... Ah, Denis, it appears that the colonel wishes to be my guest this evening." Her eyebrows flickered in disbelief at the entire ridiculous business and the head footman bowed his understanding.

"Make Colonel Montaine comfortable. I shall take dinner in my boudoir, as I had instructed earlier." She glanced at the colonel. "Do make yourself at home, Colonel. My staff will take care of you, I'm sure. I shall be in my boudoir."

It was such a masterly performance that for a moment Montaine was unable to think of a response, but then he remembered the general preparing for an assignation in a deserted cottage. He knew it was a trap, knew it in the core of his soul. Madame Giverny must not be given the opportunity to send a message to her partner, whoever he might be.

"I am desolated, Madame Giverny, but I must ask you to remain in this room."

"By whose instructions?" she demanded, her hand already on the door latch.

"By the authority invested in me by the Republic of France."

Nothing could counteract that invocation, Meg thought.

She inclined her head in faint acknowledgment. "Then I trust you will do me the honor of dining with me, Colonel Montaine... Denis, I will dine downstairs after all. In the small parlor, since we are being informal, is that not so, Colonel?"

"I am honored to accept, Madame Giverny." What else could he do? Montaine bowed and assumed the role of invited guest in the house of the woman he had intended to hold under house arrest.

Chapter 26

Cosimo was aware of the passage of time merely as a mental process. He had no timepiece and the inglenook was almost pitch black, but he knew that it was soon after nine o'clock when he heard the first hoofbeats. But it was not one horse. He listened intently. Three, he thought. Had Bonaparte brought an escort after all? Or was this an advance guard intended to sweep the place before the general's arrival? If so, he could only hope they would leave when they found nothing.

He reached up into the chimney and his fingers found purchase on a shallow ledge. He pulled himself up until his legs were in the chimney, then leaned his back against one side of the shaft and flattened his feet against the other. It was hideously uncomfortable but he was confident he would be invisible to anyone below.

The door opened and a shaft of lamplight penetrated the inglenook. Cosimo held his breath; even his heartbeat had slowed so that it was barely perceptible. Footsteps moved around the single room downstairs. He heard oth-

ers on the ladder to the loft, then the sound of feet overhead. Only one man spoke and he issued instructions in a
curt undertone. A lamp was thrust fully into the inglenook,
the light sweeping the deep recess. Cosimo was motionless, hanging just a few feet above the bent head of the
searcher with the lamp. Then the light receded and he inhaled slowly.

It didn't take long to complete the search of the cottage.
Another curt order was issued and they trooped out to
search the grounds and outbuildings. But they left one
man behind. Cosimo heard the scrape of a chair, the clink
of a sword as the man sat down heavily.

His muscles were shrieking from the cramped position
but he ignored the pain as he had long ago taught himself
to do, and concentrated his mind on the present problem.
Was Bonaparte going to come at all? Or had the plot been
discovered?

He couldn't imagine how that could have happened.
Only he and Meg knew of it.

Meg. If he was cowering in a chimney to avoid detec-
tion, what was happening to her? If they suspected enough
to search the cottage ahead of the general's arrival, then
Meg too must have fallen under suspicion.

But maybe this was just a routine search. They would
leave, certain that the location was safe, and Bonaparte
would arrive as planned.

He heard the door open again and listened as one of the
men said they'd found nothing but a goat, a handful of
chickens, and a nest of spiders in the privy.

"All right, we'll take up positions around the building
and down the path," the man in charge said. "Keep the
general covered from the moment you see him. Charlie-
boy's not in here and not outside, so I'm guessing he hasn't

arrived yet. When he does he'll get the surprise of his life," he added with a grim chuckle.

"Aye, Sergeant." There was a short silence, then the same voice said, "You really think the general's in danger, sir?"

The other man snorted almost derisively. "God knows, but Colonel Montaine's got some bee in his bonnet. You know what a fusspot he is, always muttering that the general takes unnecessary risks. Well, he's convinced himself this time that Bonaparte's love nest is a nest of vipers and the lady waiting with her legs spread is as poisonous as Cleopatra's asp."

"The lady ain't here, though, is she?" commented his companion.

"No, and she won't be, neither. Montaine's got her sewn up tight as a nun's arse."

Both men laughed coarsely and left the cottage, banging the door behind them.

Cosimo let himself down slowly, clinging to the shadows in the rear of the inglenook. They wouldn't search again. They'd be watching from outside and if they saw no one enter they would assume the place was as empty as they believed it to be. At this point he had but one thought. Bonaparte was going to keep the appointment. All was not lost. He would complete his mission.

He reached down to remove his boots, sliding the short dagger out of the sheath nestled against his calf. Then he crept soundlessly on stockinged feet to a position behind the door. A small unglazed window was set into the wall to his right, the shutters fastened back to let in the evening air. He cradled his pistol in his right hand, balanced the knife in his left. He could throw as well with either hand, but was a better shot with his right. When Bonaparte rode up he would have a clear sightline. He would fire first, and then throw the knife. He was confident enough in his marksmanship to know that both weapons would reach their target.

His inner sense of time warned him that it was close to ten o'clock, and his instinct told him that his quarry would arrive early, eager for his tryst. Cosimo waited, motionless in the shadows behind the door. He could hear nothing of the men outside but they too were waiting in hiding.

He heard the sound of hooves, at first so faint he guessed they must be several hundred yards away down the path. His grip tightened on the pistol, his eyes fixed upon the moon-washed garden beyond the window.

Bonaparte rode up on an unremarkable gelding. Clearly taking anonymity to heart, Cosimo reflected, before he banished all thought from his head, concentrating only on his target.

Bonaparte dismounted and looped the reins over the stone gatepost that marked the opening in the hedge that bordered the cottage garden. He set foot on the path.

Cosimo raised his pistol, sighted over the heart, where for all his anonymity Napoleon wore the golden eagle of France pinned to his coat. The assassin's hand was steady, his eyes narrowed as he cocked the weapon.

And then it happened. Meg's image blocked his view of his quarry. He blinked, shook his head, but it wouldn't go away. He could kill Bonaparte now. He would not survive himself, he had known that from the moment the guard had taken up positions outside. They would shoot him down before he set one foot on the path. But that was a price he had always been willing to pay.

But not Meg.

Montaine had her somewhere. There was no evidence against her at this point, but if Bonaparte was assassinated tonight, and the assassin identified as Madame Giverny's majordomo, Meg's life was not worth a sou. And before she died, she would suffer as Ana had done, and he would be unable to organize her escape as he had done for Ana.

Slowly his hand fell to his side.

He could not do it.

This time he must fail. The previously unthinkable was now a fact. There was something more important to him than the successful completion of a mission so vital the lives of hundreds of thousands of people depended upon it. He could sacrifice his own life, not willingly but because it was necessary, but he *would* not sacrifice Meg.

He moved backwards into the inglenook and once again hitched himself up into the shaft. The door of the cottage opened and Bonaparte entered. He went to the table and lit the lamp, his back to the chimney, and Cosimo in the shaft closed his eyes on the knowledge that with one thrust of his knife he could accomplish his mission.

Bonaparte climbed the ladder to the loft and waited there. Cosimo heard the thump of his boots as he took them off. He heard the general come down again, his stockinged feet slithering on the rungs of the ladder. Time stretched. Bonaparte went back into the loft and put on his boots again. He came down and went outside, leaving the door open. He went out onto the path and looked up and down. He came back into the cottage.

This went on for over an hour until finally the frustrated lover extinguished the lamp and stalked out of the cottage, slamming the door in his wake.

Cosimo lowered his feet to the ground and waited. He waited until the sounds of the general's horse had faded into the night, and then he waited until the watching guard had left. Even then he remained still and silent for another half an hour until he was certain there was no human presence anywhere in the vicinity. Then he slipped out of the inglenook, pulled on his boots, and left the cottage, closing the door softly behind him. If the old couple noticed any sign of disturbance, they would assume it had been caused by the visitor they *had* expected.

It was well past midnight as he started to walk back to the olive grove where he had left his horse. He could make no assumptions about Meg's whereabouts. Montaine could be detaining her anywhere. So he would have to go back to the house. They had very little time to make the rendezvous with the *Mary Rose*. The fishing boat that would take them to Hyères would leave on the dawn tide and not return for two days. The *Mary Rose* couldn't risk standing in too close to Toulon for more than twenty-four hours. All this had been planned down to the last detail with his crew, and they would follow his instructions to the letter. But he couldn't leave without Meg.

He put his horse to the gallop until they reached the outskirts of Toulon and then he reined him in to a sedate trot. A mad horseman galloping hell for leather through the nighttime streets of the port would be remembered. He turned onto the street behind the church and drew rein. All the lamps in the house were burning, and there were guards at the front door.

So Montaine had Meg in there. Relief was a tidal wave, invading every pore and cell. Unlike anything Cosimo had experienced before. He rode around to the mews and put his horse in a stall, loosening the girth but not unsaddling him. At the rain butt he washed as much of the chimney soot as he could from his face and hands, then he let himself into the house through the kitchen door. A group of servants huddling around the range looked at him, startled, as he entered.

"Oh, M'sieur Charles, such goings on," the housekeeper said. "Madame is in the salon with that colonel, and he won't let her go to bed. Denis said she's told him he don't know how many times that she has the headache, but he's insisting she stay. Isn't that so, Denis?"

"Yes, M'sieur Charles," the footman affirmed. "And all these soldiers. It's not right in a good household."

"The times are not right, Denis," the majordomo observed somewhat loftily, keeping himself out of the lamplight as far as possible, knowing that his hasty cleanup in the stable yard wouldn't pass muster under a bright light. "I'll find out what's going on myself. You people should be in your beds. The fires will have to be lit again in four hours." On which instruction he disappeared into his own apartments in the basement.

The long case clock in the salon struck one. Meg yawned, leaning her head against the high back of the elbow chair in the salon. She regarded her companion with an ironic lift of her eyebrows. "Colonel, would you explain to me why I must sit up all night?"

Montaine, who was yawning himself, dragged himself upright on the sofa. "I await a messenger, madame."

"I wish you'd tell me why you have to await him here, in *my* house," Meg protested. She stood up and walked to the windows, drawing back the curtains to look out on the street.

Where was Cosimo? Was he alive ... imprisoned in some dungeon? Lying mortally wounded somewhere?

She could do nothing to answer the questions. She

knew what she was to do if Cosimo didn't make the rendezvous in the stables by midnight, but she couldn't do it. Not with this great lump of a colonel in the room, watching her every move. She could feel his eyes on her back even now.

And then the door opened. "Madame, may I offer you some fresh coffee... a cognac for the colonel, perhaps?"

Cosimo stood there, immaculate in his black major-domo's garments, a tray in his hands. He offered the colonel a courteous bow as he stepped forward and placed the tray on the sideboard.

Meg didn't miss a beat. She glided across to the sideboard. "Thank you, Charles. That's very thoughtful. You passed a pleasant evening, I trust?"

"Very, thank you, madame." He reached for the cognac decanter and flicked his eyelids at her.

"Colonel, you'll join me in a cognac?" Meg said, not certain what the flick meant but certain she was supposed to act upon it.

Montaine was bored, anxious, and frustrated enough to throttle someone. The hospitality offered him thus far had been rudimentary and cognac now had its appeal. "Thank you," he said shortly.

Cosimo held a tiny vial over the goblet and four brown droplets fell into the glass. He poured cognac over it liberally and gave the goblet to Meg. "Coffee for madame," he stated, pouring a cup, and despite the desperation of the situation and her own turmoil she had to swallow an appreciative grin. Cognac, doctored or otherwise, was not on offer for her tonight, just a plentiful supply of stimulant.

"Colonel." She set the glass at his elbow and sat beside him on the sofa. "Perhaps we should play backgammon to pass the time. Charles, would you bring the backgammon board?"

Montaine shrugged and reached for his glass. "I'm an indifferent player, madame."

"At this hour of the night, sir, so am I," Madame Giverny stated acidly, as her majordomo set the backgammon table in front of the sofa and then a chair opposite the colonel. "But if I'm not to fall asleep where I sit, I must do something." She moved to take the chair, and took a sip of her coffee.

Montaine took a much larger sip of his cognac and leaned over the board. The majordomo went to stand in attendance beside the door.

Meg moved her first piece, the questions tumbling in an incoherent jumble in her head.

Cosimo was safe. So was Bonaparte dead? How had Cosimo evaded the trap that Montaine must have set for him? And there had to have been a trap. Holding her here made no sense unless it was only one side of the colonel's plan. But if Bonaparte was dead, Cosimo would not be standing there. Surely they would have taken him . . . killed him.

But she mustn't distract herself with pointless speculation. She had to concentrate on the game now being played, and it wasn't backgammon.

She kept her eyes on the colonel as she drank her coffee, noticing that every time she sipped, automatically he followed suit. It was like a marionette dance. So she kept lifting her cup to her lips and moving her pieces and within fifteen minutes the colonel's goblet was empty. She reached for it.

"A little more, Colonel?" She gestured to her majordomo. "Bring the decanter, Charles."

"No, no, I think I've had sufficient," the colonel said, and Meg could detect just the tiniest slur in his voice.

Charles filled his glass nevertheless and returned to his station at the door.

It happened so slowly that Meg was hardly aware of it despite her close observation. Colonel Montaine's hand became a little less sure as he moved his pieces, he slumped a little on the sofa, and then the piece he was about to position on the board fell from his hand and his head fell forward onto his chest.

Cosimo was there instantly. He lifted Montaine's wrist, checking his pulse. "Good," he pronounced. "He'll be out for hours but *we* don't have that much time." He pulled Meg to her feet. He clasped her face between his hands for one instant and then released her. "Go and change into your britches and meet me in the stables. And for God's sake, Meg, *hurry*."

"There's no need to be so peremptory," she said, feeling the warmth of his hands on her face, aware now of a warmth within her creeping into the cold detachment that had insulated her from the fear and hurt that seemed to have been her companions for so long. "I'm not about to dawdle over anything at this point." She whisked herself out of the salon.

The soldiers were still in the hall and they stiffened to attention as she entered. Ignoring them, Meg ascended the stairs. In her bedchamber she changed quickly into Anatole's garments that she had kept hidden in the back of the wardrobe. She looked once around the room, wondering if there was anything else she should take. The jewels?

Then she shook her head. If Cosimo had wanted her to bring them, he would have said so. Perhaps they were stolen. The thought brought a choke of lunatic laughter.

She left the room and crept down the back stairs to the kitchen. It was silent, but still well lit. A pot boy snored in front of the fire. She tiptoed past him and let herself out into the narrow courtyard beyond. The stables were in darkness and she felt her way until an arm came around her, making her jump and gasp.

"You scared me," she hissed, turning angry eyes on him.

Cosimo offered only a rote apology, but Meg was not to know how much he relished the anger that returned the liveliness to her eyes. He urged her into the narrow lane behind the church where their horses waited, and gave her a leg up onto the mare.

"We've lost close to three hours," he murmured. "Stay close."

And Meg stayed close as they left the port by an unfamiliar route and rode along the coast until they reached a secluded cove. Cosimo didn't speak and neither did she as the dark night gave way to the gray of the false dawn and then the pink tinge in the eastern sky that heralded a new day.

They rode down a narrow path to the small beach, where a fishing boat bobbed in the shallows.

"What about the horses?" Meg asked, hearing her voice as if it was that of a stranger.

"Payment for services rendered," Cosimo replied before greeting the small group of fishermen waiting on the edge of the beach.

Meg gave the mare's neck one last stroke and bade her a soft farewell. The animal was too valuable a beast to meet with anything but the best treatment. Cosimo as always had not neglected a single detail.

Except that the details were for nothing if Bonaparte was still alive.

"Come, quickly now. We have to catch the tide." Cosimo lifted her and carried her through the shallows, depositing her in the bow of the fishing boat. He hitched himself in beside her and two of the fishermen jumped into the stern while a third pushed them off the sandy bottom. The foresail and jib caught the swelling breeze.

The sun rose as they sailed out of the cove and into a stretch of water between the coast of France and a small group of islands. They sailed around the biggest of the islands and Meg drew a deep breath as the familiar shape of the *Mary Rose* stood out against a gray cliff.

She glanced at Cosimo. He too was looking at his ship, and there was a strange cast to his countenance. Not exactly a darkness, more a question. As if aware of her scrutiny he turned his gaze towards her. The blue eyes were full of light. As if he'd seen something he hadn't known existed.

As they drew closer to the *Mary Rose* the rope ladder dropped over the side. Men appeared along the rail and one of Cosimo's nephew-lieutenants, Meg wasn't sure which one at this distance, climbed down the ladder ready to pull them in. The fishing boat came alongside and one of the men tossed Frank Fisher the painter. He secured it, bringing the boat against the ship's side.

"Welcome aboard, Captain . . . ma'am." He offered a hand to assist Meg onto the ladder.

"Thank you, Frank. Go on up, Miss Barratt can manage without help." Cosimo stood back watching with a tiny smile as Meg grasped the ladder and swung herself easily onto the bottom rung. She went up hand over hand as if she'd been doing it all her life. Her fatigue dropped away from her as she hitched herself over the rail and felt the sloop's deck moving gently beneath her feet.

"G'day... g'day."

At the familiar squawk she turned, laughing. David Porter, with the macaw perched on his shoulder, emerged from the companionway. "I thought it must be you," he said, smiling, even as he looked her over with a professional eye. "You seem intact."

"I am," she said, holding out her arm for Gus, who flew instead onto her shoulder and pecked her ear. "So is Cosimo."

"So is Cosimo what?" the privateer demanded as he jumped to the deck. Gus rose with a delighted squawk of greeting and abandoned Meg for his master.

"Intact," she said. "David was asking."

"David." Cosimo held out his hand to the other man. "Everything all right on board?"

"Smooth sailing," the physician said. "You?"

"Not all the time," Cosimo said and the physician nodded as if satisfied.

Cosimo, standing at the rail beside Meg, scratched the macaw's poll, murmuring to him. And Meg could feel the tension that the privateer had carried from the moment they'd left the ship at the Bordeaux estuary leave him like an unwanted cloak. Whatever he'd been through that night, waiting for Bonaparte, was over. Whether the mission was accomplished or not, it *was* over.

Cosimo strode to the quarterdeck, where Mike at the helm nodded a laconic greeting. The captain of the *Mary Rose* stood behind the helmsman and called, "Make all sail."

Meg leaned back against the rail of the mid-deck and gazed upwards, watching the familiar routine. Men crawled all over the rigging, hanging precariously over the deck some twenty feet below as they set the sails. The sloop sprang across the water under full sail and Meg turned to look behind her at the little fishing boat, now heading out to sea.

She felt Cosimo behind her before his hand came to rest on the nape of her neck. Gus flew onto the deck rail and regarded them, bright-eyed, head cocked. "Poor Gus," he murmured experimentally, and when he received no response, muttered it again with more conviction and tucked his head under his wing.

Meg leaned back into the warm clasp, closing her eyes against the dazzle of the early sun. "You didn't kill him," she said.

"No," he agreed, his fingers moving upwards into her hair.

"Why not?"

He looked over her head at the receding coastline. "Love," he said. "An odd feeling. I've often wondered what it was like." He turned her towards him. "Now I know." He traced her face with a fingertip. "You could say it, Meg. I am so sorry it took me so much longer. But I love you. You are all and everything to me."

She didn't respond immediately, but looked at him seriously, still unsure. She could still hear his words: *I don't risk failure, my dear.*

"It must matter to you that you failed this time."

He palmed her cheek, running his fingers over her eyelids. "Yes, it matters, but not enough. Can you accept that?"

"Yes," Meg said, reaching a hand to caress his cheek. "Yes, I can accept that."

She turned within the circle of his arm and looked out over the sea. "Where are we going?"

"I promised I would take you back to Folkestone," he

said, his hand flattening against her hip. "I will keep my promise."

"And if I release you from it?"

He drew her closer against him. "Then the *Mary Rose* will follow Bonaparte to Malta."

"And the captain of the *Mary Rose* will try his mission again?"

"In one way or another," Cosimo said. "Nelson's waiting for Bonaparte. If we don't sail back to England, then the *Mary Rose* will join the admiral and the navy in this fight."

Meg turned to put her hands on the rail, feeling his body come up close, molding itself against her back. "Then I too will join this fight."

"Out of conviction or out of love?" His breath rustled across the top of her head.

"Both," she said after a moment. She turned again, reaching her hands up, linking them behind his neck. "But love takes precedence. I *love* you, privateer." Her eyes glittered with a sheen of tears.

He kissed her eyelids, stroking her face. "You are all and everything to me," he said as he had done earlier. "I love you, Meg Barratt."

ABOUT THE AUTHOR

JANE FEATHER is the *New York Times* bestselling, award-winning author of *Almost a Bride*, *The Wedding Game*, *The Bride Hunt*, *The Bachelor List*, *Kissed by Shadows*, *To Kiss a Spy*, *The Widow's Kiss*, *The Least Likely Bride*, *The Accidental Bride*, *The Hostage Bride*, *A Valentine Wedding*, *The Emerald Swan*, and many other historical romances. She was born in Cairo, Egypt, and grew up in the New Forest, in the south of England. She began her writing career after she and her family moved to Washington, D.C., in 1981. She now has more than ten million copies of her books in print.